Manifest

Anthony P. Sardina

First Printing, 2015
Second Print, 2018

ISBN: 978-1-7294-0355-6

About the Author:

Anthony P. Sardina is a retired United States Army First Sergeant, having retired in May of 2013 after 22 years of honorable service to this great nation. Anthony is currently the Building and Grounds Supervisor for Caesarstone Technologies in Richmond Hill GA, where he resides with his wife, Maria. Anthony and Maria have two grown sons, Alexander and Adrian.

Acknowledgements:
I would like to thank my wife, Maria V. Sardina, for her love, companionship, and dedication. Additionally, we all must give thanks to the brave men and women of all five branches of Service, Law Enforcement agencies, Fire Departments, Health and Medical professionals, and anyone who places the needs of others above their own.

MANIFEST

PART ONE

Chapter 1

Monday, January 27th 10:43 A.M.

*Everyone has a trigger and eventually, something will make
them pull it...*

DAVE LOOKED UP FROM HIS book to see who dared interrupt
his reading. His eyes squinted at none other than Gail. *Of course,
who else would be so inconsiderate,* entered his mind as he turned
his attention back to the latest James Patterson novel. Despite
the obvious lack of interest displayed by Dave, Gail continued to
ramble on. Captivated by the story he held in his hands, he kept
his gaze on his book and turned the page. He picked up the book
in Atlanta yesterday after his conference to read on his flight back
to Savannah. Being his first day back in the office, he wanted to
ease into the Monday morning grind by finishing the book that he
started.

He had decided to come in a little late this morning. It was
bad enough being a Monday, but this morning was particularly
rough since he had spent his whole weekend conducting work related business. Thursday was travel time, Friday was preparation,
Saturday the conference itself, and Sunday was travel home. Why
they'd schedule a regional conference on a Saturday he'd never
know. He should've taken today off, but there was really no reason

for that. He wasn't that tired. He just didn't feel like dealing with Gail. Gail's full name was Gail Watson. She was sixty-two years old, but from the way she dressed and acted you would think she was eighty-two. She was short, fat, and clearly a lonely, old woman.

Together, Dave and Gail ran this branch of Endeavor Insurance for the past seven years. Despite sharing a workspace for that entire time, Dave knew nothing about his co-worker on a personal level, nor did he want to know. He'd been with the company for nearly twenty years, but Gail has only been on for the seven that they shared, which is why Dave was considered senior and therefore given the additional responsibility of attending conferences. Their branch handled auto, home, and life insurance for a few hundred clients in Savannah and the surrounding areas. They even had a couple billboards in the town, each featuring a head shot of Dave and Gail beneath the company logo, with the company motto, *"You're why we're here,"* plastered across a white background. It was a pretty horrible motto.

Horrible mottos aside, Dave looked extremely handsome in his head shot. Dave celebrated his 40th birthday in October, but he could easily pass for someone in their mid-twenties. He stood at about six-foot-one, was a slim and muscular 174 pounds, and kept his brown hair in a neat and trim, military style appearance. He always dressed sharply, today in a grey Executive 2-button wool suit. Dave flirted with every attractive woman he met, and it worked. He shared his hotel bed with a different woman on every occasion when business had called him to Atlanta. None of them would've guessed that he had a wife and son at home. Traveling for the company wasn't without its perks.

By now, he really should be sharing with Gail the information he gathered from the conference, but he didn't feel like it. He would get to it eventually, probably before he left for lunch and his afternoon appointment. Gail was blathering away about the things that had gone on while he was away last Thursday and Friday. He didn't want to hear it right now so he tried his best to ignore her, but it was becoming increasingly difficult. She stood, basically lingering, behind his right shoulder, her words drilling into the side of his head. He was finding that he continuously needed to reread what he already read due to her distractions. This was becoming more and more frustrating. The feelings of anger and frustration were not consistent with his usual calm and relaxed demeanor. He was an arrogant douche bag, but he was relatively calm most of the time. In fact, his tolerance for her had actually grown over the last few years. When she was first hired he could barely look at her without becoming annoyed. Over the years that they worked together, Dave gradually had grown to accept her with all of her annoying quirks and was, for the most part, able to function at the office. Today was different. It was as if he had taken one hundred steps backward in his efforts to maintain a healthy and professional work relationship with this woman. A faint whisper entered somewhere between the sentences as Dave read. *Do your duty*, were the words tickling his ears and seeming to flash before his eyes, adding to his increasing irritability.

He was having trouble identifying where these thoughts, which were leading to feelings of anger and rage, were coming from. He only understood that he needed to do something quickly to suppress these feelings. His blood began to boil. His skin began to crawl, as if there were tiny spiders taking up residence somewhere underneath the first layer of his skin. His heart rate increased and he started to have chest pains. He thought that he might be having an anxiety attack or maybe even a heart attack. As his chest ached, his book began to tremble within his grasp.

Gail hadn't seemed to notice the rolling of his eyes, the deep inhales and long exhales, and the overall defensive posture that Dave's body language suggested. She continued to spew incoherent gibberish from the hole in her face, seeming not to notice the devastating effects it was having on the ears of her audience. Dave looked up from his book, surveying the objects that were laid out on his desk. He had his laptop, with a 22 inch monitor next to it, for the extended dual screen desktop that made his job easier. He had his office phone to his left, next to his printer. Miscellaneous papers were randomly scattered across the desk directly in front of him. There was also a small business card holder, about half full. His coat was resting on a nearby chair that was often used by clients. To his right was a small desk organizing cup that contained three highlighters, orange, pink, and blue, two mechanical pencils, several pens of varying color, and a pair of brown handled scissors. Scissors. He would need these in order to follow through with the plan that was quickly manifesting within his brain.

In one swift, seemingly uncontrollable movement, Dave dropped the book, rose to his feet, and brought his right elbow, in a rearward and upward thrusting motion, into full contact with Gail's nose and mouth area, causing her to immediately silence her pointless talking, mid-sentence. Upon contact, she released some sort of muffled grunt. Blood escaped her nose in a quick burst followed by a rapid flow, hitting the desk, floor, and Dave's shirt; a mess that would need attention soon. Her dentures were also knocked out of place by the blow. She staggered backward for a few shocked and disoriented steps, as Dave moved behind her and wrapped his right arm around her neck. The force of the elbow assault had caused Gail's head to jerk backward, thus exposing the neck and making it easier for Dave to gain access to the area required to cut off blood flow to the brain. He allowed his right arm to encircle Gail's neck, he then grasped his left bicep with his right hand. With his left hand, he pushed forward on the back of her head, thus expediting the process of a combined blood and air choke. The prolonged airway and blood flow restriction caused Gail to lose consciousness rather quickly.

Once the body had gone limp, Dave used his left leg to swivel his office chair around so he could gently place Gail into a seated position within his own chair. Once she was as secure as she could be in this condition, Dave surveyed the immediate area for items he could use to tie her to the chair. He moved quickly, as she would not stay out for long. First he closed and locked the door to the office in which they shared. The last thing he needed was for a client to enter the room, thus doubling his workload. In a filing cabinet across the office, Dave found a series of extension cords. Three that were about four feet in length and brown in color, along with a much longer white cord, that looked to be about double the length of the others. There were also two surge protectors with short cords, which he grabbed, as they might come in handy. He fashioned the cords together to create a securing device which he used to tie her to his chair. It wasn't the most effective method, but given her age and condition it should hold her in place.

He removed his purple and black Calvin Klein tie and used it to secure her head in an upright position by placing it around her forehead and tying it to the back of the chair. Dave secured another chair, sat, and grabbed Gail's sixty-two year old face with his left hand, applying pressure in an attempt to get the mouth to remain open. With his right hand, he reached in, past the disgusting yellow tobacco stained dentures, knocking them out of her mouth and onto the floor. He was trying to fish out that annoying tongue. The slippery bastard was as evasive as an eel soaked in extra virgin olive oil. Frustrated, he grabbed his tie clip, which he placed on the desk earlier when he removed the tie. This tie clip was about an inch and a half long, constructed of metal, and had a decorative, zig-zag pattern of slightly raised lines across the front. The clasp, which was designed to hold the tie to the shirt in a neat and uniformed fashion, had more than enough pressure to hold the wet, slippery, smoke smelling tongue in place.

Dave held the clip like a pair of tweezers and went in for a second attempt to grab the muscular organ that was creating those annoying noises earlier. At this point, he almost felt as if he was having an out of body experience. It seemed as though he was hovering above himself and his captive co-worker, watching along as someone else pulled the strings. Regardless of who was in control, this was going to happen. This was his duty. There was no preventing this inevitable transaction of expedient amputation using nothing more than handy office supplies and small articles of the average man's wardrobe.

As Gail began to come around, Dave squeezed the tip of her tongue tighter with the tie clip, making sure he had full control of it. He then forcefully pulled it from her mouth, to the full extended position. She spurted more random garbage from her toothless mouth, as she continued to slowly regain consciousness. Gail began to feel the realization of the severity of the situation. Her eyes became wide and fixated on Dave's. They filled with salty tears which ran down her blood stained cheeks, as she writhed and jerked her head from side to side, trying to break free from the grasp of the tie clip and the tie which held her in place. Her fingers wiggled and squirmed against the arms of the chair, beneath the confines of the tight extension cords. Her legs, which had been secured to the bottom portion of the wheeled office chair, began to kick and jerk in feeble attempts to break free or possibly roll away. These movements caused Dave to increase the pressure of his hold on the tongue, which in turn caused Gail to groan and grunt in a series of pathetic, puppy-like whimpers.

Without hesitation, with his right hand, Dave removed the scissors from the area where they were stowed and used them to remove the tongue from Gail's mouth. The blades from the scissors passed through the soft, moist flesh of the tongue much easier than Dave had expected, meaning that they were either extremely sharp or the tongue was extremely weak. Whatever the case, the mission was accomplished with only three passes. Blood and saliva came spewing out of Gail's face, past the blood from earlier, which had already coagulated and crusted in and around the nose and mouth area. Her body began to twitch and jerk insanely, as if she was having some type of seizure. She continued to contaminate Dave's ears with her annoying, toothless, tongue-less shrieks, moans, and groans. She had evidently lost control of her bladder as well, as Dave could see her tan slacks start to show signs of excessive moisture in the crotch area. This racket was far worse than the noise she was making earlier. There is no way Dave will be able to read with this going on!

With extreme frustration, Dave put his foot on the chair cushion in between Gail's legs, and gave the chair a firm push, causing it to roll haphazardly across the room and into the corner, leaving a trail of blood and piss on the floor. She came to a gradual stop, facing the wall, with her back toward Dave. She continued to cry and cower, tongue-less. This isn't going to work. He had to figure something else out, because this actually made matters worse. Much, much worse. Smearing Gail's blood across his forehead and cheek, Dave wiped his own sweat from his face, and began to calculate his next move. As his gaze traced the outline of the room, he heard that soft voice enter into his mind once again. It was faint at first, but as he focused his attention in an effort to understand it more clearly, the volume of the phantom voice increased slightly. *This isn't enough. You need to kill her.* As if a light bulb had illuminated over his head, it occurred to him what he needed to do. He stood up and began searching the office for something flammable. Some type of accelerant...

Chapter 2

JEFF WAITED PATIENTLY AT THE intersection of Highways 17 and 144. Jeff was on 17, facing south, with the intention of turning right onto 144, as indicated by his blinking directional arrow. He wanted to be back to the site as quickly as possible. He really should've brought his lunch today, knowing that his schedule would be as tight as it is. He was usually a better planner than this. Now here he was, in traffic, rushing to get something to eat at a fast food restaurant, when he could've already been eating at the site if he had planned accordingly. He could've grabbed some lunch somewhere closer to the site, but he had to pick up a certified letter at the post office on 144, so he figured he'd kill two birds with one stone.

He felt as though he was letting down his crew lately, having been off site all day Friday and Saturday and now it appeared that he would be gone tomorrow as well. He hated being away from the job any longer than absolutely necessary, but something had come up regarding his mother-in-law up in Beaufort and he promised his wife that they would drive up this afternoon when his step daughter got out of school. It's going to be very tight. He'd have to change out of his uniform at some point, as well. Driving to South Carolina in clothes and work boots that held the stench of the day would be pleasant for no one. Jeff impatiently checked his watch as the mid-day sun was shining off the hood of his white 2014 Dodge Ram. The light was red; therefore he could turn right if it was clear, however, a small blue sedan, perhaps a Nissan Altima, was approaching on 144 towards Jeff's location. Jeff planned on turning right as soon as the Altima passed him, falling in right behind it on Highway 144. *Hurry the hell up*, Jeff thought as the little blue car closed the distance, slowed, and turned right onto Highway 17, without using a turn signal.

If this asshole had signaled, Jeff could've been well on his way, traveling on 144 towards the cheeseburger that would cure his growling stomach. At that moment, something within Jeff that was not quite Jeff, took over. He felt a small flutter in his mind, almost like the butterflies that show up in a teenage boy's stomach when he got near a girl he had a crush on. Jeff began to assume a submissive posture to whatever it was that meant to control him, and began to alter his plans. *Do your duty*, he heard faintly inside the cab of his truck, or his mind; he couldn't be sure which. Where ever they were, the words provided Jeff with a solacing feeling of pleasure and reassurance; a sense of enlightenment that filled him with warmth all over. With his left hand, he sharply jerked the turn signal lever down, changing his blinking arrow from a right to a left, and took off in a dramatic, screeching U-turn, heading back north on Highway 17 and towards the blue Nissan Altima. His Ram used the entirety of its 6 cylinder engine to catch up to the Altima in a timely fashion. Both hands clutched the wheel with such force that his knuckles began to turn white. Jeff's brow lowered as his chin was drawn in, displaying his focus and determination. Nothing else on earth was more important than getting to that little blue car.

Manifest

The Altima slowed and stopped at the red light at the intersection of 17 and Mulberry Drive. Jeff knew that this was a newly installed light and that it didn't stay red for long. His right foot pressed the accelerator hard into the floor, as if attempting to actually push it through the floor board and onto the street below. 30. 40. 45 miles per hour. Toward the red tail lights of the idling Nissan Altima. There was no slowing down. A horrific crashing noise interrupted the midday air as Jeff's truck collided with the stationary Altima. The airbag deployed into Jeff's face immediately upon deceleration. The force in which the Ram made contact with the motionless Altima caused the entire rear portion of the Altima to seemingly become engulfed and devoured by the front of the Ram. The increased momentum caused both vehicles to howl through the intersection in a violent crash of glass, metal, and plastic. The Altima continued to slide forward a few feet after the Ram had stopped. Although Jeff was expecting the blast of the air bag, it still caught him off guard somehow. He saw a series of spots and flashes in front of him as his eyes watered from the impact of the bag. His nose stung from the white powder that was launched everywhere within the cab of his truck. The fumes from the igniting of sodium azide, which makes air bags do what air bags do, left Jeff a little shaken and disoriented, but not completely without focus. He knew he still had a job to do. A barely detectable sound reinvaded his thoughts, the same whisper from earlier that almost hissed in his mind. The angelic sound morphed into words as it repeated *do your duty*, causing a smile to manifest across Jeff's lips. He couldn't understand how he could be filled with such anger and peace at the same time.

Jeff hopped out of his Ram and began to move forward to the Altima. Much to his advantage, there was nobody on the scene as of yet. No witnesses of any kind, not that he could see anyway. He had to move quickly because he knew this privacy wouldn't last. It wouldn't take long for the looky-loo's and rubber-neckers to show up. As he got alongside the blue sedan he noticed that it appeared that its trunk was now a permanent part of its back seat. Mostly all of the glass that the vehicle contained had been smashed and was now scattered in the street, with the exception of the front windshield. Surprisingly, the front air bags had deployed. Jeff thought that a rear impact accident such as this wouldn't make the front bags pop. Oh well. The stranger appeared to be completely disoriented, his face was red and swollen from the air bag, and he had several cuts and gashes on the left rear of his head. A small amount of blood was visible in the stranger's blonde hair. He also appeared to have a significant amount of blood in his mouth. Without hesitation, and with the full force of his frustration and built up anger, Jeff punched the stranger directly in the center of his nose.

He felt bone and cartilage crunch under the force of his fist, which was still tight and sore from the combination of clutching the wheel and the impact of the crash itself. He then grabbed a firm hand-full of the stranger's hair with his left hand in an effort to hold the head steady. With the palm of his right hand, Jeff applied pressure to the stranger's forehead and began to slowly insert his thumb into the man's right eye socket. The stranger attempted to scream through his blood soaked teeth, but the pain that was inflicted by the hemorrhage and eventual bursting of his right eye caused his cries to be reduced to an almost inaudible shriek. Perhaps a dog in a nearby neighborhood might hear his pleads, but no human ever could. Once the thumb was as deep as he could get it, Jeff rotated his hand so he was able to insert his index and middle fingers into the stranger's left eye socket. He really wanted to be able to create a modified version of the universal symbol of "ok" by touching the tip of his index and middle fingers to the tip of his thumb within the skull of the asshole who doesn't know how to use turn signals. But that was proving to be difficult with the eyes getting in the way and with the amount of squirming the stranger was doing.

The stranger continued to scream silently, as he grabbed onto Jeff's arm with both hands. This actually made it a lot easier for him to be pulled from the vehicle through the destroyed driver's side window. At some point in the process of dragging his victim from the vehicle, Jeff's hand ripped completely through the bridge of the man's nose, spilling blood, snot, and bone particles everywhere. Jeff staggered back a step or two when his hand broke free. Once he regained his balance, he secured the man by the shoulders, pulled him from the vehicle and threw him onto the pavement. Jeff then connected with a brutal kick to the mid-section, certainly breaking a couple ribs in the process. In the act of pulling the stranger out of the vehicle, Jeff had noticed through the peripheral of his vision that there was an aluminum baseball bat on the floor of the passenger's side. Next to it was a worn out glove. Perfect. Jeff reached into the Altima, having to actually enter the vehicle up to his waist in order to get the object he was reaching for, and pulled it out.

He held the bat firmly with both hands, almost like a warrior would clutch a sword or possibly a battle axe. He then raised the bat high above his head and brought it down onto the stranger's skull with as much force and power as he could muster. The initial dent in the stranger's skull put a devastating amount of pressure on the brain. It only took two more swings for the skull to crack and the brain to spew forth onto the street. A puddle of blood, brain matter, and chunks of skull fragments began to pool in the middle of the street just north of the intersection of Highway 17 and Mulberry Drive.

With a sigh of relief, Jeff dropped the bat, causing a metallic ping to echo as it bounced off the street. It bounced once more, rolled, and came to rest next to what was left of the stranger's face and skull. Jeff was going to need a ride back to the site, since his truck appeared to be un-drivable. He'd need a new vehicle eventually, however; he felt satisfied that he had checked another task off his list of things needing completion before he could head out to Beaufort this afternoon.

His watch read 11:25, which was still enough time to accomplish what he needed to before heading back to the job site. He began to pick the dried blood from under his finger nails as he walked back to his truck, hoping to find his phone in working condition. *Good job.*

Chapter 3

CRAIG ATWOOD SPRAYED THE SOAPY water off the hood of his car. He was taking advantage of the unseasonably warm weather that this Monday morning had to offer. Elvis Costello's "(I Don't Want To Go To) Chelsea" echoed from his old school tape recorder. This tape recorder looked like something used in an old fashioned police interrogation room back in the day. He purchased the cassette in '78, "This Year's Model" was the name of the album, and as far as he was concerned it sounded as great now as it had then. He planned on enjoying his time off.

He was on what he had calculated to be about a three month vacation starting today. He just got back in town yesterday and he had laid a few things in motion that could possibly lead to him being able to take more than just the three months off. He might never need to work again, unless he wanted to. Actually, Craig didn't consider his work to be a job; it was more of a calling. Like a wise man once said *if you love your job, you'll never work a day in your life.* He had to squat down low to the ground in order to spray away the soap that had accumulated toward the bottom of his car.

His driveway ran alongside the house to a small two car garage in the back, next to which was a small backyard. Although tiny, the backyard was gigantic for downtown Savannah. The house itself was located in Savannah's historic district. It was a beautiful colonial home, encased with several large trees cascading Spanish moss over the entire area. Craig was told when he purchased the house that it was built in 1839 by Isaiah Davenport and during the civil war it had housed General Sherman and General Lee. By the looks of the home's exterior, there had been little or no upkeep since the Generals' visit. The grass was waist high, the porch and house were in desperate need of a fresh coat of paint, and the wrought iron fence surrounding the front yard and flanking the driveway was rusty and falling apart. It was a shame that a home with such a vast history and potential for curb appeal was left unkempt by its current owner.

Craig's attire consisted of dark brown corduroy pants, pulled up high above the location of proper placement and held there with an equally ugly brown belt complete with an oversized buckle. He completed his ensemble with a mustard brown polo shirt which was at least two sizes too small. He was average height and weight; however he had boney shoulders that were far more broad than normal. He wore eyeglasses that were slightly too large for his face, which were equipped with thick lenses that possessed no anti-glare properties and were completely covered with greasy finger prints. The frames were of a vintage 80's gold aviator style; although "hideously ugly" would be a better description. He had a drastically squared jaw with a beastly under bite and he wore his brown hair short and parted at the side. His teeth were dressed in braces, despite the fact that he was in his mid-fifties at least.

His bleach-white generic K-mart sneakers became soaked as he gave his car a final blast with the hose. His car was a beige 1984 Plymouth Reliant, which lived up to its name as the odometer had rolled past the 99,999 mark for the third time just last year. This vehicle was god-awful ugly. It looked like something someone's grandmother might drive if she also had a horrible taste in cars. He rarely cleaned it, but since it sat under this Spanish moss for the entire time he was out of town, he figured he better get some of the crud off. The nearby tape player released the recognizable clunk noise, indicating that the tape needed to be flipped. As Craig walked over to flip the tape he sang an annoying TV jingle, "Call Harrison and Smith, don't cha know, just dial 976-432 - oh."

Chapter 4

SERGEANT SETH HOLLOWAY WAS STILL exhausted from the challenging physical training session that his Platoon Sergeant administered this morning. He should've known better than to go for his entire 21 days of leave without doing any type of exercise. SGT Holloway was by no means out of shape, just a little out of practice. Today was his first day back to work following a much deserved stretch of good old fashioned R&R. Generally speaking, Holloway was a model Soldier and an outstanding junior leader. He would always achieve the maximum score allowable on the Army's physical fitness test, he regularly received high marks on his monthly evaluation reports and he was an excellent marksman. Additionally, despite his tiny 5-foot-5-inch, 157 pound body, he could hold his own against anyone in his weight class when conducting Army combatives training.

SGT Holloway's dedication and potential did not go unnoticed. Recognizing that he was ready for increased responsibility, his chain of command recently recommended him for promotion. The Army uses a point system to grant promotions once someone is recommended. They assign soldiers points based on performance, education, training, marksmanship, and physical fitness. The Department of the Army's Human Resources Command will raise or lower the points on a monthly basis to exercise control over how many people are promoted within any given career field. At the end of each month, if the Soldier has enough points based on the minimum number the Army dictates, then that Soldier will be promoted. Holloway has met every prerequisite to be promoted and as a combat engineer, he should have enough points to be promoted in February. He will soon be known as Staff Sergeant Holloway.

As the normal departure time for chow was approaching, Holloway decided to ask his Platoon Sergeant if he could leave a little early to run some errands during his lunch hour. Holloway's Platoon Sergeant was a Sergeant First Class named Eric Johnson. The rank of Sergeant First Class was abbreviated as SFC, but the individual was addressed as Sergeant. SFC Johnson was an exceptional leader of soldiers, both in combat and peacetime. He had the respect and admiration of his subordinates and his seniors alike. SFC Johnson was a powerhouse of physical strength and endurance, resembling a young Carl Weathers. He would routinely destroy his Platoon when he led physical training, which was often. He was the one who had recommended to the Commander that they considered SGT Holloway for promotion; so naturally, he had complete and total confidence in his protégé.

SGT Holloway reported to his Platoon Sergeant's office at 1100 hrs.

"SFC Johnson, is it cool if I take off for chow now? I need to get my license renewed at the DMV. I know there's gonna be a line," Holloway said as he stuck his head into the cramped office that SFC Johnson shared with the Lieutenant.

"How are you going to take three weeks off and then ask to leave early? Why didn't you take care of personal business on personal time?" SFC Johnson said in his authoritative voice that everyone around here recognized.

"I need a Georgia license. My Kansas license expired while I was on leave and I'm a Georgia resident now. I flew in yesterday and the DMV was closed." SGT Holloway responded with what seemed like an acceptable excuse. SFC Johnson agreed.

"Yeah, that's fine. Be back at 1300, 1315 at the absolute latest. At 1330 Lieutenant Aker has to brief the Battalion Commander on the demo range that we're in charge of tomorrow. He's gonna want you there in case the BC has questions about the classes you're giving."

"Roger," Holloway said in acknowledgement as he departed the area at a double time.

The nearest DMV was on Airport road in Hinesville, Georgia, right outside one of the gates of the Army installation. During his short drive, he thought about his recent trip home and how much fun he had. He was only 22-years-old and most of his high school buddies still lived in his home town of Lyndon, Kansas. With a population of less than 1,000, everyone in this tiny town loved their two time combat Veteran and they showered him with praise whenever he was home. SGT Holloway made the decision to be an Army careerist almost immediately upon enlistment, but he thought that he would eventually move back home once his service was complete. After all, home is where the heart is.

Seth exited the gate, traveled on Highway 84 for a few miles and then turned right onto Airport road passing several places where he could've stopped to grab a bite to eat. He decided against stopping as he most likely was going to have a long wait at the

DMV. He was the type of person that would ignore his personal needs until his objective was complete. He could eat some other time. Always place the mission first.

His assumptions were confirmed as he pulled into the DMV parking lot, which was overflowing. At a glance, he could see the green shirt of the last person in line just inside the building. He eventually found a spot, parked his truck and ran up to the door.

Demonstrating his attention to detail and instinctive characteristics, Seth immediately surveyed the layout of the interior of the building as he entered. It appeared to be consisting of an open area of about 1,500 square feet directly to the front of the entrance. There was a counter that ran the entire length of the space, dividing it into two separate areas, each with its own function; one for clerks and one for customers. Directly to his left, there was a universal gender rest room, door ajar. To his right was a slanted metal cabinet which was cluttered with brochures and pamphlets displayed in a random fashion. Many of them had fallen and were scattered all over the floor, underfoot. By extending his short body onto its toes, he was able to see beyond the crowd that there were only three clerks working in an area that was equipped with eight work stations. He could see behind the workers that there were a few cubical walls and possibly an office encased in glass walls. It also appeared that there was an employee rest room and break area back there. Everyone could hear talking and laughing coming from beyond those cubical walls.

The entire open area was filled a series with waist high metal poles. Each pole had a retractable blue strap attached to its side, which was extended and connected to the next pole. These commonly used straps were assembled to control the flow of the line, guiding it into an "S" pattern across the room, similar to the metal guards used at an amusement park to control lines at popular rides. On the top of each pole was a metal sign that had a message within a document protector taped to it. Holloway couldn't quite make out what the message was, but he could tell that each pole had the same message affixed to it and they were all of varying color. Some were red, some blue, and orange, green, yellow. The columns created by the poles and straps were far too narrow. The building was clearly in violation of its maximum occupancy fire code. People bumped elbows, knocked items out of each other's hands, and became more and more irritated with every step they took around this winding path. There was bad breath and BO everywhere as people marched forward like mindless drones with each and every annoying cackle of "NEXT!"

SGT Holloway took up his spot at the end of the line, which felt like a few hundred miles from the counter. His watch indicated that it was 1113, which he felt would give him enough time. Or at least he hoped. He planned on keeping an eye on the time, leaving if he needed to. Seth was a natural optimist, possessing the ability to make the most of a bad situation. He decided to create a list of items he would need to gather this afternoon in preparation for tomorrow's range. Seth was assigned to assist the Lieutenant with safety duties and the overall functioning of the range; teaching a few classes, making sure that Soldiers were doing the right thing, and anything else that might come up. Standard rifle ranges were easy to run; basic procedures were understood by everyone involved because they did it all the time. But this was a little different, this range was a demolition range. It was a little more complex and a lot more dangerous. "NEXT!"

These ranges were only conducted a few times a year. Soldiers receive training on the construction of different types of charges, the proper procedures for preparing those charges, and detonation procedures. It would be a great day of training, since soldiers learn more when they're having fun, and who doesn't like blowing things up? Seth pulled a small green notebook from his left cargo pocket and began scratching out an inventory checklist and a timeline to follow tomorrow morning. "NEXT!"

As Holloway stepped forward, he finally noticed what those colored signs that were displayed everywhere around the room where saying:

ACCORDING TO PARAGRAPH 17, TITLE 12, GEORGIA STATE CODE - IT IS A FEDERAL OFFENSE TO THREATEN OR HARRASS A GEORGIA DISTRICT OF MOTOR VEHICLES EMPLOYEE. VIOLATORS ARE SUBJECT TO A FINE OF UP $5000 OR 60 DAYS IN PRISON OR BOTH

The message repeated itself on the paper as many times as the paper size would allow. Seth looked around the area of the line again and saw that there were at least twenty of these ridiculous warnings, all in different colors. It seemed that no matter where he looked around the room, he saw one of these things. They were plastered everywhere. Looking at the signs had caused him to look at the people in the line a little closer than he had when he first arrived. There were people of all ages and ethnicity; some on their phones, some holding a paperback book in their face, and some leaning on the metal poles. He noticed that many of the folks that were leaning on the poles were older. He didn't like the idea of an elderly person having to stand in a line like this for an extended period of time. He also realized that the only chairs he saw were the three that the employee's behind the counter were occupying. "NEXT!"

In his little green notebook, next to his checklist, Seth began to scratch out a diagram of a more efficient layout for this DMV. He envisioned a series of chairs arranged in a uniformed fashion and an area where customers would take a number. This wasn't a new concept. He didn't understand why they weren't doing it this way in the first place. "NEXT!" Seth took a step forward and glanced at his watch. 1139. Since arriving, he had changed directions twice in the zig-zagging route that the line took around the room. He felt pretty confident that he'd get his license, but lunch would be out of the question if he intended on getting back on time. This wouldn't be the first time he had skipped lunch. "NEXT!"

Chapter 5

LAURA JONES ENTERED INTO HER third year of teaching last September. As someone with a few years' experience under her belt, one would think that she would be more prepared to deal with disobedient children. She taught seventh graders, which would make her students between twelve and thirteen years old, with the occasional student being either slightly younger or older depending on their individual situation. The student that was taking up most of her attention this year was a fourteen year old boy named Jason Spears.

She knew Jason from last year, as he was in seventh grade then as well, just in a different classroom. Jason is disruptive, never completes assignments on time or to standard, disrespects Laura and the other students, and is currently failing Math and English. He is also a bully and now that he's bigger than his classmates, it's easier for him to intimidate his peers. For these reasons, Laura called this impromptu parent conference to discuss the future of young Jason before matters got out of hand. Her students were at lunch now and would report to physical education with Mr. Grimly immediately after. Her meeting was scheduled for 1:30 P.M. today, which gave Laura a full hour and a half to prepare for her discussion with Jason's parents. This meeting was long overdue, actually. She wanted to discuss the situation with his parents weeks ago but it's a little difficult to arrange a meeting when the parents don't return phone calls or respond to emails. Laura had the impression that the boy's parents had no interest in his performance or behavior at school. Stacy Cooper, Jason's teacher last year, had given Laura some advice about dealing with his detached parents.

"I tried several times to get them involved," Stacy had told her back in August, "but they just don't care. Make sure you save your sent emails and keep a log of all the times you tried to get them on the phone. This way you can defend yourself if they ever try to say that you didn't do anything. They actually called Dr. Ruthfield and made a complaint about me, saying it was my fault that their "little angel" was acting up and that I never tried to let them know. Luckily, I was able to show Big Jim the records I was keeping, otherwise Dr. Ruthfield might have acted on their complaints. I mean, that's what a superintendent is supposed to do, right? I eventually got them in for a conference after the third quarter progress reports went out. Complete waste of time. Blamed me for everything. Yeah, they denied ever filing a complaint against me, but I obviously knew they did it. I just left it alone. I didn't even talk to them when Principle Stapleton told them he was being held back. Good luck with those people, Laura. Watch your back."

Laura planned on taking her friend's advice into consideration, but she had to make her own assessment. After this meeting, she would draw her own conclusions as to what her next step would be regarding young Jason. Over her short teaching career, she had parents that were actively involved in everything that their child did at school. Many parents would email her weekly, checking up on things or just to maintain contact with their child's teacher. She had parents that were receptive to her outreach, took the information she provided, and made the necessary corrections with their son or daughter at home. She also had parents that would simply say "thank you" and leave it at that. She never had to deal with parents as counter-productive as Stacy had described the Spears'. These would be her first defiant parents and today's discussion was going to be a challenge.

As Laura stood by the large window in her Mercer Middle School classroom, gazing out into the warm Savannah air, she wondered if this is where she wanted to be at this point in her life. She was still very young at age 26, her whole life ahead of her. Her petite frame, shoulder length auburn hair, and deep hazel eyes made her extremely attractive. Many of the male faculty members had made feeble attempts to court her, none successful. Her dedication and commitment to her students would always supersede any personal agendas. She deemed any type of relationship with a co-worker to be inappropriate and one with someone senior to her to be fraternization, a fact that the assistant principle, Mr. Jim Reynolds, constantly needed to be reminded of.

Mr. Reynolds' unsolicited and unwelcomed advances could be considered borderline cases of sexual harassment. She had warned him once at the end of the last school year that if he didn't back off she would file a formal complaint and, so far, he hasn't done anything this year. But, it was still early. She had altered the way she dressed over the past two years, which was unfortunate. Today she wore a conservative Ann Taylor blouse that was light purple, and a simple pair of black Worthington dress pants and she looked amazing.

A beautiful young woman should not have to worry about being harassed at her workplace, especially when that workplace is a middle school. At times she almost wished she had filed a formal complaint against Mr. Reynolds. She put too much thought into how the faculty and the community would take it. Here was an assistant principle with nearly twenty years' experience, not to mention the fact that he grew up right next door in Bryan County, and here she was, new teacher right out of college, wearing short skirts and shirts with low necklines to school. She figured it would be better to keep it in house. She did, however make it perfectly clear to Mr. Reynolds (she never called him Jim or Big Jim, even though everyone else did) that if he did anything else she wouldn't hesitate to blow the whistle. She made every attempt to avoid him throughout the school day, although some days' contact was inevitable.

Laura continued to look out the window into the faculty parking lot, at the Spanish moss hanging from the trees, creating a dome-like effect over the semi-secluded area towards the back. That area was prime real estate towards the end of the school year since it kept your vehicle relatively cool for the afternoon commute. She thought about her mother in Atlanta and the visit she had just returned from. Her mother's health was deteriorating rapidly so she tried to make the short flight to visit her whenever she could. It was tough to do during the school year, however; unless it was over Christmas or spring break, but their last conversation left Laura feeling a bit worried about her mother's state of mind. Her mother seemed sad and withdrawn, which is why Laura had decided to make this unscheduled trip to Atlanta this past weekend. The woman was also suffering from the beginning stages of dementia and her condition was worsening with every visit. These thoughts clearly made Laura sad as her mind continued to wander while she watched the birds flutter outside her window.

She shuttered, shook her head from side to side, eventually snapping out of whatever trance she was in and began to regain focus on the task at hand. She sat at her desk and opened her school issued laptop. She opened the program used to maintain grades and highlighted Jason's name. She then placed a blue folder on the desk next to the laptop, opening it to display the disciplinary reports that covered the last four months. At 12:08 P.M., Laura began to rehearse her opening statement for the upcoming meeting that she dreaded so badly. She tapped her foot under her desk to the beat of Elvis Costello's "Veronica" as it started to play on the satellite radio station opened on her laptop.

Chapter 6

As the clock on the wall in the shared office indicated that it was now 11:08 A.M., Dave found a small bottle of hand sanitizer in Gail's desk. Although flammable, he doubted that it would be enough to do what he needed to do. At this point, Gail had passed out due to blood loss or perhaps shock. Either way, it was good news for Dave. One less thing to worry about as he planned out step two in the completion of his duty. He rolled Gail across the office to a small area behind a cubical wall. This way she would be out of sight, should anyone decide to look through the window of their office door. He didn't have time to deal with the mess on the floor just yet. He would have to take his chances on that, although the condition of the floor wouldn't be relevant once the building was engulfed in flames.

Dave rolled his sleeves up, so that when he donned his sport coat, nobody would be able to see the blood and drool that was covering his shirt from wrist to mid bicep. He doused his hands with some of the sanitizer and rubbed them together briskly, as the instructions indicated. Then he squirted the remaining liquid into his pocket handkerchief. He wadded up the handkerchief and dabbed his face in the areas where Gail's blood had solidified, hoping that he got it all, but without a mirror, he had no way of checking. He put his coat on and buttoned the top button. At a glance, he was looking pretty sharp for a guy who had just brutally removed a woman's tongue with a pair of scissors. There were a few areas where you could see blood and moisture on his shirt, but the coat would cover most of it. He doubted anyone would notice, especially since they wouldn't be looking for it. He could see it easily, but he knew it was there. He threw the hanky in the trash, exited the office, and locked the door behind him. As he walked down the hall toward the reception desk, he happily sang Elvis Costello's lyrics: one's named Gus, "one's named Alphie, I don't want to go to Chelsea."

Their office occupied an 1100 square foot section on the second floor of a three story office building in which three other companies shared. The entirety of the first floor was occupied by a company named Instinct that sold commercial grade cleaning equipment and other large specialized appliances. They had a show room and a few offices. The second floor was shared by Endeavor Insurance and Harrison and Smith, Attorneys at Law. The third floor housed some real estate company's regional office, he always forgot their name. All three floors came equipped with a restroom and a small break area. There was also some attic space that all four companies shared for storage.

It was convenient sharing a floor with the lawyers. They were a couple of pompous assholes with ridiculous, low budget local commercials, complete with idiotic jingles, but they did have a lot of great clients hanging around. Given that they practiced family law, there were always a few newly divorced young ladies coming in and out of the area, many of which ready to mingle. In fact, Dave had christened the break area after hours last year with a fine, young soon-to-be-single lady; another perk of the job.

In order to get to the area of the second floor's communal restroom, break area, and elevators, Dave would have to walk past his company's cubical drones and check out with their receptionist. Their receptionist was Rachel Green, an attractive 23 year old African American woman who'd been with Endeavor for about two years. Actually, the word attractive didn't do her justice. She was drop dead gorgeous, resembling a young Vivica Fox. Dave had made a run at her when she was first hired, but apparently she wasn't into married men that were nearly twice her age. Oh well, her loss. Dave walked up to the reception desk, rested on one elbow, and leaned forward in an attempt to see down Rachel's blouse.

"Hey beautiful, I have to run across the street for a second," Dave said while looking her up and down, taking in the sights from toes to chest, without making eye contact. "I'm not expecting anyone, I'll be right back."

Without looking up from her smartphone, Rachel said "K. Is Gail back there?"

"Yeah, but she's tied up and can't talk right now. Just take a message."

Dave chuckled as he pushed through the door toward the common area they shared with the lawyers and then toward the elevator. He headed into the men's room first to check himself in the mirror right quick. Can't really walk into a store with blood on your face. Looking in the mirror, Dave noticed that he looked a little flustered, slightly red in the face. *Hurry up, get back to work.* He splashed himself with cold water, dried off, and headed toward the elevators. *Good enough. You look great.* He got in the elevator and mashed the button for the first floor. In the short elevator ride, Dave thought about what he had just done and what he was still doing. By no means did he regret his actions, he was just a little surprised by them. He had never been violent with anyone before and he rarely lost his temper. He kind of liked this little surprise. He was really enjoying doing his duty.

He exited the elevator, walked down the hall and past Instinct, and departed the building onto Abercorn Street. From here he had many choices within walking distance. He chose the BP station across the street. He jay walked, having to pause in the middle of the busy, four lane road for a break in traffic, and eventually, he trotted into the convenience store which was attached to the gas station. He had initially planned on buying a five gallon gas can and filling it up. But he figured it might look a little too conspicuous if he was running across the street and into an office building toting a jug of gas. Upon reconsideration, he selected a large bottle of lighter fluid, which was displayed next to the charcoal. He had no idea why there was a display of barbecue items in January. Perhaps it was because of the recent unseasonably warm weather of late or that the Super Bowl was coming up. Who knows and who cares. He grabbed a large handled lighter, the kind that folks use to ignite their grills, a roll of duct tape, a bottle of Dasani water, and a Milky Way.

At check out, he decided to grab a five dollar scratch ticket. You never know. Like he always told his wife, "You can't win if you don't play." *Let's go.* He paid the clerk, who was a funny looking man with ugly glasses and a lisp, "Thanths," the man said as Dave left with his bag and headed back to the office. Using the same procedure to cross the street and enter the building, Dave reported back to his company's area.

"Did I miss anything?" he asked Rachel, not bothering to stay and wait for an answer.

"Nope," she answered, not noticing he had walked right past her, not waiting for a response.

Chapter 7

DOUG MASON WAITED FOR HIS ex-wife Samantha to respond
to the calls he had made to her earlier this morning. He wanted
to discuss the details for his upcoming visit with their daughter,
Jessica. Her phone rang until it went to voicemail both times he
had tried to reach her. He hadn't left a voice mail, but he planned
on calling again as soon as he finished his lunch. He sat at a small
kitchen table inside his modest apartment in Pooler, Georgia and
slurped on a bowl of Campbell's vegetable beef soup, spilling
some on his shirt. He planned on changing before he left anyway.

Doug was a handsome African American man in his early
forties. His height and build armed him with the physical attributes that were appealing to members of the opposite sex. He was
handsome enough that he could easily be employed as a stand in
for Hollywood actors such as Idris Elba or even Will Smith. Samantha was a few years younger than Doug, a little shorter as well,
and she had beautiful shoulder length blonde hair. At one point,
they were a loving, extremely attractive, interracial couple and
together they produced a beautiful young lady in their daughter
Jessica.

Samantha was somewhat flexible when it came to his visitation, given the type of work that Doug did. His duties as an airline
pilot with Sierra airlines had him traveling across southern United

States for extended periods of time, sometimes at a moment's notice. For this particular visit with his daughter, Doug was to pick her up after school today and keep her until Wednesday morning, which was when he was due out of town again, this time for about a week. Since he was going to be gone this weekend, he thought it would be nice to spend a few days with his daughter during the middle of the week, before he had to leave. Samantha and Jessica both agreed. Although living in the same town as your ex-wife could be a little disheartening, since you were subject to the occasional uncomfortable run in with each other or the new love interest, Doug didn't mind at all because he was able to see his daughter almost every week. Jessica had just turned eleven in November and she was the love of Doug's life. She was rapidly changing into a beautiful young lady, a little too quickly. Doug was always appreciative when it came to the amount of time he and Jessica were able to spend together. He worked with several divorced men that never saw their kids; Doug knew that he could not live that way. He could not live without his daughter.

Doug and Sam had joint legal custody; therefore they made decisions on behalf of Jessica as a team, with Jessica's best interests being paramount, of course. However, due to Doug's hectic schedule and the amount of time he was away from home, the Judge decided that Sam be granted primary physical custody. Doug paid Sam $750 per month in child support payments, which he was happy to do.

Samantha had re-married about two years ago. Her new husband's name was Jeff Arkenson and he was some type of general contractor in the area, Doug wasn't sure the exact details about his job. Apparently, Jeff was working on some commercial project on Highway 204, near the I-95 ramp. The company that Jeff worked for was headquartered in Atlanta and he was required to travel there a couple times a month. Doug had even bumped into him at the airport a time or two. Sam and Jeff had discussed moving to Atlanta many times, but Sam was a little apprehensive as her mother lived in Beaufort, South Carolina, which was a short drive from Savannah, also she didn't want to take Jessica away from her father. It was a tough decision. A move would make things more convenient for Jeff, would probably come with a minor promotion as well. But Beaufort was just fifty miles away, so Sam was able to visit her mom whenever she wanted, also Doug was a great father and he deserved to have his daughter nearby. Additionally, her mom was currently in breast cancer remission, so Sam wanted to stay right here in case there was ever a recurrence.

Even if Sam's mom was in perfect health, she wouldn't want to move away from Doug. The divorce was not messy and there were no grudges between Sam and Doug, or Jeff for that matter. Sam and Doug had simply grown apart, as people often do. Doug's occupation kept him out of town a lot and Samantha had emotional and physical needs that were going unfulfilled. Despite their differences, they had maintained a cordial and professional relationship over the years for the sake of their daughter.

Before Doug could make a third attempt to call Sam, his phone vibrated across the table. Samantha's name appeared on the screen, along with her picture.

"Hey Sam," Doug said through a mouthful of peas, carrots, and processed beef chunks.

"Hi, Doug." Samantha answered. "Sorry to not pick up before. I was on the phone with my Mom. It looks like she's having a recurrence. They're talking about lumpectomy being the next step. She's really scared and confused. She's got another appointment with Dr. Allen tomorrow."

"That's horrible. I'm so sorry, Sam. Give her my love and let her know she'll be in my prayers. Keep me in the loop," Doug responded. "I'm still good to pick up Jessica tonight, right? I was gonna take her to Olive Garden."

"Well, that's what I was going to talk to you about. I was hoping you wouldn't mind postponing until this weekend. Jeff and I were gonna head up to Beaufort this afternoon. Mom wants to see us. Me and J. I want to go with her to see the doctor tomorrow. Now that Dad's gone, I don't think she likes going alone. I don't think she understands everything. I was gonna keep J out of school tomorrow and Wednesday. I'll run in when I pick her up and get her assignments. She'll be okay if she misses a couple days of school."

Slightly disappointed, Doug responded, "Really? I'm out of town this weekend. I leave Wednesday at around noon, I told you that. That's why I was going to get her today. Can't Jeff just meet you up there this weekend? Maybe he can go up late, bring J with him?"

"I'm sorry. I forgot you were going to be gone that long. My mind's a little screwed up, dealing with this. We'll make it up to you. I promise. My mom really wants to see her little J-bird. I'm worried about her, Doug. I've never heard her this way."

Just as he was preparing his lips to respond with something like "yeah, it's no problem" or "sure, give your mom my love and tell J to call me tonight when you guys get there," something triggered in Doug's mind. He had his words prepared; he could almost hear them. He just couldn't say them. Something was blocking his voice, preventing him from projecting anything from his mouth.

"Doug? You there?"

After a deep exhale, Doug spoke. The sounds that came from his mouth were not the words that he was saying. Somehow, some type of a filter had been placed over his mouth; something that changed what he was saying into something else. He felt as though he had no control over himself; as if he was somewhere sitting on a ventriloquist's lap; completely submissive to the will of the operator.

"What about me, Sam?" Doug finally responded, as he got up from his chair. "I wanna see my little J-Bird, too. She's my daughter and I don't really care if your mom wants to see her. You're always pulling this shit with me. We have joint custody. Don't you get that?! Why can't you get that through your thick skull?!"

Shocked, Sam said, "Doug, calm down. I..."

Doug cut her off before she could finish her point. "Shut up, Samantha, just shut the fuck up. Don't fucking tell me to calm down. You don't get to tell me what to do, ever again. I'm fucking sick of it. I'm picking up Jessica today and if you try to stop me I'll call Rick Harrison's office and we can deal with it that way. Try me. JUST FUCKING TRY ME!"

Even when their marriage was at its worst, he had never spoken to her like this. They fought, of course, sometimes loudly, but he never cursed at her before. He never really cursed at anyone. In the twenty years they have known each other she had never heard him raise his voice as loud as he was now or with as much of what sounded like pure rage. Overwhelmed with concerns for her ill mother and now the verbal barrage she was taking from her ex-husband, Samantha's emotions got the best of her as she broke down and began to sob uncontrollably.

Through her tears, she said, "Doug, what is wrong with..."

Doug pressed the end call button on his smartphone and threw it against the wall, smashing it to pieces. He dropped himself back into his seat at his small kitchen table. His breathing was short and rapid. His body trembled. He had never been this furious. He hurled the bowl of soup he had been eating towards the same wall that had just been struck by his phone, shattering the bowl and causing vegetable beef soup and slivers of broken bowl particles to paint the wall and floor underneath. As he sat in his bachelor pad style apartment he suddenly had an epiphany. He knew what he needed to do. He gradually submitted to the voice that pierced his mind, the voice that would certainly provide guidance, direction, and a sudden sense of purpose. *Go get her.*

Chapter 8

DAVE UNLOCKED AND ENTERED HIS office without locking the door behind him. Being discrete didn't really seem to matter much to him anymore. He decided to gather his items now so he could make a quicker departure once the fire started. *Fine, just make it fast.* He disconnected his laptop and stuck it into his computer bag, making sure to grab the loose papers that were scattered across his desk. Papers that he didn't need, he balled up and threw towards Gail in order to help with the fire. He paid special attention to his expense reports. He didn't want to accidently use them for kindling as he needed to complete them tonight, thus ensuring the reimbursement for his travel expenses. He snatched his slightly bloody Patterson novel; ensuring that the page where he had been interrupted was dog eared, and chucked it in the bag. The book was only a little stained with blood; he could still finish it later. He dropped his bloody tie clip into the inner pocket of his coat. Once his desk was cleared of everything, other than the tongue and the items he left there on purpose, he extended the heavy duty telescopic handle of his computer bag to its maximum length and rolled it towards the door.

He thought for a second that Gail had died, *nope.* Upon further examination he could see a very slow and weak raising and falling of her chest. He removed the contents of the gas station bag and laid them out on his recently cleared desk. He secured the duct tape and began wrapping it around Gail's head, covering the mouth. Three complete turns should do it. He held the tape with his teeth, tore the roll from the rest of it and placed the roll gently on Gail's lap. He tore the wrapper off the Milky Way also with his teeth and ate it in two greedy bites. He then used about half the water in the Dasani bottle to wash it down. *Hurry up.* He carefully popped off the cap of the lighter fluid bottle, removed the safety foil, and sprayed its contents over Gail's head. He doused a nearby filing cabinet with a generous portion of liquid and finally, for good measure, made a few circles around Gail's chair with a steady stream until the bottle began to spit and sputter indicating that it was empty. He then placed the empty bottle gently on her lap. "Whoops," he said out loud as he realized that he forgot to remove his tie from her head. *Leave it. Let it burn.*

He used his key to scratch the lottery ticket, scattering crumbs on the floor. Nothing. Oh well, once again, "You can't win if you don't play." *Quit stalling.* He folded the ticket and wedged it between his tie and Gail's forehead, slightly off center. She started to come around again, probably from the splashing of the fluid or the fact that he just touched her forehead. She moaned softly from under the tape, opening her eyes slightly, looking at Dave. It took him three attempts to get the child safety device on the lighter to function. Once it worked, he held the small flame to Gail's chest until the fire ignited. Gail convulsed and struggled with a suppressed series of squeals from beneath her tape-gag. Flailing wildly, causing the chair to roll around the room in a frenzy of fire and smoke, she crashed into the fluid soaked cabinet, setting it ablaze. *Get out.* Dropping the lighter onto the floor, Dave walked toward the door, grabbed the handle of his computer bag, and left. As he walked down the hall, Dave felt as though a huge weight was lifted off his shoulders. Almost as if he repaid an outstanding debt or finished a project ahead of schedule. He was relieved and it felt amazing. Arriving at the reception desk, he saw that Rachel's face was even more striking as it was illuminated by the light of the multi-touch screen of her phone.

"I'm heading out again," Dave said to Rachel. "I probably won't be back until later. I have this parent/teacher conference thing."

"K," Rachel said, "Is Gail back there?"

"Yeah, but she's on fire. The alarm should be going off in a few minutes."

"K."

Dave walked at a brisk pace to the elevator, his computer bag in tow, changing sounds as its wheels rolled across different surfaces. He didn't run, but he definitely moved faster than normal. This suit was much too expensive to have city water sprayed all over it once the sprinklers went off, which they most certainly would. As he stepped into the elevator he noticed that the voices he had been hearing all morning seem to have stopped, he guessed most likely at the exact moment of Gail's death. Dave departed the elevator once the doors opened. As he passed through Instinct's lobby, he noticed a salesman that seemed slightly familiar. He looked eerily similar to the cashier across the street. This gentleman was resting on one knee, demonstrating some kind of industrial strength carpet cleaner to a potential customer. As Dave left the building, the goofy looking salesman gave him a friendly nod, which caused his ugly glasses to slide down his nose. *Good job.*

Chapter 9

LAWRENCE WINFORD PULLED HIS LINCOLN Town Car into the Kroger's parking lot on Gwinnett Street in Savannah at a little past noon. He used to walk to the store when he needed items, since he only lived about a quarter of a mile up the street, but about six years ago, the worsening conditions of his disabilities had put an end to the walks that he enjoyed. There was once a time he was able to kill two birds with one stone; get his daily exercise and his groceries, thus following his doctor's orders. Those days were over.

Dr. Darcy has helped Larry deal with the pain of his service connected disabilities, his osteoarthritis, and other health issues for the past decade and they had established quite a rapport over the years. Dr. Darcy has been concerned lately with the fact that getting around had become more and more difficult for his friend. Larry was a retired Marine Colonel and Dr. Darcy had complete respect for his service to this great nation. At times, it broke the doctor's heart to see COL Winford's body deteriorate. The Colonel will celebrate his 70th birthday next week and the man could feel every one of those years in his knees, hips, feet, and lower back. His active duty service and his life style in the years following his military retirement had certainly taken their toll on the old Colonel's body. About a year ago, Dr. Darcy had actually suggested that he get one of those scooters that some elderly folks ride around in but he refused. There was no way in hell Larry was going to reduce himself to a tiny old man puttering around on one of those over-sized roller skates. He called Dr. Darcy an insane person when he suggested that if he was not willing to use a scooter that he should at least try using a walker. Larry told him that a walker was worse than the scooter. Finally, after blackmailing him with one of his Jacksonville Jaguar season tickets, the good doctor convinced him to carry a cane, which Larry agreed to reluctantly, perhaps just to humor him. Dr. Darcy had even given him a custom made mahogany cane with the recognizable Marine Corps Eagle, Globe, and Anchor emblem encased in acrylic glass and mounted to the top. Dr. Darcy certainly admired the Colonel and the feeling was mutual.

Not all of Larry's conditions were related to his service. Some were just a result of old age and a life time of using the body to its maximum potential. He tried not to bring too much attention to his combat related injuries. He didn't speak much about his combat experience, not even with his son, who was also in the Corps. He shared a few details with his wife before she died, but not much. He did, however, have to explain the fact that he still had a large amount of shrapnel embedded in his lower back, each piece a special souvenir from first visit to south-east Asia so many years ago. He often had to convince TSA personnel of his innocence when he would set off metal detectors because of his tiny chunks of extra baggage, an event that happened as recently as yesterday at the Atlanta airport.

Manifest

COL Winford had an appointment with Dr. Darcy this afternoon at 1630 hours, which is precisely why he chose to get his shopping done around mid-day. This particular Kroger's had only 6 handicap spots near the entrance, and as the Colonel steered his giant car toward the last remaining space, a bright red sports car sped into the spot. Larry could see that the vehicle did, in fact have handicap plates and a handicap placard hanging from the rear view mirror on the inside of the vehicle. For these reasons, he was not that irritated. As the saying goes, you snooze you lose. His attitude quickly changed when he got a glimpse of the driver as she exited her vehicle.

The driver of the red sports car, of which the make and model were unrecognizable to COL Winford, was a middle aged blonde woman in an extremely tight blue dress. The woman stepped out onto the pavement in a pair of ridiculously tall, high-heeled black stiletto shoes which made her struggle to gain her balance. While clutching a giant, expensive looking purse, she staggered across the parking lot and into the store. This woman didn't struggle to walk, she eventually had no problem staying erect on idiotic shoes that made her about three feet taller than normal, and she was able to trot into the store with no visible difficulty. Larry looked in disgust from his town car, which still sat facing the stolen handicap spot that was rightfully his. This woman was either issued a handicap status that she clearly didn't need or deserve or she was borrowing someone else's vehicle. Either way, she deserved to be dealt with and dealt with swiftly.

Larry slowly navigated his boat through the parking lot in search of a spot that could accommodate this beast. He passed several open "compact car" spaces, but there was no way he was getting this monstrosity into such a small space. He finally dropped anchor in the furthest possible location within the parking lot. Larry grabbed his unique cane and crawled out of his vehicle with a new found sense of motivation, as a soft voice tickled his ears from the inside. *Get that bitch.*

Chapter 10

AFTER DIGGING AROUND THE CAB of his Ram for what felt like an eternity, Jeff found his phone, or what was left of it. The impact of the crash had caused it to rattle around the cab of the truck, bouncing off the dashboard, windshield, and steering column, causing significant damage. The outer casing was broken and the entire face of the touchscreen suffered a spider-web looking crack, rendering it totally inoperative. It was times like this that he wished he hadn't let his wife Samantha talk him into upgrading to this stupid smartphone. If he had his old phone, which was a durable thing that had actual buttons and not some stupid screen, he would probably be in business right now. He was in construction after all; he should have a more durable phone. A few years ago, his company issued all employees those Nokia walkie-talkie phones for use on the job site. Those things could take a beating, not like the cheap crap they have nowadays. Eventually, one of the higher-ups in Atlanta had decided that it would be more cost-effective to use actual walkie-talkies, but the ones they purchased were garbage. They didn't have the range or sound quality of the Nokia ones. The jackass that made the decision to save a few bucks probably never set foot on a job site in his life.

Realizing that he was wasting valuable time, Jeff thought *maybe he has a phone*. Or at least he thought he thought. He was having trouble differentiating between what were his thoughts and what were the voices he was hearing before. This was most likely his thoughts, because they didn't come with the same feelings as the one's he was hearing earlier. These were just regular old thoughts. Shrugging, he walked back over to the trashed Altima, not seeming to care that he was covering his work boots with the stranger's blood. After noticing that he was being watched from the Auto Zone across the street, Jeff knelt directly in the blood and brain that was on the pavement. A larger chunk of sharp skull had actually caused him to flinch a little in pain as he knelt directly on top of it. As he stained his jeans with the stranger's fluids, he rolled the body over, trying to see if he had a phone in his pocket. Success!! He secured the phone and checked its functionality. After discovering that it still worked, he started to make a call and then immediately thought against it. He wasn't even sure if he knew anyone's number, all of them having been programed into his phone for so long that he forgot what they were. Not to mentioned the fact that it might not be wise to make a call from a dead man's phone, especially when you murdered him five minutes ago. He decided he would at least take it, so he turned it off and then slid it in the front pocket of his jeans. He then walked with a sense of purpose back to his truck, a purpose of what he still wasn't quite sure. People had begun to assemble and point in his direction from the Dollar General on the opposite side of the street than Auto Zone. He noticed a short man with a black and red checkered sweater seated on the hood of an old beige vehicle. Jeff had a feeling that the man had witnessed the entire event from start to finish. He could clearly see other people with their phones pressed to their faces, some were pointing in his direction as they howled into their devices. Some of them were quickly headed his way.

Jeff felt like tearing his own hair out in frustration as his mind was wandering around aimlessly. The focus he had five minutes ago was gone, having exited his mind at the same moment that life had exited the stranger he just murdered. The voice he was hearing earlier that was giving him a little guidance was now nowhere to be found. He had to use every ounce of the strength he once had to determine his next move. He knelt next to his totaled truck and tried to gather his thoughts. He removed his Atlanta Hawks cap and rubbed the top of his had vigorously. His eyes were still burning from the white powder of the airbag, its odor still lingering. Pinching the bridge of his nose with the thumb and index finger of his right hand, he struggled to develop a plan in terms of steps. One step at a time. Step one – depart the area immediately. All remaining steps – figure out somewhere else. The Richmond Hill police station was less than a half a mile away, so as they sparked their sirens, the sounds were all too clear in Jeff's confused ears. Run. His own thought. No help. He bolted towards the woods across Highway 17 in a north-west direction, knowing that he would eventually run into I-95, which he could follow to 204 and the job site. Surely he could get a vehicle there. Maybe even some lunch. He had to move fast. The sirens were getting louder.

Shouts of "Hey!" and "Stop, Get back here!" came from the spectators that had gathered in the parking lots on either side of the road. Jeff ignored their commands and increased his pace from run to sprint, as he galloped across the tall, wet grass that flanked the highway. A couple middle aged males darted out of the Auto Zone parking lot in pursuit of the man they both had just witnessed commit a brutal murder.

At a high rate of speed, Jeff entered the heavily vegetated area that consisted of varying trees and bushes. His face was getting whipped repeatedly as he weaved in and out of the objects in his path. His vision was blurry to his flanks due to his speed. He dared not look back at his pursuers at the risk of running into a tree or some other obstacle. Although he couldn't see them, he was sure of their presence as they continued to scream commands as they gained on him. The chase continued for about a quarter mile north-west of the murder site, and eventually led to what appeared to be some kind of fitness trail just inside the tree line. This made his evasion easier since the area was actually landscaped by someone. The trail curved around trees and had several apparatuses for doing various exercises along the route; pull up bars, sit up bars, and other random obstacles; each station complete with a sign describing the actions to take once there. Taking advantage of the forgiving terrain, Jeff looked over his shoulder as he ran, discovering that he had a significant lead on the two assholes who don't know how to mind their own business. He couldn't see them, but by the sounds of the breaking branches, he could tell that they were still in the thick stuff.

Jeff was somewhat familiar with this area, a fact that would help his current escape and evade operation. His exact location was still unknown to him, but he had an idea. He knew that there was a Georgia Fish Hatchery south-east of his position, and if his calculations were correct, he knew from a previous job that he would run into a residential area soon. Entering that neighborhood was probably not a good idea, as he was sure that the police would be wise to the direction he was fleeing based on what the witnesses were most likely telling them right now. The cops would definitely try to intercept him there. They would also be looking for him on I-95, he was sure of that.

Surprisingly, the excitement of the chase and the increasing adrenaline rush was causing him to regain some of his focus. When he got to a chain link fence at the edge of someone's property, he ripped off his dark green shirt, causing buttons to scatter. He dropped the shirt by his feet, removed his red Atlanta Hawks hat and threw it like a Frisbee over the fence and into the yard. Wearing nothing but a grey wife beater and bloody jeans, Jeff headed in a north-east direction, making sure to keep the outer portion of the neighborhood's connecting property lines within sight to his left. He meant to skirt around the housing area and stay within the thickening forest until he found I-95. A grin appeared on his face when he thought of the rouse he created to fool the would-be do-gooders that followed him. Hopefully they'd see his green shirt and red hat and assume he had gone jumping fences through people's back yards. As he picked up speed in his new direction, he softly sang his new favorite Elvis Costello song, "You tease, you flirt, and you shine all the buttons on your green shirt..."

Chapter 11

DAVE SPEARS PULLED HIS SILVER 2004 Dodge Avenger Coupe douche-mobile into his garage. He was excited that he had gotten his *work* done quickly, which gave him plenty of time to grab a quick shower before the teacher conference he was supposed to be at. He had never met his son's teacher but he knew who she was, he had seen her around last year. She was smoking hot, so Dave really wanted to get out of his bloody shirt and into a nicer suit, plus had desperately wanted to wash the filth of Gail off his body. There was no way he'd be able to impress this sexy young teacher if he had an old lady's musk lingering around. This wouldn't be the first time he flirted with another woman right in front of his wife. She never noticed and a lot of women found it flattering that a man would hit on them right in front of his wife. One could easily make a connection with an interested member of the opposite sex using nothing but eye contact, facial gestures, and body language, and they're always interested.

He decided that it was probably best to leave his soiled clothes in the garage. He didn't feel like explaining the blood on his shirt to his wife, Linda. Not yet anyway. He was pretty confident that she would find out what he had done soon enough. He would then deal with her accordingly. He stripped down to his leopard skin bikini underwear and placed his stained clothes under some random junk in the corner of the garage. After catching a glimpse of himself in the mirror on the wall, he paused for a moment and looked into his own eyes. He enjoyed looking into the eyes of a killer. It was exhilarating. He felt more alive than he had in years. Decades. He flexed for himself, like he did after the ten minute workout that he did every night, admiring the body that looked great for a 40-year-old. After pounding his chest a few times like Tarzan, Dave headed into the house.

"Linda!! Are you getting ready?" Dave screamed into his 1900 square foot two story home as he entered from the garage. Dave and Linda, along with the boy, shared a standard, cookie cutter house in the Wilshire estates subdivision in Savannah, which was about three miles from his office. The downstairs open floor plan consisted of an upgraded kitchen, complete with an enormous island covered in decorative high-end granite, which overlooked the main living space. There was a small half bath directly off the foyer. There was no formal dining room, which was fine since they rarely ate together. Dave walked through the laundry room, which was adjacent to the garage and was now standing in his bikini drawers in the kitchen. They kept the temperature in their house a chilly 66 degrees, so naturally Dave's nearly naked body shivered as he stood and looked around. Everything seemed to look better than before, more crisp and clear. Dave liked it. He liked that fact that he had just murdered someone.

They had a little over an hour to get to the school, but his wife took forever to get ready. Linda didn't work, so there really was no reason for her not to be ready. Dave took a few giant gulps directly from the milk container, threw it back in the fridge, and trotted up the stairs.

"Working on it!" she responded from the on suite master bath. As Linda was using her curling iron on her flowing blonde hair, Dave jumped into her line of sight. "BOO," he yelled, arms out to the side like a professional wrestler. This little playful demonstration caused Linda to jump and almost burn herself with the curling iron. Dave laughed hysterically after scaring the shit out of his wife.

"Why are you in your underwear, babe?" Linda asked while laughing.

"We need to take your car, I got a frigging flat. Got a little dirty changing the tire. I don't want to drive on the donut if I don't have to. I'll take care of it after this meeting, don't think I'm going back to the office. I'm gonna jump in the shower right quick, we have time."

"From the looks of it, it's pretty cold out, huh" Linda said as she set the curling iron down and grabbed her foundation. This was the type of banter that kept their marriage spicy, that and the fact that Dave cheated repeatedly.

"Very funny," Dave said as he climbed in the shower. "When I get out I'll show you how small it is."

Chapter 12

ABOUT THE SAME TIME DAVE was starting his shower, Rachel Green was surprised with a shower of her own as the building's sprinkler system engaged. The alarm that followed was loud enough to pierce the brain of anyone within earshot. Rachel grabbed her valuables; her iPhone, iPad, laptop, purse, and the Neiman Marcus shoes that she had removed and rested on the floor under her desk. She tried desperately to protect her gadgets from the water that was pouring from above. Without bothering to check on Gail, any of the other Endeavor employees, or the attorneys, Rachel vanished through the door and headed towards the stairs. She made a rapid decent through the stairwell and blasted herself through the doors of the main entrance and to safety. Eventually, the other Endeavor employees made it out, seemingly without injury. A middle age woman that worked as one of their claims adjusters had taken charge of the group and started to gain accountability of everyone, asking Rachel to help. Rachel reminded her that Dave was at an appointment. In an adjacent parking lot, it appeared that the employees of Instinct Appliances were conducting a similar drill.

The legal secretaries and paralegals that worked for Harrison and Smith had attached themselves to the Endeavor group. One of them reported that both the attorneys were in court. The distinct sound of a fire engine siren echoed throughout the area, getting louder by the second. This area fell under the jurisdiction of Firehouse 3 of the Savannah Fire Department and it appeared that their response time was going to be impressive. The last few stragglers from the Berry Realty regional office on the third floor came staggering out of the side exit from the stairwell. A senior employee from that office began to count folks, making sure that everyone made it out. There was a lot of heavy coughing, but for the most part, there were no significant injuries.

About six minutes had elapsed by the time the fire fighters assigned to Firehouse 3 arrived on scene. They arrived in a convoy consisting of a mini pumper, an engine, a ladder truck, and an ambulance. It seemed like over-kill for what didn't appear to be that large of a fire, but it was important to be prepared for anything. It was always better to have too much than not enough. They responded in record time, arriving with a fourteen man element which included two paramedics. An Arson Investigation Unit had been placed on standby, which was protocol for this type of situation. These gentlemen had a standard operating procedure to follow and they displayed perfect execution. There was a Lieutenant shouting commands but these men didn't need it. It looked as though they were operating instinctively; displaying the type of discipline that comes from the muscle memory of having rehearsed it so often. They initially blocked off traffic in both directions, allowing themselves enough room to maneuver, but as they gained control of the situation they allowed a modified flow of traffic to move through the area in a controlled manner. The building's exterior had dark black discoloration above the southernmost windows on the second floor. Other than that small charred area, the building looked fine from the street. The firemen would have to enter the building to survey any internal damage.

The woman who had taken charge of establishing a head count for Endeavor earlier had consolidated reports from the other company's representatives. She then informed one of the firemen that everyone that was in the building was accounted for except one. She explained that the woman they couldn't find worked on the second floor and she was over sixty years old. The fireman acknowledged and then told her to get back. Crowds had begun to gather in the other parking lots near the building, but all of the on-lookers kept their distance without being asked to do so. The firemen separated into their individual teams and began to execute their duties. They tagged a nearby hydrant and prepared to attack the fire. Within minutes it was discovered that the sprinkler system had done its job, although everyone could pretty much tell that from outside.

The firemen broke into two man teams and began searching for the missing woman, as well as for people that might have been in the building without anyone knowing. The men were covered in protected gear, wore masks, and carried axes and Haligan tools. The first and third floors were virtually clear of any evidence of fire, other than the mess left from the sprinklers. It was obvious that the fire had been isolated to a small office within a section of the second floor and, based on the visible exterior damage seen from the street; it was on the southern side of the building. The two firemen, who arrived at the office, opened the door and announced their presence.

The sight that the two men witnessed as they walked into the office once shared by Dave Spears and Gail Watson was disturbing, to say the least. These men were trained professionals and they both had seen the devastation and destruction that fire can cause to property and human life, but this was different. This was torture. Although these two gentlemen were not investigators, they had enough experience to know what the burn markings on the floor around the body indicated. It didn't take a detective to decipher what had gone on.

Due to the amount of blistering that had appeared on the areas of exposed scorched skin, it was obvious that this woman suffered terribly before she died. Hopefully she died of the carbon monoxide, one fireman thought; otherwise she would have felt her organs liquefy until the point that her brain shut down. What was left of this woman's face projected a frozen look of horrific terror that would haunt these gentlemen for the rest of their days. They could clearly see the charred duct tape around the woman's mouth, holding her head to the chair. Although most of whatever was use to tie her up had melted away, it appeared that she was still tethered to the chair. From the few patches left, they could make out that her hair had once been grey. They couldn't be sure, but they assumed that she was once someone's mother and grand-mother. She didn't deserve this.

There was a trail of blood that extended across the floor from one of the desks in the office to the middle of the room and then back again. There were tracks within the blood from where the wheels of the chair had rolled through it and spread it around. The floor was soaked with the water that had come from the sprinkler system overhead, which had mixed with the blood and the smoldering papers scattered around the room. Adding to their increasing revulsion, the men noticed that there was a small bloody object on the desk where the blood trail had originated. Based on the mess on the floor and the blood all over the front of this poor woman, it was obvious that the object was her tongue.

There was a cabinet next to the woman that had obviously been covered in the same accelerant that someone used on her. They ignored their desire to remove what was left of whatever she was tied with and to remove the tape from her mouth. They knew that the investigators would need everything in place. It was horrible having to leave her displayed in this disrespectful manner, but they knew that they had to. At that moment, both men had visions of someone they held dear having suffered like this. Having never before seen an act of such severe brutality, heartfelt sorrow for this poor woman enveloped these two men, as they began to make their way back outside to report their findings.

Chapter 13

SGT HOLLOWAY WAS NEARING HIS turn as he got closer to the counter where the three clerks occupied the eight workstations. He could see another message that was similar to the one located in multiple places within the line area behind him. This message was also duplicated like the other one and displayed in multiple different colors. This sign read:

DO NOT USE YOUR CELL PHONE WHEN AT THE COUNTER. VIOLATORS WILL BE SENT TO THE END OF THE LINE OR TOLD TO LEAVE

This announcement made him chuckle more than the last one. It wasn't necessarily the message itself that made him laugh, he agreed with that, but the manner in which they announced it. *Who did they think they were? Oh, you're going to send me to the end of the line? What am I, 12? You gonna put me in timeout, too?* He actually made himself laugh out loud as he pictured someone being scolded by one of these fat old ladies and then being sent to the corner wearing a pointy dunce cap.

Once again, he agreed with the rule. He considered it rude when someone played with their phone while they were being served. For that reason he decided to send SFC Johnson a text now, providing him with an update. The time on the screen of his smartphone read 1241 and he had only one person in front of him in line, so Seth figured he should be back on time, or at least by the no later time of 1315 that his Platoon Sergeant had indicated. As he examined his phone, he realized that he had no signal, which was most likely due to the cinder block structure and metal roof of this old building. Oh well, he'll be back in time anyway. "NEXT!"

Seth took a step forward, returned his phone to the left breast pocket of his Army Combat Uniform blouse so he wouldn't get in trouble, and removed his wallet from his back pocket. He removed his Department of the Army Active Duty identification card and his expired Kansas driver's license and he waited patiently for the upcoming announcement of "NEXT!"

Holloway moved swiftly to the woman who barked the command. She was an old Hispanic woman who could barely see over the counter. A small name plate resting at her work station indicated that her name was Claudia. She had on too much make-up, too much perfume, and she had horribly thinning black hair. There was no greeting, no "How may I help you?" there wasn't even a simple "Yes?" She sat there like a dead fish, mouth open, empty eyes staring into Seth's.

"Um, good afternoon ma'am. I need to get a Georgia driver's license. Here's my expired Kansas license and my mil..."

She interrupted him and handed him a form to fill out. "Step aside and fill this out. I'll then need two forms of ID and twenty five dollars, NEXT!"

"I just fill this out right here?" Seth asked, stepping to his left.

"Yes, move aside, please." She said, as she stared at the person that stepped up, no greeting for him either.

As Seth filled out the simple form, he wondered why they didn't have these forms at the beginning of the line. Possibly with a few clip boards, so patrons could fill them out when they moved through the line at a snail's pace. He filled it out quickly and stood patiently and obediently, waiting for her to finish with the person that was once behind him in line. After the gentleman left and before she could spew out another "NEXT!" Seth slid back in front of her and set the form down along with his military ID and his old license.

"Sir, you need to have a second form of ID. I can't accept this expired out of state license as one of those forms of identification," the tiny woman said.

Starting to become frustrated, Seth announced, "What's wrong with it? It expired only five days ago? What other kind of ID can I use?"

"Your Social Security card or a medical insurance card or a ..."

At that exact moment, a switch was engaged within his mind. He could feel his body temperature increase as he interrupted her with a voice so loud it captured the attention of everyone in the room, "I just waited two fucking hours! Why don't you have a fucking sign in the front saying this shit, so you don't waste people's fucking time!? You got all these dumb signs everywhere!" he said, as he pulled down one of the twenty warning signs and held it up in front of her.

"Sir, you need to calm down, it's on our website. NEXT!"

A voice entered into what seemed like the edge of his subconscious. The voice was calming and tranquil, which made him relax almost instantly. *You'll take care of it later*, the voice said.

Relax before you ruin everything. Seth gradually realized that he was making a scene. He was an Army Non-Commissioned Officer, wearing his uniform, and shouting at a tiny woman in a government building. Not a very good idea. *There's a better way to do this.* He agreed with the angelic suggestion fluttering in his mind.

"Thsir? Esthuse me?" said the gentleman behind him, with an exaggerated lisp. The man behind him wore stone washed Bugle Boy jeans, neatly pegged above a perfectly clean pair of first addition white and red Air Jordon high top sneakers. The man's outfit was completed with a navy blue "Member's Only" jacket and a black leather fanny pack. He was removing his wallet from his fanny pack as he spoke again, through a mouth full of braces, "..esthuse me..."

You'll take care of it later. "I'm sorry, sir," Seth said as he stepped away from the counter. "Sorry I raised my voice, ma'am. I'll take care of it later. Have a nice afternoon."

Holloway headed toward the exit, making a quick detour to use the rest room. He closed and locked the door behind him and then examined his face in the mirror. He appeared red and flustered, but there was a new look of confidence in his eyes; a look that suggested he could take on the world. He splashed himself with cold water, then leaned his head under the faucet and drank in several deep gulps.

Seth looked around the small, windowless rest room. It was a tiny space, about 10 feet by 10 feet with a toilet in the right corner. Next to the toilet was a large vanity that covered the remaining length of the wall. Above the vanity was the large mirror that extended the length of the counter. There was a large plastic cabinet on the opposite wall, most likely filled with cleaning supplies, next to the cabinet was a mop bucket filled with disgusting grey mop water. A smelly mop-head rested in the strainer and the handle itself leaned against the wall.

Seth confirmed his suspicions when he opened the cabinet and saw various spray bottles filled with different colored solutions. Along with the cleaning products, there were a few packages of cheap brown paper towels, unwrapped packages of rough toilet paper, and a few urinal cakes. He smiled at the thought, *John Wayne toilet paper, rough, tough, and don't take shit off no one... Focus.* He closed the cabinet and moved to the vanity. The cabinet under the vanity had three doors, all of which opened into the same space underneath the sink. He opened the one on the left, knelt on the floor, and looked inside. He saw two large unopened boxes of those paper towels and several brand new containers of the same types of cleaning products he saw in the plastic cabinet. He gathered the bottles from under the sink and placed them next to the others. Then he neatly stacked the two big boxes of paper towels on top of the plastic cabinet, making it appear as though they belonged there. He crawled into the space under the sink and pulled the door closed.

Seth lay on his back in the dark and gazed at the underneath portion of the cheap Formica vanity. The elbow joint of the sink's plumbing was about half a foot away from his crotch. He kicked his legs around, trying to determine how much more space he had down there. *This'll work.* If there was ever a time he was grateful to be tiny, it was now. He rolled himself over and crawled out from under the sink, dusted himself off, relieved himself in the nearby toilet, washed his hands, and exited the rest room.

Amongst the brochures and pamphlets on the floor by the exit was a standard sized piece of white paper with a small piece of tape on it. The tape had lost all of its adhesiveness and the paper had a dirty foot print on it. Seth picked it up and noticed that there was something written on the opposite side. He turned it over and read the crudely written message that was scribbled with a black marker:

IF YOUR HEAR TO RENEW EXPIERED OUT OF STATE LISENCE YOU NEED TO HAVE TWO FORMS OF ID AND YOU'RE OLD ID CANT BE ONE OF THEM

SGT Holloway laughed at the spelling and grammatical errors on this moronic sign as he crumbled it and threw it in a nearby trash barrel. He pushed through the doors and exited the stuffy, over-crowded DMV. He turned and faced the sign posted on the entrance, making a mental note of their hours, specifically when they close. Then, with a new found sense of direction and purpose, Seth marched happily through the parking lot towards his vehicle. He would have to add a few things to the checklist he had created earlier. While walking, Seth removed his phone. The time at the top of the display read 1321. *Fuck.* He also noticed that he had four new text messages, eleven missed calls, and two new voicemails.

He climbed into his truck and paused for a moment to mentally prepare for the inevitable ass-chewing that he was most certainly waiting for him. *Let's go. You've got work to do.* As he was pulling his seat belt across his lap, SGT Holloway mashed the buttons on his satellite radio, searching for the 70's station in hopes of hearing a little classic Elvis Costello. He pulled out into traffic and headed towards post.

Chapter 14

AROUND THE TIME SOME OFFICE building was being evacuated a few miles away, pain was radiating the entire length of Larry's spine as he struggled to make his way through the grocery store parking lot. He was on various pain medications and he had several techniques to help him alleviate his pain, but today was worse than normal. It seemed like the entrance to the grocery store was a hundred miles away and it got further with each agonizing step. He used his cane to assist his forward progress and it helped a bit, but by this point he wished he had taken Dr. Darcy's advice and gotten that stupid scooter.

As he slowly hobbled to the distant entrance of the store, thoughts faded in and out of his tired old mind. COL Winford hated the man he had become. In his prime, he exhibited the physical capabilities of an Olympic athlete. When he was still on active duty in the Corps he could physically outperform anyone in his Command. Anyone. Even the young pups right out of boot camp. He took pride in the fact that he could hold his own against the young folks. It's been 14 long years since the Colonel retired and his health had decreased a little each and every year since. He first began to feel the effects of his osteoarthritis in his knees and feet about six years ago. Add that to the fact that he had enough shrapnel in his lower back to make a hood ornament and you'd understand why he has gotten a bit grumpier over the years. A whisper of the words *You can make it* sparkled inside his thoughts. "I know," he replied out loud.

As he marched on, he thought of his wife, Tabitha, and how much he missed her. She had succumbed to pancreatic cancer nine years ago. They had been married 41 years at the time of her death. Tabby was a dedicated Marine wife, fully supportive of him during even the most challenging assignments. Sometimes it seemed that she loved the Corps more than he did. She marched forward through the years, by her Colonel's side, taking charge of the homestead each and every time duty called him away. She was a wonderful wife and he missed her dearly. Together they had a son and two daughters, along with seven grandchildren. Travis was the oldest of his children and was now a Major in the Corps, stationed at Camp Pendleton, CA. His daughters, Ashley and Tracy, were both in North Carolina with their families, close to Camp Lejeune, which was where Larry had retired from.

He and Tabby had moved here to Savannah shortly after she was diagnosed so she could be treated at the reputable Anderson Cancer Institute. It was time for them to down-size anyway and Larry liked being in Savannah, he wasn't too far from the girls and he still got to see Travis from time to time, depending on the Major's schedule. Sometimes Travis would make travel arrangements for his Dad, bringing him out to sunny California. Larry enjoyed those trips, one of which he just returned from yesterday. He knew that soon enough, the Marines would send Travis somewhere else and maybe he'd end up closer to here this time. A smile had begun to appear on Larry's face. *Don't lose focus, Colonel.*

As that reminder manifested in Larry's thought process, he began to pick up pace slightly. The bottom of his beautiful mahogany cane drug on the pavement, causing it to scratch and split. He didn't seem to care. He really should add some type of rubber end to the bottom of the thing. He'll ask Dr. Darcy about it this afternoon. *FOCUS*. He could almost picture that bitch in blue from earlier. *Who did she think she was, parking there?* He wasn't sure which was worse, her using someone else's handicap plate or her having one of her own. At that moment, a thought entered Larry's mind that made him see red. *She draws disability benefits. She probably gets paid.* That thought made the bridge of Larry's nose crinkle and his upper lip twitch at the corners. His feelings toward the bitch in blue had quickly progressed from irritation, to repugnance, to pure hatred.

The agony in his knees had nearly doubled since he started this expedition across the colossal parking lot, but he couldn't feel it. Nor could he feel that his feet were nearly swelling out of his shoes, or that his lower back was on fire and getting hotter. He felt nothing. He continued to march on, in the center of the aisle within the parking lot, requiring people to drive around him. A driver of one of the vehicles that had gone around him had made eye to eye contact through the dirty lenses of his goofy glasses.

Larry forgot what groceries he was here to get. He forgot what groceries were. He had no appointment this afternoon. Who is Dr. Darcy? Who are Tabitha, Travis, Ashley, and Tracy? Colonel Winford had one purpose in this life and one purpose alone. *Get that bitch.*

Chapter 15

As an old Vietnam veteran limped through a nearby grocery store parking lot, Samantha Arkenson tried for a third time to reach her ex-husband. Once she started to hear Doug's voice in his outgoing voicemail message, she hung up and set her phone down, ignoring the desire to slam it on the table. Tears trickled down her pretty face as she paced back and forth through her kitchen. Her mind was racing, ruminating on the worst case scenario regarding her mother's recent recurrence of breast cancer, confused by her ex-husbands outlandish overreaction to her request to postpone his visit. Doug was one of the kindest, gentlest, and most understanding people Sam knew. His outburst on the phone earlier was completely out of character. This was the first time she was frightened by her ex-husband. There was something else wrong with him, something happened at work, or something with his personal life that she didn't know about. Something. Samantha believed that the outburst was the tip of the iceberg; the straw that broke the camel's back, something lay under the surface and she hoped she could find out what it was before things got worse.

As she rubbed her eyes with the palm of her hand, Sam felt like she was having a mini-nervous breakdown. She was usually in control of her emotions; she was the one that kept it together in the roughest of times and was the shoulder to cry on when her friends needed it. She had been the supportive best friend when her co-worker Martha's father past away last year. Sam could always remain strong in the darkest of times. Today it felt like everything that was strong about her was disappearing. If she planned on being supportive for her mother, she was going to have to pull it together.

Giving up on trying to reach Doug, she decided to call Jeff. She usually tried not to bother him during the day, but right now he was probably off site having lunch anyway. Sam thought about suggesting that they grab Jessica and head up to Beaufort right now, but almost immediately she thought against it, knowing what he'd say. She knew he wouldn't want to. He hated leaving work early. Not knowing what Doug was going to do and now realizing that Jeff would probably dismiss her request, Sam began to sob again. *What is happening?* she thought.

Picking her phone back up, she pressed contacts and scrolled to Jeff's name. She was going to ask him anyway. She'll make him understand. If he didn't, she planned on getting Jessica herself and heading out, or perhaps she'd get Martha to join them. His phone went straight to voice mail and it was obvious to her that he had turned it off. Sam was looking through loose papers on her entry-way table, trying to find the number to the trailer at the job site, when her door-bell rang.

Samantha was shocked to see two uniformed police officers standing before her. She was deeply concerned and visibly nervous as she exited her home onto the steps out front. *What did Doug do?* she thought. *What did he do?*

"Can I help you?" Sam said in a weak, confused voice, still sobbing.

"Samantha Arkenson?" one of the officers said.

"Yes"

Notebook and pen in hand, the same officer began, "Ma'am, I'm Officer Fernandez, this is Officer Terry. When was the last time you saw your husband?"

Sam, thinking that she knew what this was about, "You mean my ex-husband?"

"No, I mean your husband. Jeffrey Arkenson."

"I saw him this morning before he left for work. Is something wrong?" She was clearly beginning to panic.

"Ma'am, could we come in. You're going to want to sit down."

Chapter 16

MIKE CHRISTIANSON WAS A SEASONED detective with the
Savannah-Chatham Metropolitan Police Department. Although
only there for the last seven years, Detective Christianson had
been in law enforcement for going on thirty-four years this March.
He was a tall, burly, fifty-six year old man with average length
black salt and pepper hair. He once wore a disgusting bushy
mustache, but his second ex-wife convinced him to, as she put it,
"lose the Magnum P.I. look. It's not 1985." Of course, he shaved
it for her. He decided to leave it off once she left him. His second
divorce was a lot messier than his first. He had to leave his position
with the Atlanta Police Department because of the repeated alter-
cations between him and ex-two, often in public. At the risk of this
ex-wife jeopardizing his career and not wanting to be in the same
city as that woman, Mike requested to be reassigned to SCMPD
seven years ago. He's been here, and single, ever since. Things are
much quieter here in Savannah, which was fine with him.

Mike sat at his desk within the bullpen, shuffling through old
papers, pretending to work, when Captain Ted Garrison called
him into his office.

"Hey Mike, got one for you. I need you down on Abercorn,
past Eisenhower on the left. Some office building. I'm pretty sure
you'll find it. Brantley, with the Arson Investigation guys will

meet you there," the Captain said, rather quickly. The Captain was a pear shaped, fifty-nine year old with a receding hair line. He had once been fit, when he was a young man, but those days were long gone. The stress of this job had caused his hair to thin and his waist to thicken.

"That's all we got?" Mike asked.

"I'm getting there. They said someone tied up some woman and torched her. Get with what's-his-face down in forensics so..."

"Tell him to meet me there," Mike said as he left the office.

Nobody in the department liked working with Mike. It wasn't that he was a bad detective or even a bad person. He was a wonderful person with a great personality. He just smelled horrible. Mike was a heavy smoker and he would usually only bathe once a week. To add to his odorous musk, he always wore his clothes much longer then he should. He had once said that the only clothes that should be washed every time you wear them are socks and underwear, even then it's a maybe. In fact, the grey suit he currently wore was going on day six, including the shirt. He only wore clip on ties, simply because he didn't like the idea of a ready-made noose around his neck. His tie usually doubled as a napkin and sometimes a handkerchief. He usually took grief from the guys about the dirty clip on tie that he wore day in and day out along with that grey suit. People stayed clear of Mike because he always reeked of a mixture of locker room, body odor, and a pile of week old laundry covered in tobacco, with the occasional sprinkle of coffee breath, just for good measure.

Mike worked better alone anyway, therefore he couldn't care less what people thought. The way he saw it, his relaxed personal hygiene practices were his own business. If you didn't like it, then stay the hell away. He was however, courteous about where he chose to smoke, always taking into consideration the effects that second hand smoke has on non-smokers, but he couldn't control the smoke that clung to his body and clothes upon leaving the designated smoking area outside. In the unlikely event that he had to work with another person, they would usually take two cars. Although it was against regulations to smoke in a department owned vehicle, Mike still got in at least one smoke every time he was called away from the office.

Mike drove his motor pool issued silver Impala south on Abercorn, towards where it intersected with Eisenhower, as the Captain had instructed. He arrived at a three story brick building on the left side of the road, a little past the intersection. It was easy to find since fire trucks were still on scene and a squad from SCMPD had cordoned off the area with yellow police tape. The uniformed policemen outside the building kept the employees of the evacuated building off to the side and segregated from the other crowd that had formed, as the detectives would want some information from them.

Mike wanted to yell out the old cliché "Nothing to see here folks, move along," but decided against it. Sparking up a Marlboro red, he asked a few questions of the officers standing by; just some common questions regarding security and the crowd, pretty much just killing time until what's his face got there. One officer explained that the woman who fried shared the office with a guy named Dave Spears and he had left the office right before the alarm went off. He explained that the guy told the receptionist, who he pointed at while explaining, that he had a teacher conference.

"Anybody find out what school he went to? Anyone going there?" Mike asked, knowing that he hadn't heard anything over the radio about it.

"I think so, we called it in."

"Bring her here," Mike said, as he pointed at Rachel, crushing out his cigarette on the sole of his shoe and cramming the butt in his back pocket.

The officer gestured Rachel and she reported promptly. By now, news of what had gone on inside had made its way through the crowd. People who knew the woman that was murdered had a look of sorrow and visible tears on their faces, while those who didn't displayed looks of shock and disbelief. Rachel had both.

"Miss, my name is Detective Christianson, I like to ask you a few questions," he said as he removed a note book from the inside pocket of his jacket. "What time did David Spears leave here?"

Through trembling lips, Rachel said "Well, he left at like 11:00, but then he came back"

"How long was he gone?"

"I'm not sure, only a few minutes. Ten Maybe. Ten minutes. He said he was running across the street."

Mike glanced across the street and saw a few commercial establishments, one of which was a gas station with a convenience store. That was probably where he went, Mike assumed, but he would make sure, of course. Probably get their security tape as well. He'd need to request that. Mike continuously scribbled in his notebook during the line of questions.

"Did you notice if he brought anything back with him?"

"No. I didn't notice anything. I didn't really look at him. He didn't stop, I figured he was in a hurry or something."

"Ok, how long did he stay before he left again?"

"Not long," Rachel said. "He said he had an appointment or something, I couldn't remember at first, but then I did and I told that officer that he said he was going to a teacher conference."

"And the fire alarm went off right after he left?"

"A few minutes later, yeah."

"We're almost done, ma'am. What else can you tell me about David Spears? Has he been acting strange lately? Anything you can think of. Anything at all...."

"No. He seemed fine to me. He was just tired, I could tell that. I know he was at a conference in Atlanta all weekend. I think he said he didn't get home until late last night."

"When did he leave for Atlanta? Do you know?"

"He was out of the office Thursday and Friday last week. I guess he left Wednesday night or Thursday morning. I don't know...I'm sure he got back last night, though..." Rachel said, starting to sob again.

"Ma'am, here's my card. If you think of anything else please call me. Any time is fine. The officers are going to need your official statement. I'm sorry for everything," Mike said as he handed the young lady his business card.

The sadness and confusion that radiated off this woman got to Mike a little. Even after over thirty years of police work, Mike still got choked up by the effects that senseless acts of violence have on the people involved. He would never allow his personal feelings to taint his judgment, however; Mike knew when to turn off his empathy and focus on detective work. He lit another cigarette as he waited for the forensic team to show up.

About six minutes after Mike arrived, a white van pulled up and a team of four people poured out of the back, followed by two from the cab. The person in the passenger's seat was what's-his-face. Brett. Or Brad.

"Hey, man," Mike said as he shook Brad's hand. "You ready to do this?"

Brad nodded as the small group of people headed to the building. Mike pinched the head off his cigarette and stuck it in his pocket. He couldn't stand litterers. He would empty his butt filled pockets at the end of the day, usually on to the floor of his back seat. Pausing to issue a few commands to the officer he had spoken to earlier, Mike said:

"Some guy named Brantley from the arson team is en route. Let him up when he gets here. Get on the radio and make sure they sent out an APB on this David Spears guy."

Mike then caught up to and followed the forensic team into the building.

"Roger," the officer said as he was waving his hand back and forth in front of his nose once Mike's back was turned.

Chapter 17

AN APB EXPLODED ACROSS THE net, alerting all law enforcement agencies within Chatham, Bryan, Liberty, and Effingham counties to be on the lookout for Jeffery Nicholas Arkenson. The broadcast was complete with a physical description of the suspect, an explanation of what he had supposedly done, and his last known location. The perp's identity was provided by the vehicle registration left inside the totaled Dodge Ram. His physical description was provided by eighteen different witnesses, half of which had actually seen him commit murder, while the rest only saw him flee the scene. The message also came with a prediction of where he was headed and instructions to arrest on sight.

The crash site north of the intersection of Highway 17 and Mulberry Drive was secured by officers responding from the Richmond Hill Police Department. Over the last ten minutes, thirteen calls regarding this situation had flooded the Bryan County emergency dispatcher. The dispatcher alerted Richmond Hill authorities after the first call and went on to explain to all subsequent callers that the situation was being attended to. Based on the information provided by the multiple callers, the dispatchers were able to alert Chatham county authorities since it appeared that the perp was heading that way. Additionally, the crime had taken place about two-tenths of a mile from not only the Richmond Hill/Savannah line, but also the line that separates Bryan County and Chatham County.

Two police cruisers secured the area surrounding the wreck, lights rolling. Similar to the crime scene miles away in Savannah, yellow police tape cordoned off the area, keeping spectators at bay. The fugitive had brutally murdered someone in what appeared to be an amplified case of road rage. Paramedics had arrived on scene a moment ago, as well as another Richmond Hill cruiser and an unmarked police sedan carrying Bryan County Sheriff's Deputy Matt Wheeler. Given the amount of law enforcement agents looking for Arkenson, Deputy Wheeler decided to post himself at the scene of the crime for the time being.

Matt Wheeler was a thirty two year old Sheriff's Deputy with six years on the job. He and his wife of eight years live in Pembroke, GA and have no children. Deputy Wheeler and his wife were high school sweethearts in their home town of Metter, GA, which is about sixty miles from Pembroke. When he was discharged from the U.S. Army seven years ago, he and his wife decided to stay in the area rather than return home to Metter. He was stationed at Fort Stewart, GA when his time was up and they already lived in Pembroke, therefore it made no sense to leave. Matt was a military policeman in the Army and his initial goal was to re-enter service as a member of the Army's Criminal Investigation Command. Those plans hadn't worked out for a few reasons, one of which was his lack of education, so he decided he would get a few years' experience in the outside sector, while taking a few college classes, before trying again.

Being so close to a military installation had its advantages for Matt; he still had several connections with members of CID (Criminal Investigations Division) and the Military Police Head-quarters. That type of networking can come in handy since a lot of the people that lived in Bryan County were active duty service members.

While Deputy Wheeler spoke with one of the paramedics, what they thought was a repeat of the current APB came across the airways:

"Attention all law enforcement agencies within Chatham, Bryan, Liberty, and Effingham counties: Be on the lookout for David Johnathan Spears. Wanted for questioning about possible arson and homicide. Possible location - Units alerted and already en route to Mercer Middle School 201 Rommel Ave. Savannah. Suspect is 40 years old, 6 feet tall, 180 pounds. Last seen wearing grey business suit. Arrest on sight."

Deputy Wheeler and the paramedic gave each other a strange look of confusion. It was rare that there were two unrelated circumstances involving murder suspects evading police in this area. The Savannah area was not without crime by any means, *But, two? At the same time?* It was strange. When he woke up this morning, Wheeler was not expecting his Monday to consist of two simultaneous man-hunts spanning a four county area in broad day light. In his six years as a Sheriff's Deputy there had been only five murders in Bryan County and never on the same day as one next door in Chatham County.

"Today's gonna be a long one," the Deputy said as he walked over to the man with half a face lying dead beside his destroyed

Altima. The paramedics had placed the man on a gurney and covered him with a sheet prior to putting him in the back of the ambulance. The area of the sheet that covered the poor man's face was soaked with bright red blood. Although the area was cordoned off from nearby onlookers, people still cried and gasped as the paramedics executed their duties. It was clear to everyone in the area that the man's face was obliterated Deputy Wheeler began to assist the other officers with gathering official statements from the crowd. A long day, indeed.

Chapter 18

As Jeff executed his wide right flank into the thickening woods attempting to bypass the residential area, he could hear dozens of sirens from what seemed like all directions. He made a feeble attempt to try and detect exactly which directions the sirens came from, but it was unsuccessful. The sounds blurred together. He needed to stick with his plan. Move to the highway. He was confident that his attempt to trick the two men that were following him had worked, or perhaps he had outrun them. Whichever the case, he could not see or hear them anymore; therefore, he no longer considered them to be a threat. They were probably bouncing around the residential area; *hopefully they would bump into the police, maybe get mistaken for me,* Jeff thought.

He was surrounded by trees in all directions now, the houses in the neighborhood to his south west were no longer visible. He hadn't been paying too much attention to the distance that he covered; therefore he really had no idea when to expect to make contact with I-95. Whenever he did, he planned on staying in the woods and using the highway as a handrail, keeping it on his left to lead him north to Highway 204 and eventually his job site. He would have to cross I-95 at some point, there was no avoiding that; or he could use the 204 overpass to get to his destination. He would eventually have to deal with the river as well. Either way, he would not have the comfort of the concealment provided by the trees for his entire evasion. He would eventually have to expose himself. He would have to be smart about how he did that, since the cops most likely have anticipated this. Speed, stealth, and timing were keys to his survival.

As he pushed forward through the woods, Jeff tried to manifest the voice that had once bounced around his head. There was warmth within that voice; it brought him a sense of contentment. If he could only get his suppressed friend to come back and provide just a little reassurance; a small slap of stimulus, he might begin to feel better. It became more and more obvious that the voice wasn't coming back and he was going to have to motivate himself somehow.

The heavy vegetation and swampy terrain that was common in this area was reducing his chances of escape as it slowed his movement significantly. It brought Jeff a small amount of comfort to know that his pursuers were navigating the same terrain he was, so they were probably slowing down as well. He had the advantage of his water proof work boots that were resisting the mushy swamp water he was trekking through; the cops were probably in dumb cop shoes. Jeff assumed that the authorities would place road blocks along I-95 and 204 and they most likely had deployed some type of K9 unit by now, although he couldn't hear any barking. Hopefully the swamp water would reduce his scent and confuse the dogs. Doubtful. Very doubtful. His optimistic attitude was depleting rapidly as he stumbled through the squishy marsh. Sweat trickled down his bare arms and into the many cuts and scratches that were caused by the green environment. The skin around his eyes, face, and neck was becoming extremely irritated as the sweat and body heat combined with the powder still covering him from the airbag that punched him in the face earlier. He was beginning to feel the effects of minor dehydration as well, black spots were starting to dance in the air in front of his face. His legs and abdomen were cramping, he needed a break. Now. Grabbing a tree to slow his momentum, Jeff slowed himself; he had to take a knee and catch his breath.

Chapter 19

SHORTLY AFTER AN ARSON INVESTIGATOR arrived at the location of a fire nine miles away, Doug Mason turned off of Rommel Ave. and parked his Toyota 4-runner outside Mercer Middle School. As he shut off the engine, a thought manifested within his mind, almost feeling like an itch on his brain that he obviously couldn't scratch. *This isn't what I want. Don't fuck this up.* He shook off the words in his head and glanced at his wrist. His watch read 12:57, but he thought it might be a little fast. He ran from his vehicle to the school's main entrance, not at a pace that would draw suspicion, but merely looking like someone trying to get somewhere a bit faster than just walking. Doug slowed down upon arriving at the school's double door entrance, caught his breath, and he calmly went inside. He was on the list of people authorized to pick up Jessica and he's been here several times before, therefore; Doug felt confident that there'd be no snags. *Unless the bitch called and warned them. She wouldn't dare.*

Doug shook his head at that thought; he didn't like the idea of referring to his daughter's mother as a bitch. *But that's what she is.* Trying to focus on something else, Doug remembered that the last time he told the office that his daughter had a doctor's appointment they gave him a friendly reminder to have little Jessica bring a note from the doctor the next day so she wouldn't get marked as missing time from school. He knew that these comments were coming again, so he prepared himself for them, maybe saving himself some time. Even a few seconds. After all, seconds add up to minutes.

Before arriving at the window opening into the office's reception desk, Doug caught his breath and prepared his handsome voice by clearing his throat. He indulged in a few deep, relaxing breaths. Breathing in through the nose and exhaling through the mouth; calming his mind, regaining his composure and confidence. He was well aware of the effect he had on women and he would use it to his advantage from time to time. Once he was ready, Doug leaned through window and projected the enchantment of his good looks upon the woman in the office.

"Good afternoon, ladies!" Doug announced through the window.

Across the office, he could see that there was a wide screen TV mounted to the wall with a crowd of faculty members huddled around it. He couldn't hear anything, but he could see police vehicles and a fire truck behind the reporter that spoke into an oversized microphone. There was a message at the bottom of the screen, white font on a yellow background, scrolling from right to left. Doug was too far away to read anything specific in the scrolling message, but he could definitely make out the red letters in the upper right corner of the screen. "ALERT!"

One of the women peeled herself away from the TV in order to see what the gentleman at the window needed. The woman was African American and large.

"Can I help you, sugar?" she said.

"Yes ma'am, I need to pick up my little girl for a doctor's appointment," Doug answered. "I'll be sure to get a note from the doctor. She's Jessica Mason. She's in Mrs. Cole's class," Doug sang to the woman, using his charm in an effort to expedite things.

It clearly worked because she smiled back at him from ear to ear, said something like "Absolutely!" and waddled over to the intercom. She used the intercom's feature that enables the administration people to communicate directly with a specific classroom. She spoke into the receiver: "Mrs. Rodman, please send Jessica Mason to the office, her father is here."

The woman smiled at the man that she knew was divorced and available. Doug smiled back.

"She'll be right up, sugar. You can have a seat right over there once you sign her out," the woman said as she handed Doug a clip board with a student sign out sheet attached to it.

"Thank you," Doug said as he filled out the spreadsheet on the clip board. Once done, he sat in one of the chairs directly outside the office where parents and students sit and wait to be served by the administration.

This school was a single story building and was very small; therefore it only took Jessica four minutes to report to the office. As soon as Doug was in sight, she ran into his arms while screaming.

"Dadddddy! I thought you weren't getting me 'til the end of the day! This is awesome!"

"Ssshh," Doug said, "I told them you had a doctor's appointment."

They smiled at each other as they headed toward the exit. *Better not fuck this up,* glistened in his mind.

"I won't," Doug said, as he pushed through the doors and exited the school. As he left, he held the door for a man he recognized from a giant billboard he'd seen earlier. He watched as the man and his wife entered the school.

Chapter 20

JIM REYNOLDS HADN'T BEEN PAYING attention to the TV that so many of his staff had been watching as he passed through the office and headed towards Laura Jones's classroom. Laura was a little surprised to see him show up for this conference, as he had never shown an interest in the discipline of the students before, although it was his responsibility as the Assistant Principle. This man definitely gave Laura the impression that he was at that school to draw a pay check, nothing more.

"Hey, Miss Jones. Dr. Ruthfield asked Principle Stapleton that I attend this meeting with you. They both want a witness here in case the Spears try to accuse you of anything. I hope it's ok with you." Mr. Reynolds said.

"Of course it is, Sir. Why wouldn't it be?" Laura said in a respectful manner, making completely sure that she wasn't giving him the signal that her polite response meant anything. Hopefully he didn't misinterpret her professional attitude to be anything other than just that. Professional. She didn't think she could handle a repeat of any of his previous behavior. Not today.

Mr. Reynolds was probably telling the truth and it made Laura happy to know that her superiors were thinking of her welfare when they decided to send a little protection in case she had to deal with accusatory parents. Although, Reynolds was just the type of creep that might say something like that just to have a reason to get close to her. If it *was* directed from higher, he probably jumped all over it when Principle Stapleton gave him the assignment, seeing it as an opportunity to look up her skirt or down her blouse. She imagined that "Big Jim," which was a nickname used by the staff, was disappointed to see her in slacks today.

Jim Reynolds was an older man and a tad portly, hence the nickname. Laura didn't know how old, but based on his receding hairline, greying hair, and belly that hung over the belt, she guessed he was in his mid-fifties. Laura didn't pay much attention to his personal life, but she knew that he had been married for a very long time and that he had a few grown kids. She gathered that information the very first time she sat in his office from the pictures on his desk. She thought back to that day just over two years ago.

Her first impression of the Assistant Principle was that of pure disgust. She felt dirty just sitting in his office during their initial meeting, surrounded by pictures of his family as he undressed her with his eyes. Luckily Laura did not allow her first impression of the filthy Assistant Principle to influence her opinion of the school itself. If she had, she wouldn't have taken the position. The fact that this man was blatant about his intentions infuriated Laura. *He probably does this to all the new young teachers*, she thought that day, *how could this fat old man think that a young teacher would be interested in him?* Laura was by no means a shallow person. She did not base her opinion of him just on his appearance, but it turned out that this specific man happens to be ugly on the inside as well as the outside.

Mr. Reynolds and Laura stood in the doorway of her class-room, waiting on either little Jason or the parents, whoever arrived first. Jason was the first to arrive, having just finished lunch. He reported as ordered and entered Laura's room about three minutes after the Assistant Principle did. Jason was disappointed by the presence of Mr. Reynolds, as he was a little intimidated by him. Young Jason showed Laura no respect whatsoever, but he feared Big Jim Reynolds. Most kids did. Laura began to think that Mr. Reynolds presence at this meeting might not be such a bad idea after all, as it will certainly keep Jason in line.

"Hi, Jason," Laura said with a friendly smile as she instructed the boy to sit in his regular seat.

Dave and Linda Spears entered the school and walked right past the office administrator's window. Dave didn't think anyone even noticed that they came in, as everyone was staring at a TV mounted to the wall. If they had noticed, they would've asked for ID and had the couple sign in on the register. As they approached Laura and Mr. Reynolds, both having returned to their position in the doorway, Dave extended his arm to the Assistant Principle, in the universal gesture of the hand shake. Jim Reynolds hadn't known that the man whose hand he shook was all over the news and was the subject of an all-points bulletin that covered four counties. He did, however; recognize him from his billboards.

"Please come in," Laura said as she led the couple into her classroom. The Spears took up the two seats in front of young Jason; Dave directly in front of the boy, and his mother directly to the left of Dave. Mr. Reynolds and Laura turned two student desks around so they could sit and face the Spears. Laura placed her laptop on the desk as she sat down and opened it, the blue folder having been stowed inside the closed laptop. Mrs. Spears pulled out her phone and began fiddling with it the instant that she sat down. Laura could feel the unwelcomed eyes of Mr. Spears while he looked her up and down. He had just finished licking his lips when Laura spoke.

"Mr. and Mrs. Spears, the reason I asked you to come in today is because I don't like the direction that Jason is heading. I think that if we don't work together to help him turn things around, we're going to run into some problems in the future," Laura said, as respectfully as she could. They wouldn't have wanted to hear what she really thought and she would have never said it out loud.

She continued to go over the grades and missing assignments with Jason's parents, every so often Mr. Spears would say something to Jason and the boy would either shrug his shoulders or say he didn't know. Mrs. Spears thumbed the screen of her phone the entire time, every once in a while she'd chuckle or groan as a result of something she read in an email or text. Mr. Reynolds would occasionally chime in to the conversation, citing the schools disciplinary standards or talking about detention or something, he wasn't really adding anything substantial to the meeting, although Laura was still grateful that he was there. If he wasn't, Jason would've said or done something inappropriate by now.

Out of nowhere, Dave said, "What do I have to do to get my son moved to another class?"

"Well, Sir, we've tried that already," Mr. Reynolds answered, "It didn't seem to help much. Did it, Jason?"

A shrug was the only response Jason gave. Laura was obviously a little frustrated by this point in the conversation. Talking to the Spears wasn't like talking to rocks. She felt that rocks would be more receptive. The young teacher was saddened by the lack of anything even close to a nurturing attitude for poor Jason from his parents. Laura had initially thought that Jason was a mean, lazy little kid. She was starting to understand the reason why. Her attitude towards Jason was slowly changing from one of resentment to something a little more sympathetic. She began to think that perhaps he wasn't that bad, maybe he just lacked any kind of attention at home and he was acting out at school to get it, as many children do.

Laura looked towards Jason with sympathetic eyes as he sat quietly with a frown on his little face. From behind his father, and while Mr. Reynolds was engaged in conversation, Jason made an obscene gesture toward Laura. He curled his fingers around an invisible penis and pretended to shove it in and out of his mouth, using his tongue to depress his cheek from the inside, as if he was performing oral sex. Mr. Reynolds and Mr. Spears had been focused on each other when it happened and Mrs. Spears had her face permanently affixed to her phone, so of course she hadn't seen it either. Laura's jaw dropped.

This boy's disgusting display caused Laura's right eye to begin to twitch, it almost felt as though someone was gently touching her eye with a feather from the inside. As she sat there, staring at this filthy little boy who now wore a devilish little grin, she started to hear the faint sounds of a word she couldn't quite understand. *Doodeeculls. Dudiekowls?* Finally the muffled word fell apart into two clear and distinct individual sounds as she heard it for a third time. *Duty Calls*

"Laura?"

Mr. Reynolds voice snapped Laura out of her momentary daze. *Duty Calls* gently whispered in her mind again, starting from the inside of her right ear and seeming to travel around the front of her forehead, dropping slightly and softly circling around the insides of her eyes, with small sparkles of pleasure, before stopping at the left ear. The path of the sound passionately massaged her from within as it moved across her mind, making her giggle a little inside. The charming voice filled her soul with a feeling of pure enlightenment; it made her feel as though all of her problems would be over shortly.

She brought her luscious hazel eyes to meet Mr. Reynolds's eyes and paused there for a more dramatic effect. She slowly opened her mouth as she spoke, gently licking her lips, allowing them to stick together before lightly pulling them apart as she said his name.

"Jim? Do you mind going over these disciplinary reports while I go to the ladies room, please?" she said in a voice that was just sultry enough to not go over the line.

"Shu-sure," Jim responded while gulping.

"You're a dear," she said as she stood, placing her hand affectionately on his shoulder. "Duty Calls."

The suggestive look she had temporarily used to distract the Assistant Principle faded from Laura's face as soon as she was no longer within his sight. It was replaced with a face that radiated pure focus and exhilaration. She moved swiftly, but not running, past the office and towards the front door, her clicking heels echoing through the empty halls. Once outside, she marched to her grey Honda Civic, pressing the button on the keyless entry device that was in her extended hand. She opened the passenger side door, reached into the glove box and secured her pistol. It was not uncommon for a young lady to have a hand gun for self-defense. Even now she could hear sirens everywhere around her; this area clearly had the potential to be dangerous. This Ruger SR9 compact center-fire pistol was completely legal and registered; she even had a Georgia concealed carry permit. She racked the slide back, chambering the first of its ten round capacity magazine. The extensive training she had undergone imbedded a sense of respect for firearms in Laura, therefore she never kept one in the chamber unless she was about to use it. She stuffed it into the front right pocket of her slacks, causing a small bulge.

Laura walked with a sense of determination through the halls of her school, heading back toward her classroom and the duty that awaited her. She passed a janitor mopping the floors in an adjacent hallway. Making sure not to walk on the portion of the floor that was still wet, she nodded at the goofy, four-eyed man as she passed. As she entered her classroom, Laura removed her pistol from her pocket in a smooth, fluid motion and fired a single 9mm round through the phone in Linda Spears hands. Half of the woman's right hand disappeared as the phone shattered into flying chunks of plastic and glass. The round continued to travel into the woman's sternum, expanding as it ripped through her flesh, pulverizing bone and tissue in its path, causing her to fly backward within her chair and crash to the floor.

Laura kept her head facing the target that she had just destroyed, but she turned the corners of her eyes towards David Spears; her eyes opened wide enough that the whites of them was surely the last thing seen by the man. She bent her right arm slightly so that the barrel of her weapon was now pointing in his direction. She squeezed the trigger, putting a round in his face. The round traveled through the cheek bone on the right side, rattled around aimlessly, exited through the back of his head, and embedded itself in the dry erase board behind him. Dave Spears hunched over slightly, but died upright; similar to the way Gail Watson died about two hours ago. Jim Reynolds had gotten up by now, attempting to flee. A pair of bullets in his chubby back put an end to that, causing him to fall forward and land on his fat face.

Little Jason Spears sat frozen in his seat, his eyes as wide as saucers, his face freckled with small splatters of his parents blood. Laura took two steps in Jason's direction; she raised her weapon and squeezed off two rounds in rapid succession into the little boy's face.

Laura reengaged the safety of her pistol, dropped the magazine, pulled the slide rearward, and caught the ejected round in mid-air. She re-inserted the ejected round back into the magazine and set both the pistol and the magazine gently down on the desk next to her laptop. Safety first. *Good Job!* Laura picked up her laptop and returned to her desk, leaving the pistol and magazine on the desk where she temporarily sat during the pointless meeting that she had just adjourned.

Chapter 21

IT WAS 1337 HRS. AS SGT Holloway waited for his Platoon Sergeant to return from the meeting that he and the Lieutenant had with the Battalion Commander. He sat in the office that his two superiors shared, much like the way an insubordinate school boy would sit and wait for his father to come home from work to administer punishment. As he waited on his inevitable ass chewing, Seth remembered the information he had gathered from his reconnaissance of the DMVs layout. He removed his green note book from his pocket and began to add a few things to his timeline and inventory checklist for tomorrow's range. On the next page in his notebook, Seth began to scratch out a second inventory for his side mission:

Nonelectric delayed initiating/detonating assembly
M14, electrical tape –Burn rate? 3 min? 4?
Igniter
4 blocks C4? 5 ???
Buffer Material – whatever...
4-6 cans
Shock tube
Stuff – nails, glass, screws, etc.
Green tape, one roll
Cordless drill?

Before he could label his drawing, Holloway heard SFC Johnson and LT Akers approaching in the hallway. He tore his new list out of his notebook, stuck it in his pocket, and got to his feet just as the two men entered the room. SGT Holloway assumed the position of parade rest, which is modified position of attention and is always the position of those who were about to receive an ass chewing; which he most certainly was.

"Ah ha, if it isn't SGT *promotable* Holloway, and I use the term loosely," SFC Johnson said as he entered the small office. "Can you excuse us, LT?"

Lieutenant Aker left the two Non-Commissioned Officers alone, and SFC Johnson began to read SGT Holloway the riot act. SFC Johnson could teach a course on the proper way to reprimand a subordinate. At no time did he ever belittle the recipient, but he would still make the walls vibrate. SGT Holloway hated letting down his superiors. They were the ones who recommended him for promotion, after all, and he considered it a violation of the trust and confidence that they have for him should he foul up. SFC Johnson went on to explain that it was the Battalion Commander who was disappointed, since he wanted to speak directly to the people who are planning on giving classes at tomorrow's range. Sometimes it's necessary to place your own needs on hold for the good of the unit. The DMV would be there later, SGT Holloway should've altered his plans once he realized that the line was too long. Seth knew he had a minor excuse; he tried to send a message from the DMV but he was without a signal. He decided that it might be a good idea to keep that to himself. He just stood at the position of parade rest and took it like a man. SFC Johnson didn't hold grudges and it would be over soon.

"Did you at least get it? Your license?" SFC Johnson said, after the ass chewing.

"No. I didn't have the right ID. It pissed me off, I was there the whole time and I didn't even get it. I'll get back there eventually, take care of it later," Holloway answered.

"Well, don't wait too long. You shouldn't be out there with an expired license."

When the conversation was complete, SFC Johnson called the Lieutenant back into the office so they could discuss tomorrow. The three men went over minor details, just a few changes that the Battalion Commander made to his expectations that Holloway would've heard if he was back on time. The LT and SFC Johnson would have another meeting with key participants to discuss these changes at the end of the duty day. SGT Holloway could make a few changes to his plans at that time as well. He would have to prepare a solid plan if he was going to complete his mission to the standard that his internal guest demanded.

Chapter 22

"ATTENTION ALL LAW ENFORCEMENT AGENCIES within Chatham, Bryan, Liberty, and Effingham counties: Update on situation regarding suspect David Johnathan Spears. Wanted for questioning about possible arson and homicide. Possible location - Units on station Mercer Middle School 201 Rommel Ave. Savannah. Shots fired. Active shooter inside school. David Johnathan Spears suspect," barked across the open net spanning a four county area.

Two units from Savannah Chatham Metropolitan Police Department arrived shortly after shots rang out from inside Mercer Middle School. The officers had already been deployed earlier in search of Dave Spears in regards to the fire and murder at an office building ten miles away at the corner of Abercorn and Eisenhower. Now it appears that he is inside the school and opening fire. All active members of SCMPD's SWAT have been altered and were en route to Mercer Middle School, including both Hostage Negotiation Teams and all six Tactical Paramedics. Faculty members had initiated their rehearsed "active shooter" drill and had begun evacuating students.

In some areas students and teachers hid within their classroom, while in other areas they were completely evacuated and assembled in their pre-determined assembly area outside. SWAT teams had arrived and begun to deploy to their areas of responsibilities. Some provided outer cordon security while others secured the interior windows and doors of the school. Another team prepared to enter the school, while snipers covered the school from elevated positions on a rooftop across the street. These professionals had quickly achieved a coordinated 360 degree containment of the objective building.

Unaware of the commotion outside, Laura Jones sat peacefully at her desk, amongst the bodies of the four people she just murdered, grading the tests that her students took this morning. Except Jason's exam, of course. That she balled up threw in the garbage. The pleasant, calming voice she once felt within her was now gone. She was a little uncertain about what to do now. There was no regret, however. She was glad that she had executed a family of three and a fat sexist pig. She just wished she put more thought into what to do next. *Oh well,* she thought with her own mind, as she continued to grade papers and wait on the police to show up.

Detective Mike Christianson left the arson investigator and the forensic team back at the Endeavor office and headed to Mercer Middle School. They could wrap things up back at the crime scene on Abercorn without him; he wanted to be there when David Spears was either apprehended or killed. He drove at a high rate of speed through the streets of Savannah and arrived at the school within eleven minutes. As the detective arrived, he witnessed who he thought was the principle talking to one of the

Negotiation Team leaders. Crushing out his cigarette and sticking the butt in his pocket, Mike approached the two men and identified himself, although he already knew the Negotiation team leader.

Cleary distraught, Principle Stapleton said, "We're w-working on getting accountability right now, Detective. I know that Mr. Spears was supposed to have a meeting with Miss Jones this afternoon. I don't know if he's here yet. I can't ch-check the sign-in sheet because it's inside. Oh God. Jim Reynolds was supposed to sit in on it and, and I-I-I don't see him anywhere either, I don't see Laura, or-or the boy. Oh my God, my secretary? Um, I don't know..."

"Sir, calm down," Mike said, "They're going to find everyone that's still inside and take care of this the best way possible. You need to pull it together for the sake of your students. Your top priority is accounting for your children and staff. Please let us know as soon as you have everyone accounted for."

"I know...y-y-yes sir.." Principle Stapleton said as he scurried away to talk to some senior members of his faculty that he could see taking charge of some children in a nearby parking lot. When he left the area, Mike approached the Negotiation team leader whose name he couldn't remember.

"What do you know?" Mike said.

"Not sure yet," the man replied, "I guess this guy set a fire or something, back at his office, then he came here and started shooting. The principle said he heard six shots, but who knows. Might be more. They're getting ready to go in, start clearing."

"He didn't just start a fire, I just came from there. This fucker tied a woman up, cut her tongue out, and then torched her," Mike said, as he stuck another Marlboro in his mouth.

"Holy shit. I didn't get all that. What a sick fuck. Man, I hope this fucker didn't shoot any kids."

"Me too," Mike said, as he exhaled smoke into the unseasonably warm Savannah afternoon.

Chapter 23

"MA'AM, RIGHT NOW I'M BEING told that he is somewhere in the woods between Highway 17 and I-95. There are multiple units searching for him, along with two K9 units and we've got a helicopter on the way," Detective Grant Wright explained to Samantha Arkenson as they sat in a small room inside SCMPD head-quarters. Grant Wright was a 31 year old detective that had eight years of law enforcement work under his belt. He was of average height and weight, but he had a freakishly large and square shaped head, a feature that didn't seem to bother Maria, his wife of five years. Shortly after the hysterical Mrs. Arkenson was brought in, Detective Wright was ordered by Captain Garrison to act as a liaison for her regarding the situation involving her husband.

Two uniformed officers had explained to Sam about an hour ago in her living room that her husband, Jeff Arkenson, had been involved in some kind of accident in Richmond Hill, that there were injuries, and that Jeff had fled the scene. Confused and upset, Sam had agreed to accompany the two officers to the police station, so she could be abreast of new information and to assist in any way she could. She had sat for the past 45 minutes in this small holding room, trying to reach Doug and Jeff on the phone. Periodically an officer would enter the room with small updates about the situation, nothing too significant. Nobody had told her that her husband had mutilated a man's face with his bare hands and then bashed his skull with a bat until his brain fell out, but eventually the Detective would.

Now Sam and Detective Wright sat in the small room. Samantha said between her sobs, "I don't understand why he would flee the scene. They told me that someone was injured. Is the other person ok? How bad was the accident?"

"I'm sorry to say this, but the other person didn't survive," the detective said, "If you know where he's going, you have to tell us. It looks like he's heading to the job site he's assigned to. It would make sense based on where he was seen running and what you already told me, unless you think he's going somewhere else..."

Sam had buried her face in her hands when the detective said the words "didn't survive." Trying her best to maintain her composure and speak clearly, she responded, "I don't know where he would go, it sounds like he's heading that way. It's right there on 204. Why would he do this? Oh my God," She broke down again.

"Has anything happened recently that would make him behave this way? Anything you can think of. Fighting at home, trouble at work. Anything?"

"No. I don't think so. No fighting. Work? I mean, I know he's getting sick of having to travel for work all the time, but I didn't think he was that mad about it."

"Where does he go? For how long?"

Sam paused to think before answering, "He just goes to Atlanta, maybe once a month or every other month. Never for more than a couple days each time, he just got back yesterday."

Outside the room there was a large amount of distracting commotion, which Sam could only assume had something to do with what her husband had done. Detective Wright knew otherwise. He stood up, explained that he would be right back, and began to leave. As he turned to walk away, Sam's phone rang. Detective Wright pointed at her phone, anticipating that she would say, "It's my husband," but she shook her head and said "sorry, it's my mother."

Sam answered without saying hello. "Mom, I don't know what's going on. I'm losing my mind here. Jeff's been in an accident and now the police can't find him and Doug freaked out on me about bringing J up to see you. I don't..."

"Sam," her mother interrupted, "aren't you watching TV? Where are you? What's Jessica's school?"

"Mercer. I'm with the police. You're scaring me," Sam answered through trembling lips.

"There's been a shooting there! Turn on the TV!"

Sam screamed out something that resembled "Oh my God!" as she burst through the door of the little room she was in and nearly ran over Detective Grant, who was on his way back.

"What's up?" he said.

"My daughters at that school!! Where the shooting is!"

Detective Grant, feeling like an idiot for not putting the pieces together earlier, said, "Let's go."

He led Samantha outside and into his police issue vehicle, placed the removable police siren onto the roof, and peeled out of the parking lot, headed toward Rommel Ave. As Detective Grant locked his seat belt into place, a nasally, overwhelmed voice announced across the radio, "Need a unit near East Gwinnett St. Respond. Unit 12. Unit 12? Kroger on East Gwinnett. 217. 217. Woman assaulted inside the store. Unit 12?"

Chapter 24

Normally a dispatcher's request like the one issued for the events on Gwinnett St. would warrant more than one unit, but this was a unique day. When Officers Benavides and Ivory pulled into the Kroger parking lot, the paramedics were already bringing out the victim on a gurney and placing her into the back of the ambulance. One of the paramedics was controlling the IV bag while the other was manipulating the gurney. The red flashing lights of the ambulance combined with the blue lights of the police cruiser reflected off the glass entrance of the grocery store. The woman's head and face were bandaged and the front of her blue dress was saturated with blood. The bandage over her face bulged excessively, looking like there was something under it, wrapped up with her face. Officer Benavides noticed that the woman wore only one black high heel shoe.

"Where's he at?" Officer Benavides asked one of the paramedics, slowing down only slightly for an answer.

"All the way in the back. To the left. The store manager is with him," answered the paramedic without losing focus on what he was doing.

The two officers ran through the grocery store in the direction that the paramedic had said, announcing themselves as they maneuvered through shoppers and wagons filled with groceries.

When they arrived in the back left corner of the store, they saw an old man seated on the floor, leaning against a refrigerated compartment where assorted cheeses were displayed. The man had blood on his pants and shirt, as well as on both hands, which rested on his lap. There was a large amount of blood smeared on the floor, as if someone had rolled around in it. He had a confused and bewildered look on his face as he stared up to the ceiling with wide eyes. There were two young gentlemen, about the age of average college students, standing as sentries on either side of the old man, a broken wooden cane was on the floor behind one of them. As the officers arrived, they were greeted by someone who looked as though he would be the store manager.

"Officers, I'm the store manager, Bill Duncan. These two gentlemen witnessed the whole thing. I'll let them explain."

"Just a second, Sir," Officer Ivory said to the store manager, as the two officers rolled the old man over to secure his hands behind his back with handcuffs, raising him to his feet. Officer Benavides asked the two witnesses and the manager to follow them outside. The officers then escorted the Larry Winford through the store, past frightened customers and through the front doors. They gently placed the man into the back of their cruiser, ensuring not to bump his head on the way in, and closed the door.

"Ok, so what happened here? I'm going to need your names first," Officer Ivory said to the two young men, as he pulled out the standard form used during these types of situations.

The two men provided their names and contact information, then one proceeded to tell the specifics of the event that they both had witnessed.

"Ok, so, we were in the back, by the lunchmeat, grabbing cheese and meat for sandwiches. This good looking blonde was over there, by the sour cream or whatever that is, when all of a sudden this guy nails her in the back of the head with his cane! It was crazy! I couldn't believe that old man could swing it so hard. It broke and she fell into the sour cream and everything and then she fell on the floor. That's not it, though. Then the old guy crawls over to her feet, pulls off one of her shoes, rolls her over and sits on her and starts stabbing her in the face with her shoe!! It was friggin' nuts! I couldn't believe it, she was knocked out so she wasn't fighting; he stabbed her like four times before Josh tackled him."

"Anything to add?" Officer Benavides said to the one named Josh.

"Not really, I started running over there as soon as she fell, but that old guy moved fast! I mean, he rolled on top of her and started stabbing like a crazy person. When I tackled him the fucking shoe stayed stuck in the lady's face. It was horrible. I held him down until he stopped fighting, then he just sat there. He hasn't said anything since, unless he said something to you guys. Some people came over and put some frozen vegetables on the back of her head, where he hit her. Um, but someone said we shouldn't pull the shoe out. I was gonna do it."

"Have you ever seen this man before? Did you see him in the store, before he attacked her?"

"I did!" the guy that was not Josh said. "I saw him a few times. He was walking around with an empty wagon, all over the place. I thought he was nuts even then. He had a crazy look on his face and he was rolling around everywhere, looking for something or someone, I guess. I mean, I saw him by the fruit up front, then I saw him by the coffee, then in the back where he hit her. He had his cane up on the back of the part of the wagon, but he had nothing else in there. I was thinking 'what the hell are you looking for, Gramps!' I guess he was looking for her, cuz, Pow!!"

"Ok, thanks fellas. We're going to need and official statement. If you could meet us at the station sometime this afternoon, that'd be great."

The officers gave them both a card and then moved over to the side of the vehicle where the old man was sitting. After opening the door, Officer Benavides read the gentleman his rights. Based on the psychotic look on the man's face, the officers decided not to ask him anymore questions. They turned off their rolling police lights as they headed out towards Chatham County Jail. As they pulled out of the parking lot, the old man spoke.

"I did. I already did," he said into the plexiglass that separated him from the two policeman. "I already fucking did it!!"

Chapter 25

CRAIG ATWOOD WIGGLED THE COAT hanger antenna of his 13 inch black and white TV in an attempt to get a better signal. He had no cable or satellite so he would have to settle for local news, if he could get the damn antenna to pick up the signal, that is. Frustrated, he went into his large, old fashioned kitchen and grabbed a roll of aluminum foil from the space under the sink, causing a few cockroaches to scamper away. This kitchen looked like something out of a history book about old colonial homes. Everything was original; there was no electric stove, only a wood burning stove with an exhaust pipe that exited through the wall. Craig's refrigerator was a General Electric from the 1930s. He wouldn't call it old, however; it's vintage. There was a thick coat of dust on every surface in this room and the light pouring in through the open window created a creepy cloud in the air as Craig moved around. He tore off a giant piece of foil and loosely attached it to the coat hanger, in hopes of increasing its reception. Success!! The screen filled with the beautiful black and white images of a reporter outside of a small school, right here in Savannah. He turned the volume of the TV all the way down so it wouldn't interfere with the confused, blithering of law enforcement coded jargon flowing out of his nearby police scanner. He really didn't need to hear what the reporter on TV was saying; he already knew. Given how long it took last time, he was a bit surprised at how fast things were beginning to take shape.

Craig kicked off his wet K-mart shoes and jumped into his ugly brown recliner. An excessive amount of dust had puffed out of the recliner when he plopped himself down, causing the beams of light shining into the creepy living room to almost appear solid with dirty air. The other pieces of furniture within the downstairs of the 3200 square foot colonial were covered in filthy white sheets. He removed his finger print covered glasses and placed them gently in his lap. Leaning back and reclining, he closed his eyes, breathing deep the sustenance that today's events were providing. He somehow heard the frantic muted words of the little person on the TV, which added to his pleasure. He opened his eyes as he exhaled slowly through his mouth, savoring the essence that he had just taken in. As he slid his glasses back on, a ghoulish grin extended across Craig's face, mouth closed at first, but eventually opening into a full smile, exposing the metal wires of his braces and the crud trapped therein. He knew that this was just the beginning; soon he would be replenished with the nutrients that he requires and, based on the size of this implant, he calculated that he had just secured a few months' worth of nourishment.

Craig eased out of his recliner and turned the dial of his vintage Ferguson black and white beauty, in search of another broadcast, hopefully covering a different event. It seemed that the only broadcasts he could raise were focused on the school. Oh well, at least he has his trusty scanner. As exciting as this morning's activities were, he knew he may have to continue providing motivation to those who were still dragging their feet. Although most of the subjects of his pollution were close to the edge, many of them still required a slight push. Looks like Craig couldn't relax just yet. Duty Calls.

Chapter 26

DOUG MASON HAD THE CRUISE control of his 4-runner set at 70 miles per hour as he and Jessica headed north on I-95, stereo set to Jessica's station. He daren't speed, he didn't want to take any chances; the last thing he needed at this point was a nosey cop pulling him over. Confused by his own behavior, Doug began to question himself and his actions. He felt as though he had a job to do; something that needed his immediate attention and he knew that he could not rest until it was done. The strange, internal itchy feeling he was experiencing before had gotten much worse. Earlier, it seemed as though that haunting voice was helping him; providing him purpose and motivation. Now it felt as though the voice that was once calming had slowly transformed into something more threatening. The itchy feeling was slowly being replaced with feelings of nausea and discomfort. Bags formed under his eyes; he felt feverish and his skin was projecting a grey, ashy appearance. *I hope you know what you're doing. This is not what I want. Don't fuck this up*, kept repeating in his mind; a voice that sounded like a hiss or a strong gust of wind on a cold autumn night. Doug rubbed the sweat from his face as he drove, his sickly condition was becoming more evident to his daughter.

"Daddy, are you OK?" Jessica asked with concern.

"I'm good, J. I'm just a little sick. I must've caught something from someone on the plane. It's all good," Doug said, smiling while lying to his daughter.

"Where are we going, anyway?"

I wish I knew, Doug thought with what he hoped was his own mind. The truth is, Doug had no idea what he was doing. The voice in Doug's mind changed slightly as he was trying to formulate an answer for his curious daughter; this voice was not haunting or comforting, it was not relaxing or calming. The voice that stabbed his brain from what felt like all directions did so with a thunderous roar that made Doug gasp in shock and pain - *KILL HER!!* - the sound screeched in an antagonizing noise that initially came from everywhere, but gradually isolated itself to the temples, pulsing with Doug's rapidly increasing heartbeat. The voice sounded as if whatever was making it was tearing its vocal cords with every word. Doug started to understand his purpose. He knew what was expected of him and what was now his mission; his duty. He was going to kill his daughter.

"Sweetie, you mind if I change this? I can't take this right now," Doug said to Jessica, referring to the boy band tune that was playing. The vomit that was bubbling up in his throat slowly began to subside.

"Yeah, but where are we going? You didn't answer me."

"It's a surprise sweetie. Grab my iPad. Watch a movie. You'll know when we get there."

Jessica popped open the center console storage area that was in between her and her Dad in order to grab the iPad. It was in its usual storage space; she had ridden in her Dad's truck often and had always grabbed his iPad when she wanted it. This was the first time she noticed his gun.

"Dad, I didn't know you had a gun. Why do you have that?" she asked her dad, surprised. This was the first time she had ever seen a gun for real.

Doug attempted to speak through his teeth, as he clenched his jaw tight enough to cut metal. His body vibrated like a frightened lap dog, as he fought the words that *someone* was trying to send through his mouth. *I have this so I can kill* you intruded his thoughts as he struggled to articulate a replacement statement; the feeling of brewing vomit had returned to his stomach.

"S-Self-defense, baby. Please don't touch it." Doug answered, almost letting the vomit fly. He used nearly all of his strength to get those seven words out of his mouth, fighting whatever it was that had a choke hold on his mind. He was starting to feel a sensation which suggested that there was something moving under the skin on his face. The itchiness and tickling from earlier had returned, but had isolated itself around his eyes, causing them to squint and twitch; almost as if there was an eyelash in both of them. He rubbed his eyes with the back of his left hand as he took the next exit. Doug knew he needed to stop before he passed out. *Don't fuck this up. Kill her.*

Chapter 27

JEFF TRIED TO MAKE THE most of the short break he took, but he was exhausted, physically and mentally. As he tried to take off running again, the black spots fluttering in front of his face returned. Shaking them off was pointless, it only made him dizzier. His body was void of fluids, the dehydration making him feel faint and disoriented. He took a knee again almost immediately after standing. If there was once a sense of purpose and direction within this confused man, it was gone now. He tried to spit, but nothing except what felt like dusty pieces of cotton came out of his mouth. He needed to drink something now. He considered grabbing a mouthful of the muddy water forming around his wet boots, but decided against it. As police descended upon Jeff from basically all directions, a sense of helplessness engulfed him. When he started his escape, he was full of confidence. Now he was beginning to think of the possibility of surrendering. Surely some lawyer would help him get a reduced sentence, especially once they heard the story of the voices that had poisoned his mind. The faint sounds of dogs in the distance broke his limited concentration.

As he looked around the surrounding woods, breathing heavily through his mouth, tears of fear and sorrow began falling from Jeff's eyes; sorrow for himself, of course, he really had no remorse for the man whose face he destroyed. What was once a strong dedicated man, was now a cowering murderer, kneeling lost in the woods as the sounds of dogs and their handlers closed the distance on his position. As the sounds of policemen communicating to one another were getting louder, Jeff realized that if there was any shred of resourcefulness left in his depleted self, he would have to get moving. He thought of his wife Samantha. He loved his wife with every ounce of his being. His future with his wife and step daughter was slowly fading away as his thoughts began to enter into a downward spiral of negativity and helplessness. He had to snap out of it. There might still be hope. Maybe. Maybe if he got up now and headed across the highway he could make it to the job site. He'd need a car, he and Samantha could go get Jessica from school and just drive. *We could do it*, he allowed himself to think. He got up and headed directly for I-95, the sounds of dogs feeling as though they were right behind him. It was almost as if the dogs were panting directly over his shoulder, into his ear, their warm dog breath causing the hairs on his neck to stand up and twitch.

The vegetation became much thicker as he got closer to the highway, the marshy swamp land still trying to swallow the boots off his feet. He hadn't been able to see the highway yet, due to a combination of trees and bushes, along with the distance he still needed to cover, but he could certainly hear the traffic as vehicles hissed by; the sounds of his freedom. His waterproof boots had done their best but his feet were soaked by now, he had painful blisters from where the socks balled up, creating uneven, wet surfaces rubbing up against his feet. The balls of his feet throbbed as if they each had their own tiny heartbeat. The recognizable sounds of the highway were becoming clearer with every step, giving him confidence and drive; unfortunately so were the sounds of the dogs and cops hot on his trail. Jeff did his best to focus on the one direction of highway sounds rather than the multiple directions of dog's barking and cops yelling his name.

He was beginning to see flashes of different colors break through the bushes and branches in front of him, as he was getting closer to the highway. He could tell based on the distance that the traffic flew by that there appeared to be a few feet of short grass from the edge of the wood line leading up to the highway itself. Jeff's feet screamed with stabbing pain from the blisters and hot spots on the balls and heels of his feet. *Never run in soaking wet work boots*, he thought with his own mind. He was sure that his internal helper was gone for good. The dogs were getting louder now, much louder. He could hear distinct commands coming from officers. Not miscellaneous, random cries of his name, but actual sounds of "Hey!" and "Freeze!" and "There he is!" meaning that they could obviously see him now.

The fact that the officers actually made visual contact and positive identification of him gave him a burst of adrenaline. With that adrenaline came speed. He was able to crash through the last bit of thick vegetation and into the shorter grassy area, adding to the scratches on his face and neck. He broke through the brush like a marathon runner running through the tape at the finish line. Unfortunately, he wasn't finished, he was still about 20 feet from the road, and he still had to cross it. The cops that meant to stop him were still behind the last bit of thick stuff and Jeff knew he needed to use that to his advantage. He was going to need to get across the highway before the forces behind him broke free. This particular stretch of I-95 consisted of two lanes running north and south, complete with a grass covered median in the center of the four lanes. Jeff dropped his head and began to expend the last of his energy in order to cover more ground, aiming for a break in traffic.

Jeff was nearly at the shoulder of the highway when the first handler and his dog broke through the branches and shrubs, into the short grass. They were to the right rear of where Jeff was currently about to head into the highway. The handler released his dog, at the same time other officers had emerged from the wood line in various locations, weapons drawn. Sirens echoed across the distance as the pre-positioned police vehicles made their way down I-95. Officers screamed at Jeff, attempting to convince him to stop fleeing, as the dog quickly began to gain on him from the right rear. The barking dog caused him to slowly turn to the right, attempting to see over his shoulder as he continued to push forward.

The truck that struck Jeff did so at about a speed of 75 miles per hour. Due to the speed that Jeff was running, he was able to make it out in front of the truck a few feet, causing the grille to be the part that made contact with him first. The red Peterbilt 389 had a flat vertical face, and given that Jeff was turning when he was hit, the momentum of the turn caused him to be projected under the vehicle as his upper body was slammed into the pavement, face first. The wheels took his legs, causing muscle and bone to explode within his work pants. His torso was removed from what was left of his legs as it bounced around under the truck and wheels, striking the various components of the truck's underbelly.

Most of the flesh had been removed from the torso when it was detached, causing muscle and ribs to be fully visible as the organs were stretched across the highway. Finally, the vehicle's rear wheels drove over the mushy pile of goo that was once a human body, causing what was left to roll violently in the road, following the truck. Lifeless arms flung skyward and slapped the pavement like a pair of dead fish as the body rolled, eventually slowing down to a hideous stop, leaving a trail of elongated intestines behind it. At some point in the process, the skin, and most of Jeff's face, had been erased by either the road or the undercarriage of the truck, leaving a half skull, cracked and twisted, exposing brain and torn facial muscles. This pile of road kill was a brutal mess of bloody devastation consisting of bone, hair, organs, and muscle; totally unrecognizable.

The driver of the truck lost control of his vehicle almost immediately. Once the rear wheels of the truck ran over the body, the trailer began to jack knife to the left, causing the tires to smoke and screech as the trailer slid sideways. It almost appeared as if the trailer was attempting to pass the cab. The jack knifed vehicle pushed forward for a few feet past what was left of Jeff's body before it slid across the median and into oncoming traffic, bringing with it the small car that was traveling along-side the truck at the moment of impact. A few vehicles were able to do some evasive maneuvering to avoid hitting the big red truck sliding toward them, but others were not so lucky. The identifiable sounds of tires screeching followed by the sound of crushing metal and breaking glass and plastic repeated itself at least three individual times as cars drove directly into the jack knifed truck. I-95 was quickly painted in oil and fuel as the cruisers that were pre-positioned darted to the crash site and began to take charge of the situation. Both directions of traffic began to congest and would probably stay that way for the rest of the day.

Chapter 28

LIEUTENANT RICK POWELL DISCUSSED THE scheme of maneuver with SCMPD SWAT Team 2 team leader Officer Dean Stinson. The gentlemen received a copy of Mercer Middle School's floor plan from the SWAT database about six minutes ago and have been discussing strategy ever since. Lieutenant Powell had ruthlessly drilled his SWAT teams in methods for dealing with an active shooter in all of the schools within their jurisdiction, so when it was discovered that they would be entering this specific school, they already had a basis for the procedure they would use. They would simply need to tailor their plan to support the current conditions. Each of the thirty operators under Lieutenant Powell's command had been required to commit the layout of every school to memory in preparation for an event such as this. Lieutenant Powell did not settle for mediocrity when it came to the preparedness of his SWAT teams.

Officer Stinson was a charismatic leader and has led Team 2, which consisted of eight operators, for the last nine years. Together with the Lieutenant, Stinson decided that based on the school's floor plan and the location of supporting elements, it would be best to enter the school from the west and clear room by room. Mercer Middle School was a single story building consisting of 28 classrooms, a gym, and a medium sized cafeteria, which doubled as their auditorium, a large band room in the west wing, and a small library near the front entrance. The team would enter through the band room, which had its own access to a small faculty parking lot. Any further delays could result in more casualties inside the school, therefore; the nine man team of operators received a quick briefing from their leader and moved out smartly to the west side of the building. It had been almost twenty minutes since the last shot was fired when Team 2 executed a text book deliberate entry and began clearing the objective with military precision.

Detective Wright arrived with Samantha Arkenson just as Officer Stinson and his men entered the school. As Detective Wright pulled into the school's parking lot, Samantha frantically looked from the passenger's window at the crowd of assembled children in the parking lot next to the school, searching for a glimpse of her daughter Jessica. What was once several small formations of children in different areas had since been consolidated into one large group and moved to a safer area next door. She could tell that the large group was actually segregated into what she assumed were individual classroom groups. The kids were seated in neat rows and the adults were all standing and walking amongst the children. Her heart pounded as she moved her eyes from face to face within the crowd, growing more and more terrified with every child that wasn't her Jessica. It was hard for her to see, since the vehicle was still moving and the occasional standing adult would block her vision. Before the vehicle came to a complete stop, Samantha jumped out, leaving the door open. She ran over to the large assembly area, where several other parents had arrived to make contact with their children. As Samantha got closer, she saw Mrs. Cole, who was Jessica's fifth grade teacher. She made a direct line to Mrs. Cole and noticed that her daughter was not among the kids sitting on the pavement. Unable to form coherent words, a clearly distraught Samantha grabbed Mrs. Cole by the shoulders and showered her with a series of frenzied questions about her daughter.

"Dear, her father picked her up about thirty minutes ago. I'm so sorry, I thought you knew. I sent her to the office about ten minutes before the shots started," Mrs. Cole said to Samantha in a calm, nurturing voice.

The enormous lump that had formed in Samantha's throat began to reduce slightly as she looked back toward the school's parking lot. Much like the way her eyes had darted from child to child earlier, she began to visually search the parking lot for Doug's 4-runner, eyes jumping from car to car. Her imagination began to run wild again; just because Jessica had reported to the office didn't mean she made it out with Doug. Additionally, the fact that he even picked her up made Sam feel uneasy. He wasn't supposed to get her until the end of the day. Her mind reverted back to the conversation they had this morning, when Doug had the conniption over the phone about the change in visitation. *Fuckin' try me* he said. He didn't just say it, he screamed it. Samantha's tears returned as she entered into an internal comparison; Jessica was safe from whatever is happening in the school, but what was happening to her ex-husband and was Jessica safe from him? The conversation she had with Doug this morning had left her confused and scared. He never spoke to anyone that way, as far as she knew. He certainly never spoke to her like that; not when they were married and not since they were divorced, either. Something was wrong, and now he had their daughter. After trying Doug's phone and reaching his voicemail again, Samantha made her way back toward Detective Wright.

Detective Wright had linked up with Detective Christianson shortly after Samantha had jumped out of his car. The Detectives gave each other a rundown of the bizarre morning they were each having. These two men weren't really friends, but they weren't enemies either. They had a professional relationship that revolved around police work, with the occasional chit chat about last night's game or whatever. Grant had a slight level of admiration for Mike; after all, Mike had more experience and was nearly twenty years his senior. Mike also had the unique ability to train and mentor young detectives and officers without even realizing he was doing it. Most of the force looked up to Mike; Grant was no different.

Detective Christianson went in depth about what Dave Spears had done back on Abercorn to his co-worker and that he was most likely the shooter here.

"You wouldn't believe it, Wright. What's his name said he thinks she was alive when Spears set her on fire, but he won't know til the autopsy. What the hell makes someone do something like that?" Mike said as he exhaled smoke away from Detective Wright.

Wright responded, "I heard some of it over the radio. Its nuts, man. This guy from the hit and run tore someone's face off and now he's running through the woods east of 17. They got K9, air, plus like half of Bryan County Sheriff's office after this asshole."

Both Detectives agreed that today was a unique one. Detective Christianson was no stranger to bizarre crimes, he served in Atlanta for many years and had headed up several cases involving human brutality towards their fellow man, but this one seemed different. He couldn't help but feel the connection between the people involved. Mike's suspicions were confirmed a little when Detective Wright's phone vibrated in his pocket.

"This is Wright," the Detective said into his police issued Blackberry.

"Don't you monitor your damn radio?" Captain Garrison said.

"It's in the car. What's up, Captain?"

"Is the Arkenson woman with you? Is her daughter ok?"

"I'm working on it. I'm getting a briefing from Mike Christianson,"

"Well, her husband ran into a truck over on 95. He's done. Bring her back here once you find out about her daughter. What's the status over there?"

"Oh shit. Um, here? Well, SWAT just went in. I guess there's only a few people not accounted for. Only one student, one teacher, and the Assistant Principle. They can't confirm or deny whether Spears is in there, but he probably is. His wife, too. We'll let you know." Wright hung up his phone and explained the call to his fellow detective.

"What the hell is happening?" Wright said to his cigarette smelling peer.

"Who knows, man? Who knows why people do what they do?" Mike answered.

"I'm going to go check on the wife. What a fucking day she's having."

Samantha found Detective Wright and was about to speak when he turned around.

In a frenzied mess, Samantha said, "My daughter left with my husband before the shooting started. I can't get him on the phone. I think he's taking her. We fought this morning. I-I-I don't know what was the matter..."

"Your husband? Did you say she's with your husband?" Detective Wright asked for clarification.

"I'm sorry, I meant my ex-husband. She's with my ex-husband. He's, he has visitation today, but he-he-he wasn't supposed to pull her out of s-s-chool early. I don't know where she is. He won't answer his phone." Samantha began to cry again.

"Can you call your daughter? Does she have a phone?" Wright answered, trying to calm her down.

"She can't have it in school. It's at home." She buried her face in her hands and trembled as she cried.

"Ma'am, I'm sure everything is ok with your daughter. It might be a blessing that your ex-husband picked her up early. He might have saved her from whatever went on inside the school. I'm sure she's fine. He must've just had a change of plans," Detective Wright said in an attempt to comfort the poor woman. "We need to head back to the station. There's been some updates with the situation involving your husband. We'll keep trying to get in touch with your ex-husband when we get to the station, I'm sure your daughter is safe with him."

Gears were turning in Detective Christianson's mind as he listened to Wright speak to this hysterical woman. *Dave Spears kills his co-worker – comes here and starts shooting. Jeff Something kills someone on 17, flees from police, and gets run over on I-95. Jeff Something's wife has daughter at the school that Spears shoots up, but ex-husband removes daughter. Jeff Something's wife thinks ex-husband kidnapped daughter...* Mike's thoughts were going a hundred miles an hour as he sparked another Marlboro. *What the hell is happening?*

As Detective Wright led Samantha to his vehicle, Mike intervenes, "Ma'am, I'm Detective Christianson. Here's my card. If you need anything, anything at all, please, don't hesitate to call. I'm terribly sorry for all that's happened."

"Thank you, Detective," Samantha said as she took the card and slid it in her pocket. She walked around the front of Detective Wright's vehicle and entered in the passenger's side. She removed her phone as soon as she sat down to call her mother. Sam intended on telling her that Jessica was fine, she just wouldn't share too many details. Her mom had enough to worry about.

"Good luck with everything here, Mike. Try not to smoke too much," Grant said as he started to open the driver's side door.

"I might want to talk to her later, Grant. Something weird is going on," Mike replied.

As Detective Wright and Samantha Arkenson drove away heading back towards SCMPD Headquarters, Mike checked his watch. 2:14. Still a long way to go. As he lit a new cigarette with the tip of the old one, Mike refocused his attention back to the school and awaited the inevitable contact between David Spears and SWAT Team 2.

Chapter 29

SWAT TEAM 2 HAD CLEARED 15 of the school's 28 rooms, including the cafeteria and library, as the two Detectives spoke outside. They moved at a methodical pace from room to room, covering each other's movement, focusing on the mission at hand; which is to make contact with and eliminate the threat. Each operator was trained to understand that a shooter's behavior can be spontaneous and unpredictable, therefore they must be prepared to kill without hesitation. Hesitation can cost an operator his or her life, or worse, you risk another potential innocent victim. Officer Stinson felt that they were dealing with a static shooter, since it had been nearly thirty minutes since the last shot and the spotters across the street have not reported any movement inside the school. They may need to deal with the suspect having barricaded himself in a room; or some other kind of last ditch effort. These types of situations rarely ended well for the shooter. They may even be dealing with a murder/suicide, although that type of thinking can cause an operator to become complacent and potentially let their guard down. For these reasons, Stinson never used the murder/suicide scenario in training exercises. The static shooter training scenario was much more effective, as it kept operators more alert.

These men were well equipped to deal with a barricaded static shooter if need be, which is where Stinson thought the situation was going. Each operator had four flash bangs and every third man had a small battering ram, door spreader, or Halligan tool. There were also two sets of heavy duty bolt cutters with the team. A barricaded shooter was not always the best case scenario when clearing a building. There was always the possibility that the shooter had a hostage. Stinson had been receiving updates through his headset pertaining to the accountability of students and faculty during the clearing process. At this moment, the team knew that there were two faculty members and one student unaccounted for, plus the possibility of another potential hostage; David Spears's wife. They hadn't yet confirmed if Spears was even in the school, or his wife, for that matter; most of the information on Spears were assumptions and predictions. The Principle had said that there was a scheduled conference that he was almost certain the Assistant Principle had attended. He couldn't be sure of any other details.

An element consisting of four operators entered the northern most hallway of the school approximately six minutes after the initial entry. A two man team consisting of Officers Bracken and Fox prepared to enter the first room in the north wing as the other two men provided security down the hallway in the direction of travel. They had learned throughout the process of clearing rooms in this school that all doors opened inward and that they did not lock. The technique they've been using thus far has been allowing the first man to enter by gently opening the door and then forcing it open completely with his shoulder as he went through it. Although each room was equipped with a small vertical window in the door, the men have not been exposing themselves by looking through it. It was better to enter weapon first, rather than making a target of yourself by peering through a little window.

Bracken entered the room first, flinging the door open with his shoulder, causing it to make contact with the wall. He assumed his sector of fire, which was straight forward along the wall, and then back toward the center of the room, visually clearing the area as he moved the red dot site of his weapon across the space. Fox was directly behind Bracken, entering almost simultaneously. Fox executed a right button hook maneuver, focusing his attention on the opposite corner of the room, sighting through his optics and scanning the room in the process. As Fox scanned the area, he detected some bodies across the room on the floor, a body slightly closer to him, face down, and a young lady (clearly still alive) seated at the teacher's desk. The red dot aperture of Fox's optics acquired a center mass position on the woman's chest.

"Let me see your hands!!" Fox screamed, as Bracken announced that his area was clear and moved to the bodies.

The woman immediately complied with the commands by raising her hands high above her head. Fox slowly moved closer to the woman, stepping over the male body which was face down on the floor in a pool of blood, two small entry wounds in the center of his back. Fox kept his red dot fixed on the woman as he moved. Bracken made note of the young boy on the floor, who appeared to have suffered multiple gunshot wounds to the face, he observed the woman who was on her back, closer to the windows, who appeared to have a single gunshot wound to the chest, and a possible defensive wound in her hand. There was also a man seated next to where the woman lay on the floor; the man had a small hole on his right cheek and a large hole in the back of his head. The room was covered with blood and brains. The man who was missing the back of his head had his eyes open and a half smirk on his face. Bracken noticed a small pistol and magazine on the desk in front of the teacher's larger desk.

"You got her?" Bracken asked.

"Yeah." Fox answered.

Officer Bracken picked up the pistol to ensure that it was cleared and then placed it back where he found it. He removed a zip tie from one of his many compartments of gear on his body and secured Laura Jones's hands behind her back. Officer Fox lowered his weapon once the threat was detained and called Officer Stinson over the radio.

Chapter 30

"I DON'T OWE YOU ANYTHING!!!!" Lawrence Widford screamed into the plexiglass that divided the police car into its two distinct spaces. Voices consumed his mind, submerging him in a terrified claustrophobic feeling of helplessness that was amplified by the tiny confines of the back seat of this police car. *Do it do it do it* hissed in his ears, alternating from left to right, feeling as if someone was sticking the words into his head with a white hot poker. His head throbbed with every syllable, it was the worst head ache he had experienced in his 70 years of life. *Oh, you'll do it. You owe meeeeee....* he envisioned a snakes tongue fluttering in his mind as the voice stretched the message across his thoughts. "SHUT UP!!!!!" Larry screamed, causing spit and phlegm to splat against the window.

"Calm down, sir! You're only going to make this worse." Officer Benevides yelled into the backseat as they pulled into the garage attached to the Chatham County Jail. The jail housed as many as 300 inmates, most of which were awaiting trial, but some were convicts that were sentenced for short durations. It was conveniently located next door to the station itself and within walking distance of the Chatham County Judicial Complex. Seven correctional officers had been waiting for their new guest. Based on the information provided from the arresting officers, the correctional officers came prepared with all the protective restraining equipment available, in case the inmate became combative; a restraint chair, restraining belts and shackles, and a spit hood.

Officers Benevides and Ivory accompanied the seven correctional officers as they escorted Larry inside to begin the booking procedures. The Colonel looked like an insane person as his eyes were as wide as they could open, his hair was sweaty and sticking out in all directions, and he was still covered in the blonde woman's blood. Despite his deranged appearance, Larry had been somewhat calm for the last few minutes.

"He hasn't been belligerent with us," Officer Benevides said to the other officers, "He's just been talking to himself. Well, more like screaming. He spit up on the glass a little, but I think it was because he was screaming so loud."

During the short walk through the garage and into the building, Larry continuously jerked his head from side to side in a frenzy. He was twitching his neck back and forth, almost as if there was something swarming around his head, the way someone might swat at a fly if their hands were bound. "FUCK YOU!!" the old man screamed at the ceiling as he was placed in front of the first station in the booking process. There were two yellow painted foot prints on the floor where Larry was instructed to plant his feet. "Fuck you..." he said again, this time much quieter, like a man defeated.

"Sir, that's not nice. You need to calm down sir. We're going to remove your cuffs now. Can I trust you to gently place your hands on the counter?" said the tiny correctional officer seated behind the desk at station one. Two gigantic correctional officers flanked

Larry, ready to pounce if he made any sudden movements. Larry nodded at the tiny man, eyes still opened as wide as humanly possible. Officers Benevides and Ivory placed the personal effects they had confiscated from Larry on the counter; keys, wallet, old flip phone with big buttons. "Good luck, sir," Officer Benevides said to Larry as he and Ivory headed into a nearby office to start the necessary paperwork required for detainee transfers.

A third enormous gentleman in standard correctional officer garb gently removed Larry's cuffs and guided his hands to the yellow painted hand prints on the counter. Larry did not resist. The tiny man opened the wallet and began to inventory its contents.

"Have you ever been arrested before, Colonel?" the tiny man asked in a respectful manner as he held the Colonel's retired Marine Corp ID in front of his face. "Sir?" No answer. A new voice manifested in Larry's mind. This time at his left ear, he could almost feel the warm breath as the words gently poured into his head. This voice was different than before. Nicer. It was his wife's voice. His dear Tabitha. Not his interpretation of her voice, but her actual voice. It was as beautiful as he remembered it. *Larry, you're going to have to do this. Please. It won't stop. Just do it, honey. Do it now. Now's your chance, baby. Now. Now. Do it Do it Do it – it won't stop until you do it...do it baby...* It was as if she was whispering in his ear; her warm, loving breath comforting the back of his neck. Tears formed in the Colonel's eyes as the pain of losing his Tabby nine years ago was reborn in this moment. "Sir?"

Tabitha's voice morphed into another familiar sound, a voice he could not understand but he recognized, *Làm ngay bây gi□. Anh n□ tôi làm ngay bây gi□ làm ngay bây gi□ bây gi□ bây gi□*

làm nó l `àm đi□u đó ngay bây gi□ M□ ch□t ti□t ... the Vietnamese taunting haunted his mind, it brought vomit to the edge of his lips, as his whole body vibrated, his hands still affixed to the counter. "Sir?!" The Vietnamese voice slowly translated itself to English as it became louder inside the tired old man's mind.

The sound of the voice spun around his brain; he heard it starting from the left, traveling across his forehead, past his right ear, and then the back of his head, repeating this route as it continued to get louder and faster, causing the room to spin, the vomit at the top of his throat rising; *Do it now. You owe me do it now do it now now now now do it do it now fucking American*, as the horrible suggestion rotated around the poor man's brain, the voice changed from what sounded human into a sound that resembled something underwater, he could hear and feel bubbles in the words, a clearly audible squishing and squashing of a fish drowning in shallow water, words that were wet and sloppy gradually built up to a loud and thunderous pop inside Larry's forehead – *NOW!!!*

Projectile vomit spewed forth from the Colonel's mouth and onto the tiny officer seated behind the counter, covering the man and the counter itself in the process. The mustard yellow pile of puke which contained the contents of the man's stomach seemed to squirm and writhe across the counter; appearing as though some of it was alive. The vomit that was plastered across the tiny man's face seemed to be living as well. Larry surged over the counter, almost immediately after his hurl, and got his hands tight around the small vomit covered correctional officer's neck. The Colonel clenched his jaw tight, exhaling more particles of spit and living vomit from the corners of his mouth, as he meant to strangle the life from the officer with his bare hands.

His assault was short lived as the two flanking correctional officers brought the Colonel to the ground with a series of choke holds and arm bars within seconds of the attack. Every correctional officer within ear shot had come to the aid of the man at the counter. The jail's Emergency Response Team (ERT) arrived at the booking desk within seconds to take charge of defusing the situation. Larry was immediately placed into a restraint chair, secured to the chair with straps virtually everywhere, and his face was secured under a spit hood. The ERT wheeled Larry into an isolation cell used to allow inmates to decompress before booking, or to sober up.

The tiny correctional officer, who had also heaved on himself due to the odor covering him, ran directly into the single inmate shower, clothes and all, to get the disgusting product of the old man's insides off his body and clothes. The correctional officers that had gathered up front looked at the pooling puddles of bile on the counter and floor, covering their noses and mouths. Something was moving. Something was alive in that vomit. Whatever they were, there was a lot of them.

Chapter 31

STUNNED STUDENTS AND TEACHERS LOOKED with unbelieving eyes as police officers escorted Miss Laura Jones from the school's main entrance and into the back of a squad car. Her own students were understandably emotional as they saw the woman they loved and admired hauled away in shackles. Everywhere confused children sought explanations from nearby adults. Paramedics tried to be as discreet as possible as they wheeled four separate gurneys with sheet covered bodies to the waiting ambulances; one body much smaller than the rest. News cameras from four different networks followed as the police vehicle containing the woman who was suspected of murdering four people headed towards Chatham County Jail.

Detective Christianson pulled a final drag off the cigarette between his lips as he hopped in his car and lit another one. Mike needed to talk to this woman. He had been expecting to be interrogating David Spears this afternoon, but apparently he had a bullet in his face, thanks to this tiny teacher. Something wasn't adding up. He tried to use this short drive to gather his thoughts; to calculate what type of questions he was going to ask her; *what set her off? why did she just commit this cold blooded quadruple homicide, and why did she just sit calmly and wait on SWAT?* So many questions needed answering. This day was becoming stranger by the minute. Mike parked his silver Impala in an open spot outside the Chatham Sheriff's Department Headquarters and climbed out. Getting a nose full of his own odor, He reached into his vehicle and grabbed the little tree air freshener that hung from the rearview mirror. *Something's better than nothing* he thought as he rubbed himself across the chest, neck, and armpits with the little green tree. He removed his clip on tie to get closer to his neck, hoping that he could cover at least some of his funk. Normally he didn't care about his unique musk, but he was going to be in a small room with this woman and there was to be no distractions. He wanted her to focus on the questions he was asking and not the rippling stink waves coming off his body.

Mike had explained to the officers back at the school that he wanted her taken directly to an interrogation room before she went to central booking. He had to get some answers now. He worked out of Savannah Chatham Metro but he's used rooms over at Chatham County Sheriff's Department multiple times. There was an understanding among all law enforcement agencies in the area that it was a joint effort in the war on crime. Everyone was cooperative when it came to using each other's facilities. *One team one fight* was the motto that pertained to situations like this.

Officers escorted the attractive young lady through the rear entrance of the station. The blood that was splattered on her blouse had dried and appeared more brown than red. Her hair was in a slight state of disarray, but other than that she looked amazing. The tiny interrogation room was 11 feet by 11 feet, with a small table in the middle, complete with two chairs. There was another chair in the corner behind where Laura was currently sitting. To her right was the one way mirror that all rooms of this nature contained. Above the mirror in the corner rested a small camera mounted to the ceiling. The red light that indicates that the camera was recording displayed a steady glow. The entire set up consisted of the stereotypical surroundings seen in hundreds of police stations across the nation. Laura rubbed her wrists once the officer removed her cuffs. She waited patiently, her hands interlaced and resting on the table; occasionally looking at the mirror, knowing that someone was watching her.

Detective Christianson entered the small room adjacent to the interrogation room and waited for a few minutes. Years of detective work and training in psychological tactics had taught him that it was always best to keep the suspect isolated for a while, as it usually leads to the suspect entering into an increased level of fear and anxiety; gives them time to think about not only what they've done, but what we were doing on the other side of the mirror. Mike knew that he needed the confession. The evidence against her was damning, but that confession would seal the deal. From the moment he saw her being escorted from the school, Mike had the impression that she would confess. She couldn't wait to. She had a sort of arrogance about her, in the way she carried herself, even now as she sat in this little room. If the look on her face and her body language could speak it would assuredly say *Yeah, I did it. So what?*

The spectating room was reaching its maximum occupancy as the officers poured in. Mike figured that at least half of these apes were there only to ogle the pretty little teacher, while the rest might actually care about the outcome of the interrogation. Feeding his ego, Mike assumed that a few were there to learn from the master. *She better not say 'I don't like Mondays'* Mike thought, like that 16 year old girl back in '79. She shot up an elementary school and then told reporters 'I don't like Mondays' when asked why she did it. The Boomtown Rats wrote a song about it. Enough delays; after a deep, calming breath, Detective Christianson proceeded into the room to begin his interrogatory style of questioning.

"Miss Jones, I'm Detective Mike Christianson, I'm going to ask you a few questions. I understand that you've elected not to invoke your right to counsel? Is that correct?" Mike said as he took the seat across from Laura.

"That's right, Detective. I didn't think it would make much difference at this point," Laura answered.

"Ma'am, could you give me your full name and date of birth please?"

"Laura Victoria Jones. November 16th, 1988"

"Thank you," Mike said respectfully "Do you need anything, ma'am? Were there any issues with how the officers treated you?"

Laura shook her head. This conversation felt as though it was a meeting between old friends and not the beginning of a police interrogation. Mike decided to stick with this technique for the time being, knowing that things might go south quick if the woman stated to change her attitude.

"Before we begin, ma'am, I just want to remind you that you have the right to legal advice either on the telephone or in person; this is an ongoing right and we can stop the interview at any time should you change your mind and want legal representation."

"Thank you," Laura said with a small smile, "That's sweet of you to say that."

"Ok, I want to discuss everything that happened in your classroom starting with when you arrived at school this morning and ending with when the SWAT team found you at your desk," Mike said as he scribbled in his note book.

"Well, this morning was like any other morning, maybe a little worse than others because I got in late last night," Laura said as more officers crammed in the room next door. "Um, I released my class for lunch a little bit before noon and I waited for the Spears family to show up. I believe you know the rest, Detective."

"I know that four people are dead. I know that a Ruger SR9 pistol that's registered in your name was found in your classroom. I know that much. I need to know how all this happened. You said you got in late last night? Where were you?"

"I was visiting my mother in Atlanta."

"You drive?"

"No, I flew. I got in to Savannah at around 9 last night, which is late for me."

Mike thought back to the questions he asked the woman outside of Dave Spears' office earlier. The receptionist at the insurance building. A strange connection was brewing in his mind. What was her name? *Rachel Green?* he thought as he flipped through his book and read his words from a couple hours ago, igniting a new question.

"Did you know the Spears? Have you ever met Dave Spears or his wife, Linda?" he asked while confirming the wife's name in his scribbles. *Was it really so strange that both of them were in Atlanta yesterday? Maybe even on the same flight? Who knows?* he thought to himself.

"No, never met them. I've seen his face on billboards before. I was trying to have a meeting with the parents of one of my worst students. Jason Spears. That's the only reason I even knew their names. Our Assistant Principle, Jim Reynolds, also showed up to my little meeting. Those parents, my God, those parents were ridiculous. They don't know the slightest thing about what it takes to do my job. To deal with rude little shits like Jason." Laura slowly raised her left hand towards her neck and gently allowed her index and middle fingers to barely caress her skin, moving from her jaw bone, tracing the outline of her chin, dropping and lightly running across her collar bone, deeply exhaling and appearing to enter into a trance like state, she added, "Sometimes, sometimes, you have to just do what needs to be done."

Laura thought of the voice that had submerged itself within her soul earlier. Although it was gone, its presence lingered in the young woman. The stimulation of the memory of her enchanting guest caused her to smile again and squirm a little within her seat. It almost appeared that she was becoming aroused as she thought about her actions. A series of several different emotions filled the crowded little room next door. A few of the officers got turned on by the sexy young woman who was giving this provocative performance, but most were appalled by her lack of respect for human life, Mike was a member of the latter group. *What needs to be done?! Are you fucking kidding me?* he thought.

"What needs to be done?! Are you saying that you shot and killed these people? Is that it? Is that what you're saying?"

"You know the answer to that, Detective."

"I want to hear you say it, Miss Jones. What *needed* to be done?"

Laura took in a deep breath and exhaled slowly. She first looked over at the mirror which led into what she imagined was a room full of police men with their faces pressed to the glass. She then brought her alluring hazel eyes to meet Mike's.

"Linda Spears cares, excuse me, *cared* more about her phone than her son. I shot her in the chest. David Spears was a pompous ass who thinks it's ok to stare at young women when his wife is two feet away. I shot him in the face. Jim Reynolds was a fat, sexist pig who should've been fired years ago. I shot him in the back when his fat ass tried to run away, and little Jason Spears, I shot him *twice* in the face because he was a little shit that would've turned out just like his father."

Chapter 32

AROUND THE SAME TIME POLICE had detained a young teacher, Doug Mason pulled into the Days Inn parking lot in Port Wentworth, Georgia. He found a spot near the main entrance so he wouldn't need to walk that far; the lightheadedness and nausea had become overwhelming. He wouldn't be able to walk straight for more than a few feet. The words *WHAT ARE YOU DOING?!* flashed within the darkness of every blink.

Doug closed his eyes and read the words for an uncomfortably long time before he spoke to his concerned daughter, "Baby, I s-s-still have a surprise for you. I just need to take a break for a little while...I need to lay down. J-J-Just for a little while. You can watch a movie, right? I just need an hour or so. I promise..." He struggled to get the words out without vomiting everywhere. He pushed his rearview mirror aside after he caught a glimpse of himself in it, disgusted by his sickly appearance.

"Ok, Daddy. We can call mom if you're sick. She can come get me if you want," Jessica said with genuine concern for her father.

"No, baby. I'll be good. I just need a nap," Doug said with a strained smile.

Making sure to grab his Glock 30 out of the center console, Doug got out of his 4-runner and was instantly forced to his knees. As his ability to steady himself was failing, the feelings of vertigo had become too much for him; he leaned forward and placed his palms on the ground. Vomit appeared in his mouth, which he quickly swallowed. By now, little Jessica had come around the truck and saw her father on his hands and knees on the ground, not noticing his gun next to him.

"Daddy! Are you ok? Stand up!" the little girl said, fighting back tears.

Get up. Do it. Do it now!! muttered around in between Doug's ears as he spit and then rose to his feet. The hot, stuffy feeling that comes with the muscle spasms involved in the act of almost vomiting began to ease off a little, allowing Doug to answer his daughter.

"I'm good, girl. I just thought I was going to throw up. I'm ok now. Let's go in."

He stuck his Glock under his belt in the small of his back, took his little girl by his clammy hand and together they walked to the entrance of the hotel. Doug could barely contain his feelings of nausea as he paid for the room with his credit card. This hotel had its rooms located on the building's exterior; the first floor doors opened onto a side walk that ran next to the parking lot and there were stairs that led to the balcony that held the second floor rooms. While walking toward their room, Doug had nearly rubbed his eyes out of his skull due to the amount of itching and burning he was feeling. As he dug his finger into the corner of his right eye where the upper and lower eye lids meet, he could feel something that didn't belong there. Something that was slimy, seeming to slip free from his finger-tips as he tried to grab it. Both eyes were blinking and watering so severe that he forgot about the puke that was still lingering around the inside of his mouth.

He and his daughter arrived at their room on the first floor, facing the highway. Doug could barely hold his hands still in order to swipe the access card for their tiny room. Once the lock released, he pushed through the door, entered the bathroom, and closed and locked the door behind him. He had to see what the hell was in his eye. He removed his Glock from the small of his back and rested it on the vanity next to the sink. Jessica was fine for the time being, as she hopped on the bed and started playing Candy Crush on her dad's iPad.

Doug leaned against the vanity so he could get as close to the mirror as possible. Through his tear filled, rapidly blinking eyes, he stared at a man who he did not recognize. He looked as though he had lost fifty pounds since this morning. No longer was he a handsome, confident black man. Now he looked more like Golum, from J.R.R. Tolkien's "The Hobbit". His skin was more of a light grey color than the medium brown that it normally was. He struggled to identify what was coming out of his eye. It looked like a small grey bump; he couldn't tell if it was actually in his eye or just resting there. He tried again to pinch the object with his index finger and thumb, but was unsuccessful once again. This thing was just too damn slippery.

As Doug stood bewildered in this tiny hotel bathroom, staring at this stranger in the mirror, his bothersome little internal guest returned and started to chant into his brain, from the inside. *DO IT DO IT DO IT DO IT* came in the form of a pulse, starting at the back of his head and pushing itself forward with every syllable. The little grey thing in his eye got longer and longer with every pulse of *do* and *it*, until Doug realized what it was. He pinched the worm with the thumb and index finger of his right hand and slowly began to extract it from his eye. Both of his watery eyes had shifted their focus onto this slippery little intruder as he pulled it gently as to not tear it half; fearing that if he did, the torn half would retract back into his skull. Doug's head was leaning slightly back, his mouth hung open like a broken trap door as he gradually removed the worm from his eye. A generous amount of thick, dark blood had begun coating the worm at the halfway point of its extraction, until finally it came free; writhing and wiggling as it dangled beneath Doug's grip.

He gasped as he dropped it into the sink; watching through trembling, bloody eyes as the worm continuing to twitch and roll around the basin, leaving a light coating of blood everywhere it went. As the urge to retch could no longer be contained, Doug heaved once, holding his mouth closed. The second heave broke through his lips and launched the contents of his stomach onto the sink, vanity, and mirror. The bloody worms that had once populated his stomach now climbed and crawled on top of one another amongst partially digested pieces of vegetable beef soup. Hundreds of common earthworms slithered within Doug's blood on the sink in this small Days Inn bathroom just off I-95. *Get up and do it* was the last thing he heard before darkness engulfed him and he passed out.

Chapter 33

A CLEAN UP TEAM CONSISTING of four personnel reported promptly to the booking desk of Chatham County Jail shortly after Larry Winford was placed in an isolation cell. The area had been cleared of all non-essential personnel due to the amount of human vomit that had been sprayed everywhere. Decontamination and sanitation of random bodily fluids is taken extremely seriously in jails and prisons. Illness can spread like wild fire when people are required to live in the close quarter's proximity that is common in all correctional institutions. Each team member was outfitted with rubber gloves, head to toe plastic smocks, and surgical masks covering the nose and mouth, to combat the stench. They each had a biohazard bodily fluids pick-up kit, which included a small shovel, surface disinfecting towels, a spray bottle of disinfecting solution, and two large yellow bags marked "biohazard" to be used for proper disposal of regurgitation.

Two workers linked up with the small gentlemen that had absorbed the full wrath of vomit as he stood outside the shower in nothing but a towel, trembling. The other two began to tackle the mess on and around the counter. One man readied the biohazard bag on the edge of the counter, while the other aligned the shovel; like a small snow plow, preparing to slide the bulk of the puke over the edge of the counter and into the waiting bag. As he got closer, he began to notice what everyone had been telling him all along. This pile of vomit was moving. There was something living, several things actually; crawling around, possibly drowning in the puke. The masked man used a pen from his breast pocket to slide one of the things out of the puke and into one of the few remaining clean areas on the counter, leaving a slippery trail behind it.

The squirming thing was a little less than a half an inch long, had two small antenna on one end and a pair of forceps-like pinchers on the other. It was tough to tell due to the fact that it was covered in mustard yellow vomit, but it appeared to be a common earwig. The man sprayed several full blasts of cleaning solution on the thing in hopes of cleaning off enough puke to be able to be sure of what it was. Upon further inspection, there was no doubt. This thing was a common, run of the mill earwig. Earwigs were located all across the country, but were especially common in Georgia and the rest of the south. There were at least three dozen of these tiny insects squirming around in Larry Winford's puke; some had died in the process of vomiting while others were crushed in the commotion of the struggle, but many were still alive and well, climbing across the counter and floor, covered in puke. "Oh my God," said the man through his surgical mask, while fighting the urge to make his own contribution to the vomit still twitching on the counter.

Outside of the isolation room where Colonel Winford sat secured in a restraint chair, one of the enormous correctional officers initialed the mandatory checklist that hung on the wall. Inmates placed in isolation need to be checked every half hour for safety purposes. This was the first time anyone checked on Larry's status since the ordeal and the officer holding the clipboard was not aware of the discovery involving the contents of the Colonel's stomach a moment ago.

"How are you doing, Colonel? You feeling any better? Are you ready to cooperate?" the large man asked as he opened the door and walked in. Colonel Winford trembled within the chair, mumbling incoherent gibberish under his breath. The officer got closer to the Colonel in order to see through the screen of the spit hood, just to confirm that he was still breathing and hadn't thrown up again under the mask. Larry's face projected a look of pure insanity from under his hood. His eyes were blood shot and opened as wide as possible, his mouth hung open as his lips vibrated furiously. The officer could notice several tiny black dots under the screen of the hood; these dots seemed to blink on and off with no discernible pattern. He couldn't be sure of what these dots were without getting a closer look. These tiny black dots were moving from Larry's face to the interior screen of the hood and then back to the face again. The closer the large officer got to the hood, the clearer the dots became. The dots were fleas. The entirety of the inside of the spit hood was filled with fleas; jumping and crawling across Larry's face. Having trouble comprehending exactly what he was seeing, the officer moved even closer to the old man. He could clearly see the tiny legs of the microscopic fleas springing themselves aimlessly around the small air pocket created by the spit hood. Some of the fleas weren't jumping or springing like the others. They were burrowing. Several random fleas were actually inserting themselves into the Colonels skin, through the large open pores in his face. The officer looked in disgust as several fleas would climb into the old man's face in one area and escape in another. The officer held his hand over his mouth.

A bubble began to form on the right side of the Colonel's forehead; similar to the way an air bubble might form in pizza dough as it rises in the oven. The giant pimple slowly grew larger and larger directly on the hairline, causing some areas of the bubble to be covered with Colonel Winford's grey hair. This disgusting boil continued to grow until it was roughly the size of a golf ball sliced in half. The officer squinted and leaned in even closer, mouth hanging open like a confused fish. A split formed on the center of the zit, small at first but then opening in all four directions, creating an "x" configuration as it opened like a blooming flower; blood and puss covered earwigs crawled and fell out of the Colonel's head, hundreds of them. The hood was slowly filling with fleas and earwigs as the officer screamed into his radio "Medic!!!!"

Chapter 34

A⊤ 3:02 P.M., A CONFUSED detective returned to his desk at SCMPD headquarters. Detective Christianson had heard many confessions over the years; perps from all walks of life, confessing to crimes ranging from petty theft to grand theft auto to homicide. Never in his 30 years of law enforcement had he ever heard a confession as chilling as the one just provided by Laura Jones. Right now, Miss Jones was writing out a full confession back at Chatham County under the supervision of the officers there. Mike wasn't sure if her written confession would be as cold as the verbal one she just gave him, but essentially it didn't matter. Prosecutors would have the video confession in conjunction with the formal, hand written one. Should be what those guys call a "slam dunk."

Looking through his notes, Mike rubbed his brow; trying to make heads or tails of this awkward day. His hand moved from his brow to the top of his head, where he scratched his itchy scalp, causing dandruff to cover his desk and notebook. *Spears kills Gail Watson, Laura Jones kills Spears family and Reynolds, both Spears and Jones were in Atlanta yesterday. Does that matter? Why would it? People travel from Atlanta to Savannah all the time. Sierra airlines does that run every day. Is it really that strange that two people that were in Atlanta yesterday committed a brutal murder today? Were they even on the same plane? And if so, does that matter?* Mike's mind was swimming as he leaned back in his chair, interlocking his hands behind his head. This wasn't the weirdest thing he'd ever seen, but pretty close. He had heard some officers over at Chatham County earlier talking about an old man that assaulted a woman at a grocery store earlier today, *was he in Atlanta yesterday?* He'd have to check. *Oh shit!* Mike thought. He almost forgot about the guy over on 17. How the hell could he have forgotten that? *Arkansas? Was that it? His wife, Samantha, maybe?* Mike pondered as he stood up and looked around the open space full of desks, searching for Detective Grant Wright.

Mike found Detective Wright sitting in one of the department's conference rooms. The interior wall of the conference room consisted of thick glass that ran from floor to ceiling. Wright was seated in a chair with his back toward the window and Mike could see that across from Wright was the woman he had met earlier. *Samantha*, he finally remembered. She was clearly distraught, having obviously been notified about her husband's demise. There was another woman sitting next to Samantha, comforting her. Probably a friend or relative. The conference table was littered with crumbled tissues. Captain Garrison was also in the room, leaning on the wall next to Wright; arms crossed, looking like an afterthought. Mike cleared his throat and entered the room.

Everyone in the room moved their eyes toward Detective Christianson as he walked in and sat down next to Detective Wright. Captain Garrison and Detective Wright looked at Mike with an expression that said *what the hell are you doing here?*

"Ma'am, I'm Mike Christianson, I'm terribly sorry for your loss," Mike said as he slid another one of his cards across the table toward Samantha and one to her friend. "Could you tell me if your husband was out of town yesterday?" Ignoring the strange looks he was getting from his peer and his boss, Mike added, "Was he in Atlanta by chance?"

"Yes, he was," she struggled to answer, looking at the other two men as she did, "but...but he goes all the time. For work. Why?" Samantha was restless in her chair, becoming defensive and concerned about these new questions. He friend held her tighter.

Mike thought of this woman's ex-husband and the concerns she had earlier when she discovered that he had picked up their daughter. *What if...?*

"I'm just trying to establish a time line for everything that went on today, ma'am. I'm so sorry, just one more question. Was your ex-husband in Atlanta yesterday?" Mike asked.

"Well, yeah. He's a pilot. He flies for Sierra airlines," Samantha answered, starting to panic. "Why, what difference does *that* make?! Doug does the Atlanta-Savannah run all the time! Why are you..."

"Ma,am, it's nothing. Detective Christianson just wants to make sure everything is covered." Detective Wright intervened.

"But why? Doug has my daughter. W-w-hy is he asking me this?!" Samantha said as she broke down crying again, resting her head on the conference table, her friend continuing to console her.

"I'm sorry Mrs. Arkenson, there really are no more questions. I think you might be more comfortable if you were to head home," Detective Wright said as he was motioning to her friend, signaling for her to help Samantha to her feet. "I'm sure that your ex-husband will call you as soon as he can. We'll stay in touch, but make sure you call me if you need anything. Anything at all."

HO-LY SHIT, Detective Christianson thought as Detective Wright and the other young lady escorted Samantha out of the conference room. Wright directed a dirty look at Mike as he walked by, but Mike didn't seem notice as his mind was racing when the door to room slammed shut.

"What the fuck is wrong with you?!" Captain Garrison barked the instant that the door was closed. "We just got that poor woman to calm down about her husband *and* ex-husband!! Are you fucking stupid? She thinks her ex took her daughter, we can't do anything about it yet, maybe not ever – he has visitation and today's his day. We just calmed her down and you got her all worked up again with your fucking questions. What the hell are you thinking?!"

"Captain, there's a connection. I don't know what it means, but there's a connection. Every one of these people flew in from Atlanta yesterday. Every one. And her ex-husband's a fucking pilot! Are you kidding me? He probably flew the damn plane they were all on!!" Detective Christianson said, starting to get excited.

"So fucking what?! People fly from Atlanta to Savannah all the time. It's not that strange, Mike, it really isn't," Captain Garrison argued.

"It's strange when they start killing people the next day. Would you agree to that? Captain? Hmmm?" Mike said, starting to become insubordinate. "Something is going on here. I need that flight number. I need to go see Laura Jones. Get the flight number. You know the guy that assaulted the woman at the grocery store? I bet he was on that plane, too. I need that flight manifest."

"Absolutely not. You're losing it, Mike," the Captain said, "You're not getting that without a warrant. Why would a judge give you a warrant for that? It's all coincidence. What are you gonna do, use the list, go door to door and..."

"Yes!! Are fucking kidding me?! If we can talk to the people that were on that plane we might be able to stop them from doing something crazy like these people did. How can you not see that?!" Mike shouted as he pounded the table with his fist, clearly getting upset.

"These are delusional fantasies, Mike. Just 'cuz you want there to be a connection doesn't mean there is one. It's a strange coincidence, that's all."

"Bull shit. There's more to it and you fucking know it. If you don't see it, then you're a fucking idiot. I'm going over to Chatham County to get that flight number. I'll send it over. Call in a favor, I know you still know folks over there. Any Judge will agree that getting this list can potentially save lives. You'll see, that guy that fucked up that woman at the grocery store will be on that manifest, along with David Spears, Laura Jones, Jeff Arkansas, or whatever the fuck his name is, and that woman's ex-husband's name is gonna be at the top of the list. I guarantee it. You'll see. We better hope it was a small plane. I'll call you in a minute with the flight number," Mike said as he stormed off, slamming the door to the conference room hard enough to make the windows shake.

Captain Garrison headed back to his office and sat behind his desk. The day was really taking its toll on him as well. He was responsible for everything that happened or failed to happen at this precinct, after all. The stress was starting to get to him.

"What the hell was that about?" Detective Wright said as he entered the Captain's office, having seen Samantha and her friend off.

"That smelly bastard's really starting to lose it, Grant. He thinks that somehow everyone that flew from Atlanta to Savannah is gonna go crazy and kill someone. He wants me to get him a warrant so he can get the flight manifest," the Captain answered.

"I don't know, Captain. It is pretty crazy. What would it hurt to get it, though? You think a judge would give it up?" Grant asked.

The Captain's phone vibrated across his desk. He snatched it up and read the message from Mike:

LAURA JONES on Sierra Flight 1289, dep ATL2007hrs arr SAV2112hrs make sure order says crew info too - - - GET IT

"I guess we'll find out," said the Captain as he picked up his office phone and started to dial.

Chapter 35

AT 1500 HRS, 45 MILES away from SCMPD, 2LT Aker and SFC Johnson held a final meeting to coordinate efforts for the demolition range that they were in charge of tomorrow. Seven people crammed in their tiny office to discuss the duties and responsibilities of those involved. Although 2LT Aker was the officer in charge, SFC Johnson gave all the orders:

"Alright, I'm going to range control on the way home tonight to sign for the range flag and radios. I need someone to go with Staff Sergeant Brunick in the morning to sign for all the stuff, the explosives, MDIs, everything," SFC Johnson said.

"I got it," SGT Holloway said without hesitation. He didn't think his eagerness would be misinterpreted as anything but a means to be forgiven for being late earlier today.

"Roger that. They're gonna meet you guys there as early as 0530. Don't screw around. Load the truck tonight and be there by 0515. Call me once they drop it off and keep a copy of the receipt. Brunick, you need to be meticulous about keeping an accurate count as we're doing this thing," SFC Johnson stressed.

"Don't worry, Sergeant. I'll help him keep accountability," SGT Holloway said with a creepy grin that made everyone chuckle.

After a good laugh, SFC Johnson got serious and started to drill people one their responsibilities tomorrow. He ensured that everyone understood their job; who was assigned as safety personnel, who was in charge of operating the radio, who was conducting the classes and safety briefing, and, most importanyly, who was keeping track of all the explosives. *Perfect*...hissed between SGT Holloway's ears.

Chapter 36

THE LATE AFTERNOON HOURS TICKED away and were for the most part uneventful, as far as Mike knew, anyway. He had decided not to go back to the precinct after he spoke with Laura Jones for a second time and sent the Captain that text message instead. In hopes of avoiding another confrontation with the Captain, Mike chose to walk over to Chatham County Jail and see if he could get any information about the man suspected of assaulting the woman at the grocery store. He was hoping that he may even be able to talk to the guy, perhaps confirming his suspicions that the man was in Atlanta yesterday. Mike headed to the administration entrance which was used by officers and other authorized personnel. There was a buzzer, intercom, and a large camera peering down on anyone who requested access. Mike pressed the buzzer and waited for someone to speak to him through the intercom.

"Can we help you?" a woman's voice said through the speaker, partially distorted.

"I'm Detective Michael Christianson," Mike said, holding his badge and ID up to the camera overhead "I wanted to talk to someone about the gentleman that was picked up today for assaulting someone at a grocery store."

After a few minutes of silence, a loud, distinct buzzing sound emerged from the door, indicating that the person on the other side had activated its release mechanism. Mike pulled the door open and went on in, making sure to check that the door securely locked behind him.

Two correctional officers were waiting for Mike on the other side of the door. One of them was the gentleman that had witnessed the Colonel's gruesome insect infestation earlier.

"They moved him to the infirmary, Detective. He had some kind of infection, I've never seen anything like it," one of the officers said. "It was pretty disgusting. He vomited all over another officer and there were bugs in it. Bugs in his vomit."

"Excuse me?" Mike said, "You mean literally? Bugs? What kind of bugs."

"Well, we had placed him in restraints because he was combative. He attacked the officer that he threw up on. I didn't see the bugs in his puke, but I was the one that did his initial thirty minute check after he was in isolation and, let me tell ya, it was disturbing," the officer said, clearly displaying that he was affected by what he had witnessed.

Mike had withdrawn his notebook by now. "What happened?" he asked.

"There were fleas under his spit hood, hundreds of them. I mean, this thing was filled with fleas. They were crawling and jumping all over his face, his nose, his eyes. They were digging themselves into his skin. It was insane."

"Oh my God," Mike said, trying to contain his emotions. He was beginning to believe that his suspicions were correct. This man was on that plane. Mike was sure of it.

"That's not all," the officer added, "he had more bugs under his skin. A bump on his head swelled up, like a pimple, and popped open. It was the same kind of bugs that were in his throw up, that's what they told me, anyway. Earbugs, I guess there called. I'm not sure."

"Earwigs," the other officer corrected.

"Yeah, earwigs. Whatever the hell they are, that old man has some issues. It was the grossest thing I've ever seen, and I've seen some shit! Trust me," the burly correctional officer said as he shuddered the willies away.

"Is he talking to anyone? Or is he out of it?" Mike asked, in hopes of confirming what he believed he already knew.

"I don't think so. I haven't been down there yet. I was going to go check on him in a few. I'm curious what the hell's wrong with him. I knew there were bugs that could get in the body, you know, parasites and shit, but these were friggin' huge. I didn't think you could see the bugs that could get in you without a microscope," the big guy said, reigniting his heebie jeebies.

Mike placed his pen to his notebook and eagerly awaited the answer, "What's his name?"

"Colonel Lawrence Winford," the officer said mockingly, demonstrating an improvised courtesy by bending slightly at the knees, "old guy sounds like royalty."

"Thanks fellas. Here's my card. Call me if he comes around," Mike said as he walked out and headed back to SCMPD HQ, hoping that the Captain had his warrant. *This man was definitely on that plane,* Mike thought as he increased his pace from walk to a run.

Chapter 37

"WHERE'S THE CAPTAIN?" MIKE SAID to Detective Wright after looking into the Captain's empty office. Mike threw himself into the seat at his desk, feeling his exhaustion starting to grow.

"He's over at the Judicial Complex trying to get your warrant. You owe me one by the way, I talked him into it, and so, you're welcome," Detective Wright answered.

"Admit it, youngster, you know I'm right. Well technically, you're Wright, I'm correct," Mike said in a horribly feeble attempt to be funny. "Check this out," he said as he pulled out his notebook. "You know that guy, well, that old man that attacked a woman at the grocery store this morning? Well, he attacked a correctional officer, too and now he's in the infirmary..."

"So?" Wright interrupted.

Mike snapped, "Let me finish. He threw up all over the officer, they said that there was earwigs in his puke. Tons of them. They stuck him in isolation, in restraints, you know, spit hood and everything. When they checked on him, the hood was full of fleas. Can you believe that? Then they said that more earwigs came out of his forehead."

"What do you mean 'came out of his forehead'? Earwigs are those little bugs that have the little pinchers on their ass, right?" a very confused Wright asked.

"Yup. Creepy little fuckers. And I don't know, they said a bump formed on his head, like a zit or something. Then it cracked open and more little bugs came out. Sick, right?" Mike said as he stood up and went into the conference room that they were all in earlier. Detective Wright followed.

In the back corner of the conference room there was a large dry erase board. It was the type that was on wheels, so you could roll it around the office, it also had a surface that would rotate 360 degrees on a pivot hinge; giving you two separate dry erase boards. The side facing the room had some things written on it in varying colors, so Mike spun it around so he could use the clean side on the back. He grabbed a black marker from the little tray and wrote the words "Ex-husband" centered at the top of the board.

"Hey, Grant, what's the name of Mrs. Arkansas' ex-husband?" Mike said.

"Her name is ARKENSON. Not Arkansas. And her exes name is Mason. Doug Mason," Grant answered.

"Oh yeah," Mike said as he erased "Ex-husband" with his tie and replaced it with:

"DOUG MASON – pilot (flight 1289)".

He began to create a flow chart on the board, writing names in black and drawing a red line through the name if that person was no longer alive. He connected everyone that he knew had flown from Atlanta to Savannah yesterday by drawing a line from their name up to Doug Mason's. He had Laura Jones, David Spears, and Jeff Arkenson all connected to the pilot. He wrote Colonel Lawrence Winford off to the side with a big question mark next to it. Under David Spears' name he wrote Linda, Jason, and Jim

Reynolds, all with a big red line through the name, as well as through Dave's, he then drew a red line to Laura's name, writing on top of the line "killed by." Next to Jeff Arkenson's name he wrote "someone on 17" and then drew a red strike through those words. Mike took a few steps back from his masterpiece of scribbles and lines. "Oh yeah," he said as moved forward and wrote "someone at grocery store" next to the Colonel's name. He drew a green line from Doug Mason to Jeff Arkenson. Along the line he wrote Samantha Arkenson, he then reached up next to Doug's name and wrote in all caps: DAUGHTER?

"You have to admit," he said as he cleared his throat "there's a connection here, Grant. You know there is. Don't let anyone erase this, I'm gonna go burn one."

"You're gonna what?" Detective Wright asked.

"I'm gonna go smoke a cigarette. Jesus," Mike said as he headed out back to pollute his lungs.

One cigarette turned into five, so Detective Wright had some privacy to take this whole thing in. He stood in front of the dry erase board, arms crossed, and a stern look on his face. *The old bastard's right*, he admitted to himself, *there's something going on, somehow, but what? What the hell is going on?* He grabbed a green dry erase marker and moved towards the words "someone on 17" and "someone at grocery store" and double underlined both, tapping the tip of the marker repeatedly at the end of the last line. Grant went over to his desk, leaving the door to the conference room ajar. He took up a seat at his desk chair, grabbed the phone, and called over to Chatham County Jail.

"Chatham County Corrections," a pleasant voice answered.

"Yes ma'am, this is Detective Wright over at Savannah Chatham. I'm trying to get some info about the inmate you have over there in the infirmary, something about bugs..." Wright said.

"Oh yes, him. I'll connect you with the doc working tonight..."

Grant cut her off, "Ma'am, I really only need you to tell me who the arresting officers were. I'm only interested in the woman he assaulted right now. I'll come by later tonight about the old man."

"Hang on," she said.

A few seconds later, Grant was provided with names Officer Benevides and Officer Ivory. He held the phone's handset between his head and shoulder, and pressed down on the plunger. Once he heard a new dial tone, Grant started to mash the buttons for Chatham County Sheriff's Department, but he hesitated. He needed to go over there. He rested the handset back in its cradle, stood up, and headed outside.

As Grant walked through the side door of the building, he was greeted by a cloud of Mike's cigarette smoke. "Uh, God, this is disgusting!! Why the hell don't you quit?!" Grant yelled and coughed at the same time.

"I'll quit when I'm dead," Mike said, "What's up?"

"I'm heading over to Chatham County, talk to the arresting officers about the bug guy's victim. I think we should head over to Bryan County to find out about Arkenson's victim, as well. Or at least call over there," Grant answered.

"I'll drive, text the Captain. Tell him what we're doing. I don't want him to come back with that warrant and not call us. I'll be pissed if I find out that warrant was just sitting here," Mike said as they headed over to his Impala.

"Got it," said Grant

They climbed into Detective Christianson's department is-sued vehicle and Grant was immediately disgusted. The front seat and floor board was covered with random cheeseburger wrappers, candy bar wrappers, empty soda cans, and other miscellaneous crap. The back seat had double the contents of the front, com-bined with a few thousand cigarette butts. Grant was pretty sure there were clothes back there amongst the filth. The odor could be compared to a stale ashtray placed next to a few pounds of ground beef that had been left out for a week.

"Dear Lord!!" Grant scolded, "This is fucking disgusting! This is a department issued vehicle! I can't believe you put this thing back in the motor pool every night!"

"Don't worry about it," Mike said, "You mind if I burn one?"

"Huh?"

"You mind if I have a smoke?"

"Fuck yes, I mind!! You're not supposed to smoke in here anyway!!"

The two detectives continued to bicker back and forth as they made the short drive over to Chatham County. They had to get a move on, as it was approaching 5 p.m., which was irrelevant to them as a detective knows no typical work schedule. Not everyone works detective hours however, and therefore it can get difficult getting things done as the day progresses into evening. Junior Officers generally did shift work; these two officers were most likely gone for the day. Grant and Mike might have to settle for the police report rather than an actual sit down with Benavides and Ivory.

Detectives Wright and Christianson walked into Chatham County Sheriff's Department at about 4:52 p.m. and were told by the desk sergeant that they just missed the officers they wanted to talk to.

"Yeah, they just left, Detectives. They had to stay past their shift to finish up the paperwork for that craziness with the old man," the desk sergeant said.

"Got it," Detective Wright said. "We're actually here to see whether or not their perp had anything to do with some other open investigations. Can you give us a copy of their report? Witness statements?"

"Yes sir. Grab a seat, I'll go make you a copy," the desk sergeant told the detectives.

Mike and Grant took a seat at the uncomfortable bench that was outside the desk sergeant's window and waited impatiently for the report. After a few minutes, it was Detective Wright that broke the awkward silence, "What makes people do things like this, ya think? I mean, what makes people snap?"

"Who knows, man? Could be a lot of things. Stress. Depression. This guys a Vietnam Vet, could be post-traumatic stress disorder. Or, what did they call it? What'd they call it before PTSD? Battle fatigue? I mean, those emotions can manifest years after the traumatic event. He could've imagined he was attacking the VC, or something. He's like 70 years old, maybe he's suffering from dementia. Who knows?" Mike answered. "People snap, man. Tip of the ice-burg, ya know. Something that seems tiny on the surface turns out to be something huge underneath."

"Yeah, but what about all the others?" Grant challenged. "The teacher, Arkenson, Spears?"

"We'll figure this out, man. Arkenson was road rage, I'll tell you that right now. I don't need to be a detective to figure that one out. Laura Jones is a cute little seventh grade teacher. The stress must've gotten to her. I'm sure they all have some kind of stressor that made 'em finally snap. A trigger. The straw that broke the camel's back, or whatever," Mike said, as the desk sergeant reappeared with their report. "I just don't know why they're all connected."

"I guess we'll figure that out too," Grant said as he grabbed the folder from the desk sergeant and led the way out the door.

Chapter 38

YOUNG JESSICA HAD HER EAR buds in when her father had fallen, so she didn't hear the thud when Doug had bounced off the linoleum a couple hours ago. He had laid motionless on the floor for the entire time his daughter sat captivated by her 20th viewing of the "Twilight Saga – Breaking Dawn part 2" on her dad's iPad. She stood up once the movie concluded and walked over to the bathroom door. Realizing that it was locked, she knocked on it lightly. "Daddy?" she said, "Are you ok? I'm getting hungry. Can we call mom?"

A few minutes, which felt like hours, had elapsed when her father finally answered. "I'm ok, baby," Doug said in a faint, weak voice. "I'll be out in a second. Grab the phonebook and see what you wanna eat. We'll order something. Whatever you want."

"Where is the phonebook?" Jessica asked.

Standing up and looking at the slowly squirming worms on the sink, "Um, check the drawers in the desk, baby. You'll find it." Doug said, as he stood frozen, staring at the mess he created. He needed to clean this up, there was no way he'd be able to explain to his daughter why there were bloody worms all over the place. "Found it!" Jessica yelled.

"Ok, baby! Figure out what you want and I'll order it when I get out." Doug hollered. He actually was feeling a little better;

much more rested. The nausea had eased back a bit, the way it does for anyone who throws up. He hadn't heard any voices or seen any words since he woke up, so he wanted to get this cleaned up while he was free of distractions. He used both hands in a scooping fashion, securing as much of the worms and puke as he could, and carried it over to the toilet. The mess splashed in the toilet with a noisy plop when he opened his hands to let it fall out. Doug continued this until he got most of his spew into the bowl, then he used all but two of the towels to soak up the rest. Satisfied that he cleaned as much as he could without cleaning products, he took one last look in the mirror before heading out to talk to his daughter. His face had regained some of its color and the bags under his eyes had reduced significantly. He noticed that his eyes were no longer bloodshot, as he looked through the smudged lenses of his glasses. *What the fuck?* Doug thought, as he looked at his confused self. Doug was wearing glasses. Big, ugly glasses with gold frames and dirty lenses. He yanked them off his face like they were on fire and threw them across the room. Dizziness and nausea began to return as Doug exited the bathroom, looking back to where he'd thrown the glasses that had appeared out of thin air on his face. A voice suddenly shouted with authority into his delusional mind: *KILL HER!!!*

Chapter 39

"HOLY SHIT!!" DETECTIVE CHRISTIANSON SAID as he and Detective Wright sat at the conference table going through the arrest report, "Listen to this statement, *'I left the shoe stuck in the woman's face because someone told me I shouldn't pull it out'*. This Winford character hit a woman in the head with his cane and then stabbed her in the face with her own fucking shoe. It says here that the shoe was left stuck in her face!"

"My God, that's nuts," Wright agreed.

Mike stood up, walked over to the board and secured a green dry erase marker. Under the words "someone at grocery store" he wrote "attacked with cane. Stabbed with shoe". He looked at his watch, frustrated, he said, "Where the fuck is the Captain? How the hell long does it take? Hey Grant, can you call over to Bryan County and see if they'll send over the report on the Arkansas homicide?"

"ARKENSON!! The name is Arkenson. Yeah, I'll call 'em," Grant answered. "You need to calm down, Mike. You're gonna have a heart attack."

"Don't worry about me, young man. You just worry about holding up that giant head of yours. I'm going to burn one," Mike said as he left.

Grant laughed as he headed over to his desk to call Bryan Country Sheriff's office; shouldn't be an issue getting them to fax over a copy of the witness statements and police report. He heard that Jeff Arkenson had been torn apart by the truck he ran in front of so there was really no reason to pursue the autopsy reports just yet. If Arkenson was just a pile of mush, the results from autopsy probably wouldn't be able to give them much to go on anyway. Grant figured that Mike would be more interested in what Arkenson had done to his victim, and not so much about what was left of him. Not yet, anyway. The documents that Grant requested had arrived through the fax machine just before his chain smoking buddy returned. Grant updated the "someone on 17" part of the board by writing "no nose/baseball bat" under it.

Together they sat in the conference room, going over arrest reports, witness statements, the random scribbles in Mike's notebook, and their flow chart on the board. These two gentleman started the day as associates, mere co-workers. But as the day has progressed, they began to turn what was once only a professional relationship into the beginning stages of an actual friendship. Experiencing traumatic events and devastation with someone usually brings people closer; they begin to develop a bond. That bond is what gives groups of professionals a certain feeling of cohesiveness and brotherhood, not unlike Soldiers who serve together in combat or the brave men and woman who were first responders on 9/11. As unfortunate as tragedy can be, it almost always brings out the best in people; it brings people together. These two were by no means as heroic as the people involved on that terrible day, but the bond is the same. These two detectives were slowly establishing a stronger admiration for one another. That type of admiration will always lead to a team that functions more efficiently.

"I said it before, man," Mike said "this is only the beginning. I got a bad feeling that there's gonna be more people up on that board, if not by the end of the night, by tomorrow, I'm sure of it."

"Dude, you stink so bad I can't even concentrate," Grant said candidly, "You need to quit smoking and start bathing, like now."

"Well, you know, I might reek, but I can always take a shower. You can't do nothing about that giant square head of yours, fucking dick. Oh wait, let me guess, you don't have a big head, you just have a lot on your mind, right?" Mike said.

There laughs become so loud that some of the other people in the office came by to see what was so funny. Mike was going to explain but then decided against it. The little joke had lost its spontaneity.

Chapter 40

SAMANTHA ARKENSON WAS OUT COLD on her sofa while her friend, Martha, tidied up her house. Martha was called on by police to help comfort and support Sam during the notification process of her husband's death. Her dear friend Martha was a friend of the family, so Jeff's death had hit her hard as well. Since leaving the police station a couple hours ago, Martha had been helping Sam make phone calls, notifying other family members, making initial contact with the funeral home, and a call to check on her mom up in Beaufort. They were both unable to get Doug on the phone, a fact that was adding to Sam's misery. Martha continued to reassure Sam that everything was fine with Doug and Jessica up until the point where she nodded off on the couch. She really did believe that. Martha was friends with Doug as well and she couldn't think of a man who loved his daughter more than Doug Mason.

Martha sat at Sam's kitchen table and sobbed once she was done cleaning up. Little Jessica still hadn't learned about her step-father's death and Martha believed that she didn't know about the school shooting either. It was going to be a difficult time for the little girl once she learns of everything that's happened. Martha regained her composure and started to draft a to-do list for her friend, starting with things that needed attending to first thing in the morning. She would be expecting a call first thing from the insurance company, Jeff's boss said he was coming by at some point, and the police said they would come by again as well. There's a lot for a surviving spouse to take care of when someone dies suddenly. Martha intended on staying here as long as necessary to help her friend during this troubling time. It was a little after 6 p.m. when Martha finished her list and sat down on the loveseat next to Sam. She turned on the TV, making sure to mute the volume, took a deep breath, and leaned back into her seat. It was going to be a long night.

Chapter 41

THE SUN WAS BEGINNING TO set outside of SCMPD HQ when Captain Garrison returned. Mike jumped to his feet as soon as he saw the Captain pull into his assigned spot outside. Grant needed an elbow in the ribs, since he had nodded off sitting there at the conference table. Once awake, he shared in Mike's eagerness as they waited like a couple of anxious school boys for the envelope that contained what they needed.

"Apparently, Judge Scott has total confidence in your hunches Mike, 'cuz she gave it up. Phil agrees with you too, I guess, because he was the one who convinced her. They both said that getting this manifest might save lives. So, you're welcome," Captain Garrison said as he opened the warrant, using it to help guide what he was saying. "This warrant is only for Sierra flight 1289 Atlanta to Savannah. It'll get you a passenger name record from the airlines computer reservation system. They should include the names, addresses, and phone numbers that the passengers provided when they reserved their flight. There's also something on here about crew member information. Don't make me regret this. I expect you to keep me informed. Roger?"

"Thanks Captain," Mike said. "You did the right thing, I guarantee that we're gonna prevent some craziness. Check this out..."

Mike went on to brief the Captain about all the connections that he and Detective Wright had discovered, as well as updates on the people in custody. Captain Garrison was shocked to hear of the brutality of the Arkenson and Winford assaults. He knew that they had attacked people, that Arkenson committed a homicide and Winford basically attempted one, he just didn't know how violent the attacks were. He obviously hadn't heard about the bugs. The initial skepticism the Captain had for Mike's theory had slowly begun to fade.

"You ready to go get this?" Mike asked Grant.

"I gotta make an appearance at home sometime tonight. Let me know when you have it, I'll come back in," Grant answered.

"Alright, man," Mike said, sounding a little disappointed. "Captain, thanks again. I'm heading over there."

Detective Christianson headed out to his Impala, sparking up a Marlboro as soon as he cleared the building. Before cranking the engine, he radioed dispatch and requested that a couple of uniformed officers meet him outside the Sierra terminal at Savannah/Hilton Head International Airport in about twenty minutes. The sun had completely set by now, causing Savannah to open up into what looked like was going to be a clear night. The airport was about 15 miles away from SCMPD HQ, although Mike didn't always associate distance in terms of miles. He used cigarettes. People knew not to ask him for directions as he'd usually answer with something like head down 204 for like 3 butts then turn right on...

Mike threw the butt of his forth cigarette into the cache of butts in his back seat as he pulled up to the area just outside the

Sierra terminal. Leaving his vehicle in one of the spaces allotted for dropping off and picking up passengers, he felt confident that his law enforcement plates and SCMPD decal on the windshield would protect him from potential towers. For good measure, Mike flashed his badge and gave a quick explanation to the airline representative outside.

Savannah/Hilton Head was a small airport, hosting about 50,000 flights annually on two functioning runways, and provides service from six different airlines. Four of the six airlines had terminals spread out on the main floor, distributed equally across the space with two on either side of the escalator, which was the focal point for those entering the airport. The remaining two airlines operated out of the floor below, directly next to the baggage claim area and rental car companies. Sierra was located to the far left off the main entry doors. Mike moved swiftly towards the left after he entered the airport, fighting back the urge to run. He had become obsessed with confirming his theory; and that's all it would be, a confirmation. He already knew the truth. There was no doubt in his mind.

Mike was greeted by two SCMPD officers once he entered the area of the Sierra terminal. There were four people in line at the counter, consisting of a couple and two individual travelers. There were an additional three people pressing screens at the kiosks. "Stand by, fellas," Mike said to the officers as he headed up to the counter.

Mike bypassed everyone and headed directly to the nearest agent, interrupting the passenger that was checking in. Badge up, Mike said, "Ma'am, I'm Detective Christianson from Savannah

Chatham Metro. This is a warrant instructing you to provide me with all information you have on Flight 1289 from yesterday, Atlanta to Savannah. I'm going to need the complete passenger manifest, to include names and addresses, crew information, plane type, and any other information pertaining to that flight."

A little startled, the woman responded, "Um, ok. Could you wait a minute detective, while I finish with this passenger? I'll get my supervisor to help you with whatever you need."

"That's fine, ma'am," Mike said as he stepped off to the side, giving the passenger her space back at the counter. The supervisor walked up a few seconds later, apparently having heard what Mike said to the woman.

"Sir, I'm Chris Armstrong. I'm the supervisor for this shift. How may I help you?" the tiny, nervous gentleman said.

Mike repeated what he said earlier, nearly verbatim. The tiny man escorted Detective Christianson into the back area as to not cause concern or panic in the travelers within earshot, the officers followed. The four men went behind the counter, past the little conveyor belt that takes your bags away forever, and into a small office. They all took up seats at a small conference table as Mr. Armstrong examined the warrant. Mike felt the beginning stages of irritation start to build up as he looked at this man who appeared like he was 15 years old. The man had a mild case of acne and still had the wet behind the ears look. *Do your parents know you work here?* Mike thought, giving himself a small internal chuckle that helped settle his growing frustration.

"Sir, I think I need to call my supervisor. Information such as this is only released following some type of aviation disaster. I don't see anything like that here," the young man said.

"Look, Mr. Armstrong, this warrant says all it needs to say. See this seal and signature at the bottom?" Mike said while tapping the bottom part of the paper, "That's all you need, my friend. If it makes you feel better call whoever you want. Just understand that the longer I sit here, the more lives are going to be affected."

"What is it all about?" Armstrong asked, starting to show true concern.

"We're wasting time. Call your supervisor or give me what I need," Mike said.

"Yes sir, excuse me," Armstrong said as he got up and walked out.

"What's this all about, Detective?" one of the officers who resembled a young Mike Tyson asked.

"Well, we're trying to see if the homicides from earlier have any connections. It looks like some of the people involved might have been together on this flight. I really want to just confirm or deny that suspicion," Mike said, purposely being as vague as possible. Rumors can destroy an investigation once they start progressing through the grapevine. Mike discovered years ago that when young officers started talking they could tear down an organization with gossip and hearsay. It's best to keep it simple, say only enough to answer the question and do it in a disinteresting way. He didn't intend on keeping the force in the dark forever, they would eventually know when they needed to know and right now they didn't need to know.

"Yeah, they said today was a crazy one," the other officer said. These two had just come on shift a couple hours ago, at 4:00 p.m. Savannah County Metro did change over at 8, 4, and midnight for the officers that did shift work. These shift changes came complete with an in-brief for those who were beginning their day. Today's briefing must've been something.

After about ten minutes, Armstrong came back into the room with a young lady beside him. "Detective, this is Miss Fisher, she'll be able to print out everything for you. I'll just need a copy of the warrant."

"Of course," Mike said as he stood up and followed the young lady further into the back area. She led Mike to another office where she logged onto her computer. This office was far too small for the whole group, so the uniformed officers went back into the terminal area to wait on Mike. "You guys are good," Mike said as they were leaving, giving them a gesture with his hand, saluting off his brow, indicating that they could leave for good.

The woman continued to peck away at her keyboard, displaying skills that far exceeded Mike's two finger approach to typing. She came to what looked like some type of official data base where she was prompted to input the date and flight number. She entered "1289, Jan 26, 2014" in the search bar and awaited the results.

"Sir, this is our computer reservation system. It will have the information provided by the passengers when they purchased their tickets, minus the payment method. Our supervisor told us that there's a different type of warrant for that kind of information. This will have names, addresses, phone numbers, and the seat they were assigned. The phone numbers are only as accurate as what the people provided at the time of reservation, you have to understand," the woman explained in a professional manner.

"Thank you, miss. You're being very helpful. What about the crew information, where do we get that?' Mike said, trying to subdue his enthusiasm.

"We'll get there, sir. It's a different database." she said as she leaned back, giving Mike a better view of the screen. "It looks like there was 97 people on that flight, yeah, see there, it's missing some phone numbers. That happens sometimes. I'll go ahead and print this for you, and then we'll pull up the crew info."

Mike resisted the urge to push her out of the way and start scrolling for the names; Arkenson, Spears, Jones, Winford. "Thank you" he said with a smile, as she removed the pages from the printer and placed them in a Sierra airlines folder. He continued to look over her shoulder as she pulled up the database for crew information, although he wanted to rip open the folder in his hands and confirm his suspicions. The young lady went through a few pages, typed in a user name and password at one point, and finally arrived to the area where she plugged in the flight info.

"Here it is: Flight 1289, departed Atlanta at 262007JAN2014 and arrived at 262104JAN2014. Oh, looks like they were eight minutes early. So, it was a Boeing 737-600, which is pretty standard for that route. Um, flight crew of two and it looks like there were three flight attendants..."

"Pilot, where's the pilot?" Mike asked as his eyes tried to look everywhere at once, no longer able to contain his excitement.

"Here," she said, pressing her finger directly on the screen, "Douglas Mason. Looks like Chad Beecroft was co-pilot."

Mike's heart rate increased a little as he watched the woman's finger tap the screen. A small lump appeared in his throat,

"P-please print this for me as well, ma'am. Thanks again, you've been extremely helpful," Mike said, as his eyes became fixated on those two words: DOUGLAS MASON

Chapter 42

Colonel Lawrence Winford stared at ugly old ceiling tiles from his bed in the infirmary at Chatham County Jail. This was a tiny facility, consisting of only ten beds, a staff of three during the day and only one at night. Memorial University Medical Center was only a ten-minute drive away, therefore anyone needing more than just basic medical attention would be transferred there. The entrance to the infirmary led directly to a large, "U" shaped reception desk that was on an elevated platform, giving the person working there a better view of the floor. Under the reception desk was a large red button used to alert the jail's ERT in the event of a belligerent inmate. The beds were distributed equally, five on each side of the reception desk. Behind the spot where the receptionist/nurse sat were two additional rooms for the privacy required to treat certain patients and a third room occupied by the doctor on shift. There were six locked supply closets along the front wall which housed various medical supplies used for routine care.

The Colonel lay in the bed directly to the receptionist's right; the first one to the left of anyone entering. He was secured to the bed with restraining devices for his protection, as well as the protection of the staff. His spit hood had been removed earlier to tend to the wound on his forehead and the infestation of insects, and since he hadn't lashed out at anyone yet, the nurses decided to leave the hood off. Larry was looking much better than he had an hour ago. He still appeared comatose, just lying there, oblivious to his surroundings, as he soaked in his second IV bag, replenishing the electrolytes that his body had thrown up earlier. His skin had regained some of its color, the boil on his head had been drained of all puss and insects, disinfected with hydrogen peroxide, and dressed with clean, dry first aid dressings.

The doctor on shift had initially planned on having the inmate transferred to Memorial University Medical Center, since the Colonel's condition was quite alarming and they were only equipped for minor conditions here. However, the doctor reconsidered his assessment after consulting his colleagues at the university, since Larry has been showing drastic improvements. Before the doctor left for the night at 7 p.m., he instructed the night nurse to continue to monitor the patient and refer to Memorial if necessary. Apparently, a patient spewing bugs from his body is a common occurrence here, since the doctor hadn't seemed too concerned when he left.

The Colonel continued to lay motionless, eyes open and unblinking. His breathing had returned to normal, as well as his fever. In fact, the nurse was going to contact one of correctional officers shortly to see about beginning the booking procedures again. The only factor that would prevent that was that Larry was still not responding to verbal commands, he was simply laying there, mesmerized by the ceiling, mouth hanging open. His pupils had responded to light stimulation earlier, as they should, he just wasn't responding to verbal stimulation. The night nurse decided that she would give him a few more hours before suggesting to send him back out front. He would eventually need to complete the processing in order to answer to the judge tomorrow.

The young woman stood over the Colonel and waved her hand in front of his face. "Sir? Sir, can you hear me?" she said, "I'm going to remove your IV, ok?" She placed a small 2x2 gauze over the IV site and removed the catheter from the arm, she then used a small piece of white medical tape to hold the gauze in place. There was no reaction from the Colonel at all during this process or when the nurse wheeled away the stainless steel IV bag holder. She headed over to the supply closet directly in front of his bed, unlocked it, and returned a few un-used supplies. In direct violation of standard operating procedures, the woman left the closet unsecured as she returned to her perch behind the reception desk. Some classic Elvis Costello played softly on her iHome as she opened her copy of James Patterson's "Zoo" and began to read, hoping to God that her shift went on without incident. She was unaware that the Colonel had closed his eyes.

A faint whisper had reentered the Colonel's thoughts. This voice was not as loud and threatening as before, this one was more of a quiet taunt. It was almost inaudible at first, like the small series of bleeps you almost hear when you're administered an audiology exam; not sure if you actually heard it or if you made yourself hear it. The noise gradually got slightly louder, until Larry could start to make sense of what he was hearing. It seemed as though there was a small person standing on his pillow, whispering softly into his ear. The night nurse hadn't noticed that the supply closet door had creaked open slightly.

You're a coward you're a coward and a baby killer you're a fucking worthless old man that can't even walk you need a fucking scooter old man you should just fucking kill yourself coward failure worthless coward disgrace to the fucking uniform fuck your dead wife coward... the words breathed into his ears, rattled around his puzzled mind as they tickled his eyes from inside, causing rapid twitches and jerks. The sinister and dismal voice continued to ridicule the tired old Colonel until his feelings of nausea returned, thus ensuring that the distracted night nurse would soon have to stop reading her book.

Chapter 43

DETECTIVE CHRISTIANSON RIPPED OPEN THE Sierra folder that contained the passenger and crew manifests as soon as he climbed into his grungy vehicle, which was still parked illegally. He could hardly contain himself as he searched for the familiar names that he had spent all afternoon scribbling in his notebook and on the dry erase board. He started with the passenger list, ignoring the crew list as he had already seen Doug Mason's name on the monitor earlier. His eyes darted to the top of the three page document to the first name: *Arkenson, Jeffery N., seat* 26C, followed by his address and complete ten digit phone number. His eyes scanned down the list, reading each name aloud in a muffled grunt, until he found *Jones, Laura V. seat* 10A. His excitement continued to grow as he frantically flipped the stapled page over to see the second sheet, *shit*, he thought as he ripped the page free from the stapled group, accidentally. Nobody he knew on the second sheet, *dammit*, he thought as he tore sheets two and three apart, clutching sheet three tight within his grasp. Midway down the page, there it was: *Spears, David J. seat* 17B and finally, the last name on the list: *Winford, Lawrence A. seat* 21D. Mike sat exhilarated as he breathed heavily through his mouth, fumbling with his phone. He intended on calling Detective Wright, but he didn't have his number. He'd have to settle for the Captain with whom to share the excitement of his discovery.

Mike didn't let the Captain get through his complete greeting as he answered the call.

"Captain, its Christianson. They're all on here. Every one of them. The ex-husband was the pilot and they're all..."

Mike stopped himself mid-sentence as he thought of something that should not have eluded him this long. A lump bulged in his throat as his heart sunk; thinking of the worst case scenario like all good law enforcement personnel do. *What if?* he thought, *what if the other pilot, what's his name? Bee-something, what if he takes control of another plane? What if he's in the air when he "snaps"? What if he's up there right now?*

"They're all what?" the Captain asked. "Mike? They're all what?"

"I'll call you back." Mike said as he ended the call and dropped his phone on the seat. All good law enforcement personnel are natural pessimists, always thinking of the worst possible outcome of any situation. In order to implement control measures to mitigate risk, one must be able to predict hazards before they occur and anticipate tragedies and failures. These attributes provide some people with an anticipatory instinct which helps them keep bad things from happening. In most cases, detectives are called upon to discover how and why something horrible happen, but occasionally they can be given the opportunity to prevent it. Mike jumped at this opportunity.

This time he ran into the airport, seeing no need to hide his enthusiasm. He ran directly up to the Sierra terminal, leaned on the counter and said in a loud, authoritative voice "I need to see Armstrong. I need to see the young lady that helped me before."

Mr. Armstrong appeared almost instantaneously, hoping to get the detective to lower his voice and stop causing a scene. "Yes, Detective. What else did you need?" he said, indicating with his quiet voice that Mike should lower his.

"I need to know when..." he forgot the name of the other pilot and he left the manifest in his car. "The other pilot, on flight 1289 yesterday, when is he scheduled to fly again? I know pilots have a recovery time, or whatever. When is he flying again? Beecraft? Beecroft! The name's Beecroft. When is he flying again?!"

"Sir, please lower your voice. I don't believe that information was requested on your warrant. I can't give you that information without talking to my supervisor. I'll need..."

Mike didn't let the little man finish, he reached over the counter and grabbed the toddler by his shirt collar. "Look, you little shit, people that were on that plane are acting crazy. Four people from that flight have attempted murder, three succeeded. One of them succeeded four times. You watch the news today, you fucking twerp? Every one of *those* people were on *this* plane. The other pilot kidnapped his own daughter. If this guy's gonna snap, we want him to snap when he's on the ground and not in the air, controlling a fucking 70 ton jet. You go back there and find out when Beecrotch, or whatever his fucking name is, is scheduled to fly again"

Mike pushed the skinny supervisor away, causing him to use the momentum of the push to head into the back room faster. People from all the airlines had begun to look over in Mike's direction. Everyone on this floor, and possibly the floor beneath, had heard everything, and Mike didn't give a shit.

A shaken and disheveled Chris Armstrong returned and said, "Sir, Chad Beecroft is scheduled to fly the Atlanta run at 9 a.m. tomorrow." he said as he handed Mike a small business card. "His address and phone number are on the back of this card."

"You might want to call you supervisor after all, you're gonna need someone else to fly that plane," Mike said as he left.

Chapter 44

NORMALLY, 1930 HRS. WAS FAR too early to go to sleep, but SGT Holloway knew that tomorrow was going to be a long day. He used a backwards planning sequence in nearly everything that he did; starting from the event and planning backwards, ensuring that he allotted enough time for everything to be accomplished. He and Staff Sergeant Brunick were ordered to be at the range at 0515 tomorrow to sign for the explosives and the associated gear that went with it, which means that they would need to leave the company area no later than 0415, which means that he would need to meet Brunick at the company no later than 0400. Holloway lived in Pembroke, GA which was about a thirty minute drive normally, but since there would be less traffic than there was during the regular commute time, Seth figured he could do it in 20, hence his planned 0340 departure time. He liked to have a little time to play with before he left his house in the morning, so a 0245 first call seemed early enough.

Another habit instilled in Seth through months of Army training was the staging of equipment. By the front door, Seth placed his uniform and boots, his individual outer tactical vest, his helmet, gloves and eye protection, and his assault pack. The assault pack had been stuffed with some cold weather clothing and a rain parka. It also included what every Soldier affectionately refers to as their "woobie." A woobie was the term used to describe a piece of standard issue equipment called a "poncho liner" which was simply a small quilted blanket that had strings on the corners that allowed its owner to tie it to their poncho, hence the name "poncho liner." Nobody used it as intended, it was almost always used as a small, compact blanket that could be used virtually anywhere. It was small enough to cram into any pocket or pouch, which made it a Soldier's best friend when it got chilly outside.

Seth referred back to the checklist he had created earlier. Black tape. Green tape. He searched in his small garage for a roll of black electrical tape and a roll of 2 inch green duct tape, both of which he knew were in there somewhere. Once found, he went back inside and he threw both next to his assault pack. Back to the garage. Cordless drill. He snatched the drill off his workbench, grabbed the charger as well, just in case. Stuff - nails, glass, screws, etc. He filled a small mason jar with as many nails, nuts, washers, screws, and bolts as he could find. As he screwed the lid back on the jar, the words *you can get more when you get the cans*, dashed across his mind, visually and verbally. "Yeah, you're right," he said out loud.

He went back into his house and closed the door to the garage. He placed the new objects inside his assault pack with the rest of his stuff and zipped it up. Immediately after he closed it, he un-zipped it, having forgotten something. He went to his night stand and grabbed the book he had gotten in Atlanta yesterday, Dean Koontz "Innocence," and stuffed it in with the rest of his gear. There would probably be some downtime at the range tomorrow and tons of time to kill after. "Oh yeah," he said, out loud again, as he went back to his garage and got his tactical head lamp. He'd need this to be able to see his book tomorrow night.

Looking at his prepositioned pile of gear by the door, Seth breathed a sigh of relief, knowing that he would soon be able to fulfill his obligation to the wonderful voice within his head. His excitement began to build as he started to look forward to doing his duty. *Get some rest, Sergeant, tomorrow's going to be a long day, and tomorrow night's going to be even longer...* he heard and felt the words pass through his body, providing comfort. "Yes it is," SGT Holloway said out loud, as he crawled into bed, "yes it is."

Chapter 45

MIKE HAD TWO MISSED CALLS when he returned to his car and his phone. One number was the Captain's. The other, which he didn't recognize, was most likely Detective Wright's. He held his phone in his left hand and the card that Armstrong had handed him back at the terminal in his right. Flipping over the card, he mashed the numbers that Armstrong had provided him for Chad Beecroft. After five rings, an outgoing voicemail message started to play, which he didn't listen to. Gears were turning in Mike's detective-mind, as he twirled the business card in his hand like some kind of magician. He grabbed his hand mic and radioed dispatch, requesting a unit to meet him at Beecroft's address. Mike then went to the other missed call on his phone, the one he didn't recognize, and hit "call back."

"Detective Wright" a familiar voice said.

"Grant – Mike. I got the manifest. All those people were on the plane that Mason flew. I have the address of the co-pilot. He's supposed to fly again tomorrow, man. I'm going over there," Mike said, as he pulled his seat belt across his lap.

"You call him? I heard you on the radio," Grant said. "Want me to meet you there?"

"Yeah, his address is 17 Chandler. See you soon."

Detective Christianson arrived at the Beecroft residence just before 8 p.m., fourteen minutes after hanging up with Grant. He had been so preoccupied with his ruminating thoughts that he hadn't noticed the large amount of police sirens piercing the night air, or maybe he was immune to them. Killing his engine and sparking a cigarette, he looked across the street and saw that Grant was already standing in the street in front of the house. Chandler Drive was a thickly settled development with several large trees with low hanging moss, causing the drive through the neighborhood to seem like driving in a tunnel. The Beecroft house was recessed back about fifty feet at the end of a long driveway. There were large trees on either side of the driveway, almost like arches. There were no exterior lights on at the house and the nearest street light was about a quarter mile away, which would give the detectives the cover of darkness should they need it. Mike got out of his car and headed over to Grant, the cherry on the butt in his mouth causing his face to glow.

"You're not gonna believe this shit, they're all on the manifest, all of them," Mike said, cigarette bobbing. Grant responded, "I heard you call dispatch, you're not gonna be able to justify pulling a unit on a night as busy as this one sounds."

"Huh?" Mike said

"You didn't hear all the sirens? Sounds like its World War III out there!!" Grant said, as a series of gun shots echoed far in the distance.

Not acknowledging Grant's statement or the distant gunfire, Mike said, "Look at that," as he drew his revolver from his shoulder holster and move swiftly toward the house.

The door to the Beecroft home was slightly ajar. Mike continued to creep forward until Grant lost him in the darkness. "Hey!" Grant whispered "So what? What are you doing? Don't go in there, Mike."

"Relax, I'm not." Mike said as he used the barrel of his revolver to open the door a little wider, allowing him to see into the well-lit house.

The Beecroft home was beautiful, the foyer was spacious and a decorative crystal chandelier hung overhead. Travertine floor tiles led from the foyer into the hard wood floors that appeared to cover the rest of the downstairs. Mike's eyes scanned the area that he had within his sector of fire, his eyes started scanning at chest height and worked their way downward. He traced the floor, from the tiled area as it transformed into hard wood. There was a pool of blood on the floor about six feet past where the hard wood began. He could only see this pool of blood partially as it was appearing to have originated well past the foyer and around the corner, he could only see what looked like the outskirts of it, and it clearly had been there a while, the top of the pool had a dull look to it, like the skin a bowl of soup will form if you leave it out for too long.

"Blood," Mike said softly over his shoulder. "Get a unit here."

After radioing for backup, Grant instinctively drew his weapon and moved alongside Mike, as they pushed the door open. Grant moved to the left while Mike continued to cover the direction of travel, noticing that to his right was a deadbolted door that, based on the houses exterior, led to the garage. To Grant's left were two small rooms, one was an office, the other a guest bed room, which he quickly cleared. Together they moved forward, covering the large open living space of the Beecroft home. They stopped a foot short of the right hand corner, pausing for a fraction of a second. Although the two had never worked together in this manner, they moved with the tactical precision and synchronicity of a seasoned SWAT team. Mike executed a large step forward with his left foot, thrusting the barrel of his weapon around the corner to the right, while Grant moved forward slightly, still covering 12 o'clock.

A woman lay in the center of the pool of blood. She was on her back, eyes looking up at the ceiling, frozen in a horrifying gaze. She had been slashed repeated across the face in a fashion so brutal that her nose hung off to the side. Other areas were so deep that her white skull was exposed under the hanging flesh. Her chest and upper thighs had also been stabbed an undeterminable amount of times, causing the clothing she wore to be soaked with blood and unrecognizable. The body was in a small open area within the house's main living space. Behind the body was a small, load bearing wall which was the only wall that separated what appeared to be the kitchen from the rest of the down stairs. Smeared bloody footprints led from the body to the area behind that wall. Grant had a door about four feet ahead on his left, on which he kept his gun fixed.

Mike made a hand and arm signal gesture to Grant, indicating the he was going to move forward and clear around the corner ahead, into the area that was probably the kitchen. Grant nodded, as he widened his sector of fire, covering Mike's movement. Mike moved forward slowly, bobbing up and down like a velociraptor about to strike. He gently leaned up against the load bearing wall as he prepared both mentally and physically to take the corner and what lied beyond. Mike stepped around the corner, following his barrel, and was face to face with Chad Beecroft.

Chapter 46

JESSICA WAS ENJOYING THE LITTLE sleep over her Dad had improvised in the hotel room. She loved her Dad sooo much! She was allowed to order whatever food she wanted, she got Chinese food. She loved Chinese food. She probably ordered too much, but who cares? She couldn't understand why the lo mein noodles made her Dad run into the bathroom and slam the door. She made a fort with the cushions of the couch, covering it with the blankets off the bed for more privacy. She started her fifth episode of "Glee" on Netflix, with the intention of watching the whole season if her Dad would let her. Tonight was awesome. Her life was awesome. Jessica loved having a black dad and a white mom; she loved being an interracial child. So many beautiful famous women were interracial and Jessica knew she was going to be just as beautiful as any of them. She didn't like that her parents were divorced of course, but at least she got to see both parents equally; plus at Christmas and birthdays she got spoiled, her parents trying to out-do each other. She loved Jeff, too. She never called him dad, or even referred to him as her step father, but she loved him just the same.

Her Dad came out of the bathroom a few minutes after the episode started, the sound of a flushing toilet behind him. She heard him lay down on the bed with a groan. "You ok, Daddy?" she said.

"I'm good, baby. I'm gonna try to get some sleep. Watch whatever you want," her Dad said in a weak, raspy voice. He started to snore almost right away. Jessica had never heard her Dad snore. Not like this anyway. She was worried he might choke to death. It sounded gross. It was so loud and gross she had to turn the volume on the iPad all the way up. She wished she had her cell phone. She liked to text her friends from under the covers late at night. Oh well. She looked at the little battery icon in the corner of the iPad's screen. 40%. She was going to have to wake her Daddy up in a little while if she was going to watch more "Glee." She didn't know where the charger was. Hopefully he wouldn't be too mad when she woke him up.

Chapter 47

DETECTIVE CHRISTIANSON STARED INTO CHAD Beecroft's dead eyes for a few seconds, trying to get a grasp on what had happened. Beecroft sat at a small kitchen table, face locked in a look of surprise and terror, eyes opened wide. His left arm lay out in front of him with the palm facing skyward, almost looking as if it was on display. The entire forearm was open, from wrist to inner elbow, with an incision that was nearly surgical. The entire table and floor underneath was covered in blood, showing the same level of coagulation as the woman's. Beecroft's right arm hung like a dangling rope; a large, professional grade kitchen knife lie on the floor under his hand. Mike saw out of the corner of his eye a staircase to his right. "Grant!" he called. "Master bedroom clear," Grant said when he appeared. Mike gestured with his head toward the staircase and Grant ascended.

Mike was holstering his revolver when Grant came back a few seconds later. "Upstairs clear. Holy shit," Grant exclaimed. Both detectives have seen their fair share of bodies and brutalities, but you never really get used to it. The initial shock is always there. Grant had seen it briefly before he went upstairs, but now he really took it in. This man didn't just cut his own wrist, he disassembled it. His left arm looked like a loaf of French bread laying on its side, sliced and ready for someone to make a sandwich. The long gash was deep enough to severely damage the muscles, tendons, and nerves within the wrist and forearm and expose the radius and ulna bones. He wouldn't have been able to cut his other wrist even if he wanted to, this arm was totally inoperative. The accessory cephalic vein and radial artery were completely severed and, by the amount of blood on the table and floor, they drained like cut garden hoses. He probably died within a minute of the slice. As Grant and Mike stared at the mutilated arm laying on the table, something moved within the wound. Something made the tiny pool of blood in the arm ripple as whatever it was struggled to get out from inside this little canyon. A tiny black horn emerged from the pool of blood, immediately followed by another. These little things continued to wade around blindly within the giant gash on Beecroft's arm until they reached the edge and were able to climb out. Two dark black rhinoceros beetles climbed out of the wound and walked down the arm to the table. They struggled to walk through the thickening blood that was pooled there, but the beetles persevered and almost made it out of the blood. Grant quickly fetched a glass from the strainer next to the sink and used it to trap the scurrying, blood soaked beetles. He slammed the glass down on the bugs, giving them their own little dome to investigate.

"What the fuck is that about?" Grant asked.

"Who knows, we're gonna want forensics to get in touch with the university on this one," Mike answered.

"Police!" sounded from the front entrance. "Back here, fellas," Mike said. "Secure the outside. Tape it off. Might be here a while."

Chapter 48

THE NEGLIGENT NURSE WAS FULL blown asleep at her post in the Chatham County Jail infirmary. Her book lay open on the reception desk, pages having shuffled around once her hand fell limp. Colonel Winford had also nodded off to sleep about thirty minutes ago and had slept soundly until the unsecured supply closet door began to creak open wider. The sound that woke the Colonel resembled the sound you might hear from a haunted house, like a door in desperate need of a little WD40 on the hinge. The creaking door continued to cry as it gradually swung all the way open. The old man could see a strange shape in the shadows within the closet, hidden behind the supplies. The only light on in the infirmary was over the sleeping night nurse, making it tough for him to focus on what he was seeing. He was secured to the bed as well, therefore he needed to press his chin to his chest and look down the length of his body toward the open closet door. There was definitely something moving in there amongst the cotton swabs and Band-Aids. A few boxes of random bandages fell to the floor as the secret visitor emerged from the closet, leading with its gigantic antennas.

The earwig that slithered out of the closet was about the size of an average cat. It dragged its elongated body out of the closet, spilling more supplies on the floor as its antennas twitched with curiosity and wonder. It kept its large wings hidden and secured tightly against its body, perhaps due to fear of the unknown or the possibility of other predators in the area. Its upper body hugged the shelving until it could step peacefully on the floor, allowing its sharp pincers to fall off the shelving as well. Colonel Winford began to breathe more heavily out of his open mouth as he watched this thing "look" around the area, examining its new surroundings, almost the way a curious dog does when it goes somewhere new. He looked to the left out of the corner of his eye and saw that the nurse was still sound asleep.

The giant earwig began to scurry toward the Colonel's bed, until it was no longer within his sight, blocked by the foot of the bed itself. He breathed a bit heavier now that he lost sight of the thing, its actions and intention a mystery to the confused old man. Larry thought of an old wives tale about earwigs crawling into your ear and laying eggs in your brain. He had also heard when he was a child that some earwigs would crawl in there and then feast on the brain. If that was the case now, he was pretty much a meal for the taking since he was strapped to the bed. Somehow, the Colonel thought that this thing had a different agenda.

Twitchy antennas slowly became visible on the right side of the bed, alongside where the Colonel lay, at about waist level. His eyes widened as he fixated on the individual sensory cells that comprised the antenna, struggling to keep his eyes focused on their rapid movement. The creature crawled up and onto Larry's chest. He could feel the weight of the things leathery underbelly as it sidled up to him like an old friend. It moved its head closer to the Colonel's, its slippery insect mouth parts dangling inches from his face, rubbing together like bugs do. The things compound eyes were fixed on Larry's. Without standing back up, the thing maintained belly to belly contact with the Colonel and slowly began to spin around until its jaw like pincers were directly in his face. The set of pincers swayed back and forth, as if displaying to the old man their power, before they extended skyward in an offensive posture.

The pincers lowered themselves to the Colonel's right arm area and poked around blindly, missing its target multiple times as it stabbed his arm and the bed repeatedly, not causing any damage. Finally it slid one of the pincers under the strap that secured his arm to the bed. Frantically, the giant earwig clawed, pinched, and jerked at the heavy duty strap, much like the way it would fight another male earwig or possibly defend itself from a predator, or perhaps capture its dinner. It continued this struggle for a few minutes to no avail. It lay on the Colonel exhausted, moving slightly from side to side as it withdrew its pincer from around the strap. After a short break, it raised its backside up again into attack posture and began to vibrate its tail. It looked like a dog that had just come inside after a walk in the rain. The whole bed vibrated softly under the weight of this giant insect, the Colonel's teeth chattered. The two blades of the thing's pincers gradually morphed into the blades of a standard pair of scissors. The earwig squeezed the blades of his scissors opened and closed a few times, to check their functionality. Once he was satisfied, he went at the strap for a second attempt.

The scissors made short work of the heavy duty restraining straps, cutting through this one with only two pumps. The thing squirmed around on top of Larry, until it could make a similar effort on the left arm strap. It separated the blades of its scissors open and easily slid one of the blades under the strap, much easier than the last time, he was getting better at this. *Snip snip.* The left strap fell free. It squirmed lower down the Colonel's body, through the piss that had been expelled when it first climbed up here, and to the point where its head was by the foot of the bed. The two leg straps were removed easily by the earwig's scissors, he was a pro by now. Using the same squirming momentum, the thing rotated itself around so that it was once again face to face with the Colonel.

The earwig was now in the possession of a human face. An ugly, middle-aged man face that wore old, giant golden framed glasses with smudged lenses. The man-bug had an excessive under bite and a horrible square jaw. Antenna still sprouted from the forehead of this grotesque human insect, still twitching wildly. It showed its braces covered teeth when it opened its mouth to speak. "*Now sssir, Kill the bitch,*" it said with a lisp, as it vanished into thin air with a dramatic pop. Small, circular wisps of dark brown smoke remained in the shape of the creature until it gently dissipated into the infirmary's ventilation system.

Simultaneous with the pop, the door to the supply closet broke the silence in the infirmary as it slammed shut on its own. The negligent night nursed snapped awake, startled by the noise of the slamming door. She stood up and stretched, feeling much more rested after her little power nap. Looking over toward the Colonel, she noticed that the poor old man had lost control of his bladder and there was medical supplies spilled on the floor. She groaned as she realized she was going to have to deal with that and not be able to go back to sleep just yet.

Chapter 49

THE SAVANNAH NIGHT AIR WAS filled with sirens, screams, gunshots, and explosions. Tonight's events were not unlike those on any given night in Iraq or Afghanistan. Fifteen individual reports of assault, disorderly conduct, stabbings, and vandalism had flooded the airway. Every officer on duty at both SCMPD and Chatham Sheriff's Department had been dispatched. Those not on shift were alerted and given thirty minutes to report for duty. Road rage seemed to be the most common occurrence amongst the pandemonium. In addition to the other fifteen cases, there were twelve accidents reported; some including multiple vehicles, all with several injuries.

Parents attacked children, children attacked pets, husbands attacked wives, wives attacked husbands, and everyone attacked total strangers. In downtown Savannah, a woman was thrown down the steep stone steps that led from Williamson Street to the cobblestone walkway of River Street fifty feet below. The report would later say that the woman broke both legs, her right collar bone, and her neck as she tumbled head over heels, bouncing off the metal bars in the center of the staircase design to control traffic flow. Witnesses said that her head cracked like a ripe grapefruit when it made contact with the decorative cobblestone road below. Nobody saw the man that did it, therefore the officers on scene had nothing to go on. A man was strangled with his own dog leash on Murphy Ave., presumably for not picking up his dogs leavings. Someone who was also walking their dog had taken offense when the man a few feet in front of him let his dog do his business and then left a steaming pile of dog shit as he walked away. Witnesses told police that the second man let go of his dog, ran up and actually picked up the mess the man's dog left. He caught up to him, shoved the fresh dog turds into his face, threw him to the ground, and then choked him to death with the dog leash. The man's Papillon tried to defend its master to no avail. The murderer is still at large, most likely still walking his dog.

Similar events continued all along the coastal empire, as well as incidents reported as south as Tampa, FL and as north as Winston-Salem, NC. All events stemmed from some type of rage, something that caused people to snap and commit these horrible crimes. Some perpetrators were caught on site, some died while carrying out their duties, while others killed themselves after, whether due to guilt or remorse is unknown. Many people fled the area of their crime and are still out there somewhere. The death toll and the combinations of brutal crimes was more tonight than it had been in decades. Police certainly had their hands full as the events continued, showing no signs of stopping.

Chapter 50

"Colonel, are you feeling ok?" the half asleep nurse said as she left the reception area and headed over to the inmate's bed. Due to her groggy state or perhaps the dim lighting, she hadn't noticed that his restraints had been cut, some were on the floor while others dangled from the bed. Larry lay motionless, with the exception of a gentle tremble; his chin remained pressed to his chest and his eyes were facing forward, opened wide and looking down the length of his body. His breathing had calmed significantly, so much so that the nurse thought he may have died. She stood over the bed on Larry's left, held a light to his eyes and watched them react normally. The nurse then leaned over and gently placed her left ear on the Colonel's chest, attempting to feel the raising and lowering of his chest, and to feel his breath on her face.

The nurse spoke while she was raising her head away from the patient "Well, I think you're good to go, sir. Do you think you might want ttt-"

Larry clasped the woman's head with both hands, right hand on the top of her head and the left hand grasped a handful of hair from the back of the neck. His teeth tore through the flesh of her neck as easy as a lion's teeth would take its prey, causing blood to spray from the corners of his mouth. The Colonel locked on with the strength of an obedient pit bull, using the full strength of his dental implants. The woman struggled pointlessly, as Larry clenched tighter every time she twitched. She was able to muster a few screams in between gurgles as the vice grip began to crush her trachea. She had her hands planted on the Colonel's chest, trying to push free, but the grip of his jaw and his hands were too much for the poor woman to disengage.

Once Larry had crushed through the woman's neck enough to get his teeth to touch, he jerked his head vigorously back and forth, tearing more and more cartilage, muscle, and tendons in the process; until he was able to rip out a mouth full of throat parts, leaving a gaping hole in the woman's neck. The woman fell forward onto Larry's chest, her jugular spraying like one of the fountains at Forsyth Park. The old man pushed her off, causing her to hit the floor with a thud, as he sat up in his bed. Colonel Winford let out a sigh of relief through his nose, easing into the mollification of an objective being taken; a mission completed to standard.

The Colonel walked around the abandoned infirmary, in search something he wasn't quite sure of yet. He jerked on the handle of the supply closet that had manifested his little helper earlier, but it was locked. After a few more aimless walks around the area, Larry climbed up into the receptionist station and began feeling around under the desk for what he was sure was there. You didn't serve in the military for three decades and not know that places like this had security features emplaced. He pressed the silent alarm button just as soon as his hand grazed over it, he then spit out the chunk of flesh that was in his mouth on to the desk. While he waited for his guests to arrive, Larry picked up the nurses book, licked his bloody finger with an equally bloody tongue, and turned to Chapter one. He might have a few minutes to read.

Chapter 51

IT WAS NEARLY 10 P.M. when Detectives Wright and Christian-son walked back into headquarters, greeted by the Captain.

"Where the hell have you two been? It's a frigging mad house tonight. Every available unit is out there," the Captain said, flustered.

"Captain, everyone is on this manifest. Everyone from earlier today, and I bet everyone from all the bullshit going on tonight is on here too," Mike said as he walked past the Captain and into the conference room, followed by Grant. He grabbed a green dry erase marker, moved to the board, and put a big check mark next to the names of everyone that was on the list. On the manifest, he put a check mark next to everyone that was written on the board with a red ink pen, drawing a line through the deceased.

"Mike, we don't have time for your naughty and nice list..." the Captain started to say.

"The co-pilot killed his wife and then himself. Me and Grant just came from there. Check this out..." Mike said as he laid the paperwork out on the conference table and called the Captain over.

Mike showed the Captain the flight manifest and the crew list, both of which had scribbles and check marks everywhere. As he pointed to a name on the list, he'd point to where that same name was located on the dry erase board.

"First name on the list, right there *Jeff Arkenson*, next is *Laura Jones*, right here. Then *David Spears*, here. Last name on the list, *Lawrence Winford*. Check this crew list, Douglas Mason, *Chad Beecroft*. Beecroft killed his wife, then himself and Mason is missing and he has his daughter. We're going to want to check on these stewardesses first thing. We can't afford to let them on another plane."

The Captain stood like a bewildered moron, staring at the manifest, the crew list, and the dry erase board, not knowing how to make heads or tails of either. He was clearly overwhelmed with the craziness and confusion of today's events. Knowing that the night was going to continue to be insane, the Captain left Wright and Christianson alone. "J-J-Just keep me in the loop. Let me know what you're going to do before you go do it," the Captain said as he headed to his office to call the Commissioner for the fourth time tonight.

"This crew list doesn't have addresses or phone numbers on it, we're going to have to go back down there." Grant said.

"I'll call Armstrong down at the Sierra terminal, he'll give it up. We need to prioritize this manifest, maybe break it down by county. We can call in some favors, I got a buddy in Liberty County that can help with folks down there. I know a guy named Wheeler over in Bryan County, too," Mike said.

"What are we supposed to do about all the people that left the area? Or had connecting flights?" Grant challenged.

"We're gonna have to call, man. Not much else we can do. I'm sure they'll understand our concern, especially after everything that's going on tonight. We need to find out if any of the people brought in tonight are on this manifest," Mike said. "We need to call around, get names of everyone arrested tonight. So we can start to narrow this thing down." Mike's eyes were wandering around the room as his mind followed.

A young, uniformed policeman popped his head into the conference room, "Detective Christianson, you got someone from Chatham County Jail on the phone. Says he talked to you earlier today."

"Grant, I'm gonna go take this. Can you take the flight manifest and start separating people by county? There's no way we can do this alone. We're gonna need some help," Mike said as he left with the officer.

Detective Wright secured a fresh pad of paper out of the small credenza that housed various supplies one might need during a conference. He ran out to his desk and grabbed his laptop, he knew what towns were in most counties within the state, but he wanted the laptop for confirmation. He sat down at the table and began to disassemble the 97 names of the flight manifest, using the addresses that patrons provided when they purchased their ticket. At the top of the first sheet he jotted across the width of the page until he ran out of room: Chatham, Bryan, Effingham, Liberty, Long, Evans, Bullock. He went to the top of the flight manifest, by-passed Jeff Arkenson's name and came to the second one: Craig Atwood, 126 Abercorn. Savannah GA, No phone number provided. Grant wrote Craig Atwood's info down under Chatham County. Next name: Daryl Bernard, 113 Sue Ellen Dr. Richmond Hill GA 912-555-3628. Grant wrote that info down under Bryan County.

Before Detective Wright could start on the third name, Detective Christianson entered the room. Without speaking, Mike walked to the large dry erase board and, with a green marker, drew a line from Lawrence Winford's name. At the end of the line he wrote "night nurse", he then secured a red marker and put a slash through the words he just wrote.

Mike sat and spoke slowly, "This guy got out of his restraints somehow and tore out a woman's throat with his mouth."

"My God! What in God's name is going on, man?" Grant said.

"I don't know. This is the craziest thing I've ever seen, and I've been around, you know? Alright, I'm going to go call Armstrong down at Sierra. We need to make sure those stewardesses aren't flying anytime soon. Keep breaking down that manifest, I'll be back," Mike said as he headed to his desk just outside the conference room door. He pulled up the Savannah/Hilton Head International Airport directory and found the number for the Sierra representative. After a few seconds of the automated "press one now, press two now" bullshit, Mike finally got an actual human on the phone.

"Sierra Airlines, how may I help you?" a friendly female voice asked.

"Ma'am, my name is Detective Michael Christianson. I was in there earlier tonight to secure a flight manifest. I need to speak with Mr. Armstrong immediately."

"Please hold," the woman said, her tone suggesting that she knew exactly who Mike was based on the scene he caused the last time he was there.

"This is Mr. Armstrong. What is it, Detective?" Armstrong said, sounding irritated.

"I'm going to need the contact information on the three stewardesses that worked flight 1289, as well as their schedule," Mike demanded.

"Detective, I can't keep giving you our staff's personal information without..."

Mike cut him off, "You remember Chad Beecroft? He brutally murdered his wife and then committed suicide by slashing his arm open. In fact, he cut so deep into his own arm, he almost went through it. Based on the condition of the bodies, he did it sometime earlier today. Now, you tell me, Armstrong, do you think we might want to keep those stewardesses grounded for a while?"

After a few seconds of silence, Mike said "Let me guess, you have to call your supervisor."

"Please hold, Detective," Armstrong said.

Mike waited impatiently, while he listened to a music version of "That's what friends are for"; a horrible song normally, but this elevator music version of it made Mike want to kill himself. *Poor choice of words,* Mike thought.

"Detective?" Mr. Armstrong said.

"Still here, Sir. What do you have for me?" Mike said.

"Bad news actually, Sir." Armstrong said, "I can send over the information you need, but I'm afraid that one of those stewardesses is working the redeye flight to Boston right now. They took off about twenty minutes ago. Her name is Chantay Williams."

"Shit," Mike said, a little disappointed in himself for not bringing this up when he made the scene about Beecroft earlier.

If he had, he might have been able to keep that woman on the ground. "Is there any way we can radio the pilot? Let him know what's going on and that the woman is a potential risk?"

"I can try, Sir, but I'll have to..."

"...ask your supervisor," Mike interrupted. Mike provided Armstrong with the station's fax number, as well as the number to his desk. "Thanks for your help, young man. Call me once you have confirmation that the air traffic folks gave the pilot a heads up."

Mike waited by the fax machine for about fifteen seconds before giving up. "Grant!!! I have a fax en route, grab it for me, will ya? I'm going to burn one."

As Mike lit his fourth cigarette with the head of the third, he thought about the senselessness of today's events. He'd seen a lot of shit during his thirty something years, but never this much in one day and never connected like these events were. He hopped up on the railing that flanked the station's wheelchair ramp and looked down at his swinging feet. His thoughts wandered aimlessly as he contaminated his lungs and eventually his mind landed on his ex-wives. Although both of his wives had been unfaithful, which was what led to the divorces, he was by no means a model husband. He was unable to fulfil his first wife's emotional needs, or at least that's what her lawyer said. Mike loved her dearly; he supposed he still did, even though they were divorced over a decade ago. His second marriage was a total disaster; the woman was a money grubbing whore and she cheated on him repeatedly with several members of the force. She was the reason he had to get out of Atlanta. He feared that if he bumped into her in the street, he might just lose his shield. There were no children, with either wife, and that was a good thing as far as Mike was concerned.

Mike allowed himself to get his thoughts back on task. Crushing out his fourth butt, he threw it in a nearby trash can and headed back inside to see how far along Grant was in breaking down the manifest.

"Fax come in?" Mike asked as soon as he entered the conference room.

"Yeah, it's right there," Grant answered without looking up from his laptop. "I think I have this list broken down as much as we can get it. I have everyone separated by county, along with addresses and phone numbers if there was one. We can send out emails to our contacts with other departments. We can start making calls here if you want, but I don't think we should go anywhere just yet. We should wait until morning."

Although Mike wanted to get on the road now, start beating on doors; he knew that Grant was probably right, since it was almost 10:30 p.m. "Oh yeah, almost forgot, bad news" Mike added "one of the stewardesses is in the air already. She left for Boston like an hour ago. Armstrong is gonna get on the horn with air traffic control and see if they can get word to the crew. *Be advised* or whatever. That's the best we can do at this point."

"Shit, where's the flight to?" Grant asked.

"Boston. I just said that. The rest of her schedule should be on that fax they sent over. Along with the rest of them, I hope," Mike answered.

"Alright, man," Grant said, "I'm heading out. I'll get back with you on this in the morning. My brain's fried. Don't stay here all night."

"Later," Mike said as Grant left the conference room and eventually the building. Once alone, Mike began to go over the list that Grant had created. It was a well-produced product and it should make their job a lot easier in the morning. However, Mike wanted to be able to narrow the list down by calling over to Bryan County and Chatham County Jails to get a list of everyone they brought in tonight. Based on the amount of action that was going on out there, he believed he'd be able to reduce this list significantly. Mike headed over to his desk, grabbed his old office phone, and called over to Bryan County Jail.

"Bryan County Jail," a man answered.

"Good evening, this is Detective Michael Christianson over at SCMPD. I need you to send me a list of anyone that was brought in today. Anyone and everyone, for any reason. I need to run the names against a list of people potentially involved in other crimes," Mike said.

"You know you have access to that info through the state database, right? You should be able to log in with your badge number and get whatever info you need. All you need to do is check the daily blotter for whatever county you're looking for." the man said.

Feeling like a complete idiot, Mike said "Yeah, I'm not that great with computers, man. I guess that's why they call me an old timer over here. What's the web page I go to?"

The gentleman over at Bryan County Jail explained the procedures for logging into the Georgia state database where he would have access to the blotter reports for every station across the state; just one of the many resources available to detectives and other law enforcement personnel. Mike thanked the gentleman and powered up his laptop. He hardly used the thing, so when it asked him for his password, he had to dig it out of his desk. He had written it on a yellow post it note the last time he was required to change it and now he couldn't seem to find his note. *Oh yeah,* he thought, when he remembered that he had it in his phone under "notes." Mike 1 3262C!! There it is. Mike ran outside for a quick smoke to calm his nerves. He wanted a clean head when he started going through these blotter reports and comparing them to the flight manifest. He'd need to put on a new pot of coffee as well.

Chapter 52

SAMANTHA ARKENSON TOSSED AND TURNED on the sofa in her house while her dear friend Martha lie passed out on the love seat, TV on. The nightmares penetrating Sam's mind had caused her to roll around restlessly, moaning occasionally and sweating profusely. In her dream, her ex-husband Doug had kidnapped their daughter Jessica and although she could see them both clearly within the dream, she could do nothing about it. She watched as her daughter and ex-husband walked through a crowded train station and boarded a train. They were both happy and smiling, although she could plainly see that Doug had a pistol pressed into their daughters back. Her screams went unnoticed as she yelled at Doug, "Where are you taking our daughter?!" and "Answer me!" Sam boarded the train behind the two of them and allowed the doors to close. Although the station was crowded, the train itself was deserted with the exception of Doug, Jessica, Samantha, and a woman who was already seated when they entered. The woman who was seated was dressed in all black and wore a hood that covered her face. Samantha continued to scream helplessly at Doug and Jessica but they did not respond. Another person suddenly appeared on the train. It was Jeff, although it was hard to recognize him, as half of his face was hanging off and he was covered head to toe with wounds which were seeping blood and puss. His arms appeared to be hanging on by a thread, dangling from his shoulders and swaying with the motion of the train. His stomach was torn apart, causing his intestines to be hanging freely from the abdominal cavity and gathered in a moist pile on the floor beneath.

The woman who had been seated when they entered the train stood up and removed her hood. It was Sam's mother. She had several open sores on her face, specifically around her mouth and eyes. Her skin was extremely pale, looking almost like an albino. Her mother walked over to Jeff and they held each other in a deep, loving embrace, not noticing that she was standing in the pile of guts on the floor. Before the two separated from their grasp of one another, Doug shot them both. He continued to pump round after round into the two bodies after they had collapsed to the floor of the train. Sam screamed silently, nobody responding to her presence. Doug turned the barrel of his pistol on Jessica and fired. He straddled the tiny body and executed a similar routine; firing non-stop into Jessica's limp corpse. There was no need for him to reload. This was a dream gun and it was equipped with a never ending magazine.

Finally, Doug acknowledged the fact that Samantha was on the train. He looked directly at her and said, "I told you to fucking try me, bitch." He then placed the pistol in his mouth and pulled the trigger – the incredible pop of the round being fired caused Sam to snap herself awake. She was laying on her sofa, drenched in sweat, heart pounding within her chest. Although relieved that it was only a dream, Sam was nonetheless traumatized. Her husband was still dead, having committed a brutal murder prior to his own horrific ending, and her daughter was still missing, although the police had made the determination that her situation did not warrant the title "missing" since she was with her father that had joint custody. Samantha began to sob as her thoughts went to her mother and her breast cancer recurrence. She hadn't even thought about trying to make it to Beaufort in the morning to be there for her mother's appointment. Sam had nearly forgotten it.

Sam realized that Martha was still here and asleep on the love seat. She planned on asking Martha to accompany her to her mother's in Beaufort tomorrow. She needed to be there for her mother, regardless of her own issues, her mother needed her and perhaps they would be able to provide one another comfort during this ordeal. What makes us resilient creatures is our ability to seek comfort from one another during the most challenging situations. Sam needed her mother just as much as her mother needed her. She decided to wake Martha and suggest that they get on the road now.

Chapter 53

MIKE BROUGHT HIS LAPTOP INTO the conference room, so he could continue to update his board and the manifest as he discovered new information from the blotter reports. Once logged in, he decided to start with Chatham County. He scanned the list of names, disregarding David Spears, Laura Jones, and Lawrence Winford, as he already knew about them. Each entry on the police blotter had the time and place of the occurrence, the names of the individuals involved, names of anyone arrested, and the name and unit of the officers that responded and made the arrest. Additionally, there was a short write up of the event which was periodically updated as new information was discovered.

The first entry Mike read stated, "At 1327, 911 call regarding potential 240 at intersection of Chatham Parkway and Park of Commerce. 11-81 followed by physical assault. Responding officer - Jamison, Stephen. Dolan, Robert apprehended and processed Chatham County Jail. Felton, Shannon evacuated to Memorial University Medical Center"

Mike scanned the manifest with the same level of excitement he had when he first received it. There it was, plain as day: *Dolan, Robert F. seat 38B*. He stood up and went over to his board, which was starting to look like an unorganized mess, he was going to have to do something about this, later. For now, he scribbled the name

Robert Dolan. He drew a line from that name and wrote *"assault-ed woman on Chatham parkway."* He then got the idea that he should circle names of people that are currently in custody. Good idea. He circled Laura Jones, Lawrence Winford, and Robert Dolan. He put a check next to Dolan's name on the manifest with his red pen. *Oh shit,* he thought, as he jotted *Chantay Williams* on the board, with a big question mark next to it. Next to the question mark he wrote, *"stewardess, in flight to Boston as of 2200-ish."* He couldn't quite remember the exact time that Armstrong said she had taken off. *Shit, Armstrong.* He never called back. Mike grabbed his cigarettes and his cell phone, he'd call from outside while he pollutes his lungs for the 37th time today.

Before the woman could give the complete greeting, Mike said through a mouth full of smoke, "I need to speak to Armstrong. This is Detective Christianson."

"I'm sorry, Detective. Mr. Armstrong is gone for the night. Is there something I can help you with?" the woman said.

Irritated, Mike said, "Well, I hope so. He was supposed to get in touch with the aircraft that Chantay Williams is currently working on. He was supposed to give them a warning that she might do something disruptive. Who's in charge over there?"

"Sir, we checked in our last flight just now. We're getting ready to close the counter until 5 a.m. tomorrow. I don't know if Mr. Armstrong did anything. I'm not sure I know what..."

Mike cut the woman off before she could continue. He ex-plained to her everything he had told Armstrong earlier, in hopes that she would sense the urgency and take the initiative to make something happen. Based on the tone of her voice and her feeble response, however; Mike felt as though he was on his own. He smoked another cigarette and went back inside. Topping off his coffee cup, he went back into the conference room and stuck his face back into his laptop and the state's blotter reports. He removed his coat and tie in order to get a little more comfortable. He picked up where he left off in the Chatham County blotter and began to read again. He did so, intending on continuing until complete, regardless of how long it took. He needed to narrow this manifest down. *Gonna be a long night,* he thought as he chugged his coffee.

Chapter 54

FLIGHT 1049 BEGAN ITS FINAL descent at 2315, which was on schedule to meet its 2345 arrival time at Logan International Airport. Chantay Williams was a 27 year old African American woman who had been a flight attendant with Sierra Airlines for just over four years. She hadn't intended on staying with the company for this long, but when she graduated college the job market was virtually nonexistent. Sierra was the only place that was hiring, and it was only part time. She was promoted to full time after about a year with the company and, as she was a natural extrovert, she decided to stay in the job. Chantay was a well-spoken, friendly, caring person and this type of work suited her perfectly. She was single, which made the constant traveling more enjoyable since there was no family left behind. She was able to see many areas of the country that she normally would never have traveled to if it weren't for this job. Chantay really came to love her job and its many benefits; she counted her blessings every day. This particular trip was enabling her to spend some time with her brother who lived in Boston. Her supervisors worked with her schedule to allow her to have a four day break in Boston before heading back to Savannah, so basically she was able to visit her brother on the company's dime. For that, she was extremely grateful.

Anthony P. Sardina

Chantay felt her stomach raise slightly as the Captain recited a commonly heard announcement: "Ladies and gentlemen, as we start our descent, please make sure your seat backs and tray tables are in their full upright position. Make sure your seat belt is securely fastened and all carry-on luggage is stowed underneath the seat in front of you or in the overhead bins. Please turn off all electronic devices until we are safely parked at the gate. Thank you. Flight attendants, prepare for landing, please."

Chantay made her last run through the cabin to pick up trash and other miscellaneous objects and to ensure that all passengers were in compliance with the Captain's orders. She was about half way through her section when she encountered a large man, about 40 years old, with his seat back reclined and his cell phone out.

"Sir, I need you to put your seat back up and power down your phone please," Chantay said while smiling respectfully.

"Relax lady, it's in airplane mode," the man said, without making eye contact.

"Sir, I'm sorry, but that doesn't matter. I need you to please turn it off and put it away," she said. People began to look over at what was slowly becoming a scene. Passengers shifted uncomfortably in their seats when the man responded, "Do you even know what airplane mode is? It means that there's no signal. I'm not going to mess with your communications or whatever. Relax." Other passengers began to chime in, telling the man to just shut it off and be quiet. "Mind your damn business," was his response to anyone who attempted to intervene.

Chantay was becoming annoyed with this disrespectful passenger, but she held it together and did what she was trained to do in such circumstances. She began to recite the Federal Communications Commission regulation regarding passengers who fail to comply with crew instructions pertaining to electronic devices and the repercussions the violator can expect once on the ground. The man didn't let her finish her pitch as he interrupted with, "Fine, it's off. Jesus Christ, you people amaze me. You think you're some kind of authority figure? With your little smock and name tag? You're a fucking stewardess. You're a joke."

"Ok, thank you," she said, struggling to keep it together as she headed to the area where flight attendants sit during landing. She's dealt with assholes before, but never one that degraded her like this guy. As the buckle of her seat belt sounded its metallic click, a voice popped into her head, *fuck that fucker*, it said. The sound made her smile, it almost tickled her brain. She felt warm all over, like she was curled up next to a fire with a good book and her favorite blanket. Chantay rarely used profanity, therefore these thoughts came as a surprise to her. She kind of liked it. Yeah, she thought, *fuck that fucking fucker*. She laughed out loud at that one. She was seated alone in her section of the plane, which was to the rear of where the asshole was seated, therefore nobody could see her laughing hysterically, nor could anyone hear her as the engines of the plane hummed louder as it descended. *You should fucking kill him*, entered her mind. That thought made her stop laughing. Her face lost all expression as she stared at the planes exit door across from where she currently sat. The voice had changed, it was no longer her internal voice, but the voice of someone else. Someone with a horrible, exaggerated lisp. *You ssshould throw him out that fucking door right there*, the voice hissed. *You* *have to, you have to do it. He said "you people" who the fuck does he think he is kill him kill him now fuck the fucker and kill him throw him out that door open it open the dooooor....*the voice continued, causing Chantay's head to spin, like someone who stood up after having too much to drink.

"I can't open that door," she said out loud to nobody. *You better do something, fuck that fucker. It's your duty,* echoed inside her skull. She looked around her immediate area and saw that there was a half pot of coffee resting within the machine. The light on the machine was illuminated, indicating that the pot was still hot. *Why didn't I put this away for landing?* she thought to herself. *Maybe because you knew you'd need it,* her special friend answered. *That should work fine,* the voice went on to say in an approving tone, causing Chantay to nod when it spoke to her. She stood up, stumbling slightly due to the plane's rapidly decreasing altitude, and secured the hot pot of coffee. She marched with a sense of purpose toward the asshole that had disrespected her earlier, coming up from behind him, noticing that his phone was back in his hand. With the force of a medieval warrior, Chantay smashed the coffee pot over the man's head, cutting his scalp and scorching his skin at the same time. Piping hot coffee splashed on the passengers within its radius. The glass pot broke apart, leaving Chantay with a black handled weapon, consisting of jagged shards of remaining glass.

The startled man tried to get up to retaliate, but he forgot that his seat belt was engaged. Confused passengers looked on with disbelief, some cheered a little internally, as they watched the woman who was treated so rudely standing up for herself. As the asshole fumbled with his belt, Chantay went in for the kill. She plunged the shattered portion of the coffee pot into the man's neck, slicing back and forth like a lumberjack sawing a log, causing severe lacerations with every pass. People that once had secretly applauded her actions began to regret their initial assessment as blood sprayed across the entire row of passengers. More glass broke off the handle when it scratched across the man's Adam's apple, as Chantay continued to saw at his neck, essentially trying to amputate his head. Cries of pain and shock turned into gurgles as foaming blood began to flow from the multiple gashes in his neck. Chantay was tackled from behind by a random passenger just as the plane touched down at Boston's Logan International Airport. The person who tackled her used his body weight to hold her down, while another Samaritan stepped up and kicked what was left of the coffee pot away. The words, *good enough,* coursed through Chantay's mind as she yelled on deaf ears, "Stop!! I'm supposed to do this!!"

Chapter 55

Detective Christianson had made a substantial dent in the manifest as he discovered another twelve people that were on the list and also apprehended. He moved his laptop into the conference room so he could refer back to his messy dry erase board flow chart when he needed to. He sent an email to Sheriff's Deputy Matt Wheeler over in Bryan County, attaching a list of names for him to check on, assuming that he'd get the message first thing in the morning. Mike had met Deputy Wheeler a few years ago at the Great Ogeechee Seafood Festival in Bryan County. Wheeler was working the festival that night, along with several other officers from Bryan County and Richmond Hill PD. When he was attempting to get a drunken crowd to settle down, some drunk jackass attacked him from behind. Mike had been there, enjoying deep fried seafood from over fifty different vendors, when he witnessed a fellow law enforcement brother in need. Of course Mike intervened, weapon drawn, and eventually the two of them got the situation under control. Wheeler wasn't working alone, but at that moment his partners were elsewhere. If not for Detective Christianson's actions, the night may have ended differently for Matt Wheeler. Wheeler was obviously appreciative of Mike's efforts, and the two became not quite friends, but associates. Mike didn't really have any friends, although he was slowly starting to consider Detective Wright one, even though he went home early.

Mike had another associate over in Liberty County, but he couldn't quite remember his name. He'd have to dig through his desk to get that guy's information. He knew several other guys across the state of Georgia that he could call upon when he needed help; it's always good to establish a solid network across different agencies. He just had trouble remembering names, which is why he constantly had to refer to his old school rolodex or to the piles of post it notes stuck together inside his desk drawer. Mike grabbed the rolodex off his desk as he headed out for another smoke. These would be cigarettes 38-40. He had sucked in two complete packs of Marlboro reds today. Mike could usually determine his level of stress based on how many smokes he had left in his pack at the end of the day, rarely finishing off a full pack. Today was a new record for butts consumed. Mike took the last toke off cigarette number 40, pulled six more stinky cigarette butts out of his pocket, and threw them all in the trash can before heading back inside.

Noticing that the office was nearly deserted, Mike headed back into the conference room to get back to work. He was a little irritated that the Captain had snuck out. At least it was nice and quiet. There was some activity out front, but Mike had the entire back area all to himself. As he typed, his vision started to blur. Long, busy day. Tomorrow was going to be even longer. The tired, old detective stood and stretched, let out a long, satisfying yawn and sat back down. That stretch did nothing to cure his growing exhaustion. He was going to need a quick nap. Mike took his jacket and balled it up into a make shift pillow on the floor. He killed the lights and laid down, trying to control his ruminating thoughts that were still spirally around his mind. He eventually nodded off, hopefully into a recuperative sleep; even a few minutes can make all the difference.

PART TWO

Tuesday, January 28th, 5:17 A.M.

"Little triggers that you pull with your tongue. Little triggers, I don't wanna be hung up, strung up, when you don't call up." -Elvis Costello
"Everyone will pull it, or they'll die trying ..." -Craig Atwood

Chapter 56

HOLLOWAY AND BRUNICK DROVE THEIR military issued Humvee through the entrance of the range at about 0515, as ordered by their Platoon Sergeant yesterday. It was their job to sign for the equipment they would need for today's training, which was due to arrive anytime between 0530 and 0730. Soldiers from the installation's Ammunition Supply Point (ASP) were tasked with the responsibility of delivering ammunition on a daily basis. Units wishing to conduct training on any specific day were required to submit a formal request at least eight weeks prior to the day of the event. They must then have a representative waiting at the predetermined range on that date to receive the ammunition, explosives, rockets, or whatever it was that they requested.

Explosives and the demolition equipment associated with this type of training had to be delivered separate from the small arms ammunition required for other ranges, therefore; it was a safe assumption that it would be delivered either first or last, since the Soldiers dropping it off would have to do a specific run only for this delivery. Holloway and Brunick hoped their drop off would be first, since they still had to separate the C4, time fuses, igniters, detonation cord, and everything else into individual bundles for distribution. That process can take some time. The first bus of Soldiers was due to arrive at 0830, so they should be fine; but SFC

Johnson and the Lieutenant planned on arriving at around 0630 and Holloway and Brunick wanted to be set up and ready when they got here.

This demolitions range consisted of a large open area, about the size of a football field, with the long axis of the area running north to south. There was a small road on the south side of the field, which ran east to west. Directly off this small road was a large set of bleachers, used to assemble Soldiers for safety briefings, to receive classes, or to take breaks. To the right of these bleachers, away from the open area and in a spot that provides shade during the day, was the ammo point. The ammo point consisted of a small red shed, only large enough for three men to stand in. Inside the shed were various shelves to store the explosives and other gear they'd be using today. There was a large service window in the shed, the idea being that, after the safety briefing, Soldiers would file by the window to be issued the equipment they'd need for today's training. Next to the shed is where Holloway and Brunick sat in the Humvee and waited.

Directly in the center of this large open field was a man-made berm that ran east to west; separating the space into two distinct areas. The berm was about twelve feet tall, with a gradual slope that allowed Soldiers to walk over it easily. North of the berm was the impact area; the area where the explosives would be safely detonated. The area south of the berm was the safety area; the area where the classes and training would take place and where Soldiers would prepare their charges. The berm was constructed of tightly packed dirt and had been in place long enough for thick, green grass to grow along its sides and top. There were several beaten paths within the grass, where Soldiers would walk over from one side to the other. There was a larger, more prominent beaten path directly in the middle of the berm, which was the proper point to cross over, however; not everyone followed the rules. On the south side of the berm was a large "U" shaped table, crudely constructed out of old 2x4's and plywood. The table was high enough for Soldiers to stand and use the plywood surface to construct their charges. The instructor would stand in the middle of the "U" in order to make corrections and provide guidance when needed.

Within the berm itself, there were three heavy duty bunkers constructed of reinforced steel. When Soldiers completed their individual charges, they would be inspected by the instructors to ensure correct assembly. If they were correct, the Soldiers would be instructed to cross the berm, at the designated crossing area, and wait on the north side. Once everyone was on the north side, the instructor would lay the main line; which was a long piece of det cord that all other charges would attach to, thus creating a large explosion of all the charges in unison. Once all charges were attached to the main line, all Soldiers would cross back over the berm and get into one of the bunkers. The instructor would attach a length of time fuse, usually cut to at least five minutes, to the main line. He would then use the igniter to start the time fuse and join the others in the bunker. This procedure was the safest and most effective way to allow Soldiers to see the full effect of explosive charges when used properly.

"Where the hell are these assholes?" Brunick said, breaking the silence.

"I don't know, man. They better get here soon, though," Holloway said, "I got shit to do this afternoon."

Both men knew that they couldn't get the range up and running until the explosives got here. A delay in the delivery could cause a chain reaction which would create a late day for everyone. They needed to get started as soon as the Soldiers arrived at 0830 in order to get done at a reasonable hour.

"What do you got going on?" Brunick asked, in an effort to keep the conversation going, killing time.

"I have to head back to the DMV, pick up my license," Holloway lied.

Brunick challenged, "I thought they mailed it to you. They mailed me mine."

"I don't know, they told me to go there today to get mine," Holloway stuck with his story as the demolitions delivery truck pulled up. "Hey – 0606, not bad," he said, sighing a bit in relief after almost getting caught in a lie. Brunick did outrank Holloway, after all. Lying to a superior was never a good idea.

Brunick and Holloway got out of their Humvee as the much larger, tactical military vehicle backed up to the ammo shed in order to off load the supplies.

"Who's signing for this shit?" a Soldier asked. "I am," answered Brunick, as he and Holloway prepared to inventory the several boxes of explosives and equipment being delivered.

Chapter 57

DOUG MASON BREATHED IN THE chilly New England air as he walked along the beach, somewhere in Massachusetts, perhaps Cape Cod. The unique cackle of seagulls penetrated the morning air. Combined with the sound of the ocean, that was all that Doug could hear. He could tell right away that he was dreaming, the environment suggested it immediately. He wore a long, black trench coat, a white shirt underneath, black pants, and shiny black dress shoes, which were becoming scuffed by the sand as he walked. There were several billowy clouds overhead that seemed to move across the bright blue sky a lot faster than normal. For some reason, in this dream, Doug was white. He looked at his hands, turning them over a few times for a better inspection. *Why am I white?* he thought. *That's my scar,* he acknowledged as he noticed the scar he had on his left knuckle; a scar from a fight he had in college. Strange. He looked out at the Atlantic ocean, watching the waves gently crash on the beach, when he realized he was looking through a pair of glasses. *Oh well, I might as well go with it* he thought, as he removed the glasses and cleaned them with his shirt.

As Doug walked along the beach, he noticed a series of rect-angular holes within the sand, each hole was roughly 6 feet long, 4 feet wide, and only a few feet deep. These holes were aligned in a uniformed fashion, side by side, and extended as far as the eye could see. It didn't take long for him to realize that these were graves. Pre-dug graves along the beach. The meticulousness of the exact positioning of these graves' was far too precise to have been done by a human. As he moved closer to the graves, he noticed that a few of them had something inside. Bodies. There were human bodies resting at the bottom of some of these shallow graves. The first body he saw he recognized as Chantay Williams. *I know her*, Doug thought. *I just did a run with her.* Chantay lay on her stomach, her hands bound behind her back. Her head was turned slightly to the right, which is why Doug could recognize her face. She had been shot in the back of the head, execution style; a large exit wound was directly in the center of her forehead. Her eyes and mouth were locked open, displaying a look of insane terror; a look that Doug would surely remember when he woke from this horrible dream.

The next grave contained a distorted, mutilated body. What remained of the torso was wearing a blood soaked grey undershirt and lying face down, the arms were nearly severed from the body. The lower half was separated from the torso; it lay facing up, as if the body had been twisted by some deranged giant. The head, which hung from the body's upper half by a thread, was without a face; only a skull surrounded by a few mangled tendons and muscles that remained. Like the last body, there was an exit wound in the forehead of this mess, again execution style; although the gunshot looked a tad excessive, since this person was obviously already dead. Despite the fact that Doug could not recognize the face of this thing; somehow he knew it was Jeff Arkenson, his wife's new husband. *Poor Jeff*, he thought.

Chad Beecroft lay in the next grave, face down, with the same gunshot wound as the others. His hands were bound behind his back, just like Chantay's. Beecroft's left arm was slashed in a vertical fashion from the wrist to the back of the elbow. His body appeared to be void of blood, as the skin was extremely pale and the gunshot wound was simply a creepy hole; no blood to be found. Doug continued to walk along, next to the graves, surveying the area, breathing deep the cold ocean air. Two people suddenly appeared in front of him as he walked, causing him to stop, mid step. It was his ex-wife, Samantha, and their daughter. Their hands were bound behind their back, their mouths covered with green duct tape. They both knelt before their graves, facing away from Doug. Suddenly, there was a gun in Doug's hand. It was his gun. His finger rest gently on the trigger. It was the same gun he kept in his 4-runner; the same gun that currently rested on the sink in the hotel room he shared with his daughter back in the real world.

Doug placed the barrel of his gun on the back of Samantha's head and squeezed the trigger. Blood and brains sprayed forward into the hole and the surrounding sand as she fell face down in her pre-positioned grave. Jessica sobbed and cried from beneath her tape, as she turned her wide, tear filled eyes towards her father. Without even the slightest hesitation, White-Doug placed his barrel to her temple and squeezed the trigger.

The explosion of the gunshot caused Doug to snap awake; jerking upright, his heart pounding within his chest. The single bed sheet covering him was saturated with sweat. There was enough ambient light within the room for him to see the small fort his daughter had made with the cushions of the room's sofa last night, it was still covered with the other blankets from the hotel bed where he lay. The digital clock on the end table read 6:23. *Shit, she's gonna need to get ready for school soon,* Doug thought, not knowing that all Chatham County schools were closed today due to yesterday's shooting.

Doug got out of bed and peeked under the blankets into Jessica's little secret fort. The beautiful young lady was still sleeping soundly, his iPad still resting on her chest. The urge to urinate suddenly hit Doug like a slap in the face, more powerful than he had ever experienced. He headed to the bathroom at a quick pace, closing the door behind him before turning on the light. He stood over the toilet bowl and attempted to relieve himself. Within seconds, the pain hit him. The stinging within his penis was like nothing he had ever felt before, his eyes squinted and his abdomen tightened as he struggled to get even the tiniest drop out. Doug had never had a venereal disease, but he imagined that this is what it would feel like. It felt as though there were tiny shards of broken glass within his external urethral orifice, slicing into his sensitive flesh with every attempt to pass urine. A few little droplets of urine fell from Doug's penis as he moaned in agony, his body twitching as he pushed and struggled to piss. He began to feel something moving along the length of his penis. *Is this a kidney stone?* he thought. *Am I passing a fucking kidney stone? Is that it? My God, this fucking hurts!!* He had a co-worker that had explained to him what it felt like to pass a stone and Doug never wanted to experience that type of pain. If it was a stone, Doug knew that once he forced the little crystallized mineral out, his pain would subside, therefore; he took a deep breath and pushed with as much force as he could muster. He clenched his teeth and squeezed.

The stream of urine began to spray in all directions, not unlike a garden hose when you placed your thumb over the opening. There was something obstructing the natural flow. Doug groaned as quietly as he could, so he wouldn't wake Jessica, as the object eased closer to the exit. Piss continued to spray wildly, hitting the back and sides of the bowl, as well as the floor, until the object presented itself. The tiny spider that crawled out of Doug's penis was about the size of a standard aspirin. It struggled to remain on the head of the penis, its tiny legs clinging and gripping, trying to hold on within the increasing pressure of Doug's urine flow. Doug's mouth hung open as he watched the little spider finally get blasted into the toilet, unable to hang on any longer. The tiny insect struggled to remain afloat in the piss filled bowl, trying to cling to the wall and climb up, unsuccessfully. Doug recognized this type of spider, due to its unique markings along its back which resembled a violin pointing towards its rear. It was a brown recluse, common here in Savannah. As Doug reached forward to flush the toilet, he caught a glimpse of his lower back in the nearby mirror. There were four individual swollen red sores along his waist line, directly centered in the small of his back; most likely spider bites.

Chapter 58

FLASHLIGHTS DANCED AROUND THE TINY ammo shed as Brunick and Holloway inventoried the equipment they had just received. The sun had not completely risen yet and there was no electricity in the small shed, therefore the head lamps the two men wore on their foreheads were totally essential.

"Holy shit, this is a lot of crap! We're never going to use all this shit. Check this off as I say it," Brunick said as he handed Holloway a clip board which held the receipt. "30 cases of C4 - 30 blocks per box, Det Cord three rolls -1000 feet per roll, Tin Fuse three rolls -1000 feet per roll, M11 four boxes - 60 per box, M12 two boxes - 48 per box, M13 two boxes - 20 per box, M14 two boxes - 40 per box, M81 Fuse igniters 2 boxes - 300 per box, Steel pickets, 20 each #10 cans, 20 each. Electrical tape - 10 rolls, 100 MPH tape - 5 rolls."

As Brunick said it, Holloway put a check mark next to it on the inventory sheet. He also put a check mark next to it on the internal checklist in his mind of items he'll need later tonight. The two men had the items placed in the ammo shed in a neat and orderly fashion when SFC Johnson and Lieutenant Aker arrived at 0640.

"Looking good, gentlemen. Looking damn good," SFC Johnson said, as he removed his body armor and helmet, setting them on the hood of the Humvee he just drove up in. "Start breaking it down for distribution. Slight change of plans, we have to shut down no later than 1400 today. Well, 1430 at the latest. There's a 1600 Battalion awards ceremony that we all have to be at. So, me and the LT talked on the way out here: we'll put 'em in the bleachers, I'll demonstrate the Bangalore, LT will demonstrate the breaching charge on the door, Holloway, you demonstrate the grapeshot. Once we show 'em what everything looks like, we'll run 'em down range, blow the stuff we prepped, come back here, let them each make a grapeshot or something, blow that, then we're done. No lunch for us, or you can eat on the go."

"The BC wants us all there at the ceremony. We changed the bus schedule, it's gonna stay out here 'til we're done." the Lieutenant said as he started pulling a large steel door from the back of their vehicle. "SGT Holloway, gimmie a hand."

"Yes sir," Holloway said as he and the Lieutenant removed the heavy duty door from the truck and leaned it against the tailgate. "Is the BC still coming out here?"

"Oh yeah, you know he'll be here. He loves hanging out with Soldiers. He loves blowing shit up even more. He's a crusty old Sapper," The LT answered.

"Brunick, call the ASP and tell those dudes to be back here to pick up all the unused stuff at 1400." SFC Johnson ordered. Brunick nodded as he pulled out his smart phone. "Make that 1330. They'll be late or they'll wait on us. One way or the other. Ok, we got like two hours 'til the bus gets here. Let's move a couple tables over here in front of the bleachers, that way we have something to work off of when we demonstrate."

As he went towards the "U" shaped tables with his Platoon Sergeant and Platoon Leader, SGT Holloway began to decipher his plan for smuggling some explosives off the range.

Chapter 59

DOUG SAT UP ON THE vanity so he could get a better look at the four tiny blisters that had formed on the small of his back. He twisted and struggled to look over his shoulder at his reflection. He hadn't noticed any pain earlier, but now that he knew these were there, he started to feel a hot, burning sensation along his waist line; a throbbing pain that pulsed like a heartbeat. Along with the pain came the feeling of pressure in his lower back, almost as if these little sores were ready to burst at any second.

The brown recluse was common here in Georgia, therefore; Doug was well aware of the results of an untreated bite from this type of spider. As he looked over his shoulder at the four bumps in the mirror, he reached back with his finger and applied slight pressure on one. He could feel the fluid under the blister squish around, knowing that the spider's venom was doing its duty as it destroyed the tissue underneath. Damaged tissue would eventually become gangrenous and could possibly spread as it continued to eat away at the flesh in and around the infected area. Doug had seen the results of one of these bites first hand when he was in high school. His friend had been reluctant in telling anyone how severe the bite was as he feared he would miss football practice and then not be allowed to play in the upcoming game. The untreated wound in this boy's chest had gotten so bad that it looked like a mini-volcano, resembling a popped zit about the size of a baseball. The boy was eventually treated and was basically fine, but not before the venom liquefied a hole in his chest big enough to stick your fist into.

As Doug looked in awe at the disgusting bumps on his waistline, his eyes surveyed the rest of his back. He looked much worse than he had last night. His skin looked more like an elephants skin than a human's; it was grey and wrinkled, ashy and in dire need of skin moisturizer. A hot, steamy shower was in order. Doug turned on the water and left the bathroom, he intended on letting the water warm up for a while, maybe even fill the room up with steam. He needed to check the bed for more spiders before he got in the shower, anyway. Jessica still lay sound asleep on the floor; Doug wasn't planning on disturbing her, school would have to do without his little girl today.

Doug's skin crawled as he removed the sheet from the bed he had just spent the night in. Brown recluse spiders of varying sizes littered his bed; hundreds of them, crawling across one another in a large pile, jockeying for position. They seemed to be isolated in the center of the bed, right around where Doug's midsection had been as he slept. The pile of spiders was about the size of a standard soup bowl, overturned. Removing the sheet had disturbed the little guests and the pile started to disassemble. Doug quickly grabbed the corners of the fitted sheet, attempting to trap the company of spiders in a small bundle; he couldn't let his daughter see this. He brought the corners of the sheet together, creating a package of brown recluse spiders. Doug didn't want to go outside, he didn't want to go anywhere, but what to do with this makeshift bag of spiders? The toilet, he thought. He entered the bathroom, which was beginning to fill with steam. He brought the bag of spiders to the toilet and did his best to deposit all of the little bastards into the bowl. Some scurried free, but for the most part he had gotten them all inside. The spiders at the bottom of the bunch had sacrificed themselves by providing the ones on top with a surface on which to stand. Several spiders had made the effort to reach the sides of the bowl. Many succeeded in the climb up the bowls interior walls. Seeing what was happening, Doug quickly pulled the handle, crushing the escape attempt of a few hundred tiny prisoners as the toilet flushed.

"What the fuck is happening to me?" Doug said to himself in the bathroom's foggy mirror. *You better fucking pay me what's owed, motherfucker* whispered in his right ear. *This will not stop* hissed in his left. The mirror began to vibrate, causing the image of himself to warp and twitch. A loud noise popped in his head, simultaneous with the words being spelled in the condensation on the steamy mirror – *KILL HER!!* Doug's gun, which lay on the vanity, slowly began to spin in place.

Chapter 60

DETECTIVE WRIGHT STOOD OVER DETECTIVE Christianson, who still lie sleeping on the floor of the conference room at SC-MPD HQ. Wright straddled the snoring man, as he slowly bent down and tickled his nose with the tip of a ball point pen, leaving a series of black squiggles across his face.

"Asshole," Mike said, as he snapped awake. "What time is it?"

A little past seven," Grant said while laughing. Both men stood up and sat at the conference room table. Grant slid a fresh cup of Dunkin Donuts coffee across the table towards his fellow Detective. Mike opened it and immediately began drinking, nodding in appreciation. "What else did you get done last night?" Grant asked.

"Gimmie a second," Mike answered, rubbing his eyes. Mike searched through the scattered papers and notes that were on the table until he found the manifest, which looked like a toddler had attacked it with a series of different colored markers and highlighters. Mike cleared his throat, exhaling an odor that smelled like death mixed with cigarette smoke.

"These people were picked up last night, broken down by county," he said, as he tapped his finger on the list, pointing out the varying colors and the legend he created in the corner. "I was gonna call around for more specifics later today, but every one of them were arrested for some type of assault. Um, oh yeah, I emailed a list of folks in Bryan County that were unaccounted for to Matt Wheeler. I need to do a follow up on that. I gotta find my contact in Liberty County. What's his name? Oh shit, almost forgot..."

Mike shuffled through the mess on the table until he found the crew list. A large, red circle was around the name Chantay Williams. "This woman worked a flight from Savannah to Boston last night. I told Armstrong to get word to the aircraft, fucker blew me off. I talked to some woman after that, she was of no use to me either. Man, I hope nothing happened. If something happened, I'm gonna wring that sorry little fucker's neck."

"Who? Armstrong?" Grant asked.

"No, President Nixon. Yes, Armstrong! Who the fuck else would I mean? Anyway, here's a list of people not accounted for here in Chatham County. I want to talk to them today."

Mike produced a sheet of paper that was about half filled with names and addresses, some had phone numbers. The name at the top of the list read: *Craig Atwood, 126 Abercorn. Savannah GA, No phone number provided.*

Chapter 61

BRYAN COUNTY SHERIFF'S DEPUTY MATT Wheeler opened his email at around 0815, thirty minutes after he arrived at the office. Like many people, he had to ease into the day, get some coffee, make his rounds, and bullshit with whoever else was there. He wasn't one to jump right to his desk.

Scrolling through his unopened emails, one caught his eye: Michael Christianson, SCMPD Detective, Homicide. The name brought a smile to Matt's face. He thought back to the altercation he had with a few drunks at the seafood festival a couple years ago. Christianson had been there, off duty, and he intervened. The two have been buddies ever since. It was good to know that people still had your back, we were still one big team, looking out for one another. Matt read the subject line before opening the message. It was a single word: LIST.

Matt,

How are things over in Bryan County? Been a long time. Anyway, I'm working on something over here, might be nothing. I'm thinking that all of the events that went on today are connected. I know you guys had a few crazy events over there. I linked a few of them together and connected them to a flight that left Atlanta Sunday night. I got the manifest and crew list from the airline and me and Grant Wright broke the names down by county. That's the attachment. It's a list of people who live in Bryan County that were on flight 1289, ATL to SAV. Do me a favor and check some of them out, see if they've been involved in any crimes since Sunday. If not, maybe we can prevent a few. Let me know what you find out.

Mike

Matt read the email again, he usually reads all his emails two times to make sure he didn't miss anything. He went ahead and opened the attachment and saw a list of twelve names with addresses. Some had phone numbers. After examining the list for a few minutes, he sent the document to the network printer that the office shared and made the short walk down the hall to retrieve it.

Reclining in his chair, feet on the desk, he kept reading the list, seeing if he knew any of these people, if any of them had a record or any prior arrests. Nothing was popping out at him. For now, it was just a list of random names. He planned on checking the blotter report after the 0830 huddle to see if anything turned up. He knew that if some of these names were on yesterday's blotter, there might be some truth to Christianson's investigation. Wheeler liked to help out a colleague whenever possible, especially one that saved his ass once before.

At 0825 Wheeler headed into the department's conference room for the 0830 shift change and routine morning huddle. These meetings would always start with a debrief from the night shift. They would outline everything that went on from the beginning of their shift until now, including anything that was on going. Then there would be about a half hour allotted to an actual one on one handoff between the oncoming and outgoing individuals. Once a thorough hand over was complete, the night shift was released. The oncoming folks would pile back into the conference room to discuss today's events. This was routine shift change procedures and were followed three times a day.

After the huddle, Matt realized he was going to have to re-prioritize his to-do list if he was going to check on any of these names for his friend. He decided to start with the ones that had a phone number. Scrolling down the list of addresses, searching for one with a number, his eyes traced across the name *Seth Holloway*, complete with a ten digit contact number. Matt yanked the receiver from its cradle and dialed the numbers.

Chapter 62

BUSES WERE EXPECTED TO DELIVER about fifty Soldiers to the range in a little less than one hour. There was still plenty of time to prepare for their arrival. SFC Johnson lay two large steel pickets on the plywood table in front of the empty bleachers. These steel pickets were common in the Army's inventory of construction equipment, most commonly used when creating obstacles. They were about 4 feet long, with several small notches on each side, which were about a foot apart. The pickets were "U" shaped, thus ensuring that they remained more securely in the ground when you pounded them in. They were intended to be used as posts in the assembly of a wire fence. One would pound in several pickets in a row and then run wire through the small notches, creating the fence, which could then be fortified with additional wire or perhaps subsurface anti-personnel mines. Today, SFC Johnson would show the Soldiers one of the other many uses of these common metal pickets. He laid out several feet of det cord on the table. Det cord was essentially a long, hollow tube, filled with explosives, hence the name: *detonation cord*. This cord had multiple uses, limited only by the imagination of its user. It could be used independently, as demonstrated in the movie *We Were Soldiers*, when they ran the cord around the base of several trees to create a make-shift helicopter landing zone. Its primary use was to detonate blasting caps which would in turn detonate other explosives.

The senior Non Commissioned Officer would demonstrate how you could create a field expedient Bangalore torpedo by packing the "U" shaped groove of two pickets with C4. C4 was extremely pliable, therefore; it could be packed into almost any space or molded into any shape needed. It had the consistency of a glob of clay. Once the explosive was in place, one would then tie a few knots in a length of det cord and lay it on one of the pickets directly in the C4. The next step would be to place the pickets together, essentially making a long sandwich, ensuring that there was a small tail of the det cord protruding out from one of the ends. Finally, you would tape the pickets together with several turns of duct tape. When you were ready to blow it, you would connect your initiation device to the piece of exposed det cord and voila; you're done. This long bomb could be used to destroy an enemy obstacle or vehicle, you could use it to destroy a wall in order to gain access to a building; basically anything. A bonus effect was the fact that the detonation would cause the pickets to shatter into several small, lethal projectiles which would cause significant damage to enemy personnel and equipment. The field expedient Bangalore torpedo had a long, awkward shape, but it was relatively light weight, so Soldiers could carry it to the objective.

SFC Johnson had created this charge a few hundred times, usually in training, but once he had the opportunity to do it in a combat environment during the initial invasion into Iraq in 2003. He enjoyed showing young Soldiers the effects of explosives and the different techniques one could use when supplies were limited. Once his equipment was ready for his demonstration, he helped the Lieutenant prepare his class. The LT was going to show the Soldiers how you could quickly and easily breach a door with a few turns of det cord around the knob. Or, depending on the thickness of the door and the amount of lethality you could get away with, you could add some explosives to the det cord. Det cord would do the trick alone on most doors, however; sometimes you would need to add a little more punch if the door was thick or if there was a dead bolt engaged.

The last charge to be demonstrated was the grapeshot charge. SGT Holloway would do this one. This was constructed using some type of container, such as an old ammo can or a discarded coffee can; today they were provided with several number ten cans. One would poke a hole through the bottom of the can and run a length of det cord through the hole. You could attach a blasting cap to the end of the cord or you could simply tie a Uli knot. A Uli knot was a small knot which is tied on top of itself at the end of the cord; it creates a small ball of det cord which will cause a larger explosion when detonated. Once the knot was tied inside the can, you would then fill the can with C4, packing it in tight around the Uli knot or blasting cap, whichever you used. Once the C4 was in place, you would need some type of buffer material, such as cardboard, burlap, several sheets of paper; basically anything that you could place on top of the C4 to act as a buffer. Once the buffer was in place, the last step would be to add the projectiles. Anything could be used as a projectile; nuts, bolts, nails, screws, broken glass, rocks, anything. Any object placed on top of the buffer would become a lethal projectile designed to kill anyone within its path. The objects would be fired in whatever direction the user faced the can; the range and radius depending on the size of the can used and amount of explosives. Holloway had created several grapeshot charges over the few years he's been on active duty; he planned on making at least five more by the time it was all said and done.

Holloway's phone vibrated in his pocket. He had to remove his glove with his teeth in order to get to the phone which was buried deep. The number was not a familiar one to Seth, therefore he ignored it. He rarely took calls from a number he didn't recognize, unless he was expecting it. There's a lot of crazy people out there.

Chapter 63

DETECTIVES WRIGHT AND CHRISTIANSON PASSED Captain Garrison as they exited SCMPD HQ. "Where the hell do you two think you're going?" the Captain asked.

Mike looked at his watch. 8:27. *Fine time to show up, Captain,* he thought. "We're gonna check out a few names of people that were on that flight the other day. Tons of them were arrested last night. I sent out a few names over to Bryan County, so they can help us out," Mike said, as he and Grant continued to walk on past the Captain.

"We don't have time for that shit today, Mike. We really don't. There's a lot of other shit going on," the Captain said.

"Well, *this* shit has a lot to do with *that* shit," Mike said, "We'll be on the radio, we'll come back if you need us to. It's right around the corner." The two Detectives headed out to the parking lot as the Captain shook his head at the insubordinate behavior of the two men. They climbed into Mike's smelly, trashed Impala. "What's the address again?" Mike asked.

"126 Abercorn," Grant answered. "A little early, don't cha think?"

"He should've added a cell number when he booked his flight, we could've called. Maybe we'll catch him before he heads out to work." Mike said as he cranked the engine. He pulled out, heading north on Habersham Street.

"It's less than a mile from here," Grant said, "My God, you fucking stink, dude. You can't keep sleeping in the office and then wear the same clothes. It's nasty. You didn't even brush your teeth!"

"I had coffee. I'm good," Mike said, causing them both to laugh. "There's some gum in the glove box, hook me up."

Grant handed Mike a stick of gum and took one for himself. Mike realized that his buddy was probably right. He couldn't expect people to take him seriously as a detective if they had to cover their nose when they spoke to him. He was going to have to work on his personal hygiene practices. Grant removed a small bottle of hand sanitizer from his interior coat pocket and handed it to Mike. "You have pen on your face. This should take it off."

Mike's GPS led them to an old colonial home in one of Savannah's most historic areas. There were several large trees around the house and its drive way, complete with hanging Spanish moss, which was common in downtown Savannah. The home was quite beautiful, despite the fact that its owner had neglected routine exterior upkeep for what looked like a decade. The grass was waist high, the front of the house and its porch needed paint, and the black, wrought iron fence around the front yard was riddled with so much rust that it was barely standing.

"Nice old house," Mike said as they exited the vehicle. "What's this guy's name again?"

"Atwood. Craig Atwood," Grant answered as the two walked up the creepy driveway towards the equally creepy front porch. An old fashioned rocking chair sat on the porch, facing the street. The weak stairs groaned under their feet as the two Detectives headed up on to the porch and knocked on the door.

After a few seconds, Craig Atwood opened the door. He wore a navy blue robe and black slippers. Two days' worth of stubble covered his hideously square chin and his glasses were littered with grubby finger prints. He held a steaming cup of dark black coffee in his right hand.

"Can I help you?" Atwood said through his yellow grill, which was covered with ugly old braces.

"Yes sir," Mike said while flashing his credentials, "I'm Detective Christianson, and this is Detective Wright. We're investigating a series of crimes and assaults that have taken place over the last twenty four hours that we feel may be connected. Do you have a few minutes to answer some questions for us?"

"Abstholutely," Atwood said with a lisp, "pleasth, come in, gentlemen"

Craig held the door wide for the two Detectives, who entered immediately after the invitation. Mike and Grant felt as though they had walked backwards through time as they entered the foyer of this old home. Nearly all the furniture they could see was covered with large sheets, with the exception of one dirty recliner, which faced an ancient television complete with a mangled coat hanger/tin foil antenna. A visible coat of dust lay on every surface. Every fixture within eye sight appeared to be original. Every coat of paint and sheet of wall paper was equally vintage. It was evident that this home had received no upgrades during its existence, however long that was.

Craig led the detectives to the left and into the home's formal dining room. The vintage art deco dining room table was without a table cloth or place settings and had a coat of dust thick enough to write your name in. Six Winsor dining room chairs surrounded the dusty table. A decorative chair rail and fancy crown molding completed the room as it covered the entire space. There were a few other pieces of dining room furniture placed throughout the room, although the Detectives couldn't identify what they were as they were beneath drop cloths. A filthy, cobweb covered glass chandelier hung over head, projecting rays of interrupted light onto the table where the three men eventually sat.

"You guyths need thsome coffee?" Atwood asked.

"No, thank you. We won't take up too much of your time this morning. We just have a few questions," Mike said as he removed his tiny note book from his coats interior pocket. "Were you on flight 1289 from Atlanta to Savannah this past Sunday?"

"You know I wasth, Detective. I can only asthume that you're so spethific with the flight number beacusth you know I wasth on the flight," Atwood answered in a defensive tone.

"Fair enough. We're concerned about people that were on that flight because it seems that all of them have been committing random acts of violence since being on that plane. Have you been watching the news?" Mike asked. Atwood nodded. "Well, most of yesterday's events had something to do with someone that was on that same flight. 1289, Atlanta to Savannah. We're talking to everyone that was on that flight to see if we can prevent anything similar to yesterday's events."

"Interethsting. What makths you think thesth people didn't justh sthnap? People sthnap, you know? Sthometimth it only takths sthomething little to pusth people over the edge. The newsth thaid the woman who thshot thosth people in the sthchool wasth thexually harrathed by the Athithant Printhiple. They thaid the man on theventeen wasth road rage. Could be ssstressth. It might be juth coienthidenthe," Atwood struggled to say.

"Could be what?" Grant said.

"SSSStressth."

"Stress?" Mike said, seeking confirmation.

"Yesth, thasth what I thaid," Atwood responded.

"You certainly know a lot about what went on yesterday." Grant said, making an observation.

"Well, isth all over the newsth. But, to ansther your quethion, I feel fine, detectivtheths. Never better."

There was a few seconds of awkward silence as the Detectives tried to decipher what Atwood had just said. Mike's notes were a mess. The silence was broken by the familiar cackle of a police scanner in the other room. Mike and Grant looked at each other in surprise.

"Why do you have a police scanner?" Grant asked.

"Sthometimth the newsth doethent cover everything. I like to thsay on top of what goesth on in my thcity. I'm pretty thsure that itsth legal to have a scthanner here in Georgia," Atwood answered.

"You're right, it's legal," Mike said. Mike knew that there were even smartphone apps that did the same thing that the police scanners did. There were several states that had laws forbidding citizens from possessing mobile police scanners, Florida was one of them. Radar detectors were also illegal in several states. Mike continued, "I was just wondering why you feel that you need it."

"Well, Detective, that's none of your fucking business," Atwood said as he winked at Mike; his words out came clearly without his lisp.

"What was that?" Mike asked.

"What wasth what?" Atwood responded.

"The little wink."

Grant looked at Mike with a confused expression on his face, as if asking *what are you talking about?* Grant made an effort to interrupt the awkwardness of the moment as he asked "What kind of work do you do, Mr. Atwood?"

"I'm an independent communicationsth conthultant. I have to travel all over the country for my work," he answered, directing his answer to Detective Christianson and not to the man who asked the question. Mike and Grant both felt it a little strange that a man that was so clearly detached from the advances in technology was a communications consultant. Neither Detective knew the exact job description, however; they both assumed that someone with that title would need to have a grasp on social media and information technology, which it appeared that, based on his living conditions, Mr. Atwood had neither.

Feeling that this conversation had run its course, Mike pulled out one of his business cards and slid it across the table, leaving a small trench in the dust. "Mr. Atwood, we're sorry we took up so much of your time this morning. Please give us a call if you think of anything you'd like to share with us, or if you start to feel strange or like you're going to do something you might regret." Grant gave up one of his cards as well.

"I'll walk you gentlemen out." Atwood said, as he led the way.

The three men walked through the front door and down the creaky stairs of the porch. Mike noticed that Atwood was walking entirely too close to the Detectives; uncomfortably close. He was invading their personal space as they walked, almost rubbing elbows as they descended the steps. He continued to sidle up to both Detectives as they walked the length of the winding driveway.

"I think we're good, Mr. Atwood." Mike said, although he wanted to say *back the fuck off me!* This guy didn't seem to mind Mike's horrible body odor.

"I could come with you, gentlemen. I know the area well. If you're planning on looking up other people that were on that flight. I could come with you to the polithe sthathion, ansther thsome questions, maybe." Atwood said in a creepy manner. Almost as if he was saying *please, take me with you...* He followed them all the way into the street where the car was parked, hovering alongside Mike like a lost puppy.

"No, sir. We're fine. You give us a call if you think of anything else" Mike said, as he attempted to open the door to the Impala. Atwood was almost nose to nose with Mike by now, preventing the door from opening. The Detective lost what little remained of his calm demeanor. "Back up," he demanded, opening the door towards Atwood, forcing him to move. Mike got in, started the engine and drove off. Atwood walked into the street behind the vehicle, waving his arm skyward as if saying goodbye to a pair of old friends.

"What a fucking fruitloop..." Mike said.

"What was that shit about? That shit with the wink?" Grant asked.

"He fucking winked at me. When he told me it was none of my business why he had a scanner." Mike answered.

"He didn't wink at you. I was looking right at him. He just re-peated what he said before about the news. He didn't say anything about whether or not it was your business." Grant explained.

Mike pulled a cigarette out of his pack with his teeth and sparked it up. "I'm smoking this, I don't give a shit that you don't like it."

Chapter 64

BRIAN REYES STARTED HIS ELEVENTH consecutive round of Call
of Duty: Team Death-Match at a few minutes past nine. School
was canceled today because of some shooting at one of the middle
schools in Savannah, so he was able to sleep in until about an hour
ago. His mother didn't get home from work until sometime after
midnight, so he thought she was still sleeping. Brian planned on
doing absolutely nothing today. He'd been playing Call of Duty:
Ghosts on his PlayStation 3 since he woke up and he saw no reason
in stopping. It was going to be a good day; lazy and full of video
games. Brian wore a bulky headset, complete with a microphone
to enhance the gaming experience. The earmuffs on this headset
covered half of his head, making him look like a male version of
Princess Leia. The microphone that was affixed to the headset had
a large foam cover, which blocked the lower half of his face. Brian
didn't really care what he looked like, he was happy that he could
communicate with his teammates as he played each round, as well
as talk trash to opponents in between rounds. Today was going to
be a blast.

After his team's most recent victory, a tiny boy with an Australian accent polluted the airways of the PlayStation network with
his ten year old trash talk. "Dude, how old are you? Shouldn't you
be in school?" Brian asked him through the mic. "It's nighttime,

douche. I'm in Australia, you dumb-shit," the little brat responded. Everyone in the session got a laugh from the little kid, so did Brian. It was pretty funny, especially since the boy had an accent. It was always fun to play with people from different countries. As he played on, Brian was starting to look forward to the intermission so he could hear this little shit again; he could only hear this kid's comments in between rounds, since he was on the other team. During the round itself you could only communicate with your own team.

As the next map loaded, Brian's thoughts wandered, thinking about school, his childhood. He had started his sophomore year at Alfred Ely Beach High School this past September. So far his school year had been uneventful. He passed his classes easily, but he was by no means an honor student. He did the minimum; no more, no less. Brian was an average kid in general; not many friends, or enemies, for that matter. He had turned 16 in December, five days before Christmas, which usually sucked, since people would generally give him one gift, *this is for Christmas and your birthday,* kind of thing. *Fucking rip off.*

His father had sent him this PlayStation 3 and the 40 inch Sony TV which it was hooked up to for this birthday/Christmas. His father's name was Mark Jenkins and he lived in Phoenix, Arizona with his second wife and Brian's half brother and sister. Brian had only just met his father about five years ago, as his mother had been vague with him when he was younger about the details of his father. All Brian knew growing up was that his parents had divorced when he was very young and that his father lived somewhere out west. Sometime shortly after Brian's tenth birthday, he insisted that his mother tell him more about the father that he never knew. She explained she and his father weren't actually married at the time of his birth, which is why Brian and his mother had the name Reyes. They dated a little in high school, she got pregnant, and he went to college. When Brian was only a couple months old, his father had married another woman and moved out west to be near her family.

His father was some type of surgeon, or something, and he had been sending his mother money over the years to help care for him. His mother had made arrangements for Brian to speak to his father over the phone back when he was ten, and they continued to speak almost weekly ever since. Brian's dad would even fly him out to Phoenix about once a year for a visit. For the past three years he had spent his birthday/Christmas out west, but this year his visit was delayed because his dad had gone to Hawaii with his wife's parents. His mother and father both agreed that it would be ok if Brian missed a week of school in order to be with his dad, therefore; he spent last week in Phoenix, getting back in Savannah the day before yesterday.

Brian sometimes resented his mother for keeping his father's existence from him for the first ten years of his life. She didn't hide the fact that he had a father, but she didn't make sure they had a relationship either. Brian's dad and his wife had two young children, a four year old boy and a new born baby girl. Brian liked the fact that he was a big brother, although he rarely saw them. He was envious of the life his dad had out west. His dad was rich and Brian lived in a tiny two bedroom apartment with his mom, who was just a waitress, hardly making enough money to pay the

rent. He felt like an afterthought when he visited his dad, like a
fifth wheel. His dad had his other two kids, blonde hair and blue
eyes, like their mom, with the last name Jenkins. Now all of a
sudden, here was this 16 year old, half Hispanic son from another
woman, getting in the way. It made him angry when he thought of
his mother barely making enough money to pay the bills and his
rich dad who sent only a few hundred dollars every month. He
had asked his dad a couple of years ago if he could live out there in
Arizona, a question that was answered with a simple: *I don't think
that's a good idea.*

Tears welled up in Brian's eyes when he thought back to that
conversation when he was thirteen. He was crushed. His father
had spoken to his mother on the phone for a long time after Brian
asked the question, so perhaps there was more to it that he didn't
understand. Brian really didn't care what the reason was. *Why
wasn't it a good idea?* he thought even now, *are you ashamed of
me, dad? Am I not good enough for your new family?* Brian sobbed
as he played Call of Duty in the tiny apartment that he and his
mother shared, his mind wandering around, thinking of his childhood, or lack thereof, and his father enjoying parenthood with his
other kids. Brian's internal voice suddenly changed to something
different. He couldn't tell if the voice he heard was coming from
one of the other players in the game that he was playing, through
the headset. The voice sounded like the small child with that annoying, taunting tone, the Australian boy with the funny accent;
the trash talker he'd been hearing through his headset in between
rounds all morning. To be sure, Brian removed his headset and set
it on the ground.

He continued to hear the taunting gibberish of the annoying child in his mind after he removed the headset. The voice cracked and skipped, the way it would if it was coming through the servers of the PlayStation network. It said the same words that Brian had thought a few minutes ago, but with an Australian accent: *why wasn't it a good idea? Is he ashamed of you? Are you not good enough for his new family?* The voice echoing through his mind sounded like it was broadcasted over an old, static filled radio. *Fuck him, Brian. He doesn't care about you, fuck him. Fuck her too...fuck your mother...she didn't even tell you that you had a father...fuck his new wife, fuck that bitch.* Brian stood up, looked at the headset on the floor, in shock at the strange, unwelcomed voice that intruded his brain. He squeezed the controller in his hand until he could feel the plastic assembly start to crack. It vibrated in his hand as his character was killed in the game, his opponent's kill-cam filling the 40 inch screen. *He's too far away, he's too far away, he's too far away...*the young boy repeated in his ear. Tears fell down Brian's flushed cheek, *he's with his real kids, his real son, his real daughter, not you, not you, of course not you, you don't even matter...and it's all because of her...her...her...kill...kill...kill her kill her kill her her, her kill...kill...NOW!!!*

A flash of pain hit Brian in both temples with a force like a vice grip crushing his head. He broke the controller in his hands into two pieces and threw them both at the TV, causing the screen to go blank as a spider web looking crack formed in the upper right corner. He grabbed a small, novelty Atlanta Braves baseball bat off his floor and smashed what was left of the TV his father had sent him only a few weeks ago. The PlayStation suffered the wrath of the tiny bat next, as Brian shattered the outer casing of the expensive video game console and threw it to the floor. The little bat had splintered when Brian gave the console a final blow, leaving him nothing but a small, fractured and splintered weapon, with its little red Atlanta Braves handle. *Stick that in her fucking heart* the little boy's voice said in Brian's mind as the same words came through loud and clear through the headset that still lay on the floor by his feet. *Kill that bitch,* it repeated as Brian flung his bedroom door open, causing it to bounce off the wall. He marched through the open doorway and headed across the hall to where his mother currently slept.

Chapter 65

"DADDY, DADDY? I HAVE TO go to the bathroom," little Jessica said as she knocked softly on the bathroom door. Doug had been in the shower for nearly an hour now, letting the steaming hot water penetrate the open sores on his lower back, hopeful that the heat was flushing any damaged tissue away. The pressure and heat from the shower head had reduced his pain significantly. What was once a throbbing, stinging pain was now just a minor annoyance. The tiny room looked like a sauna as it had been filling with steam for so long. Doug pulled the shower curtain aside and shut off the water.

"I'll be out in a second, baby." Doug said as he noticed his gun was still spinning in place on the sink. It was spinning slowly, like a bottle in that pre-teen game from so many years ago. He tried to ignore it as he wiped the condensation off the mirror so he could inspect his lower back. Looking over his shoulder at his naked body, he examined his sores. The four individual spider bites looked like tiny, drained volcanos. The circumference of each hole was about a quarter inch with a deep pit in the center surrounded with a perimeter of pink and tender flesh. The skin around the area appeared wrinkled and white, waterlogged. He couldn't see any black skin, which was a good sign. It looked like the pus and damaged tissue had been rinsed down the drain. An appointment to see the doctor was still in order, he'd need antibiotics to make sure that the infection was dead. Doug's eyes traced up his back, starting to notice that the reflection of his withering body looked horrible. Although he just got out of the shower, his skin was dry and cracked. He looked like he had aged twenty years since yesterday. The vertebrae that comprised his spine were becoming visible through his ashy skin.

"I'm late for school, Daddy," Jessica said through the closed door.

"No school today, baby. We're gonna watch movies all day. We'll use the redbox outside if there's nothing else on Netflix," Doug said as he quickly tried to dry off the areas that were still wet. His little girl had to go to the bathroom, after all. He tied the towel around his waist, grabbed the spinning gun, and opened the door.

"Why's there no school today? Does Mom and Jeff know?" Jessica asked her naked, gun toting father. Her concern was beginning to show in her face and body language; she was clearly a confused little eleven year old girl.

"She's the one that told me, baby-girl. It's all good." Doug said as he caressed her cheek with the hand not clutching a firearm.

Jessica went into the bathroom and locked the door. After inspecting for more spiders, Doug sat on the bed and rubbed his eyes. *What the fuck is happening to me?* Doug thought. The faint, whispering voice that's been violating his mind since yesterday spoke to him, *you better do it soon. I'll make it worse. Much, much, much worse. You'll wish you were dead, fucker. I promise you.* Doug jumped as he felt something crawl across his foot. He jerked his feet up on to the bed, startled, as his heart leapt into his throat. The tarantula that had touched his foot walked with smug conviction across the hotel room floor, as if it were a welcomed guest. Doug quickly located the room's ice bucket.

Chapter 66

SOLDIERS WATCHED WITH ATTENTIVE EYES as SFC Johnson showed them the steps involved in making a field expedient Bangalore torpedo. Fifty two Soldiers in full combat gear filled the bleachers about thirty minutes ago, received their safety briefing from the Range Safety Officer, and started watching demonstrations immediately after. The Battalion Commander arrived just in time to receive the safety briefing with the men; he was not above the rules and liked to show people that whenever he could. SFC Johnson went through his demonstration rather quickly, giving the Lieutenant plenty of time to show them the door. The door breach charge was simple, so the LT went through the motions with a quick five minute presentation. Most Soldiers were familiar with that charge anyway.

SGT Holloway excelled when given the chance to show his skills in front of his peers, so naturally, he was excited to be able to give the demonstration of the grapeshot charge with the Battalion Commander in the audience. Holloway brought his equipment in front of the bleachers once the LT was done with the door. He provided a brief introduction: "Good morning Soldiers, you all know me, I'm SGT Holloway, I'm in 2nd Platoon, A co. I'm going to go over the grapeshot charge. I want to welcome Lieutenant Colonel Anderson to today's training. Everyone here should know that the grapeshot charge is a field expedient version of the M18 Claymore anti-personnel mine. The equipment you'll need to assemble this charge is..." Holloway held up each item as he went through the equipment one would need to prepare the simple charge.

Once complete, the BC commended SGT Holloway on his professional demonstration as Soldiers began to file out of the bleachers. The plan was to take everyone down range so that SFC Johnson, the LT, and Holloway could show them the proper emplacement of these three charges. They would then all report to the bunkers and detonate everything. Holloway had an alternative plan.

"Hey, can you cover me, I gotta piss like a racehorse," SGT Holloway said to Staff Sergeant Brunick as he ran over to the ammo shed. "Yeah, I'll take care of it," Brunick said as he took the ready-made grapeshot charge from Seth's hands. "Thanks, Dog."

Holloway relieved himself in the small wooded area directly behind the ammo shed as everyone else walked north towards the berm that separated the range into its two distinct areas. Seth was alone. He knew he would be alone for at least 30 minutes, maybe even 45. Plenty of time for him to do what he needed to do. *Right on track Sergeant. Nicely done*, flashed in his mind as he went inside the ammo shed and opened his assault pack. The C4 that lined the wall of the tiny shed was in twenty eight individual boxes, all of which were stacked neatly on the shelves. The two that were opened to provide explosives for the demonstration and the blocks to be issued lay empty off to the side. Seth grabbed a box off the top of the stack and gently removed the tape that held the box's top closed. He removed four blocks of C4 from the box and replaced the empty space with several handfuls of dirt. Using a small piece of electrical tape which was rolled into a loop, Seth reclosed the box the best he could. If someone were to inspect the box it would've been clear that it had been tampered with, but at a glance, it appeared fine. The top remained closed and the shape of the box was not altered, due to the replacement dirt inside. Surely it would rattle if someone shook the box, but he'd take care of that when the time came.

Seth placed the box underneath five others on the shelf, thus increasing the illusion that everything was normal, and he grabbed a roll of det cord. He unrolled about 50ft off the 1000ft roll of cord and stuffed it in his bag. He then secured several blasting caps with pre-attached time fuses and a handful of ignition devices and stuck them in his bag as well. He didn't grab any tape, he had enough from his house. Making sure to rearrange the placement of objects in his bag, Seth placed his wet weather parka and his poncho liner on top, so if someone were to glance in his bag, it wouldn't be obvious what he had done. *Too easy,* he thought, *am I forgetting anything? Doesn't look like it,* his friendly little helper said, *I think you're good to go, Sergeant. You will be rewarded for doing your duty. Don't fuck this up.*

Chapter 67

MIKE WROTE THE WORDS CRAIG ATWOOD on the dry erase board in the conference room, all caps and double underlined. He and Grant had originally planned on heading to the address of the next name on their list, but since they were so close to HQ, they figured it would be a good idea to stop by and check in. Captain Garrison walked into the conference room, rubbing his giant forehead, clearly overwhelmed by the events of the past day and a half.

"Who's Craig Atwood?" the Captain asked.

"He's a fucking freak, we just came from his house," Mike said as Grant nodded. "This guy has something to do with this whole thing. Somehow. I don't know how or what, but I'm gonna figure it out. This asshole has been monitoring everything on his police scanner. He's a creepy fucker."

"He is," Grant added, "There's definitely something fishy about that guy. Mike, go brush your damn teeth."

"Fuck off." Mike said as headed to the stations locker room to take a quick shower and probably brush his teeth. The Captain and Detective Wright both laughed as Mike left.

"Hey, don't go too far today. I know I'm gonna need you at some point," the Captain said to Grant. "You can play with your smelly little friend for a little while longer, then I'm gonna need you both to do some real work. That reminds me, give Mike this message."

Before heading back to his office, the Captain pulled a folded post it note out of his breast pocket and handed it to Grant. Having to pry open the self-adhesive little note, Grant read the message which was scribbled in red ink:

Christianson – Chris Armstrong called at 0850, from Sierra airlines. Call him ASAP (a number followed)

Why didn't he call his cell, Grant thought as he walked through the building towards the locker room. Mike was already done with his shower when Grant walked into the steam filled shower room.

"What's up?" Mike said as he was putting on the same clothes he had on before he got in the shower.

"Did you even use soap? What's the point of showering if you're gonna put the same nasty clothes back on? What are you? A ten year old? Armstrong from Sierra called. Wants you to call him back." Grant said through laughter. Christianson was a nasty old man and Grant was finding his antics funnier with every minute they worked together.

"Fuck. Why didn't he call my fucking cell phone?" Mike said, pulling his sweaty shirt over his head. Grant shrugged his shoulders. Mike finished getting dressed and they both headed back to the conference room.

Chapter 68

AMANDA REYES WOKE TO THE sounds of destruction coming from across the hall. The 34 year old Hispanic woman jumped out of bed, in fear that someone or something was in her home, possibly hurting her son, who she assumed was still asleep in his room. She kept a small pistol under her mattress for occasions such as this. A single mother in downtown Savannah had to be prepared to defend herself and her small family. Amanda was no different. The little hand gun she held was completely legal and registered and she was prepared to kill if anyone meant to hurt her or her son. She leaned against the wall directly next to her bedroom door, her pistol in both hands and pointing safely toward the floor. Amanda listened carefully, trying to get a better understanding of what was happening in her house.

A surge of adrenaline flowed through Amanda's body as she opened the cylinder of her revolver to check that it was loaded. The courses on gun safety she had taken were evident, as Amanda handled her gun with the care and precision of a seasoned police officer. Once she saw the shiny brass casings of her ammunition within the pistol, she flicked her wrist, allowing the cylinder to snap closed. Suddenly she heard another crashing noise from across the hall, followed by a thud, as if something was thrown on the floor. Another smash echoed through the house, followed by the sound of wood breaking; a loud cracking noise she couldn't quite place, but if she had to guess, it sounded like a baseball bat breaking, like when a pro ball player makes contact with a fast ball that splinters the bat. Both she and her boy were Braves fans, so she'd heard that sound on TV many times.

Another noise bounced off Amanda's ears; a noise that added to her already amped defensive posture. The sound was that of her son's door flying open and hitting the wall. It was loud enough that she imagined the doorknob must've left a hole in the drywall. The sound of the door making contact with the wall was immediately followed by the sound of stomping feet. The individual thuds made the house vibrate as someone marched across the hall from her son's room and stood outside her bedroom door.

Amanda could almost feel whoever it was breathing on the other side of the wall that she leaned against. She moved to a position in the center of her room where she had unobstructed view of her bedroom door. *You better not have hurt my son, motherfucker*, she thought as she widen her stance and prepared to fire at whatever came through that door. *Let's go, asshole. I haven't got all day...*

Chapter 69

"Mr. Armstrong? This is Detective Christianson returning your call," Mike said into his cell phone while he and Grant sat in the conference room.

"Bad news, Detective. Chantay Williams attacked a passenger on the flight last night to Boston. I'm afraid that the man did not survive," Armstrong said with his nasally, annoying little voice.

"So, I take it you didn't get word to the crew, like I asked you to. Maybe if there was some kind of warning this could've been prevented." Mike stood, blood boiling, "This is your fucking fault, you little shit! I fucking told you to warn somebody, you whiny little fuck. That person's blood is on your fucking hands!" Mike said as he hung up and slammed his phone on the table.

"Holy shit!" Grant said. "What the hell happened?"

Mike said nothing as he marched over to the board where he had written the name *Chantay Williams* last night, followed by a question mark. He erased the question mark and the words "in flight to Boston as of 2200-ish." He replaced those words with "attacked and killed passenger on plane to Boston because Armstrong didn't fucking warn anybody." Mike underlined his new statement and then plopped himself into one of the conference room chairs, tossing the dry erase marker towards the tray at the bottom of the board, missing the target.

"Holy shit," Grant said once again. "Did you get any other details before you hung up on him?"

Mike shook his head without saying anything. He was furious. He wanted to drive down to the airport and strangle that little weasel fuck. Without explanation, Mike got up and walked out. He exited the building and walked up to his Impala, popping the trunk as he moved. Inside the trunk was an opened carton of Marlboro cigarettes. Mike secured a pack from the carton, turned and rested his butt on the back of his vehicle, leaving the trunk door open. Slapping the top end of the pack against the palm of his hand, Mike sighed and said, "What the fuck is happening?"

Chapter 70

CRAIG DRESSED SHORTLY AFTER THE Detectives drove off. He donned the same brown corduroy pants he wore yesterday, into which he tucked his REO Speedwagon tee-shirt. It was an unseasonably warm January morning here in Savannah, so Craig decided to wear his favorite pair of Birkenstocks, complete with a dingy pair of white tube socks. He walked out his front door, deciding to enjoy the morning air, and sat in the rocking chair on his front porch, coffee in hand. Craig flipped through the morning paper, periodically looking over the top of it towards the street. Eventually, he saw what he'd been waiting for.

A young woman, perhaps in her mid-thirties, walked her small dog on the side walk in front of Craig's colonial. The tiny dog was a Yorkshire terrier and it was clearly excited to be taking this morning stroll. The woman wore some type of black and purple running suit, complete with flashy running shoes. Her blonde hair was up in a ponytail as she walked at a brisk pace under the trees of this Savannah road.

"Ma'am, exthcuse me, ma'am? Do you have a thsecond?" Craig said, getting to his feet and trotting down his drive way. As he headed down the long driveway, Craig removed a business card from his pocket and held it in his right hand. He inhaled deeply through his nose and mouth, gathering as much phlegm as his body had to offer. He then spat the mucus into his hand, on top of the card. The woman had noticed what he did, so naturally she began to take a few steps back.

As soon as he was within striking distance, Craig leapt forward and open-palm slapped the woman across the face, causing the card to stick to her left cheek. He immediately closed the distance between himself and the woman, pressing his chest to hers as her dogged barked and jumped. For about a second, the two were nose to nose, as Craig pushed her backwards with his body; as his left foot stepped forward, her right foot stepped back, almost in unison. The woman's body was jerked slightly as they both stepped off the sidewalk and into the street. She pushed Craig in the chest with both hands, getting him out of her personal space, and raised her hands in a posture that suggested she was ready to fight.

"Back the fuck off." the woman said, clearly prepared to go toe to toe with Craig, card still stuck to her face with his snot as the adhesive.

Craig darted towards the woman again, this time going for the face with both hands, attempting to grab her by the cheeks. His hands pawed haphazardly at her face, hitting her nose and mouth. The woman snapped her teeth tight around Craig's left hand, in the area between the thumb and index finger. Blood flowed around her teeth and down his wrist, as he withdrew his hands. He clutched his left hand with the right one, grimacing in pain as the woman kicked him squarely in the crotch. Craig fell to his knees, crying like a school girl as the woman ran off in the direction she was initially traveling, securing her dog in the process.

Craig limped up to his porch, holding his swelling balls. He stopped to look towards the fleeing woman before entering his home, shutting the door behind him. Once the woman was at what she considered to be a safe distance, she stopped running. The card had fallen off her face a few steps back, so she had to go back to retrieve it. Disgusted, she wiped the lugie off her face with the sleeve of her jogging parka. She was about to dial 911 on her iPhone when she picked up the dirty business card and flipped it over. "DETECTIVE MICHAEL CHRISTIANSON – Savannah Chatham Metropolitan Police Department" was printed across the card in bold font, along with an address and two contact numbers.

Chapter 71

Brian Reyes clutched the fractured piece of bat in his right hand as he stood outside his Mother's bedroom. With his left hand, he tried the door knob, knowing that it would probably be locked. *Break it down break the fucking door down kill that bitch* the little invisible Australian boy whispered in his ear. Brian stood frozen in the hallway between this tiny apartment's only two bedrooms. His right eye began to twitch, almost like someone was tickling it with a feather. He had no control over the movements his eye was making, as he stood there shaking. *You better fucking do it you owe me you have to do your fucking duty pussy* bounced around his mind in an annoying little ten year old voice.

A small trickle of blood exited Brian's left nostril. He clenched both eyes tightly shut as pain radiated across his temples with the repeating words *do it do it do it*. He fought the urge to smash the door down. He was a strong young man, fully capable of shattering this cheap door, but he held his ground against the demonic suggestions in his thoughts. He struggled to picture his Mother and all the reasons he loved her. He saw her in his mind, working her ass off late at night so she could provide for her only son. He reminded himself that she had always placed his needs above her own; she sacrificed everything for him. He saw himself as a young boy, back when his mom had to work two jobs just to make ends meet. The blood flow from his nose increased. The pain in his head doubled.

The piece of broken bat fell through Brian's fingers as he vomited on his Mother's bedroom door. The force in which this puke exited his body was like nothing he had ever felt before. It seemed that every muscle in his body contracted at once. Heat and sweat engulfed his head as he looked at the mess he had just made, wiping his chin with his sleeve. There were small, moving objects within his vomit, both the pile on the floor and the portion that was plastered to his mother's door. The things were about the size of a raison, twitching and crawling independently of one another. Brian didn't wait around to find out what they really were, he ran down the stairs and burst free of the apartment, into the fresh morning air. Words still pierced his mind, now coming through in different voices; he heard his father's voice, his teacher's, his friends, the Australian boys voice, all merged together, demanding that he march back upstairs and murder his mother.

"NO!" he screamed into the apartment complex's parking lot. Brian ran across the parking lot and into a small wooded area, just outside the apartment complex's property line. This little area was free of any vegetation and had several logs laying on their side where kids would sit and hang out. Although the spot was cleared of all bushes and shrubs, it was still not visible to the surrounding area due to the hanging moss of the trees which encircled the space. This was a common secluded hang out for the kids who lived around here, often used for sex or drugs. There were a few dirty lawn chairs amongst the logs, as well as random pieces of garbage and empty beer cans all over the ground. A large, industrial wooden spool lay on its side, used as a makeshift table.

Brian dropped himself into one of the chairs and sobbed. His head throbbed with a head ache so bad that he wished he were dead. *That'll work you fucking coward if you won't kill her kill your fucking self coward* recited in his brain as blood dripped from his nose into the dirt below. The drops of blood began to move across the ground within the dirt, leaving a small trail, similar to the way one might write in the dirt with their finger. The blood wiggled around the ground like a sperm, leaving a message in the dirt: DO IT

Chapter 72

"Christianson," Mike said into his cell phone, cigarette bobbing between his lips.

A frantic, excited voice babbled on the other end of the phone "Yes sir, my name is Tracy Brock. I was just attacked by a man while I was walking my dog on Abercorn. He hit me with your business card for some reason. I was about to call 911..."

"Where on Abercorn, ma'am? Are you still in danger?" Mike interrupted.

"No, he went back in his house. Um, the house I'm next to is 138. 138 Abercorn," she said, sounding as if she was struggling to read the house number.

"Ok, ma'am. I'm going to send a unit there immediately, to talk to you. Do you plan on pressing charges?"

"Of course. This guy spit on your card and slapped me in the face with it. The damn thing stuck to my face! Why would he do that? I don't even know him! I've never seen him before in my life. He tried to choke me or something, but I bit his hand. His left hand. I kicked him in the balls and ran. I saw him go into his house. Are you going to come arrest him or what?!" she said, becoming irritated by the whole thing.

"Yes ma'am. I'm sending a unit to your location right now. Would you like me to send paramedics? You said you bit him?

Did he bleed? I'm going to request an ambulance as well, if he got fluids on you, you're going to want to be checked out. Don't worry about him, I'll take care of that. You wait on the police officers. If he comes back, go to the gas station on the corner of Abercorn and Bull. Somewhere public. I'm terribly sorry that this happened to you," Mike said, with sincerity.

"Yes, sir. Thank you."

Mike reached inside the cab of his vehicle and grabbed the hand-mike from his radio. He quickly explained the situation to the dispatch operator, released the hand-mike, allowing it to retract back into the cab, shut the trunk, and ran inside.

"Grant!" he hollered as he entered the bullpen. "Grant, where you at?!"

Detective Wright came out of the conference room. "What? Take it easy." Grant said as Mike walked right past him and into the conference room. Mike went to the dry erase board, picked up the marker that was on the floor; the one that he threw towards the tray earlier. Under the words CRAIG ATWOOD he wrote: *attacked woman on Abercorn. She bit left hand.* He triple under-lined it.

"A woman just called me directly. This fruitloop spit on my card and slapped her in the face. She said it stuck to her fucking face! He tried to choke her and she bit him. She's pressing charges. I have a unit heading her way now. We need to go get this asshole. I want to talk to him before he's booked," Mike said, clearly excited.

"This is insane," Grant said. "Is he taunting us? Or you? Why the hell would he "give" her your card?" Grant did the universal signal of quotes with his hands as he spoke.

"Who knows why people do what they do? What did he say? *Ssssometimessth people juth sthnap,*" Mike said, mocking Atwood with a forced lisp. "C'mon, let's go get this fucker."

The two Detectives headed back outside and towards Mike's car. Somehow, Mike felt that this Craig Atwood guy was the basis for all the strange happenings of the last day and a half. He wasn't sure how, but his detective instinct was telling him something was going on. Something was up. There were too many coincidences. One or two is strange enough. This shit had dozens of things in common, going all the way back to yesterday morning. Mike's mind darted back and forth as he began the short drive to 126 Abercorn.

Spears kills coworker, Jones kills Spears and family and assistant principle, Arkansauce kills someguy, truck kills arkansauce, Mason. What did he do again? Oh yeah, kidnapped his daughter. Maybe. What else? Oh yeah, Winford kills nurse in infirmary. Stewardess kills guy on plane. Shit, almost forgot Beecroft, kills wife and self. What else? What am I forgetting?

Mike's internal rambling was interrupted by Grant's voice, "There he goes right there?"

Atwood sat in the rocking chair on his front porch and waved at the detectives as they pulled the car to the curb in front of his house. Mike and Grant exited the vehicle and started up the driveway. "Mr. Atwood, come down here and talk to us," Grant said. "Sssthure." Atwood responded, as he got out of the chair and began heading down the driveway.

As soon as Atwood was within reach, Mike secured his hands, saying, "Place your hands behind your back, you're under arrest."

Mike went on to read him his rights, Atwood never once asked what this was about, nor did he deny anything. They placed him in the back seat and drove off smartly back to SCMPD HQ. Craig Atwood said nothing during the short trip. He simply sat quietly in the back seat, eyes closed and trembling.

Chapter 73

SAMANTHA ARKENSON HELD HER MOTHER'S hand tightly as they sat together in Dr. Allen's waiting room. Sam's dear friend Martha sat with them. Martha and Sam had arrived in Beaufort late last night; they stayed in a hotel right off the highway since Sam's mom had a small apartment. She had decided not to tell her mother about her husband's tragic death or the fact that her ex-husband had basically kidnapped their daughter, although the police didn't see it that way. Her mom had enough to worry about right now.

"Ladies?" Dr. Allen said, coming to the waiting room personally, "You can come back now."

The kind doctor escorted the three women back into his office. After ensuring that Sam and her mom sat, he went down the hall and secured a third chair for Martha. "Ma'am," he said to Martha, "I don't have a problem with you listening in, as long as Ms. Davis is fine with it."

"It's fine, doctor." Samantha's mother said.

Dr. Allen directed his comments towards Samantha, "Well, your mother and I spoke yesterday on the phone. The recurrence is local, which means it returned basically in the same place it started, the same breast. It doesn't appear as aggressive as before, but as we discussed last time, it can be somewhat unpredictable."

"Yes sir," Sam said, "My mother said that you mentioned the possibility of lumpectomy surgery."

"Yes. Yes we did. That would be our next step, in conjunction with more radiation. Basically, we would actually remove the tumor and some of the surrounding tissue. It's a relatively simple procedure, takes about 20-30 minutes." The doctor directed his attention to Sam's mother, "You'll only have to stay overnight, you won't have an extended stay in the hospital. We can expect about 5 to 7 weeks of radiation therapy following the procedure. We'll see where we're at after that."

"What are the risks of this procedure, doctor?" Sam asked.

"Well, I mean, there's a risk in every medical procedure. Specifically to this surgery, there could be a loss of sensation in the breast following the procedure, the breasts may differ in size, things like that. I'll provide the three of you with some information papers that can help set your mind at ease. I've done this procedure over 200 times, if that makes you feel any better." Dr. Allen said to all three women.

"Sir, what's the difference between a lumpectomy and a mastectomy? I mean, I know the difference, what I mean is, why choose one over the other?" Sam asked.

"Well, a lumpectomy is a breast conserving surgery. I feel that, right now, there's no reason to remove the entire breast. I think we can get it. I really do. We can discuss the pros and cons more in depth if you like, but I feel pretty confident in this," Dr. Allen answered, in an effort to put the women at ease. It worked. Sam and her mom had complete confidence in his abilities.

The group wrapped up the conversation and the women headed out front to schedule the appointment and discuss the pre-surgery procedures with the nurses. Sam was relieved that she was able to be at this appointment with her mother. Her mom wouldn't ask enough questions or speak up if she didn't understand. It was important to be here to support her mother, and Sam was appreciative that she had her friend with her during this troubling time.

They all piled into Martha's car and headed to Sam's moms house. The plan was for Sam and Martha to stay for a few more hours before heading back to Savannah. Sam had to figure out a way to break the news about Jeff. She knew she needed to tell her eventually, there was no avoiding that. She definitely wasn't going to tell her that she feared Doug was going to hurt their daughter somehow. Sam tried to call Doug again, assuming that it would go straight to voice mail, which it did.

Chapter 74

CRAIG ATWOOD SAT PATIENTLY IN one of SCMPD interrogation rooms. The rooms in this station were similar to the ones over at Chatham County, same layout, complete with table, chairs, mirror, and camera; the only difference was that there was a large steel ring bolted to the table used to secure a suspect's hands. Atwood's cuffs had been removed, therefore; he sat with his hands resting on the table, fingers interlocked. Mike and Grant watched him from the tiny adjacent viewing room, through the one way mirror. There was a monitor in the little room, receiving the feed from the camera next door. Grant used the controls to zoom the camera in on Atwood's hands.

"I don't see any bite marks on his hands." Grant said "Didn't the woman say she drew blood?"

"Yeah. I can't tell from here either. I'll look closer when I get in there."

Detective Christianson always liked to make his suspects wait before walking in. Hopefully, they would become impatient and nervous, possibly giving him an advantage right from the start. Atwood didn't look to be affected at all by being made to wait. He had even waved at the detectives through the mirror a couple times.

As Mike was preparing to enter the interrogation room, Captain Garrison walked in. "This the guy? Looks like a fucking douchebag."

"Yup. That's him," Mike answered. "I'm gonna head in there in a second, if you wanna stick around, Captain."

"I'm going to. Grant, I need you out on Bay Street. Someone found a woman in a dumpster. A unit's already there, but I need you to run point. I know you wanna stick with your new boyfriend here, but I need you on this. It's a mad house and I'm short," the Captain said.

"That's sexual harassment, boss," Grant said, "I gotcha, Captain. I know the deal. Alright, Mike. It's been fun, good luck with this weirdo. I'll talk to you later on today."

"Alright, talk to you later," Mike said, as he shook Grant's hand. Mike was a little disappointed. He had come to enjoy working with Grant over the last day and a half. They had established a good working relationship and Mike was actually considering talking to the Captain about making them permanent partners. Generally, Mike preferred working alone, but the last day and a half had been a small refresher; a reminder of the camaraderie established between teammates on the job.

"You gonna do this?" the Captain asked. Mike said nothing in response as he walked out.

Before sitting across from Atwood, Mike made the standard announcement that is required prior to any interrogation, citing the time and date out loud so that the recording picked it up. He announced Atwood's name, followed by the nature of the upcoming interview.

Once Mike finished, it was Atwood who spoke first, "You know you can only hold me for 48 hoursth without a charge. Isthn't that right, detective?"

Promptly, Mike returned with, "Yeah, I got it. I don't need you to tell me my job. You'll be charged. Let me see your hands."

"Why?" Atwood responded

"The woman who accused you of assaulting her is claiming that she bit you on the hand. The left hand. This would be a lot easier on both of us if you just show me your hands."

With a minor rolling of the eyes complete with a disrespectful half smirk, Craig decided to comply and held up both hands to his front. He held his hands up, knuckles facing the detective, elbows bent with his biceps parallel to the table. He displayed his hands in a limp fashion, head slightly cocked to the right, in an effort to be as defiant as possible while still complying in some way.

"I need you to turn your hands around and extend your fingers, please." the detective instructed. Mike saw no visible signs of bite marks anywhere on Atwood's hands.

Craig followed the detective's instructions and turned his hands around so his palms were facing forward. His hands were knotted in what appeared to be a painful manner, knuckles bent at different angles, almost as if he were suffering from a severe case of carpal tunnel syndrome or rheumatoid arthritis. The joints were red and swollen and the hands trembled as he held them in front of his face, a face that did not project an expression of pain, although Mike believed that it should.

Suddenly, small flashes of what appeared to be green lightning began to flicker and flash in between Craig's fingertips.

These electric beams resembled those seen in a novelty plasma globe; one of those glass orbs with a high-voltage electrode in the center that reacts when a conducting object, usually somebody's fingertips, touches the glass. These tiny sparks of lightning moved from fingertip to fingertip and radiated up and down in the space between Craig's fingers. The color started light green, but slowly progressed to blue, purple, and red, gradually transitioning from one color to the next. The reflection of these lights flickered in the grubby lenses of Craig's ugly glasses. Mike could smell a sharp electrical odor in the air as the colored filaments crackled and popped between the man's fingers.

Without warning, there was a bright flash of light and a loud pop in the room, as if someone had taken a picture with an old-fashioned camera. Simultaneous with the flash, Craig fully extended the fingers on both hands, spreading them to the maximum interval that the body would allow. The flickering lights ceased. Craig continued to spread the fingers apart with such force that the space between them began to crack and split, initially as if he had dry and irritated skin, but quickly progressing to a full blown tear. He maintained eye contact with Mike during this strange display, half smirk still on his face. Mike stared back, not sure what to make of what was going on. The webs of both of Craig's hands ripped apart with the gashes extending about half way down the palm. Blood flowed down both arms, dripped off the elbows, and began to pool on the table.

The fingers on each hand began to grow. One inch longer than normal. Two. Three. Continuing. The fingers maintained the same girth during their growth and the location of the knuckles on each finger was moving to remain proportional to the finger's slowly changing size. It almost appeared as if the fingers were stretching, as if they were constructed of baker's dough. As the fingers grew, the hands continued to spread apart and eventually the skin began peeling back exposing the bones and tendons beneath. The tendons were completely visible and moved as they should. The thumbs on each hand maintained their normal shape and size during the metamorphosis, however; the skin between the index finger and thumb on the right hand had torn so much that the thumb began to dangle from the rest of the hand, slightly oscillating in place, causing a small circle of steadily dripping blood to collect on the desk underneath. The fingers were now at their new maximum length, approximately three feet longer than normal. Craig's hands resembled two overturned rakes that had only four prongs, a standard type of rake that was in every garage that was used to collect leaves in the fall.

Mike had been frozen solid with disbelief by this time. He was not overcome by fear, yet, he was simply locked in position, mouth and eyes opened wide. From the tips of each elongated finger a black claw sprung forth. The blackness of the claws was so deep that they resembled small pieces of volcanic rock. They stretched to about four inches in length, some a little longer than others, some in pristine condition, some displaying nicks and scratches possibly from previous encounters. These claws were not an extension of Craig's fingernails, but had actually broken through the skin, directly at the tip. This caused more streams of blood to flow from the body that was once Craig's, flowing down each finger and joining the streams of blood that were already coming from the hands. The thing that was once Craig rolled its eyes skyward, as if looking at the ceiling, at the same time tilting its head back and opening its mouth. The head continued to lean backwards as the mouth opened wider and wider, eventually tearing the flesh at the corners of the mouth, enabling it to open even wider still. It almost resembled a snake that has the ability to detach its jaw in order to swallow large prey. At this point, the eyes were facing behind the body, in an upside down fashion, as the face was torn open at the midway point. Its glasses had fallen off and bounced on the floor, not breaking.

The blood that came from the mouth did not resemble any type of bleeding that was consistent with the human arterial system. This blood looked as if someone was pouring a bucket of red paint slowly onto the table from within the mouth of the creature. By now, Mike's breathing had become more rapid, his heart pounded violently within his chest. Despite the obvious danger in front of him, he remained locked in place. Possibly without the ability to move or possibly by choice. The tongue that rolled out of the mouth appeared to be reptilian, light pink in color, about a foot and a half long, an inch thick and it had a forked tip. It fell forward and made contact with the table, creating a meaty, slapping sound as it splashed in the blood that had pooled there. It didn't appear that the thing had purposely stuck out its tongue, it looked more like gravity had caused it to fall out of the open mouth. The splash had thrown a small amount of blood splatter on Mike's face, around the nose and mouth area, some of which had actually splashed into his mouth. Mike did not flinch.

The creature remained in this state for a few seconds, blood continuing to drip and pour, its chest continuing to raise and lower, indicating life, spitting small amounts of foamy blood from the hole in its face as it breathed. Once again, there was a flash and pop within the tiny room, at which time the Craig-thing had morphed into a mass of cockroaches. Each individual roach moved independently, however; together they constructed the shape and form of the Craig-thing. Some roaches were larger than others, some fell off, due to their inability to gain a secure foot-hold in their assigned area, scurrying across the floor after falling. They continuously moved and crawled across one another in an effort to maintain the shape. Roaches had piled themselves neatly, one on top of another, in order to complete the form of the individual fingers of the Craig-thing, which were still facing skyward as it continued to hold up its hands. These roach-fingers swayed back and forth as the roaches struggled to keep the towers erect. Mike could hear the individual clicks and hisses of each roach in the formation. He could clearly identify each individual antenna, as it twitched aimlessly about. His breathing had drastically increased pace, his skin became flushed and red hot, and the pains in his chest had continued to worsen.

The Craig-thing slowly began to raise its roach-head back to normal and closed its mouth, after sucking its tongue back inside. Mike could almost make out the features of the face that was once Craig's within the twitching and squirming roaches. The roach-head turned left and then right, pausing at the point of redirection, almost as if surveying the room. Finally, it centered its head, facing Mike. Mike watched in what was now a state of terror as the Craig-thing winked its *eye* and fell apart, scattering roaches everywhere within the small room. It had appeared as though a conductor somewhere had given the roach structure the command to relax, causing them to collapse in relief. Mike fell backward in his chair, unable to maintain any of his tough -guy detective composure any longer. His upper back made contact with the wall in a large thud as he clutched his chest in pain. Mike was going into cardiac arrest.

Chapter 75

BRIAN SAT TERRIFIED IN THE filthy lawn chair within the secluded teenage hangout in his neighborhood. The large letters spelling out the words: DO IT remained in the dirt by his feet, written in blood. The long hanging Spanish moss on the surrounding trees began to droop closer to the ground, extending slowly, causing the small, cleared area to appear darker than normal. The moss was beginning to look like someone's disgusting, matted hair as it seemed to multiply; each individual strain becoming more visible. Eventually, the stuff made contact with the ground, creating a complete 360 degree cocoon around the boy. The area almost resembled a complete dome of green, dirty curtains, totally isolated from the outside world. Brian was paralyzed with fear as he looked around this newly developed tomb; he could see no sunlight, no blue sky through the breaks in the leaves and moss, no view of the parking lot or the trail leading up to this hang out.

The knots in the trees surrounding Brian slowly transformed into eyes, merged within the surrounding bark. Each eye was a different size, consistent with whatever size the knot was. Some blinked, some did not. The eyes were each a different color, although brown seemed to be the most common one. Some looked fresh, as if it had a good night's sleep, while other's appeared bloodshot. Each eye was fixated on Brian, staring at him as he sat in the lawn chair. He could feel the pressure of their gaze, as they peered down on him from every direction. A cool breeze blew through the area, although the moss made no movement. One of the logs that kids used as a seat started to roll slightly, rocking back and forth with the breeze. This log appeared to be rotten, there were several areas within the side of it that were falling apart as if moved, riddled with termites and other outdoor critters.

*Kill her....kill her....go back to your shitty house and finish your job...*whispered inside the tiny dome in a haunting voice. These words didn't feel like they were inside Brian's mind, they seemed more like they were coming from somewhere inside this newly established cocoon of moss. The words started to stretch, little by little, and eventually morphed into a continuous hum. The hum got louder and louder until it was clearly recognizable as a buzz; a buzz so loud and powerful the trees shook. The whole area vibrated with the increasing buzzing sound, all the logs started to roll around.

A small army of wasps exited one of the rotten portions of the first log. Although out of season, these wasps were common yellow jackets; hundreds of them poured out of this log, causing the buzzing to get louder and more amplified within the enclosed space. The wasps immediately engulfed young Brian's body, stinging him virtually everywhere, causing him to break out of the terrified trance that had prevented him from moving earlier. Shortly after the initial assault, the wasps began to target specific areas of his body, starting with the eyes. Yellow jackets are not the types of wasps that lose their stinger when they use it, they can sting multiple times, which they did, unmercifully. Brian screamed as he twisted and swatted, trying to defend himself. His eyes were becoming so swollen that they remained shut. Several wasps were trying to gain access into his mouth, which he kept clamped shut. A few got the idea to crawl up his nose, stinging along the way.

Once Brian had fallen to the ground, losing all hope of defending himself from the bombardment, the wasps backed off. Some returned to the log, but most simply remained at a hover a few feet from where Brian lay, barely breathing. The *ravenous flock* of wasps lingered above the boy, almost seeming to be guarding him, preventing his escape, while awaiting orders. The buzzing had grown even louder as the hovering wasps began to assemble; they began to fuse together into what was at first a large ball, but eventually took shape. A human shape. The wasp ball first sprouted legs, so it could stand. No longer requiring their wings, the buzzing began to quiet itself, becoming fainter as the wasp thing began to complete its transformation. The disgusting, squirming pile of wasps had finished its rebirth and it now stood before Brian. The boy struggled to squint his swollen eyes in order to see what was happening. Craig Atwood squatted down next to Brian, so he could whisper gently into the boy's ears, "You better take care of bussssssinesssss, young man. You have no idea what I'm capable of." Atwood faded into thin air as Amanda Reyes pushed herself through the moss curtain and discovered her son lying unconscious in the dirt.

Chapter 76

THE TARANTULA STRUGGLED TO FREE itself from beneath the ice bucket where Doug had trapped it about an hour ago. He was once again in the bathroom, checking the worsening condition of his appearance in the mirror. Jessica had crawled back into the secret fort with the iPad and, for the time being, she seemed to be satisfied. Doug had warned her to not mess with the ice bucket; "it's got a big ugly spider under it" he had told her. She hated spiders, like most little girls. If he had simply said "don't mess with the bucket" surely her curious eleven year old mind would wonder why. By telling her the truth, Doug ensured that she'd obey.

Doug stared into his own bloodshot eyes in the mirror, gun back in place on the vanity, not spinning. The skin around the eyes was swollen and there were dark bags underneath. The itchy, burning feeling he had felt in his eyes yesterday had returned, but so far there were no visitors. His lips were so chapped they began to split in several areas. The corners of his mouth were dry and cracked. Doug's muscular physique was fading away. His ribs were in full view and his arms dangled like a pair of drained gas pumps.

He thought about calling Sam. He was wrong to treat her that way on the phone yesterday. If he got in touch with her perhaps she would meet them here, maybe he could get to the hospital and find out what's wrong with him, maybe get the medical attention he clearly needed. What he was doing was wrong. He knew that. Even though he was still unsure of what he actually *was* doing. The thought of making things right started to make him feel a little better. He hadn't gone too far yet. He could easily turn this around.

The vibration in the mirror returned, beginning in the center and extending out to the ends; almost in a wave pattern. The wave in the mirror rippled to the ends and then back to the center. It followed this pattern two more times before shattering. Glass particles and fragments showered the sink and floor. Tiny chunks of glass projectiles littered Doug's face and neck, causing slashes and gouges almost instantly. Some of the glass pieces were so fine, Doug was certain that he must've inhaled them. He brought his forearms up in front of his face in an effort to block some of the blast but it was ineffective. He wasn't fast enough.

The tiny bathroom felt as though it was becoming smaller with every beat of Doug's heart. The ceiling dropped. The walls closed in. The floor even seemed to rise. The faster Doug's heart beat; the faster the transformation of the room took place. The toilet, shower, and vanity moved with the walls, slowly removing what little free space Doug had remaining; causing him to have to squat to avoid the dropping ceiling. Glass slivers pierced the soles of his bare feet as he squatted lower and lower.

"Daddy!! Daddy, what broke?! Are you ok?" Jessica screamed into the door. Her interruption caused the shrinking room to pause for a moment. Doug struggled to hide his fear and pain as he answered "I'm ok, baby. The mirror just fell off the wall! Can you believe that?! I need to clean it up. I don't know what happened." Talking to his little girl calmed his nerves slightly, allowed him to focus a bit more clearly. "I'll call the front desk, let 'em know what happened. I'll be out in a second. I got cut a little." Comforting his little girl almost made him feel like a father again. It gave him strength.

"Are you ok?" she asked, clearly becoming upset.

"Yes baby, its fine. It's just a little cut. Hey, make sure you don't mess with that ice bucket," Doug said, grasping the toilet to help maintain his balance.

The room slowly began to return to its normal shape. The interior beams within the walls creaked and groaned as they were forced back to their original form. Soon, Doug was able to stand erect. He turned on the faucet and splashed himself with cold water, cleaning the new wounds on his face and neck, hopefully rinsing out any tiny shards of glass that were in there. As he rubbed his eyes gently with the heels of his hands, his familiar friend began whispering in his ear, *next time I'll crush your ass. You better do something. Now. You can't win. You will not beat me.* When Doug removed his hands and opened his eyes, he could see a pair of grey worms up close and personal. Although unable to focus on them because they were so close, Doug knew exactly what they were. He'd seen them before. The worms were back.

Chapter 77

PARAMEDICS ARRIVED ON SCENE AND made their initial assessment of Detective Christianson within minutes of his collapse. Officers are trained in all aspects of first responder duties, therefore two members of the force were able to perform CPR and get Mike's breathing back to normal just as the paramedics arrived. Mike was still nonresponsive, however; so he was evacuated to Memorial University Medical Center for further treatment and evaluation. Due to the fact that Mike had some type of heart condition, paramedics informed the Captain that he could check on his detective in the ICU in about an hour. Captain Garrison did not intend on waiting that long.

At some point during the confusion, Craig Atwood escaped. Nobody reported seeing him leave. The Captain examined the short footage of the interrogation tape multiple times and it appeared that as soon as Mike fell back grasping his chest, Atwood stood up, picked up his glasses off the floor, and walked out. Having ran out of the adjacent room looking for help, the Captain hadn't seen Atwood walk out until now, on the tape. The two officers performing CPR didn't see anyone but the detective on the floor. It was as if Atwood had vanished. This was extremely embarrassing for the members of the SCMPD. They'd never

Manifest

had a suspect simply walk through the front door, which is what
Atwood had apparently done.

Captain Garrison had checked with the department's security detail and the team currently on duty up front. None of
the station's security videos had any footage of Atwood, except
the views of when he was first brought in by Christianson and
Wright, images of the two men escorting the prisoner down the
hall in hand cuffs and placing him in the interrogation room. The
camera hadn't even caught Atwood walking out of that room.
The strange situation was becoming stranger by the minute. The
Captain couldn't think of a single route through this building that
didn't pass at least one camera, but somehow Atwood found one.
That was the only reasonable explanation. He gave the senior
man on duty a solid ass chewing and demanded that they search
the building. "If he didn't pass anyone in the front, he must still be
in here somewhere!! Find him!" the Captain demanded, although
he already believed that Atwood was long gone.

The more he thought about the way things were turning out,
the more the Captain was starting to believe Detective Christianson's theory about Craig Atwood. Something was up with
that guy. He had watched Mike have what looked like a heart
attack after saying only a few words to this Atwood and now he's
vanished. *He wouldn't be dumb enough to go back to his house,
would he?* the Captain thought. He surveyed the area to see who
he had available. Due to the action over the last day and a half,
pickings were slim in the bull pen. It didn't look like he had any
free detectives to task. He snatched up the first uniform he saw
walking by.

319

"Grab the paperwork they have out front on Craig Atwood. I need you and another Officer to head to this guy's house and see if he's there. He doesn't live far from here. Get over there ASAP. Detain on sight. Contact me directly when you have him. Understand?"

The Officer nodded in acknowledgement and moved out to follow the order he was given as Captain Garrison headed into his office to grab a few things before he headed out. As he was grabbing his coat and preparing to head to Memorial, a uniformed Officer intercepted him as he exited his office.

"Captain, this tape just got here for Detective Christianson. It's from the gas station across the street from the burn victim yesterday. I guess he requested they send it over," the young Officer said.

"Just set it on my desk, thanks," Captain Garrison answered as he walked out. There was no time. He'd have to check it out when he got back. All he could think of right now was the condition of his best detective. He had to check on the status of Detective Christianson.

Chapter 78

AFTER HEARING THE SOUND OF someone throwing up outside her door and then running out of her house, Amanda Reyes flung open her bedroom door. Weapon up and ready, she stepped over the pile of vomit and some other object she couldn't quite make out on the floor and walked into her son's room. She discovered the smashed Play Station along with the destroyed TV and game controller. As she kicked around the broken piece of novelty Atlanta Braves baseball bat to see what it was, she realized that her son was gone. She also realized what the other object in the hall was. It was the rest of the bat.

Amanda covered her mouth as she gasped, terrified at the fact that she almost shot her son. Her son had done this. She would have opened fire on anyone who entered her bedroom. She had no idea it was Brian, but based on the evidence in his room and the hallway, it was almost certainly him. *Why did he do this?* she thought. *Why did he destroy his TV and game?* At the risk of another potential accident, she returned her gun to its resting place between her mattress and box spring. Not noticing the contents of her son's vomit, she headed downstairs and out the open front door.

Everyone in the neighborhood knew about the teenager's secret hideout, therefore; it was no secret. Amanda had an idea where her son might go if he was upset, which he obviously was. They had fought before and he had gone to this little secluded area to be alone. Several times. She felt confident that she would fine him there. As she walked through the parking lot, Amanda thought of the best approach to this situation. She wanted to scream at him, for scaring her so much and for destroying the gift that his father had given him. He was much too old to be throwing tantrums like this, he needed to grateful for the gifts he received for his birthday and Christmas. Increasing her pace, she decided that it might not be such a good idea to blow up on him. Something set him off, he was upset about something more than his game, she believed. "Aggressive, angry parent" might not be the best approach to this situation.

As the trees that covered the teenage hangout came within view, Amanda started to run. She got to a point where she could see the clearing through breaks in the moss; she saw her son lying on the ground. Her run became a sprint as she crashed through the thick Spanish moss that was hanging over the area like a curtain. She broke through with both arms, shoving the vegetation to the side as she moved. Her son lie in the dirt next to an over turned lawn chair. Amanda lay on her side next to her boy, frantically yelling in his ear.

"Brian? Brian baby, can you hear me? C'mon baby, wake up..." Amanda said as tears flowed down her cheeks. Her sons eyes were swollen shut, making him look like a boxer after a tenth round knockout. Vomit and blood stained the boy's shirt. She saw and heard several wasps buzzing around the area. *Wasps? In January?* The poor woman was becoming more and more confused by the minute. *Why the hell would there be wasps in January?* She panicked, shook her boy by the shoulders and yelled again. "Wake up, Brian. Snap out of it! Wake up! Help!" she yelled out, "Help me!!" Gaining a bit of composure, Amanda pulled out her phone and mashed 911.

She did her best to calm down, hoping to be able to give clear and concise instructions to the emergency operator. "Please, my son needs an ambulance. He's not answering me. His face is swelled up and he won't wake up!!" she said through tears.

"Ma'am, is your son breathing?" the 911 dispatcher asked.

"Yes, I can feel him breathing. Barely, though. He's wheezing. He won't wake up. I think he was stung by wasps. There's wasps flying around here and his face is all swollen. It looks like bee stings. Please help..." Amanda answered.

Amanda went on to give the woman her address and directions to this little secluded hangout. She intended on running out to the parking lot so she could guide them in. The woman on the phone made her relax somewhat, assuring her that the ambulance would be there in minutes and for her to stay with her son, to continue to talk to and comfort him. She imagined that the woman on the phone was also a mother, based on her tone and the obvious concern she had in her voice.

Due to where the Reyes's lived, the ambulance would most likely bring Brian to Memorial University Medical Center. Amanda intended on riding with her son in the ambulance, there was no way in hell she was going to let him out of her sight. As the sound of approaching sirens increased, Amanda moved to an area where she could keep her eyes on the parking lot and her son at the same time.

Chapter 79

CAPTAIN GARRISON ARRIVED AT THE reception desk in the intensive care unit at Memorial University Medical Center a few minutes past 11:00 a.m. He leaned impatiently on the desk, searching for someone to help him. A woman he assumed was a nurse stepped out of a small room behind the desk.

"Miss, I'm Captain Ted Garrison. I'm looking for Detective Michael Christianson. He was brought..."

The nurse cut him off, "Yes sir, we've been expecting you. You can have a seat right there. The Doctor will be with you shortly."

Captain Garrison sat in one of the uncomfortable seats in the small waiting area as he was told. A few minutes had passed when a frantic, young Hispanic woman sat down in the seat across from him. She was clearly distraught, covered in dirt from her chest to her toes. She sobbed into her hands as she waited. He thought about trying to comfort her but then immediately thought against it. He was in no condition to be a shoulder to cry on. Instead, as the Captain waited, he decided to call Detective Wright to get a status report on his situation and tell him the news about his friend.

"Wright," Grant said as he answered his phone.

"Grant, it's Ted. How you looking?" the Captain asked.

"Wrapping things up. Looks like it's gonna take some time. There's not much to go on. No ID, no purse or anything. No witnesses. Straight up Jane Doe. Throat cut. Forensic guys are here. I'm getting ready to start interviewing people in the stores around here," Grant answered.

"Ok, keep me in the loop. I got bad news, Grant. Christianson had some kind of heart attack or something, I'm at Memorial, waiting on the doc. I'm not sure how bad it is yet."

"Jesus. Let me know what the doctor says."

"One more thing, Atwood got away. He must've slipped out in the confusion. I got a unit heading to his house. I don't know how this guy got away. I still don't get it."

"What the fuck, Captain? How hard is it to hang on to one guy?" Grant snapped, obviously pissed off.

"Grant..." Wright hung up on the Captain before he could finish making his point. He sighed and shook his head in frustration. He understood Detective Wright's disgruntlement, however; that gave him no right to be insubordinate. He rested his head on his hand as he closed his eyes for a minute.

"Captain?" the doctor said, causing the Captain to snap awake and stand to greet the man. "Well, good news, I guess. According to his EKG it looks like everything is normal. He had a good old fashion anxiety attack. A panic attack. That's all."

"A panic attack? Are you serious? I saw it. It looked a lot worse than a panic attack." the Captain said.

"Well sir, the signs and symptoms of the two can be very similar. The shortness of breath, chest pains, dizziness, all of those symptoms can occur in both heart attacks and anxiety attacks.

That's what makes it so dangerous, it's sometimes hard to tell the difference. You did the right thing, having him brought here. It's better to be safe than sorry, I'm sure you know that," the doctor said.

"Of course, I understand that. I just don't understand why Detective Christianson had a panic attack. He's not the type of guy that panics."

"You'd be surprised how often it happens to people you'd never expect. Anything can trigger it, stress, immediate danger, anything. It can add up and cause the anxiety attack to spontaneously occur, without warning. Has the detective been under much stress lately? Any more than normal, I mean?" the doctor asked.

"Yes, actually. The nature of the job is stressful itself, but the last couple of days have been rough. I'm sure you've seen it on the news." the Captain said.

"Yes, I have. It's been a crazy week. Its times like this I'm happy we have you guys out there doing your jobs. Thank you for everything you do, sir. I truly mean that"

"Well, we appreciate everything you folks do here too, doctor. So, what now? Can I see him?" the Captain asked.

"I plan on keeping him here overnight. For observation. You know, just as a precaution. He should be free to go sometime tomorrow morning. I'll take you back to see him now."

The doctor led Captain Garrison down the hall to Mike's room, where the detective sat upright in his hospital bed. The doctor departed the area once the Captain headed into the room. Mike looked better than the Captain expected. There were various heart monitoring devices around him, beeps and numbers flashed across multiple screens, things he'd have to ask about, which he'd forget anyway, so the Captain didn't bother asking. Mike was dressed in a standard hospital outfit, he sipped water from a straw as he greeted the Captain with a flick of his chin. "How you doing, sunshine?" the Captain said, wiggling Mike's big toe.

"I thought I was gonna fucking die. I can't believe he thinks it was a panic attack. That guy is nuts. That was a fucking heart attack. My chest was on fire. What'd you guys do with Atwood? I can't believe that shit. What the hell did you guys do with him?!" Mike said, starting to twitch around in the bed, showing his excitement.

"He took off. I don't know how the hell he got by everyone, but he did. I got people out looking for him." Captain Garrison reluctantly said.

"Are you fucking kidding?! That thing can't be out there. It's a fucking monster. Didn't you see it? Didn't you see what happened? Didn't you see what he did? What he was? Is? What he is? He's a fucking monster," Mike said, his excitement starting to turn into terror.

"I don't know what you mean. He lifted his hands to show you where the woman bit him and you fell back, grabbing your chest. That's it. What else is there?" the Captain asked.

Mike didn't make eye contact. He just stared straight ahead at the wall where the unused television was mounted. After a few seconds of awkward silence, Mike spoke, "Nothing, I guess."

He started to cough uncontrollably, causing him to kick his hospital blanket off and onto the floor. He felt something come up into his mouth and rattle around, something that was just jerked free from the excessive coughing. He couldn't tell exactly what it was, but he had an idea, as its protective, membranous hind wings bounced off the back of his teeth. Small antenna tickled the roof of his mouth while the thing walked around on his tongue. Making sure not to bite into it, he immediately swallowed whatever it was, thus ensuring that none of its fatty, white guts were squished inside his mouth.

"Nothing at all."

Chapter 80

THE SAME DOCTOR THAT HAD spoken to Captain Garrison about thirty minutes ago now spoke with Amanda Reyes. "Ma'am, were you aware that your son was allergic to wasps?"

"No, oh my God, is he ok? I didn't know," Amanda said to the doctor, fearing the worst.

"His breathing is starting to return to normal. The swelling has gone down some, but not much. I'm sure it will get better with time. He was administered a shot of epinephrine, that should help with all of his allergic reactions, but it's going to take time. He was stung over a hundred times, Ms. Reyes, he's lucky to be alive. I'm grateful that he was wearing jeans and tennis shoes, they provided a lot of protection, this could've been much worse. We're going to prescribe a few self-injectable doses of epinephrine for you to take home. He really shouldn't leave the house without it," the doctor explained.

"Oh my God, I had no idea he was allergic to anything. I don't even think he's ever been stung before. It's my fault, my God, it's my fault. I should've known," Amanda cried. "Why were there bees out in January? I don't understand."

"It's not your fault. You have nothing to be ashamed of. The only real way you could've known that your son was allergic *is* if he was stung. This could be a blessing in disguise. Now you know.

So you know, they weren't bees, they were wasps, ma'am. Yellow Jackets, to be precise. He had a few still under his shirt. As far as why they're out in January, I'm not an expert on wasps, by any means, but I know that the queen hibernates in the winter, usually in a tree stump or an old log, or something like that. Maybe the unseasonal weather we've had lately sped up the process, I really couldn't say. All the more reason to keep an epinephrine injector handy, can never be too sure."

"Yes, sir," Amanda said, "Can I go see him? When can he come home?"

"I'll take you to see him now, ma'am, but I want him to stay at least tonight. He's still unconscious, but everything seems to be returning to normal. I'm sure he'll be fine. He just needs his rest. We'll keep him here tonight, just to be sure," the doctor answered as he escorted Amanda to her son's room, two doors down from Detective Christianson's room.

Amanda's sobbing returned as she saw her son lying helpless in his hospital bed. The swelling in his face had only gone down slightly, it was still hard to recognize him. She sat next to him and took his hand. It broke her heart to see her boy like this. She knew he was in pain before this wasp attack, some kind of emotional pain that caused him to freak out and break everything in his room. No parent wants to see their child hurting; Amanda would go through a hundred years' worth of emotional distress so that her son wouldn't have to suffer five minutes. She knew that his childhood was rough, without a father, and she hated herself for keeping his father from him for so long. Amanda sobbed even harder at the thought of her actions before Brian's tenth birthday.

She honestly thought that he would be better off not knowing him; she really believed that. Her actions were not devious or deceitful, she did what she thought was right and in Brian's best interest at the time.

Brian inhaled deeply through his nose, held it for a fraction of a second, and pushed it out the same way. His breathing seemed to be completely back to normal now. That made Amanda smile a little. She would deal with whatever caused him to snap later. Right now, she was just grateful that he was alive and was apparently getting better. Amanda removed her phone from her pocket. She decided to call Brian's father. He had developed a relationship with his son over the past few years and he should know about this.

Chapter 81

DETECTIVE WRIGHT WATCHED AS JANE Doe headed to the medical examiner's office in the back of an ambulance with the coroner. Jane Doe had blonde hair, blue eyes, and appeared to be about 30 years old. Although the cause of death was clearly criminal homicide, the body would still go through a forensic autopsy, which could determine whether or not other factors needed to be considered. They would be able to determine the approximate time of death, confirm the fact that the body was obviously moved here, and if the presence of any chemicals or poisons were in the body at the time of death. They would also use the sexual assault forensic exam kit to ensure that any DNA or other forensic evidence is collected properly. The evidence technician and his team had completed their duties, collected everything they needed, and agreed with Grant that this was not the crime scene. Pictures and molds of foot prints and tire tracks near the dumpster were taken.

The dumpster where the poor woman was found was on Bay Street, which was an area that was full of continuous foot traffic, both night and day. Surely, someone saw something. Directly to the north of Bay Street, and about fifty feet below, was River Street. Dangerously steep stair cases connect the two streets at various locations. The Savannah River was just north of River Street and the street followed the curvature of the river itself. Both streets were considered to be a common party area; people would frequent the bars in this area on a nightly basis. The north side of Bay Street was riddled with trees covered in the standard hanging moss that is seen everywhere around here, therefore it is possible that the killer used the cover of darkness, which is increased by the trees, when he or she disposed of the body. The dumpster was in a partially secluded area, under trees, and up against a vacant building. There was minimal blood in the dumpster with the body, therefore it seemed to Detective Wright that she was killed nearby and moved here after she bled out. The murder scene had to be one of these establishments or perhaps one of the vacant buildings. It didn't make sense that someone would kill this woman in a private place and then dump her here in public. Based on what the woman was wearing, Wright thought that this was a case of a woman turning down a man at one of the bars or clubs right around here. Maybe he followed her out to her car, or perhaps attacked her in the bathroom, snuck out a back door. It was all speculation, there was really nothing to go on other than the body.

Detective Wright had interviewed employees at every bar, restaurant, and souvenir shop within a modified three block radius of where the body was found. He decided against walking down to River Street for now. There was no way someone hauled a body up those steep stairs without being seen. He entered and inspected the vacant buildings that were open, searching for signs of a struggle, blood, anything at all. Everything came up short. His interviews were all pretty much dead ends, nobody saw or heard anything. The murder and subsequent dumping of the body happened last night, Grant was sure of it. He'd worked enough cases in the past to come to this conclusion. He planned on talking to a few more people before heading back to the station. If anyone had seen anything they would've gone home by now. He would come back later tonight to talk to the employees that come on for third shift. Perhaps by then they would have a name on the victim. A headache was starting to penetrate his temples, Grant needed to get back to the office.

Chapter 82

MIKE CHRISTIANSON FLIPPED THROUGH THE seven channels that the hospital TV had to offer. Game shows and pointless day time talk bullshit were all he had to choose from. He shut the TV off and placed the tethered remote down on the little table that folded up from within the arm of the bed. After he scratched his head of messy hair, he took a hand full of his mane and used it to pull his head to the side in an effort to crack his stiff neck. No luck. He knew that if he could get it to crack, he'd feel better, maybe make his head ache go away. He was still trying to figure out what the hell had happened back at the station. Mike liked to believe that he had things under control; that he had a grasp on reality. He couldn't have imagined that, could he? The Captain obviously didn't see anything strange. There's no way in hell he imagined that thing he coughed up before. The thing he coughed up and then swallowed.

"Fuck that," Mike said out loud, refusing to acknowledge the fact that he coughed up a live cockroach about an hour ago. "There's no fucking way." He continued scratching his head forcefully and gradually he interlaced his hands behind his head and looked skyward. Staring at the dated popcorn ceiling in his tiny hospital room, he thought *what the fuck is happening to me?*

The toilet flushed in the bathroom connected to his room. The door to the bathroom was to his left, on the same wall that the bed was against, therefore; as much as he leaned and struggled, he couldn't see through the open door. *Did I fall asleep?* He thought. *Did someone slip in there while I was sleeping? There must be another way in there, I must share it with the guy next door.* Someone turned on the faucet and washed their hands under the running water. He heard the sound of paper towels being torn from a dispenser and the ruffling sound of someone drying their hands, followed by the sounds of crumbling paper being thrown into a trash can.

"You wanna know whasth happening to you, Mike? You really wanna know?" Craig Atwood said as he walked out of the bathroom and stood over the hospital bed. Mike could see his own reflection in Atwood's dingy glasses. "You didn't fall asthleep, either. There'sth no other way into that bathroom, you know that."

"What the fuck do you want?" Mike said, not really sure of what else to say.

"I want you to understand, Mike. I really do. I want you to know that I admire you, Mike," Atwood said.

"Stop calling me Mike. You don't know me."

"Michael Paul Christianson, born November 15th, 1958. You married your first wife, Christine, in 1982, two years after you joined the force. She left you in 1989. You were single for eleven years, then you married the whore. She left you in 2007. Am I pretty close? Should I keep going? You were promoted to detective in the summer of 1988, which added to your work load, which is why Christine left you. Pretty selfish of her if you ask me. Not sure why the whore left you, other than the fact that she's a whore. I had to lose the lisp, too, by the way. I know you liked mocking me, but I just couldn't take it anymore."

"Anyone could've found that information. You don't impress me," Mike said.

"About an hour ago you coughed up a live cockroach. You had to swallow it because you couldn't take the thought of crushing it in your mouth," Atwood said, leaning in closer as he said it.

Mike returned his focus to the ceiling and lay there silently, almost refusing to acknowledge anything Atwood said, or perhaps even ignoring his existence all together. This made Atwood chuckle through his closed lips, exhaling a grunt-like laugh through his nose.

"You're too stressed, Detective. You know that? Did you know that too much stress causes the body to shut down non-essential systems, including the immune system? So, people under excessive amounts of stress are more prone to disease and illnesses. They even say that stress causes ulcers. Crazy, huh? Chronic stress can even effect the human brain, basic functions like mood, memory, decision making, and all sorts of other things. You really need to relax, Mike."

"Fuck you," Mike said, while continuing to look at the ceiling.

"People under large amounts of undue stress are more susceptible to my powers. You have to know that. I can touch submissive people much easier than dominant ones. I mean, I can touch everyone, but the submissive ones usually give in, without a fight. Dominant ones require a little persuasion."

"What the fuck are you talking about?" Mike asked, finally turning his head towards Atwood, meeting his eyes.

"I mean I fucking own you. Can't you feel it, Detective?"

Chapter 83

CAPTAIN GARRISON INTERCEPTED DETECTIVE WRIGHT as soon as he walked back into the station. Grant was frustrated to see the Captain standing there as he walked in, almost like a parent waiting on a late teenager.

"Grant, I'm glad you're back. I want to show you something. C'mon," the Captain said to Detective Wright before he even made it through the door. *Christ, let me breathe,* Grant thought.

"Can I get a second to get through the door? What is it? I need to get this report started and then go see the medical examiner," Grant said, clearly having already lost his patience.

"It'll only take a second. It's about Atwood," Captain Garrison said, leading Grant down the hall to the small room that was connected to the interrogation room.

"That's Christianson's problem now. I have this fucking Jane Doe to worry about. Do you know how long that shit's gonna take? I don't have time for this. If you wanted me to fuck around with Atwood, you shouldn't have put me on Jane Doe," Grant snapped.

"Hey, you fucking relax, Detective. I'm sharing this information with you because Christianson is still in the hospital, until tomorrow. So stop your fucking whining. It will only take a second," the Captain said, finally attempting to put an end to Grant's insubordination.

Detective Wright said nothing. He just continued to follow the Captain with a pouty look on his face. This is the first time Grant had been blatantly disrespectful towards a superior. Captain Garrison figured that the Detective was just stressed out over the last two days of craziness, God knew he was. They weren't used to having this many acts of violence in such a short amount of time. The two men entered the little room, Captain Garrison sat in the room's only chair, which was in front of a medium sized folding table. On top of the table was the small monitor that was used to watch the various recordings from the interrogation room or any other tapes that are brought in. It was equipped with an old style VCR/DVD combination unit.

"Here's the tape from the BP station across the street from where David Spears torched his co-worker yesterday, check this out," Captain Garrison said as he inserted the tape.

The two men watched the grainy, black and white footage of the gas station's checkout counter. The camera angle was pointing downward on the clerk and customers from somewhere that appeared to be above the main entrance. Grant didn't pay much attention to the clerk, he was focused on Spears, or who he thought was Spears, as he entered, gathered a few items, paid for them and left. That's when Grant noticed that the clerk was Atwood.

"You see who that is?" the Captain said, "Didn't you say he was a communications consultant, or some shit?"

"So what? You brought me in here to tell me that someone lied to police about their fucking job? Holy shit, call the fucking FBI, we're gonna need help with this one!" Grant said, obviously mocking the Captain, who was getting tired of the deliberate bad attitude.

"That's not all," the Captain said. He removed the tape of the BP gas station and held up a disc. "This is footage of WTOC covering the school shooting yesterday at Mercer."

He inserted the DVD and pressed play. This picture was much clearer than the gas station security tape, it was also in color. A news reporter spoke into the camera using the school and a large crowd of people as a backdrop. Grant could see the ambulances outside and the SWAT team members hanging around. The attractive female reporter spoke of a woman being detained and the fact that there are at least four dead, although no names have been released. She started to say something about a press release being scheduled in the future when the Captain cut her off by hitting the pause button.

The Captain stood up, leaned forward onto the table, and pressed his chubby finger to the screen. "Right there, see him? There goes Craig Atwood. Right there."

Grant squinted as he also leaned closer to the screen. After a few seconds of looking at random faces, he found him. Standing amongst the crowd of parents, almost looking as though he belonged, was none other than Craig Atwood.

"Again Captain, So what? Are you telling me that it's not possible to drive from that BP on Abercorn to Mercer Middle School? Is that what you're saying? Fucking Christianson did it. What are you saying? Why are you wasting my fucking time? I have work to do!" Grant started to walk out of the room when the Captain stopped him.

"Wait! Get back here, Detective. I'm getting sick of your attitude. That's not all..."

Chapter 84

"I own you," Craig reiterated.

"Fuck you," Mike said, starting to feel the opening stages of a tension headache. His temples throbbed, the bright fluorescent lights of his tiny hospital room began to pierce his skull.

"Let me explain something to you, when a human dies, the bond between the spirit and the physical body is severed. The human spirit is comprised of mostly raw energy, it does whatever the hell you humans think it does after it breaks free from the physical half, I don't know what it does, that's not my concern. I'm only interested in it right before it moves on, and then I'm only interested in some of it. I have a unique ability to harness some of that energy. I guess you could say I feed on it. I need it."

Mike just stared at the ceiling, no longer wanting to listen to the blathering psychopath hovering over his hospital bed. The pain in his head increased with every tick of the wall clock's second hand. The repeat pounding of the clock was unbearable, the effect it was having on Mike was becoming physically evident, as he squirmed and twitched within the bed.

"I'm not a psychopath, Detective. I just have a gift, a gift which I am required to use to survive. Now, I can't take some of every human spirit, shit, that would make things so much easier! No, I can only withdraw from a spirit that was severed as a result of one of my suggestions. See, Mike, I have another talent. A talent that's kept me going for so many years that I've lost count. Do you want to know what it is, Detective? Do you?"

Atwood paced around Mike's bed, almost taunting him with the information. Mike groaned with every tick of the clock, his head feeling like it would explode from the pressure.

"I have the ability to plant suggestions in the human sub-conscious, I guess you could call them subliminal messages. I call them triggers. I plant several little triggers within the human brain. Now, I can't control when one of my subjects pulls their trigger, but I can assure you, they *will* pull it. Eventually something makes them pull it. Something makes them snap. There's people I've touched decades ago that still haven't pulled it, but I guarantee, someday they will. Once they do, I own them. They're mine. Once they've pulled their trigger, I am forever connected to these people, they've been touched with my essence and they owe me for that. You'll see, Mike. Sometimes they need a little encouragement to do their duty, but they'll get to it, or they'll die trying. Just like you. You're mine, old friend."

Mike finally broke his silence and turned his head to face Atwood. He fought through the burning pain behind his eyes when he opened his mouth to speak, able to only sputter out a few words, "The plane? Why was it the plane?" Mike grunted.

"Close, Detective. Very close. You disappoint me, though. I thought you were better than this. It's not the plane, it's motion in general. I am only able to plant my essence if both the human and I are in motion. The faster we move, the deeper and more effective the trigger is. There was a time that I had to walk next to people, close to them. Very close, and I found that when I did it while walking, sometimes the suggestions I planted were weak. If the trigger is weak, then the amount of sustenance I get when my subject kills is also weak. I was burning through energy faster than I could harvest it. There were times I thought I might die."

Mike vibrated in his bed, his jaw clenched so tight his teeth might shatter. His face was red and flushed, sweat beading on his forehead and cheeks. A single trickle of blood escaped his left nostril and wedged itself between his lips. Vomit brewed deep within his insides. "Horseback was pretty tough, too. Have you ever tried to ride along someone, I mean right next to them, and then try to concentrate enough to connect your mind to their subconscious? I thought not. It's fucking hard. Then, then one day there was an invention called "the train." That was the greatest day of my life; when I was able to sit back, relax, and infect as many subjects as I wanted while we steamed across the countryside. I found that the faster I went, the more energy I got from the human spirit when it is ripped from the body. Well, not more energy, just better quality energy. Some of my subjects kill multiple times, every time they kill because of my trigger, I get some energy. It's made me basically immortal, my friend, and it's only getting better."

Mike forced out a question through his closed teeth, barely squeezing the words past his bloody lips, "Why are you telling me this?"

"I told you, I admire you. I admire your character. I've learned many things during my time on this planet. People who have strength of character are usually reluctant to follow through with their duties. They pull the trigger fine, but once they do, they tend to drag their feet in paying me what's owed. When they do pay up, when they finally kill, which they most certainly will, the quality of energy is phenomenal. Weak, submissive people? Well, the juice I get from them is just like them, weak. Strong people help me to harvest strong energy. It's funny, you'd think that when I infect someone that is already prone to violence and murder, I'd get a big payout. Well, it's the other way around. I guess because they were going to do it anyway, whether I blessed them or not. But, I digress, you had a question, didn't you? Well, I'm telling you this, Mike, because in my five centuries on this planet, you are the first and only person to ever knock on my door. You found me. Somehow, you found me. You have strength of character, you have determination, you care about your fellow man. These qualities are going to make your kills payoff tenfold. Your's and your big headed friend's."

Chapter 85

"GET TO THE FUCKING POINT, Captain. You're wasting my time," Detective Wright said as he hovered over the Captain's shoulder.

Captain Garrison ignored Grant's disrespectful tone as he removed a VHS tape from a cardboard sleeve. He inserted the tape into the VRC/DVD combination unit connected to the tiny TV and pressed play. A few seconds of static filled the screen and was eventually replaced by an image of Craig Atwood seated peacefully at the table in the interrogation room, hands crossed and resting on the table. A date/time stamp was displayed in the corner of the screen.

Mike walked into the room and sat in the chair opposite The two began speaking. Grant rolled his eyes, knowing what was about to happen since he saw this live a few hours ago. Mike announced the date and time and the purpose of the interview. Atwood said something about how long he could be held without a charge, Mike said something back, and then Mike told him to hold up his hands. Grant tapped his foot like an impatient teacher waiting for a tardy student. Atwood held his hands up, turned them around and spread his fingers, at which time Mike fell back in his chair, clutching his chest. As soon as Mike's back made contact with the floor, Atwood stood up, picked his glasses up off the floor, and walked through the door.

"Yeah, I've seen this. I saw it live. What's your point, Captain?" Grant said, struggling to hold back his brewing anger.

"The glasses, look at his glasses," Captain Garrison said, as he rewound the tape. He was nearly pressing his face to the screen again. He rewound the tape to the point where Mike started to fall back, pausing it just as Mike started to bring his hands up to his chest.

"Look. Look at Atwood. Where are his glasses? Did you see him take them off? He had them on when the tape started, where are they now? They're on the floor. That's what he picked up before he walked out. When did they end up on the floor behind him?"

Grant had his focus on Mike at this point in the tape, as he fell back. He hadn't even been looking at Atwood. The Captain almost had his nose touching the screen by now.

"Here, I'll rewind it again. Pay attention to Atwood. Watch his face, his glasses. They just fade away. Doesn't make any sense." the Captain said as he rewound all the way back to the beginning. "Now, don't even look at Mike. Look at Atwood."

Grant got closer, squatting down to get a better look, almost placing his head right next to the Captains. He watched without blinking as the poor quality video rolled on. Sure enough, a fragment of a second before Mike started to fall, Atwood's glasses just faded away. Grant's jaw dropped.

"I don't get it," Captain Garrison said, staring at the screen, reaching up to rewind it again. "I've never seen anything like this. I don't know if the tape skipped or something, there's really no way we could've missed that. I'm going to head back to Memorial. I think we..."

Detective Wright fired a controlled pair into the back of the Captains head, killing him instantly. Both rounds entered his head above the right ear and exited his face through the eyes and nose, covering the table and monitor with blood, brain, and skull. One round destroyed the monitor after it left the Captain. Grant let out a sigh of relief, as if he'd finally taken care of some business that was long overdue. He started to holster his weapon, but paused halfway. He decided that it might be best to keep it out as he was certainly going to be needing it soon.

The first man to enter the viewing room took two rounds to the chest, center mass. Grant was an excellent close-quarters marksman and he didn't plan on going down without a fight. He had made an immediate assessment of where to place his rounds on this target and since the man wore a white dress shirt, Grant fired at the largest possible spot on the target, which is center mass, directly at the chest. He quickly went through the steps of target acquisition and determined that there was no bulge of body armor under the man's dress shirt and a pair to the chest should do it. Eventually, people would start to arrive wearing body armor and therefore; he would have to change his sight picture to the incapacitating zone, which is below the eyes and above the mouth. Accountability of ammunition was key. His revolver now held four rounds and he had two full speed-loaders on his belt, totaling another twelve rounds. Rapid re-loading was vital if he was going to survive. He may even have to secure the weapon of one of his fallen teammates, as they would eventually start piling up.

Using the Captain's fat dead body as cover, Grant knelt in a more stable firing position and prepared to defend himself from the wave of his fellow law enforcement personnel, who were currently assembling in the hallway. He traced the barrel of his service revolver in the imaginary path that the men who entered the room would most likely take. Grant knew their tactics, he'd trained with them before, he knew that the first man would go left, as that was the path of least resistance for the layout of this particular room. He rehearsed firing a single shot at the number one man, and a controlled pair into the number two man. These shots would need to be high as these targets will have donned body armor by now. After a few dry runs, Grant placed his sight alignment back to his twelve o'clock direction and waited for the inevitable tactical assault that was most certainly on its way.

Chapter 86

"DADDY? DADDY, ARE YOU OK?" a terrified young Jessica said to the bathroom door. She'd been saying it for nearly ten minutes now, which wasn't a very long time, but to her it seemed like an eternity. The ice bucket a few feet behind her now had the hotel's Bible and phone book resting on top of it. She started hearing a pinging noise coming from under it about an hour ago, as if the spider was jumping, trying to escape, which is why she decided to weigh the bucket down. "Dad? Do you have the charger for the iPad?" she added.

Finally, a faint response came from the bathroom. "It's in the car, baby. You can go get it. Take my keys and don't forget to take the little hotel room card next to my wallet, by the TV. You'll need it to get back in," Doug's words were weak and raspy.

"Can you get it?" Jessica said, relieved that her father finally answered. She didn't want to go outside alone.

"No, baby. I can't. I'm really sick now. You'll be fine. Just don't forget the card so you can get back in. Write down our room number so you don't forget," Doug answered.

"Ok, daddy," Jessica said as she reluctantly got dressed and headed out to the parking lot to get the charger.

Doug sat on the bathroom floor, in the space between the toilet and the tub. He needed to be close to the toilet, as his vomit had been coming more frequently now, and with little or no warning. Blood covered the rim of the open bowl, some of which was smeared over the edge and down the sides. Doug was completely naked as he sat, clutching his knees against his chest. He looked like a completely different person. His size had actually reduced by what looked like at least twenty pounds. His skin was littered with random sores and bruises, along with several open cuts from the mirror that shattered into his face earlier.

He stopped cleaning up the worms that had been coming out of his body, he hadn't been able to keep up. Bloody worms wriggled and twitched on his chest, legs, and the surrounding floor. Some had been crushed accidently as he shifted his position to get more comfortable. He basically stopped caring, as another worm fell from his nose, almost as if he were some type of creepy dispenser. Another began to free itself from one of the cuts on his face, Doug pinched it between his thumb and index finger and helped with the extraction. He pulled it slowly from his face and dropped it in the toilet, soon it would be greeted by more worms, as he felt another batch brewing in his stomach.

Heat engulfed his body, every muscle flexed as he puked another load of bloody worms into the toilet. He grasped the sides of the cool bowl, squeezing with every push of vomit. The sores from the spider bites on his lower back were pointed skyward now, as he hunched over the toilet. Worms seemed to exit the wounds easily, sliding themselves out, falling to freedom. The sweat accumulating on Doug's body dripped freely into the bowl and on the floor. Once the latest batch of worms had been evacuated, he placed his temple against the side of the bowl, finding a bit of comfort in its cool temperature.

Jessica reentered the room about seven minutes after she left, out of breath. She returned her dad's car keys and hotel room card back where she found them and reported to the bathroom door. She made sure to keep her distance from the over turned ice bucket and the little prisoner trapped therein. She planned on adding a few more objects to the Bible and phone book as soon as she spoke to her father.

"Daddy, I have it. Are you ok? Should we call mommy?" the frightened little girl said, becoming a pro at talking to a door. She was proud of herself for going to the car alone.

"No, baby. We don't need to call your mom. I'll be ok. Just watch some more movies. I'll be out soon," Doug answered.

Jessica said nothing. She went over to the small desk next to the dresser where the TV was and grabbed a small lamp. Unplugging it, she took it over to the trapped spider and placed it gently on top of the phonebook, adding to the weight which held the spider captive. The young girl had noticed the phone on the desk when she got the lamp. There were instructions next to the phone, telling her to dial 9 to get an outside line, or dial o to get the front desk. She wished she had her phone, if she had her phone she could just say "MOM" and the phone would call her mom's cell. Jessica didn't remember her mom's number, she never needed to dial it. Tears built up in the little girls eyes as she crawled back into her fort. She was frightened for her sick father, she was confused about why she wasn't in school, and she was starting to miss her mother and Jeff.

Chapter 87

GRANT DROPPED THE NEXT TWO intruders almost exactly as he had rehearsed, doing it with only two rounds instead of three. They didn't even get a shot off. Three rounds left. Plus the twelve on his hip. He resisted the temptation to move forward and secure one of their guns. Not yet. The second wave could come at any time. He had to make these three rounds count. Then he could reload, maybe even grab one of those guns. Adrenaline flowed through Grant's body like a surge of electricity, his heart throbbed within his chest. He had total control of this moment and his aim would continue to be true, regardless of what came through the door next. One man was still alive, Grant could hear him struggling to breathe. The man would eventually bleed out, therefore he decided to save the round.

Any connection Grant had with the outside world was gone, all that remained was this tiny room in which he was cornered. Nothing else mattered. He had no wife. He had no friend named Mike Christianson in a hospital bed across town. There was no murder victim with the medical examiner. There were only potential targets outside the room, and that was all. He could hear them, rustling about, running up and down halls, probably evacuating non-essential personnel. A SWAT team was probably outside, maybe even the same one from yesterday. They would be here soon, Grant started to accept his fate. They would use some type of dynamic entry technique, leading with a flash-bang or concussion grenade. Maybe tear gas, if they meant to take him alive, which they probably didn't. He had killed four officers, one of which was the Captain of this precinct; there was no way in hell he was coming out of this alive.

The officer that was struggling to breathe finally faded away, ending with several coughs and a few horrible gurgling sounds. Grant lowered himself into a prone firing position, laying directly on the Captain's body. He kept his gun oriented on the door, but with his left hand he removed his wallet from his coat's interior pocket. Fumbling through the wallet with his one free hand, Grant removed a picture of his wife and stared at it for a few moments, before resting it next to him on the Captain's chest. Tears formed in his eyes as the sight of his beautiful wife had brought new perspective to the situation. Maybe it didn't have to end this way. If he turned himself in perhaps his actions could be attributed to stress, maybe he could get a light sentence or maybe he could even plead insanity. He had the tape, the tape with Craig Atwood's magical disappearing glasses. Mike would back his story, something was suspicious about Atwood anyway, he poisoned Grant's mind somehow.

Grant's thoughts were interrupted with the explosion of a concussion grenade. He was hit with an immediate blast of pressure and heat, causing instant disorientation. The one way mirror looking into the interrogation room shattered, causing Grant to lower his head, placing it flush against the corpse he lay on. The room filled with dust particles and tiny fragments of the shattered mirror, causing Grant to cough as he breathed in high levels of both. He took one last look at his wife's picture, which had fallen off the Captain when the grenade went off. Leaving his revolver on the floor, he stood and raised his hands, coughing up the crud he had been inhaling, as he waited to be apprehended.

Two members from SCMPD SWAT Team 3 simultaneously entered the tiny room and stopped short, their path blocked by three dead officers. The men assumed sectors of fire, one covering each half of the room, ensuring that the only target was the one standing before them with his hands up. Dust was beginning to settle as the two operators continued to survey the room, assessing the situation. Grant remained calm, still frozen in the center of the room, with the intention of surrendering, the dead Captain lying by his feet next to his service revolver and the photo of his wife. Struggling to breathe through the dust particles still lingering, he coughed, breaking the silence. One of the operators fired two quick rounds, both of which penetrated Detective Wright's chest, center mass, and exited in between his shoulder blades, together leaving a six-inch-wide exit wound. Grant's body fell immediately, having been voided of life, and now resting peacefully on top of Captain Garrison. The operator who did not fire moved forward, secured Detective Wright's revolver, and fired a single round into the door frame of the room's only entrance. He then rested it gently in Grant's right hand. The man spoke into his radio, "We got him, it's clear."

Chapter 88

CRAIG ATWOOD INHALED THROUGH HIS nose, it was a deep, long breath, one that he held for an equally long time. He exhaled through his mouth, he then followed this ritual a few more times, as he stood over Mike's hospital bed.

"Now you know why I gave that woman your card, so you'd pick me up and not some random cop. Your friend was just a bonus. He's gone, by the way." Atwood said, "He paid me what he owed, plus a few more. For that, I am eternally grateful. Literally." He laughed at his clever choice of words. Mike had vomited all over himself and the hospital bed a few minutes ago, the cockroaches that spewed forth had been walking all over the sheets, tracking tiny little bloody footprints everywhere. His head felt like it would burst, the throbbing continued, feeling as though there was no relief in sight. The puking had not caused his nausea to fade, as it sometimes does for people. If anything, it was worse now than before he threw up.

"Detective Wright killed four people and then some fancy cops killed him. They looked like knights in black armor. Ah, I love when someone like you and your friend pull your trigger and then follow through, when you take your time and I have to intervene, it frustrates me. The last thing you want to do is frustrate me, Mike. It's just better to just go ahead and get it over with. Sometimes people kill themselves, and to be honest, I'll settle for that. I'm able to harvest the energy of any spirit that is torn from the body as a result of my implant, even if it's the subject themselves. The quality of the energy is weak when that happens, though, I don't prefer it. So, make sure you kill someone else, and not yourself, ok, buddy? Kill several people, the more the better. You can kill yourself after, if you want."

Mike said nothing. He had to get this thing out of his room. He had to call the precinct, see if what Atwood was saying was true. Then, he had to get out of this hospital. The walls felt like they were closing in on the detective. His brain swelled in his skull, he could feel the pressure increasing. The next batch of vomit was forming in his stomach, he could actually feel the new roaches walking around inside of him.

"I need to get out of here," Mike finally said, "If I'm going to do anything, I can't do it in here, can I? Well, I could, but my weapon is back at the station. I'll need it if I'm going to do anything."

"Do you think I'm fucking stupid, detective? Are you trying to use reverse psychology on me?" Craig asked. The next words Craig said were not out loud. He transmitted them directly into Mike's pulsing mind. *You're going to do this, Mike. You're going to do your duty or I will never stop, you'll think that your mind is going to burst you'll think that bugs are everywhere your head will swell until you put a bullet through it don't fuck this up fucker....*

An enormous pop flashed in the room, similar to the one back in the interrogation room, it filled the room with a quick burst of bright light. Craig Atwood vanished, with him vanished the pain in Mike's head and the sensation of cockroaches in his gut. Unfortunately, the bloody roaches on the bed were still there, hiding from the light within the folds and crevasses of the wrinkled sheet. He knew he had to get rid of this mess. The doctor would surely try to keep him here longer if he saw this, not that Mike was planning on following proper hospital discharge procedures anyway, but if the doctor walked in right now, there'd be a problem.

Mike crawled out of the bed, secured the corners of the bloody, cockroach covered sheet, and brought them together, tying a secure knot. He threw the bundle on the floor, stomped on it a few times, hearing and feeling the roaches crunch under his bare feet, sounding like someone crushing fortune cookies. He slid the bloody roach bundle under the hospital bed, secured his clothes off the nearby chair, and started to come out of his hospital gown. He changed faster than superman in a phone booth and threw the gown under the bed as well. He stuck his phone, badge, and his wallet back into his pockets. Mike turned on the light in the bathroom then closed the door, in hopes that if anyone came in they'd think he was in there. He was starting to feel significantly better, head ache and nausea almost completely gone, but he was still far from normal. He walked confidently through the door, past the empty reception area, where the woman was apparently busy in the back room. Mike made it to the elevator without incident. The daring escape from the hospital was much easier than Mike had expected. He called the station as soon as he was outside.

"This is Christianson, what's going on over there?" Mike said, before the person on the other end had a chance to say anything.

A frantic, young officer struggled to put words together, "Detective Christianson? There's been a shooting, it's D-D-Detective

Wright. He shot the Captain. He killed him. He fucking killed him. H-H-He killed Detective Anderson, and Officers Copeland and Fitzgerald. SWAT just killed him. It's a fucking mess here. I don't und-"

Mike hung up on him and screamed into the Memorial University Medical Center's parking lot. Several concerned citizens looked towards the detective as he took to the street at a quick pace, running toward the precinct.

Chapter 89

Two ambulances were joining the one that was already idling outside SCMPD as Mike ran up. He had run less than a mile before deciding to step in front of a vehicle, holding his badge up. The fact that he was still a little lightheaded and disoriented from his vomiting made him decide against commandeering the vehicle, he simply got in the passenger side of the blue sedan and insisted that the driver take him to SCMPD HQ. The gentleman dropped him at an intersection a tenth of a mile away and Mike ran the rest of the distance.

"What's the status?" Mike said, out of breath, to the first uniform he saw.

"I thought you were in the hospital?" the young officer asked.

"Fucking answer me!" Mike snapped.

Another detective walked up, someone that Mike knew. It was Detective Hogan. He placed his hand affectionately on Mike's shoulder.

"Bill," Mike said, "What happened? Was it Grant? What the fuck did he do?"

"He lost it, Mike. I don't know what happened. He killed Ted," Detective Hogan said, fighting his emotions. "He killed Justin. Plus two officers. Copeland and Fitzgerald. SWAT just took him out before he could do anymore fucking damage."

The building had been evacuated, people that worked inside were assembled in the parking lot, comforting one another. It was truly a devastating sequence of events that had rocked this community over the last two days. The school shooting yesterday followed by the assault at the precinct today, by one of their own, was more brutality than this area had seen in decades, not to mention all of the other random acts of violence. The stress of today's events was clearly displayed on the faces of everyone involved.

"I didn't know Wright that well," Detective Hogan continued, "but I never thought he was capable of anything like this."

Mike shrugged his shoulders. He knew the truth. He knew that Grant's mind was violated by something that isn't human, something that corrupted his friend and forced him to commit these horrible murders. Mike wasn't ready to share that theory with anyone yet, he would not be taken seriously, not yet anyway. The bodies of all five victims were carried away and everyone was allowed back into the precinct. People filed into the building resembling lifeless drones, marching in, one behind the other. Morale had hit an all-time low.

Lieutenant Fred Brannon, acting Captain, called an impromptu meeting of all available detectives. The meeting was to begin in one hour, all off duty personnel were called in, even those who had just been on 24 hour duty. Mike had no intention of going to this meeting, as he sat in the conference room, where he and Grant had created their flow chart on the dry erase board. The various lists and rosters the two had created still lay scattered everywhere, the seat Grant had sat in rested a few feet from the table, still in place from the last time he sat there. Mike started to slowly gather the items on the table, placing them together in a large folder. He threw a half cup full of cold coffee at the dry erase board as he walked out.

Mike grabbed an empty box from the supply room and gathered a few more items from his desk, including his laptop. He threw the objects in the box in frustration, nearly breaking some of them. He made no eye contact and talked to no one as he headed towards the exit.

"Make sure you're at my meeting, Detective," the young Lieutenant said to Mike.

"I had a fucking heart attack a few hours ago and I escaped the hospital to run down here. I'm not going to your fucking meeting. I'm going home," Mike said. He continued out of the building and into the parking lot, not looking back.

Chapter 90

SGT HOLLOWAY ENSURED THAT HE was the one that secured the box that had been tampered with when helping the others load up the unused ordnance. They had only gone through about half the C4 during today's training, therefore; the rest was to be turned in, along with the remaining det cord, fuse igniters, and anything else that was unused. The Soldiers from the Ammo Supply Point had arrived at 1345 and SGT Holloway led a detail of Soldiers assigned to help load the truck. He took care in making sure that he was the one that handled the box that he had taken four blocks of C4 from earlier this morning. The size and weight of the box were consistent with the others, but he had used dirt to make up the space lost when he took the C4; dirt would shake. He had to be the one to get that box. Anyone else would notice the difference.

SFC Johnson had everyone on the bus and heading back to the Company area by 1330, so they could get cleaned up and ready for the Battalion Awards Ceremony, which was still scheduled for 1600 this afternoon. All that remained on the range were Holloway, Brunick, and four other Soldiers who were helping load the ASP truck. The Soldiers that worked the ASP were also there, as well as a gentleman from the installation's range control detachment, who was there to make sure the unit didn't leave anything behind and that everything was left clean and in working order. Once the shed was free of all explosives and supplies, SGT Holloway secured his assault pack and threw it in the cab of the Humvee.

The two Soldiers from the ASP checked items off the receipt in haste, after all, they were in this Battalion as well, therefore; they also had to get ready for this big ceremony. Once they were satisfied, they gave Brunick a copy of the turn in document and drove away, followed by the gentleman from range control, who had cleared the unit of the responsibility of the range. Holloway and Brunick allowed the detail to mount the back of the vehicle, and they departed the range and headed back to the Company area to join the others in preparing for the ceremony, although Holloway had no intention of being there. He had much more important plans.

The two Non Commissioned Officers dropped the detail off at the Company and headed to the motor pool to return the vehicle to its proper storage area. Seth made sure he handled his assault pack with care, as to not lose any of his precious supplies. He wasn't concerned with being too rough with it; it took a combination of heat and pressure to cause C4 to ignite. He could throw his bag around all he wanted, it would be perfectly safe. After securing the truck in its assigned spot, the two men walked the quarter mile back to the Company. They arrived in the parking lot within ten minutes.

Stopping by his truck, Seth said to Brunick, "You go ahead, Sergeant. I'll catch up, I have to make a phone call."

Brunick gave him some random response, Seth wasn't even listening; he was focused on the task at hand. He watched as Brunick hustled through the parking lot, taking care not to leave too quickly. Once Brunick was no longer in sight, Seth jumped in his truck and headed for the gate. He needed to make one stop before he went to the DMV.

Seth pulled into the Walmart parking lot on highway 84 within minutes of leaving the installation. He left his bag in the cab of his truck, there was no need to haul it around the store. He headed inside and, after grabbing a wagon, went straight to the home improvement section, walking at a brisk pace. Seth was starting to get excited about completing his task; doing his duty. He found the aisle that held nails, screws, washers, nuts, and other packages of random hardware. He grabbed a few packages of each and threw them in his wagon. He rocked his wagon back on two wheels, quickly changing directions, and headed to the grocery section of this monster of a store.

He found the aisle that contained coffee rather quickly. *Plastic? No, plastic won't work,* he thought as he surveyed his choices. *Dammit, they're plastic!* Seth was starting to get flustered as he shuffled through the choices of cans, all of which were plastic. Finally, all the way at the end of the aisle and at the bottom, he found some metal cans. He secured four 11 oz. cans of a type of coffee he'd never heard of and threw them in his wagon. Before heading to check out, Seth decided to get a pre-made sandwich at the deli, along with a giant jug of ice tea. It was going to be a long night, he'd need something. He paid and left.

It was close to 1430 when Seth pulled into the DMV parking lot on Airport road. The parking lot was packed and Seth could again see the end of the line through the front door windows. He finally found a spot all the way in the rear of the parking lot, where he backed in his truck, parking in a way that hopefully would expedite his escape tomorrow morning. He decided to leave the coffee and projectiles in the truck, he didn't have room in his assault pack right now anyway.

A Soldier in uniform carrying a full assault pack on their back is not an uncommon sight near a Military installation. Walking through the parking lot towards the entrance, Seth knew that he could move freely about the DMV and nobody would wonder why he had a full pack on his back. He entered the DMV and went around the line to the pamphlets off to the right. After securing one of the pamphlets, he held it in front of his face, as if inspecting it. His eyes traced over it, allowing him to conduct a visual recon of his objective. He saw that there were cameras mounted in the two far corners of the large area. *Fuck*, he hadn't noticed those yesterday. If it was a live feed being monitored somewhere, he might run into a problem. A recording would be irrelevant, since any tape would surely be destroyed tomorrow. He would have to wait and see.

He traced his eyes across the workers, today only two clerks worked the eight stations. One of the clerks was his dear friend Claudia, the woman that lacked any type of customer service skills whatsoever. Claudia, the fat, bloated bitch that lacked general conversational etiquette, such as "good morning" and "have a nice day" or even "how may I help you." He could see her across the room, blank idiotic look on her face. *This was going to be fun. I hope she works tomorrow*, Seth thought, as he entered the restroom and locked the door.

Chapter 91

SAM ARKENSON TRIED CALLING DOUG from inside her mother's tiny kitchen and, once again, it went straight to voicemail. She and Martha had decided to stay another night here with Sam's mom; neither had to work tomorrow, and Sam still had to figure out a way to tell her mother that her son-in-law was dead. She planned on leaving out the part where Jeff brutally murdered a perfect stranger in the middle of the road in broad daylight. That part of the story would have to wait for another time. The three ladies sat at a small table in the kitchen, sipping herbal tea.

"Mom, there's something I need to tell you. There was an accident with Jeff at his job yesterday," Sam reluctantly began the abbreviated story.

"Is he ok, baby? Is everything alright?" her mom asked, with true concern for her son-in-law.

"He's not, mom, he didn't survive. I'm so sorry I didn't tell you earlier, I didn't want to worry you on the day you were seeing the doctor," Sam said as the tears began.

"Oh my God, baby," her mom said, as her sobbing began as well, "What happened? You should've told me, you don't need to worry about me and my doctor, your husband was killed! Oh my God, Jessica! Where's J? Is she ok? Is she with Doug?" The old woman was becoming frantic now, asking question after question, not waiting on an answer. Martha rested her hand on the poor woman's shoulder.

"She's fine, mom. Yes, she's with Doug. She doesn't know yet. I can't get through to Doug," Sam said, causing her mom to gasp, placing her hand over her mouth as she did it. "It was an accident on the highway, near his work, mom. He got hit on the highway. It happened yesterday, I'm so sorry I didn't tell you."

"I'm so sorry, baby," her mom said, standing and taking her daughter in her arms, all three women were sobbing now. "Don't ever keep anything from me again. You don't need to worry about me, Samantha. I'm your mother, I can handle myself, you need to go home and be with your daughter. She needs to know what happened to her step-father."

Her mother's comments made Sam cry even harder, "Mom, I can't get Doug on the phone. Doug doesn't even know. I don't know where they are..." she began trembling, nearly hyperventilating. Her mom held her tighter, nurturing her sobbing child.

"I'm sure they're ok, sweetheart. We'll get in touch with them" her mom said, Martha agreed with several nods as she rubbed Sam's back. "I'm glad you're staying tonight, I want you here longer. Are you sure it's ok, Martha"

"Yes, ma'am. As long as you want," Martha said.

The three ladies continued to drink their tea, as Sam went on to elaborate on details about Jeff's death, details that she made up as she went. She planned on never telling her mom about the true nature of his last few hours. The tea and conversation gradually migrated to the living room, as the women sat at the couch and placed their beverages on the coffee table, on top of coasters, of course. Sam's mom loved daytime TV, not the soaps, she hated those; she was a fan of the talk shows, such as Ellen, Steve Harvey, and the like. Turning on the set, she started to flip through channels in search of one of her favorites. A special report, complete with its own scrolling "Alert" marquee, filled the screen on most stations. The report instantly caught the attention of the three women as they read the words at the bottom of the screen as they scrolled by: Five dead, Savannah Chatham Metropolitan Police Department, Detective kills four and is killed by SWAT.

Chapter 92

SETH PLACED THE CONTENTS OF his assault pack neatly under the sink in the restroom, in the area he had cleaned out yesterday, on the far right hand side. He stacked the four blocks of C4 against the back wall, laid out the det cord and igniters next to the stack, his book, his head lamp, the cordless drill, and finally his woobie. Knowing that anyone could come in while he was heading back to his truck for the next load, he decided he should create some type of deterrent; something to prevent people from looking under the sink. He opened the supply closet and set a few cleaning products on the floor next to its opened doors. Hopefully this will draw the attention of anyone who wanted to snoop around, as well as anyone coming in here in search of supplies, although based on the condition of this place, he doubted anyone would come searching for cleaning products.

He donned his empty assault pack and headed out to the parking lot, drawing zero suspicion. Once at his truck, he loaded the bags of supplies he had purchased at Walmart into his pack and headed back to the DMV. He walked at a brisk pace, without running. A Soldier walking with a purpose was also a common sight in this area. He could probably run if he wanted and it wouldn't draw attention. Understanding that, he picked up a double time.

Luckily, nobody entered the restroom while he was gone and nobody seemed to notice anything he was doing. Everyone was preoccupied with being annoyed by the line. He made sure to lock the door as he unloaded his supplies next to the other items. Once his bag was empty, Seth secured the woobie, head lamp, and his book and placed them with his assault pack on the far left hand side under the sink. He used this opportunity to relieve himself one last time, after all, the DMV didn't close for almost another four hours, might be a long wait.

After unlocking the bathroom door, Seth crawled into the space under the sink. The door needed to remain unlocked so patrons could use the restroom; a locked door would eventually arouse suspicion. *God, I hope nobody comes in here and takes a massive shit,* he thought as he struggled to get comfortable under the sink. He used his empty assault pack and his woobie as a pillow, placed his head lamp on, and grabbed his Dean Koontz book. "Innocence" was the title, he had purchased it in Atlanta on Sunday, but hadn't started it yet. He should be able to knock out a few Chapters, maybe take a nap before he needed to start working. He was a much better fit yesterday when he rehearsed this, but he didn't have his supplies then, he must've underestimated how much space they would take up. He kicked the items around at his feet, trying to get more space for his legs, knocking over the C4. If he learned anything from his two combat deployments, it's that a Soldier can get comfortable and fall asleep almost anywhere. This was no different.

After realizing that his head lamp was causing an awful glare on the pages of the book, he removed it and placed it in the corner, pointing at the underbelly of the ugly formica countertop. This seemed to provide ample light for him to read. He planned on reading until he became sleepy, which should be soon, since he's been up since 0230 and on his feet all day. Tonight would be a successful operation; he had done his due diligence, he had planned and rehearsed with military precision. It was 1445 when Seth began to read, waiting patiently for the DMV to close so he could begin his true work; his duty. *You can rest, Sergeant. You've earned it. Tonight's a big night,* whispered across his mind as those exact words actually displayed themselves in the first Chapter of his book. *At Ease, Sergeant.* As the demon gently whispered soft words of encouragement into his brain and displayed them across the pages, SGT Holloway slowly faded off to sleep.

Chapter 93

MIKE PULLED INTO THE PARKING lot of his condo development shortly after leaving the station. He lived close to work, which made his commute through Savannah much less painful. Although, the close proximity of his office had no effect on his mood during this trip. The devastating loss of the man who had become a friend over the last two days was taking its toll on the detective. Mike didn't smoke during the short drive, although he normally would've sucked down at least two. He lost all interest in the manifest, the individual lists he and Grant had created; he had no intention of checking his email or trying to remember his contact over in Liberty County. *I'm done,* he thought as he put the car in park and sat.

You're not done. You're not even close, mother fucker. You better think again, the words slammed his mind from all directions, like a shotgun blast of heat and pressure. Mike squinted his eyes and groaned in pain as Atwood increased the tightness of the choke hold on his brain. The steering wheel felt as though it might break under the force of Mike's grip. Blood began to show itself in his left nostril again, dripping on his thigh and the floor board below. The interior of the Impala began to close in on Mike, it reduced in size rapidly, the frame groaning as it twisted and buckled, changing shape, transforming into a cocoon of glass and metal around the detective. Curiously, the glass did not shatter, rather it warped and bent, altering its shape while maintaining its transparency. Mike could see the world beyond the glass slowly begin to fade from view.

The ten thousand crushed cigarette butts within the vehicle began to sprout legs and walk amongst the garbage and dirty clothing. They traveled through old, disposable coffee cups, around the crusty cheese still attached to the paper that once surrounded a cheeseburger, they weaved in and around old gas receipts and unpaid parking tickets. Antenna forced themselves through the front of each butt-roach, giving them guidance and direction, allowing them to find their target. They assembled on Mike, crawling up his pant legs, scaling the back of the front seat, jumping on the back of his head and falling down his shirt collar. He struggled to open the door to no avail. Each bug hissed and clicked within the shrinking vehicle interior, in unison with Craig Atwood's ever changing voice. The word KILL began to chant, in the form of hissing roaches and the voice of the demon that exposed his true intentions to Mike in the hospital earlier today.

Nausea engulfed the detective as he continued to hunch lower and lower within the car, trying to avoid the crushing effects of the ceiling. "STOP!!" he screamed to no one, cigarette-roaches were crawling across his face now, trying to gain access to his mouth, ears, and nose. His body heaved up the first of his vomit, which splattered across the wheel and morphing windshield, exiting his mouth and nose. The chanting continued to get louder and louder, as it flexed and pulsed, the shrinking vehicle beginning to vibrate. All available space within what was once a department owned

Impala was gone, all that remained was room for Mike, his gear, garbage and clothing, and a few thousand cigarette cockroaches.

Mike pressed the back of his head to the wheel and stared down at the small portion of floor board, blood and vomit still dripping from his face. "Please stop...stop" he whispered. The strong confident detective was now reduced to a cowering, roach covered mess. *I'll stop when you pay me what's owed!!* screamed in his mind, followed by a loud and thunderous pop and flash. The car returned to normal in an instant, not gradually like it had changed. The vomit and blood remained on Mike's chest and lap. The roaches had changed back to dirty cigarette butts, however; they remained where they were, crawling in and out of the detectives clothing. He was littered from head to toe, within his underwear, under his t-shirt, stuck to his lower back and under his armpit, disgusting crushed cigarette butts. Mike sobbed in his car as he sat in the parking lot of his condo complex, truly defeated; he was a shadow of the man he was when he woke this morning.

He departed his vehicle, the door working properly once again, and walked through the parking lot towards his unit. Thankfully, his condo was on the ground level; he wouldn't have been able to climb stairs in his condition. He moved slowly, his head hung low as he drooled into the box that he carried; his bloody saliva mixed with vomit particles pooled on top of the manifest, which was resting on a clipboard at the top of the box. He set his box on the ground so he could work the lock and gain access to his unit. Defeated, he threw himself in his recliner and began to ponder his next move, if any.

Chapter 94

SCMPD WAS A DISASTER ZONE. Blood still covered the floor in the viewing room, biohazard teams did their best to clean the contaminated area amongst the chaos of a franticly working police station. Random acts of violence within the Savannah area continued to flood the airways of the police net, every available officer was engaged in some type of emergency call. All detectives, with the exception of Detectives Wright and Christianson, were tasked to take charge of recent homicides, some with apprehended suspects and others without anyone detained. Young Lieutenant Brannon was overwhelmed with the influx of crimes and assaults.

Craig Atwood positioned himself in his filthy recliner, monitoring his police scanner as the second and third order effects of his poison were beginning to surface. People attacked one another all over town, otherwise law abiding people were committing brutal murders and assaults at will all along the southeast. Although only able to monitor the local area on his scanner, he knew that his radius expanded well beyond the range of this fifty year old device. Every time a spirit was torn from its physical body as a result of one of his triggers, Atwood fed. He breathed deep the glorious energy as the spirits prepared to cross over to where ever the hell they went. With every breath he gained strength, he gained longevity, he gained life. He decided that he didn't need to bother his procrastinators for the time being, he was getting more than enough juice from the actions of today, not to mention the gigantic payoff that one minion would provide in the morning; one explosive payoff.

The demon made himself chuckle a little as he thought of that homonym. This was truly one of his most beneficial implants. Craig's infected multiple subjects at the same time before, once as many as fifty, but this was nearly double that. This was the first time he attempted to poison such a large group; it was a risk, a risk that was paying off phenomenally. He planned on attempting a much larger group next time. Larger implants would physically drain the demon, leaving him somewhat worthless for a few days after the event. In fact, Craig had spent most of Sunday night and Monday morning in bed. Luckily, his subjects started making payments early on Monday morning, starting with the douche bag insurance salesman. He was easy. Unfortunately, the payout wasn't that plentiful from that trigger; probably because he was the scum of society, a deceitful, dishonest asshole with no strength of character. The second payment of the day was of average strength, the road raging construction worker. He paid out more than the douche, but only slightly more. The teacher paid out more than the two of them combined, and not only because she killed four, it was because she was pure of heart; still is, actually. The big headed detective has been the highest paying subject of this implant, by far. It wasn't over yet, folks have been pulling triggers all day, plus he still had the other detective and the warrior. Like old blue eyes had told him many years ago, *The best is yet to come...*

Chapter 95

BRIAN REYES EXITED THE TAILGATE of a C-130 at an altitude high enough that he could see the curvature of the earth. He was demonstrating the proper execution of a text book military High Altitude, Low Opening (HALO) insertion. With the assistance of night vision goggles, Brian navigated while free falling, ensuring that he was as close as possible to his designated drop zone prior to deploying his parachute. He was dressed in head to toe black military clothing and gear, complete with a black ski mask under his helmet. The full moon over this Arizona landscape provided him with just enough ambient light to identify the target house from above. A desert camouflaged Remington R5, complete with all available attachments, dangled from his side, securely attached to his harness. He had unlocked this weapon when he reached level 40 earlier today.

The altimeter on his shoulder indicated 2500 feet above ground level, causing Brian to promptly deploy his main parachute. The opening shock jerked his upper body skyward and caused his legs to swing forward, weapon rocking back and forth on his hip, grenades and flash-bangs bounced against each other as they dangled from his chest. He used his toggles to steer his parachute through the sky in his dream, attempting to get as close as possible to his target: his father's back yard. The warm Arizona air caused his chute to rise and fall as it passed through pockets of thermal air, filling his canopy with the hot air which gave it bursts of lift. He used these to his advantage, allowing them to help ease his descent as he pulled both toggles into his chest and prepared to land. He touched down gently in the giant red blinking bull's eye on the ground in the far corner of the back yard, the blinking circles disappeared once he landed. The parachute blew away freely in the wind after Brian engaged the canopy release assembly on each shoulder and quickly pulled his weapon from his hip, placing it into firing configuration.

Pressing down on the left analog stick, Brian was able to move at a brisk pace, out of the open area and into the concealment of trees and shrubs on the north side of the yard. Surprise was key if he meant to gain and maintain the initiative of this engagement. He meant to enter through the second story balcony through the use of his grappling hook firing attachment on his Remington R5, which he equipped in lieu of a grenade launcher. He would then quietly clear each room upstairs and slowly make his way to the main target, which was downstairs in the main living room, according to the intel provided in the mission briefing. The plan, which was rehearsed and committed to memory prior to infiltration, was to execute the wife and children and then lay in wait for the father to return from work.

He moved swiftly through the cover of the wood line, peering through the red dot sight aperture of his weapon, scanning for targets left to right. He headed directly for the area indicated with the blinking arrow, on the patio directly beneath the target balcony. Once Brian was in place, the arrow disappeared, thus allowing him to fire his grappling hook onto the balcony overhead. Effortlessly, the hook sailed through the evening air and made contact with the railing. It never missed. It would always hit its target and it would always hold his weight. Brian slung his assault rifle on his back and climbed the rope with ease, in a hand over hand fashion, no legs.

The balcony led to an elaborate master bedroom. Clearing the master bedroom and en suite were a formality, he knew where the intended targets were. He used passive clearing techniques in every room upstairs, as he didn't want to alert his targets of his presence by throwing flash-bangs around unnecessarily. With the barrel of his weapon leading the way, Brian descended the large stairway. Night vision goggles were no longer required due to the light coming from the family room, light and the recognizable sounds of a popular TV game show. The staircase turned to the left and led to a decorative, spacious foyer. This landing might be the perfect spot to wait on his primary target, once he dispatched the secondary targets. He crept down the few remaining steps and rested gently against the wall which led into the large, open area that held the family room and enormous kitchen directly to the right. Slowly he eased his head around the corner, conducting a quick assessment of the room. A large sofa, complete with a long table behind it, was centered in the room, its back facing him. He saw the back of the woman's head and shoulders and it appeared as though she was cradling the baby. From around the couch, Brian saw random toddler toys scattered about the floor and he made a quick assumption that the other child was there playing, just out of his line of sight. Assumptions got operators killed in this business, therefore; he intended on confirming this suspicion shortly. A ridiculously large TV was mounted to the wall on the left hand side, fully visible from all areas within this giant space.

After his two second visual recon, Brian rested against the wall, allowed his weapon to hang from his body while he readied a grenade. He decided to use a fragmentary grenade rather than a flash bang. Perhaps the lethality of this tiny ball would finish the job, leaving him only with the duty of confirming it. He flicked off the thumb safety and pulled the pin. Releasing his grip, he allowed the spoon to fly into the air, which made a loud clinking noise when it hit the marble floor of the foyer, no doubt heard by the woman. Brian suspected that she was looking this way. He executed a quick *one one thousand, two one thousand count,* then exposed himself from around the corner and lobbed the grenade in an underhand fashion over the couch and into the area beyond. He immediately took cover back up the stairs and on the landing.

The grenade detonated with a thunderous pop, peppering lethal fragments of its casing in a 360 degree fashion. Brian's ears rung with a continuous buzzing noise, shattered glass and fragments littered the lawn outside, as the entire area filled with clouds of dust and debris. The traveling cloud filled the foyer and engulfed Brian as he stood on the landing. As the dust settled and the ringing subsided, he walked back down the stairs and into the living area in order to survey the damage and finish off any survivors. The room was void of any recognizable furniture, body parts and miscellaneous internal organs were all that remain of the targets, one full size and two miniature. Glass fragments and chunks of decorative granite counter top crunched under Brian's military style boots.

He repositioned himself on the landing, overlooking the dust riddled foyer. His returning father would surely notice the shattered living room windows and the debris on the lawn outside; his most probable course of action will be to run through the front door, concerned with his family's safety. That is when Brian would take him, but not before a wounding, incapacitating shot to the knees. He meant to bring the man down, but keep him alive for a brief amount of reeducation training prior to his execution.

As planned, the father burst through the door, hollering the name of his dead wife. A three to five round burst of grazing fire took out his legs, causing him to fall on his face in the dusty foyer, screaming in pain. Young Brian rose to his feet and, carrying his weapon at a low ready position, walked slowly toward his wounded father.

"Do you see what happens when you start a new family and leave your son behind?" Brian said, muffled through the black ski mask. "Sometimes when you leave someone, they come find you."

The man struggled to look up at the menacing shadow in black military garb that came slowly closer. Brian kicked the man over on to his back and knelt beside him.

"Who are you? Why have you done this?" the man said, coughing on dust particles that still lingered in the area.

"You know who I am, fucker, and you know what you owe me, fucker. You know what's due." Brian said, as he raised his hand to the top of his ski mask and yanked it off his head in one fluid motion. The face of Craig Atwood stared down on the withering man on the floor. Dust rested in the greasy finger prints of Craig's glasses as he pressed the barrel of his weapon on his father's forehead, burning the flesh.

Brian jerked himself awake to the sound of gunfire within his dream, sitting up abruptly in his hospital bed. His rapid movement caused his mother, Amanda, to wake as well. She had been sleeping in the chair next her son for several hours now, and this was the first sign of responsiveness that he has shown since he arrived this morning. Sobbing, Amanda lay her arms on top of her son's chest as he lay back down, sobbing as well. The boy's face was still swollen beyond recognition due to his multiple bee stings.

Chapter 96

MIKE'S HEAD STARTED TO CLEAR as he rested his body and mind while sitting in his recliner. He was slowly beginning to regain focus, realigning himself with a clear task and purpose. It seemed that the hold that Craig Atwood had on his mind was beginning to loosen its grip. He wasn't gone completely, Mike could still feel the demon lingering in his mind, but it was reduced, diluted even. He needed to take advantage of the lapse of the exterior thoughts invading his brain. He must come up with a plan, he needed to take purposeful action and make something happen, although he had no idea what that was.

The detective started to inventory the items he took from the station, laying them out on his table. He had thrown them in the box haphazardly, therefore; he wasn't too sure of what he had to work with. He had the manifest that he received from Sierra airlines yesterday, stained with drool, puke and blood. He had his laptop, which he plugged in and booted up. He had the list of crew members from flight 1289 and a few random notes scribbled on scratch paper. Grant had done a lot of work consolidating the people by county, unfortunately he didn't have access to that information anymore. There were a few other miscellaneous objects from his desk, things he really didn't need that he had grabbed in the heat of the moment.

His cell phone vibrated across the table, indicating the fourth missed call from SCMPD this afternoon; ignoring it, Mike logged on to the website that gives law enforcement personnel access to consolidated blotter reports. Unclear of what to do next, Mike decided to pick up where he left off last night, crossing off the names of people on the flight manifest that were already in custody by local police for one reason or another. Sounds of sirens outside and Mike's again vibrating phone suggested that there would be a few more names checked off the manifest in a few minutes.

Mike checked his email once his laptop was ready to roll and saw that Sheriff's Deputy Matt Wheeler had responded to the message he sent last night. The one word response of "roger" didn't fill Mike with much confidence, but he decided to reply anyway. Mike used the same technique of a short, one word response of "well?" in hopes that Matt took care of Bryan County folks. Mike started to feel his excitement return as he fumbled through the box for a black marker.

The police blotter data base provided enough information from the events of last night and today to check off another fifteen names on the manifest. Mike was also able to account for the other flight attendants as well, one had murdered her husband this morning and was in custody and the other had been arrested for vandalizing an ATM inside a grocery store yesterday afternoon. The third flight attendant was the woman who murdered a man on her flight last night, Chantay Williams. Mike continued to notice that the severity of each offense varied. Some were brutal murders and others were minor, less violent offenses. That fact began to make sense as he thought back to his conversation with Atwood, different stress levels, different character strengths, beliefs, and values; all of these played a factor in how that person reacted to the demon's "trigger." *There has to be a way to beat it,* Mike thought. He was a practical man, every problem had a solution, and sometimes there were several viable options on how to solve it. There had to be a way to win.

It had been almost an hour since Mike felt direct contact with Atwood. The demon hadn't whispered anything in his ear, he hadn't deployed any armies of cockroaches or other insects. Mike had a few theories why this was; perhaps the monster had its fill, or maybe he was off tormenting someone else. Whatever the reason, he knew it wouldn't last long, this was just a short break, the thing would return. Without a definitive plan, Mike continued to check names off, based on the blotter reports, as he waited on a response from Deputy Wheeler, and perhaps an epiphany.

Chapter 97

AMANDA REYES EMBRACED HER SON as he lay in his hospital bed. In her eyes, he was a new born child, a child that was in pain and need of nurturing. Her emotions had taken over, she hadn't even remembered that he had destroyed his TV and gaming console earlier, she was just happy he was awake and talking.

"I'm sorry, mom. I'm sorry I broke everything," Brian quietly said through his swollen face, his eyes were barely open. Like the detective, he was also feeling the grip of whatever it was that had hold of him beginning to loosen. His thoughts were beginning to clear, his mind, once again, becoming his own. "I don't know what came over me. I was so mad, mom. I wanted to hurt you. And my dad. I'm so sorry..."

"Baby, don't worry about that now. We'll figure it out. You just worry about getting better," she said as she gently caressed the boy's face. "I called your father. He's flying in tonight to see you. He's worried about you, about the bee stings."

"He is? He's flying here?" Brian asked, as some color came back to his face. Tears fell from his eyes as he held his mother tighter.

She nodded, not realizing how much it meant to the boy. "I'm sorry I didn't know you were allergic to bees, or hornets, or whatever they were. I don't even know why they were out in January.

Doesn't make sense. The doctor gave us some injectors, in case it happens again, we'll be prepared," she said. "I'm sure you've been stung before, I don't know why you reacted the way you did."

"When will my dad be here?" Brian asked, struggling to open his eyes wider in anticipation.

"Well, he emailed me his itinerary," she said as she pulled out her phone. "Hmmm, he lands tonight just before midnight. So, he'll probably be here to see you in the morning. I'll call him sometime after he lands, find out where he's staying and what time he plans on coming to see you."

The pain and anger Brian felt earlier today was gone. What replaced it was a feeling of acceptance and worth, and the warmth of being wanted. The horrible images that haunted his dreams were all but gone. His heart filled with love and respect for both his parents, although they haven't ever been together in those roles and never would be.

"Can we call him now?" Brian asked.

"No, baby. He's on the plane now. Let me check his itinerary again. He lands in Atlanta at nine tonight, two hour layover. We could try calling him at around 9:15, if you want," his mother answered.

"Ok," Brian said, leaning back in his hospital bed. A swollen smile extended across his face. The taunting voices of earlier seemed to be gone for good, he hadn't heard or seen anything strange for a few hours now. He lay in anticipation of tonight's conversation with his father, a new found feeling of admiration surrounded his soul, admiration for his long distance dad.

Chapter 98

DOUG EMERGED FROM THE HOTEL room's bathroom wearing nothing but a pair of boxer shorts, moist worms still clinging to his back. Jessica greeted her father, who she hadn't seen in hours, with a hesitant hug. She grimaced at the look of her dad, he was skinny and ashy, as he looked down on her with swollen, blood shot eyes.

"Daddy, ewe!! You have a worm on your shoulder! Gross!!" she said, pushing past him to wash her hands.

"Be careful of the glass, J, there's still some on the floor! Don't touch the gun!" Doug said, as he admired what she had done with the bible, phone book, and lamp. He felt almost a hundred percent better. His nausea and head ache had faded, it had been nearly an hour since he discharged a worm from his body and even longer since he'd heard anything in his head that wasn't his. He still looked like hell, skin that was once light brown was now grey and cracked, visible ribs and spine.

"Daddy, why are there worms all over the bathroom? What's going on? What's wrong with you?" she said, trembling. She was still terrified, fearful for what was happening to her father. Jessica was a smart young lady, much smarter than her years; she knew that something was wrong. Her father was not well. He may say everything is ok, but she was smart enough to know when he was lying to her, telling her what he thought she wanted to hear.

"It's ok, baby. I had those with me because I was going to take you fishing, until I got sick. I had it all planned out, that was the big surprise. I planned on taking you out in the boat," Doug said, deliberately deceiving his daughter.

"Ok," Jessica said, not believing a word of her father's story. She was too smart for her own good, she knew something wasn't right. "You know I don't like fishing."

"You used to love it! What is it? Pretty girls can't fish? You getting too big on me?" Doug said, as he ruffled his little girl's hair.

Jessica knew that something was going on. She didn't know exactly what it was, but there was something different about her dad, and she intended on finding it out. What she really wanted to do was call her mother, but she couldn't remember the number. As if a light bulb had been inserted above Jessica's little head, it came to her. The iPad. She was Facebook friends with her mother, she could send her a message with her dad's iPad and it would go directly to her mom's phone, or at least it should. If her mom had it set up that way. Little J worked it all out in her head, she didn't want her dad to know what she was planning, something was going on with him.

"I guess I just don't like it anymore. I'm gonna watch some more movies," Jessica said, as she crawled back under the blankets and into her fort. She might watch another movie, but not until she sent her mom a message. She tapped the Facebook app on the iPad and it opened into her dad's account. Not knowing how to log him out, she just went to the spot to send a message and looked up her mom's profile. She knew they were friends, they all were; her, her mom and dad, even Jeff. She began to type the message: *Mom, this is Jessica. Something is wrong with dad. He is very sick. Please call his phone. We are at a hotel...* She paused and crawled out of her fort. Her dad had gone back into the bathroom and closed the door again, that was becoming his home away from home. She looked at the phone on the desk and, after grabbing a pen and post it note, wrote down the room number and hotel's address. She took her note and climbed back into her little fort, and added the information to the message. She concluded: *I'm scared mom, please call or come get me. There is something wrong with daddy. He said there was no school today, is that true? Please call. Love you*

The concerned little pre-teen mashed the send button on the app and watched the progress bar extend all the way to the right. She was truly concerned for her father's well-being. Her attitude would certainly change if she had been privy to the suggestions that have been rattling around in his head all day, the suggestions of the demon. Demands would be a better description of the voices in her father's head; demands that he end her life. If she had known the truth, she would have fled while her dad was inside the bathroom.

Chapter 99

THE SUN WAS SETTING ON the second day contaminated by the demon Craig Atwood, hundreds of lives destroyed by the effects of his poison. Families were torn apart, property was destroyed, police officers were killed in shootouts, and children were murdered by their parents. The monster grew more and more powerful with every ounce of energy he consumed, his immortality being extended with every pull of the trigger. Atwood had calculated that this series would allow him about three months' worth of sustenance, but it was becoming obvious that he had underestimated significantly.

Detective Mike Christianson took advantage of the reduced influence of the demon and rested, his body still recovering from the anxiety attack and horrible vomiting. He had twelve missed calls from head-quarters and zero intent of returning them, they would have to send someone here if they wanted him. The blood stained manifest still remained on his dining room table, along with his laptop, zero emails in his inbox. His heart ached at the loss of his friend, Grant Wright, the loss of Captain Ted Garrison, and the other members of SCMPD that had died today because of Atwood.

Brian Reyes slept in his hospital bed, his mother by his side. She had set an alarm on her phone, to remind her to call Brian's father, hopefully catching him during his lay-over in Atlanta. The swelling of Brian's face had reduced considerably, perhaps due to the medicine he'd been given. Amanda believed that his condition was improving due to a combination of the medicine and the fact that his father was on his way. Whatever had come over her son earlier today seemed like a distant memory. That thought made her smile, as she gently ran her hand across Brian's head as he slept.

Doug Mason had once again secured himself within the small bathroom of the hotel room that he and his daughter shared, the young lady waited anxiously for her mother to respond to the message she sent earlier. She was getting away with watching anything she wanted on her dad's iPad; shows and movies that would otherwise be off limits to the eleven year old. It was fun breaking the rules and watching scary movies, but what little Jessica really wanted was her daddy back.

Sam, her mother, and Martha were curling up on the couch, admiring L.L. Cool J on "NCIS – Los Angeles," while an icon on Sam's iPhone indicated that she had a new message. There was no alert, no tone. She would have to pick it up in order to see that there was a message, which she hadn't planned on doing. Sam was becoming increasingly frustrated with getting Doug's voice mail each and every time she called since yesterday, she was giving it a break.

SGT Seth Holloway slept soundly under the sink in the DMV restroom, his head lamp still illuminating the tight space. His book lay open on his chest, still at the beginning of Chapter one. His watch would sound its alarm at precisely midnight, alerting him that it was time to get up and get to work. He had a lot of work ahead of him. As the uninfected put their day to rest and lay down to sleep, SGT Holloway began his day, prepared to fulfill his obligation; to do his duty.

PART THREE

Wednesday, January 29th, 0001 hrs.

"The conductor does not need to know how to play every instrument in the orchestra."

-Detective Mike Christianson

"You've accomplished nothing!!" -Craig Atwood

Chapter 100

SETH HOLLOWAY WOKE TO THE iPhone alarm titled "constellation," which repeated in his ear as the clock reached the military time of 0001. The area under the sink was well lit, due to the combination of his head lamp and now the illuminated screen of his phone. Seth could smell his own breath as he forced his mouth open. His breath was rough. He needed to remedy his horrible cotton mouth immediately. He cracked his back with an enormous stretch after emerging from the tiny space. Although he was a small man, it still took its toll on the body being crammed under a sink for nearly eight hours.

He rinsed his mouth out with water by placing his entire face under the running faucet, cursing himself for not remembering to pack a tooth brush. How the hell could he have forgotten a tooth brush? After devouring the sandwich he brought, Seth started to work. He donned his head lamp, then opened the four 11 oz. coffee cans, using his trusty Leatherman tool that he carried whenever in uniform. Before dumping the first can into the toilet, he took a deep breath of the fresh coffee grounds, cursing himself again for not planning a way to have a cup. He emptied the remains of the other three cans into the bowl and flushed it all down.

The four empty cans were placed in a neat and orderly fashion across the sink, opened side down. Seth withdrew the small nail file attached to his Leatherman and, in a downward thrusting motion, stabbed a hole in the bottom of each can. The holes were about a half inch in diameter. Once satisfied, he removed the length of det cord from under the sink and cut four five foot pieces off the bundle. He fed the first piece through the hole in the bottom of one of the cans and tied a Uli knot on the inside. The Uli knot was essentially just a ball of cord that would act like a blasting cap when ignited, it had more than enough force to detonate any C4 that was packed around it.

He completed the same process with the three remaining cans, leaving him with four empty coffee cans, each with a ball of det cord on the inside and a tail of about four feet dangling from the bottom. Now the C4. Seth pulled the blocks of explosive out from under the sink and laid it out neatly on the counter. The unique odor of C4 hit him in the face as he unwrapped each package. C4 has been manufactured to have no smell whatsoever, but anyone who worked with it would tell you that is false. It had a tinge of old, dirty almonds; it burned the nose when smelled. Each bar of C4 had a self-adhesive strip, which could be used to secure it to almost anything. Seth needed to remove the strip, since he planned on forming and packing it into each can. He had four complete blocks, more than enough to do what he needed, perhaps too much.

He pulled the tail of det cord taunt from the bottom, holding the Uli knot tight to the bottom of the can, and began to pack the C4. It was important to fill in all areas of the can to ensure proper distribution of fragments when it detonates. C4 is completely pliable and easy to form, not unlike play-dough or a handful of clay.

After packing a full block of explosive into each can, he rested them neatly on the counter, the opening facing skyward, unable to rest evenly on the sink due to the tail of det cord that extended from the bottom.

Now it was time for the buffer material; something to help ensure that the projectiles are forced outward in the direction of the can's opening as it explodes. Seth headed to the supply closet, which still hung open the way he left it eight hours earlier. He pulled out a few packages of the old scratchy brown paper towels he placed on top of the closet Monday morning. After placing a large stack of paper towels in each can, directly on top of the C4, Seth opened the random packages of nails, screws, nuts, bolts, and washers. He distributed the contents of each package evenly throughout each can, on top of the buffer material. Once everything he brought had been placed inside each grapeshot charge, Seth realized that there wasn't enough. There wasn't enough projectiles. A gap of two inches remained at the top of each can.

FUCK, Seth thought, *what the fuck am I going to use?* He'd surely be able to search the office out in the main area of the DMV for random objects to fill the empty space, but he wanted to be out there as little as possible, due to the possibility of the cameras being monitored at some security monitoring facility. *Dammit!* Pickins were slim inside the restroom. There was nothing he could use in here that would be a suitable, lethal projectile. "Fuck," Seth said to himself in the mirror, blinding himself with his head lamp.

Suddenly, the mirror began to vibrate, similar to the way it had in Doug Mason's hotel bathroom yesterday. Seth watched as the vibrations in the large mirror radiated outward, its ripples heading to the full extent of the corners, and then back to the center. His face became distorted in the reflection as the vibration continued for another pulse before shattering into a few thousand pieces, falling into the sink and onto the counter. The raining chunks of shattered mirror pieces filled the remaining space within the cans, topping them off completely with varying shapes and sizes of sharp, jagged potential projectiles. *Does that work?* whispered in the air within the tiny, dirty bathroom. "Yes, sir," Seth answered, "that should do it!"

Chapter 101

SAMANTHA ARKENSON ROLLED OFF HER mother's couch and headed into the bathroom, almost stepping on Martha, who lay on a half inflated air mattress on the floor. Sam's mom had retired to her bedroom several hours ago and the two ladies had fallen asleep watching late night talk shows. Sam's phone rested where it had for the last few hours, on her mom's tiny dining room table, an unopened Facebook message still waiting for attention. After rolling off the worthless mattress, Martha shut off the TV and laid back down.

Sam washed her hands after doing what she had to do. Leaving the bathroom, she saw her phone on the table. She knew that her mother wouldn't have a phone charger compatible with her iPhone, so she decided she would check it one last time and power it down, saving some juice for tomorrow. She plugged in her four digit pin and brought up her home screen, seeing that she had no missed calls and no text messages. There were fifteen new emails, but that was no different than any other day; she got several emails from different department stores, announcing sales and whatnot. Sam scrolled to the right and noticed she had four Facebook messages. Realizing that someone probably liked one of her photos or perhaps someone wanted a Candycrush life or some Farmville crap, Sam decided to just power it down, she'd check it in the morning. Yesterday was a long, rough day. She needed her rest, there was still the matter of her deceased husband to attend to when she got back to Savannah.

She kicked the air mattress as she walked closer to the couch, waking her friend.

"Hey," she whispered, "you got your charger?"

"No, be quiet. You're gonna wake your mom. Go to bed." Martha answered.

"I want to leave early tomorrow. I have a lot to do. I want to go straight to Doug's house. First thing. Set your phone for like seven, seven thirty. I shut mine off." Sam said.

"Fine, shut up. Hey, switch with me. My back is killing me," Martha said, groaning as she got up again.

"Nope," Sam said, rolling over into the cushions of the couch, showing no intention of giving up the couch to Martha.

Chapter 102

SETH MADE MULTIPLE TRIPS WHEN moving his supplies to the DMVs service counter. He evenly distributed the four grapeshot charges across the surface of the eight work stations, basically placing one can between each two stations, making sure to slide the cans close to the far edge so he could reach them once he jumped over the counter. After securing his cordless drill, both rolls of tape, and the roll of det cord, Seth jumped over the counter. He moved to the far right side of the long counter and crawled underneath, drill in hand. He had placed a ¼ inch bit in his drill the other day, knowing the circumference of standard det cord, therefore; there was no doubt in his mind that the holes he was about to drill within the eight individual partition walls under the counter would be large enough to insert a length of det cord through all eight holes.

He began drilling his first hole, making sure he did it high in the partition wall and far in the back, thus giving him enough room to tape the cans to the under belly of the countertop and attach the det cord from the bottom of the can to the main line, which would eventually run the length of the entire counter through the holes he was drilling. The drill penetrated the cheap particle board that separated the work stations easily, allowing Seth to drill all of the holes within five minutes; the only challenge being that he had to crawl under each space separately, which had done a number on his already tight back.

Starting from the far left side of the counter, as seen from the perspective of the people who would be in line here in a few hours, Seth fed cord through the individual holes, pulling up slack as he went, ensuring that he tied a secure overhand knot in the cord on the far right side after running it through the hole. This would prevent it from accidently slipping out, which would reduce the effectiveness of the main line. He needed to drill one more hole in this work station, on the left side near the floor, allowing him to run the remaining det cord along the base board of the room. He used durable, green duct tape to keep the cord tight against the wall, as he ran it along the base board of the far left wall, into the corner, and along the shared wall of the restroom. Seth grabbed the drill and headed back into the restroom.

After crawling back into last night's bedroom under the counter, Seth drilled his last hole. Before heading back into the main area of the DMV, Seth opened that giant jug of ice tea from yesterday and took a few chugs. He set it on the counter top, which was still covered with pieces of the shattered mirror, something he'd need to clean up eventually. He headed back out to the DMV waiting area, in search of the tiny hole in the wall he just created. Once he found it, he routed the rest of the det cord through the hole, allowing it to roll up in the area under the sink in the bathroom as he fed it through. This marked the end of the first phase of his preparation in the completion of his duties.

Seth walked the length of the main line, inspecting it for any kinks, any loose areas. The ugly green tape he used to keep the cord neat and tidy against the floor, running along the wall, blended in nicely with the hideous green, dingy carpet. He knew it was there and he could hardly see it. This would be virtually invisible to the naked eye of the patrons waiting in line. The cord under the counter was a different matter, surely if a worker looked under the counter, he or she would see it; they'd see the grapeshot charges as well. It was a necessary risk.

The next phase in the process was to attach the individual charges to the main line. This would be done by securing the tail of each can to the main line with a prusik knot, which has been proven to be the best method for securing a free running end of rope or cord to a stationary object, in this case: the main line. Before he tied each prusik, he used several pieces of the green duct tape to secure the cans to the under belly of the counter top, ensuring that the open side that held the projectiles was facing where the employees would eventually stand. He had used a few thin strips of weak, black electrical tape on the open end of each can, extending the tape across the top in a zig zag pattern, so the mirror pieces and other projectiles wouldn't fall out when the cans were placed in a horizontal fashion. If anyone were to look under the counter or run their hand across the under portion, they would see or feel the charges; once again, a necessary risk.

The final step in this process was to attach the igniter to the end of the det cord under the sink in the bathroom. Seth used an M81, which came with a small length of time fuse. Time fuse was basically just det cord with yellow rings spaced out evenly on it. This piece was complete with three yellow rings. Each ring indicated a minute of burn time, so in this case, he would have three minutes after pulling the pin on the igniter before the time fuse would cause the main line to explode, which would cause the grapeshot charges to explode, firing lethal chunks of mirror fragments, nails, nuts, bolts, and screws into the asshole employees of this fucked up operation. Seth pulled the blade from his Leatherman tool and used it to remove two of the three yellow rings from the time fuse, leaving himself a minute to escape once he pulled the pin. Finally, he did his best to clean up the shattered pieces of mirror that covered the counter and floor. Thankfully, there was a vacuum in the small break area in the back. It was 0232 when Seth crawled back under the sink. He reset the alarm on his iPhone for 0530, which would give him a half hour to pack up his gear and wait for the DMV to open its doors.

*Too early...much too early, wait wait wait...wait for the line to build, wait for more workers to show up...don't do it too early...that's not what I want...*Seth heard these words repeat in his head, words that made perfect sense. "I wasn't..." Seth said out loud, "I still need to get outta here. I'll sit in the truck for a while, then come back in. Don't worry, I'm not fucking stupid." *I know you're not, my friend. You are a pillar of integrity and you will be rewarded....*

Chapter 103

MIKE INHALED THE LAST OF this morning's fifth cigarette as he watched the sunrise from his condo's patio. He was never one to get up this early, or to smoke outside, but he had gone to bed much earlier than normal last night, and his ruminating mind forced him up about an hour ago. He was surrounded by thoughts of his dead partner, dead boss, and his devious tormentor, whom hadn't made his presence known since early yesterday evening. He pondered for a way to permanently free himself from Atwood's grip, there had to be a way. It was unknown if Atwood was vulnerable to conventional weapons, although the woman he attacked yesterday had said she kicked him in the balls and he went down, screaming like a bitch. Maybe he could be hurt, maybe even taken out, with regular weapons. Mike was halfway tempted to go to his house, confront him now, perhaps catch him off guard and kill him as he slept, if he slept.

Taking a break from smoking, Mike went inside to fetch another cup of coffee. He planned on grabbing his phone as well, although it might be too early for him to call Wheeler. He had to get another person involved in this thing; if he could convince Wheeler of Atwood's evil power, perhaps Wheeler could take him out, as the demon had no control over him, none that Mike knew of, anyway. It would take some convincing, especial since the two haven't spoken in months. He secured another cup of coffee, his phone, and his laptop before heading back out to the patio.

Mike thought back to images he had been shown yesterday, the images of Atwood's mutating body; his hands breaking apart, the growing fingers, the roaches. Using his detective powers of deduction, he tried to think of a rational explanation; this had to be a hallucination, Atwood must've drugged him somehow. His mind wandered to the moment when he was in the hospital, when Atwood had somehow appeared in the bathroom; he could've crawled in, somehow. The illness, the head aches and vomiting; perhaps a reaction to whatever drug he slipped him, it must be that. Nothing else makes sense.

The time in the lower right corner of Mike's laptop said that it was 7:12 a.m., which was late enough to call Wheeler. Mike decided he would check his email first, maybe the deputy had responded at some point throughout the night. He had to get someone else on board, someone that wasn't infected, if that was actually what had happened. After realizing that there were no new email messages, Mike started to do a few searches for subjects such as "mind altering drugs," "demon powers of suggestion," and "teleportation." The latter two making him laugh. There had to be some other explanation.

Chapter 104

SETH SNAPPED AWAKE TO THE sound of a flushing toilet. He must've canceled the alarm when it had gone off two hours ago and gone back to sleep. Whoever had just flushed the toilet was now washing their hands, causing the draining water to pass through the elbow joint above his crotch. Hopefully this was a patron and not an employee, otherwise the missing mirror would be seen as evidence of some type of break in. Seth had done a great job cleaning, therefore; most of the particles and fragments were removed by the vacuum. He waited for this person to leave before starting to quietly pack up the few loose articles he had under the sink.

While his comrades on the Army installation were finishing their morning physical fitness training, Seth was preparing to make his escape from the DMV bathroom. He planned on waiting in his truck, at least for a couple hours, allowing the building to fill with unsuspecting people before he went back in and pulled the ring on the igniter. Surely Master would be pleased with the results of last night's placement of explosives; Seth had done well.

SGT Holloway's leaders had listed him as "out of ranks" at this morning's accountability formation, but could not indicate him as "absent without leave" until he had gone a complete 24 hours without reporting. Everyone he worked with feared the worst, simply because Holloway was not the type of Soldier to just run off; something was wrong. His Platoon Sergeant planned on sending someone to his house if Seth hadn't turned up by their 0900 formation. The last time anyone had seen him was when he and Brunick had returned the Humvee to the motor pool yesterday.

The person who was washing their hands finally finished and left the restroom. Seth gave it a few seconds before crawling out, in case someone was waiting outside. After the brief delay, Seth emerged from under the sink, cracked his back again, and locked the door. Still under the sink was his blanket, book, drill, jug of tea, and his empty assault pack. He stuffed everything in the bag, threw it on his back, and headed out. Before exiting the building, Seth made note of the people in the main area of the DMV. There were three employees working behind the counter, all of which were helping customers. There were only two people waiting in line. Seth was pleased to see that his best friend, Claudia, was assigned to the work station directly in the center of the counter. She was currently positioned in line with one of the grapeshot chargers; a few dozen nails and screws, along with a handful of broken mirror pieces, were pointing directly at her fat, bloated stomach.

Displaying a devilish grin that was not quite his own, Seth pushed through the door and headed to his truck. After climbing in his truck, he removed his phone from his assault pack and checked the list of missed calls, which totaled twenty one, complete with twelve voicemail messages, most of the numbers he recognized as members from his unit. The number that he first noticed yesterday at the range had called him four more times throughout the day. Seth contemplated whether or not to call it back, since whoever it was had called him once before he'd gone missing from work, there-fore; it most likely wasn't someone from the unit looking for him.

After staring at the number for long enough for the screen to go black, Seth finally hit the number with his thumb, initiating a call back. Seth's heart sunk and his eyes widened when the voice came through the line: "Deputy Wheeler...This is Wheeler. Hello?" Seth immediately hung up the phone and set it on the passenger seat. *Why the fuck is a deputy calling me? Why did he call me yesterday at the range?* His mind was swimming, struggling to understand. If the calls started coming after he went missing, it might make a little sense, but there was no reason for this deputy to be calling him so early in the day yesterday. The phone vibrated on the seat next to Seth, the same number was displayed across the screen. He watched it until the screen indicated "missed call", and a few seconds later, "new voicemail message." After a few minutes of consideration, Seth decided to listen to the message that the deputy just left.

He engaged the speaker, leaving the phone on the seat next to him. A deep, low voice spoke with authority as the message played: *Hello, Mr. Holloway, this is Sheriff's Deputy Matt Wheeler over here in Bryan County. I'm not sure why you just called and hung up. I left you a voicemail yesterday. I'm wanting to talk to you a little bit about your flight on Sunday. There's really nothing for you to worry about, again, um, I'm not sure why you're hanging up on me. Please call me back, you have the number. Hope to hear from you, thanks.* Seth deleted the message before the phone gave him any other options. He had no intention of calling this guy back. None whatsoever.

Chapter 105

THE LAMP, BIBLE, AND PHONE book fell off the top of the ice bucket as the tarantula bumped its fat body against the top of his prison. The second time the spider made contact with the top of the bucket caused it to make a loud pinging noise, hopping off the carpet slightly. The third and final jump made the bucket topple over and roll into the lamp, granting the tarantula the freedom he had just earned. Doug had not been out of the bathroom since early last night and little J was sound asleep in her couch cushion sanctuary. The fat spider looked like it had doubled in size since it was last seen. He crawled over the phone book, walking with determination across the hotel room floor, towards the desk. Once he cleared half the distance to the desk, the tarantula sprung itself into the air, and with pin point accuracy, landed directly under the desk. After bouncing off the carpet and hitting the wall, he righted himself once again and regained his focus, as he crawled along the baseboard and located the phone jack.

The spider's tiny fangs made short work of the phone cord, nibbling through it enough to cut the connection, but not the cord entirely. After the completion of his mission, the tiny soldier marched into the center of the room, making note of the couch cushion castle and the snoring noises coming from within. He desperately wanted to crawl inside and bite whatever was making the horrible noises that were causing the whole room to vibrate. His fangs would have already pierced the flesh of whatever was inside the castle if it wasn't off limits; he had no control or effect over whatever was in there.

Positioning himself under the bed, the hairy visitor waited idly by for orders. Surely there would be something devious in his future, he would not have been manifested for the minor tasks he'd been charged with. The large one would come through the giant portal shortly, perhaps the Master would instruct him to do more than just walk across his foot this time, maybe he could get involved like the worms and little spiders. He would exceed the Master's expectations once given the order to strike. The Master will be pleased. But, not yet. He needed to be patient. He needed to be obedient. He would be rewarded.

Chapter 106

MARTHA AND SAM THREW ELBOWS into one another as they got ready for the day in Sam's mother's tiny bathroom. They'd been up for about thirty minutes now, having coffee with Sam's mom, watching the morning news explain the various violent acts in southern South Carolina and northern Georgia. After a short delay, the two young ladies were preparing for the short drive home; minimal preparations, after all, they weren't going to a beauty pageant, but they had to conduct a modified version of typical morning personal hygiene. After taking a third elbow to the forehead, Sam decided to go check her phone and give Martha the bathroom to herself.

She grabbed her phone and sat next to her mom at the small kitchen table. Refusing another cup of coffee from her mom, Sam waited as her phone powered up and went through its routine. She realized that there were no missed calls and no new texts messages, although she now had a total of thirty two emails and eleven Facebook messages. Since Martha took forever to get ready, even in a case like this, Sam figured that she would clean out her inbox. Every email in her inbox was potential trash, with the exception of one; the one from the funeral director. Attached was an itemized list of all charges she would be responsible for. She closed it, not wanting to concern herself with that right now. The insurance should pay for it, unless the insurance company refused payments for murders who get killed when evading police.

Using the thumb scrolling method, Sam looked through her Facebook messages, of which were ten regular notifications and one message. The notifications consisted of a few liked photos, mostly from the new pictures she posted last weekend, there were a few comments, as well. She saved the message for last. The messages she usually got were from friends who noticed Sam was logged on and just threw her a "hey" or "what's up, girl?" She didn't really use the message feature for any meaningful correspondence.

Sam jumped to her feet, shouting loud enough for Martha to hear over the hair dryer, "I have a message from Doug!! Thank God!!"

"See baby," her mom said "I told you he'd get in touch with you." She rubbed Sam's lower back as she spoke.

"Oh, it's from Jessica. She's using his iPad." Sam said. She read the message silently, her eyes opening wider and filling with tears as she read. Her mother noticed her reaction to the message.

"What is it? What's wrong, Samantha?" her mom asked.

"They're in a hotel. In Port Wentworth. She said something's wrong with Doug. Mom, she's scared. She said she's scared," Sam said, through a face full of tears.

Samantha dialed the number that Jessica provided in the email and entered the room number. The phone rang nearly a dozen times before Sam gave up.

"Martha!! Let's go, I want to go to this hotel. In Port Wentworth. There's no answer. Let's go!" Sam yelled to her friend in the bathroom.

"Sweetheart, call the front desk. They'll patch you through to the room," her mom said, trying to get Sam to calm down.

"Mom, they'll just patch me into the room, that's where I just called. I need to go, now." Sam said, a little frustrated with her mom. Sam was now in protective mother mode; her daughter was scared, possibly in danger. Nothing would stop her from getting to her daughter.

Martha came out of the bathroom, rubbing her hair with a towel, having given up with the cheap hair dryer. "Sam," she said, "call the police. If you're worried about J, send the police over there."

"She just said Doug was sick, I don't want to get him in any kind of trouble. I just want to make sure she's ok." Sam said, "Hurry up, let's go."

"Call the detective. He said if you need anything to call him," Martha reminded her.

"Yeah, good idea. I still want to leave, like now. So hurry up," Sam said, as she tore through her purse, looking for Detective Wright's business card. She found both Wright and Christianson's cards inside her wallet within her fancy purse. She dialed Detective Wright's number first. He was the helpful detective, not the one that asked her all the upsetting follow up questions. The phone went straight to voicemail and Sam hung up, without leaving a message. She immediately called the other detective, the one that stunk.

Chapter 107

MIKE WAS LIGHTING A CIGARETTE with the head of his last one as his phone vibrated across the bistro table on his patio. The missed calls from last night and this morning have all been numbers he recognized, except this one. He had never seen this number before. After a few moments of second guessing himself, Mike decided to answer it.

"Christianson," Mike said, with the understanding that he can always hang up.

"Detective Christianson, this is Samantha Arkenson, you gave me your card the other day. Twice, actually. You said if I needed anything I could contact you." Sam said, being as clear headed as she could. Her emotions were placed in check for the time being.

"Ma'am, I'm actually not working today. I had a minor heart attack yesterday, so I'm taking some time off," Mike said, exaggerating about his condition, although he still didn't believe that all he had was a panic attack.

"Sir, I tried the other detective before I called you. Grant was his name. You both said if I needed anything you would help. All I need is for you to go check on my daughter. She's with my ex-husband at a hotel in Port Wentworth. She says her father is really sick and she's scared. That's all. There's nobody else I can call. You do it or have someone do it, please. I'm 40 miles away, you're two miles away, five tops." Sam said, her voice beginning to crack towards the end.

Mike took the phone away from his ear, holding it in his hand as he rested his forehead on the table. He wasn't even planning on putting on more than a robe today. There was no way to determine when and if Atwood would show his face again. The last thing Mike wanted was to be babysitting this woman's daughter when that asshole resurfaced.

"Hello? Detective, are you there? Hello?" Sam said frantically on the line.

"I'm here, miss. I'll head over there, but you have to meet me there. I don't want to be there all morning. If your ex-husband is as sick as your daughter says he is, I'll have an ambulance come over. What's the hotel and room number? What's your daughter's name?" Mike said.

Relieved, Sam gave Mike the information he asked for, adding her ex-husband's name as well. She had every intention of meeting him there, but the fact that the detective had agreed to check on Jessica right now filled her with comfort. Samantha thanked Mike in advance multiple times for his good deed before ending the conversation. She and Martha quickly gathered their belongings, said their good byes to Sam's mom, and headed out. This short drive was only 40 miles, but traveling at this time of day on 95 from Beaufort to Savannah was going to be a bumper to bumper snail's pace. Mike truly gave Sam piece of mind when he agreed to go check on the young lady and her sick father.

Mike finished another cigarette before heading in to get dressed, a task in which he wasn't breaking any records in terms of timeliness. He agreed to go check on this woman's daughter, but he never said he was going to rush. He was about to call Wheeler, but decided against it, he'd deal with that once he got back. As he was pulling his pants up, Mike noticed that there was a new email in his inbox. The message from Deputy Wheeler said:

Mike,

Well, all but two of the names you sent me are already in custody or dead. I agree with you, this is insane. What the hell is happening? I'm sorry for everything that happened over there yesterday. It's a fucking shame. You guys keep your chin up. One of the people that I haven't checked off is missing, his wife hasn't seen him since Monday. The name is Dave Sanders. The other one just called me and hung up. Seth Holloway. I think he's a Soldier, he had an out of state area code. My experience has taught me that usually around here that means they're stationed at Fort Stewart. I have a friend at the criminal investigations division over there. I'm getting ready to head on over and see what I can find out. I'll keep you in the loop. I agree with you, buddy. Something strange is going on. I'll call after I talk with Holloway.

Matt

Mike read the email again, just to be sure that he didn't miss anything. As he buttoned his pants and pulled a dirty shirt over his head, Mike thought of the response he was about to write to Matt. He had to shoot him some type of acknowledgement, hopefully they could keep this conversation going, although Mike wasn't too sure of what he'd accomplish. It was obvious that whatever the game was, Atwood was winning. Mike began his two finger, poking approach to typing as he prepared a response to Matt's message.

Matt,

Thanks for being onboard with me on this thing. I'll call you in a bit, you don't know the half of it. I'm going to do a favor for the woman whose husband was hit on 95 yesterday, I'll call you when I get back. Let me know what you find out from your criminal investigations division friend.

Thanks again,

Mike

Mike moved his cursor over the "send" button and clicked, sending the email on its way. Suddenly, pressure surrounded Mike, the pressure that a deep sea diver feels when he exceeds maximum depth without proper gear. His head felt as though it would explode, as it became immediately obvious that Craig Atwood was back. Every muscle in Mike's body flexed; his eyes felt like bursting from his skull. He lost control of his bladder as he crushed his mouse within his right hand, the jagged plastic pieces cutting his palm. He groaned in pain, grinding his teeth, clenching his eyes closed in an attempt to keep the eye balls where they belong. Words entered Mike's ears, words that were delivered with what felt like a rusty ice pick: *Now's your chance to pay up, fucker. You will go to that hotel. You will kill the man and his daughter. You will wait for the woman and her friend. You will kill them both. You will do this. This is your duty, detective.*

Mike coughed up the bloody contents of his stomach as he

struggled to move from the chair he was in. He felt fused to the chair, unable to stand, unable to even turn his head. Atwood was exhibiting the full wrath of his power with this assault, Mike feared that the demon would go too far, perhaps not realizing the limits of his powers. He lost complete control of his bowels, soiling his pants as he hurled more cockroach infested vomit onto his laptop and table. The detective lost conciseness after the violent projectile vomit left his mouth, his face falling against the keyboard, crushing a few roaches in the process. Roaches walked freely about the table, crawling in and out of Mike's open mouth. Bloody bubbles of snot formed in his nostrils as he struggled to breathe around the roaches that invaded his nasal passageway. With a high pitched voice loud enough to shatter Mike's sliding patio door, Atwood sounded his command. From all directions, the demon screamed *GET UP!!*

Chapter 108

THE WORDS, *GET UP!!* RIPPED through Doug Mason's soul as he lay sleeping on the dirty bathroom floor of his Port Wentworth hotel room. Scorching pain entered through his eye sockets, followed its way down his spine, the demon Atwood ran his scaly hand across each vertebra, before exiting the body in the form of a horrible bowel movement consisting of blood soaked worms. The sickening pile of modified feces splattered across the wall, floor, and side of the white porcelain bowl. Doug clutched the sides of his head as he rolled on his back, smearing the mess he had just created across the open sores from the spider bites. Loose fragments of the shattered mirror dug into his flesh.

The once strong black man lay twisted and helpless in his own feces, rolling around like a fish out of water, holding his head tight on the sides, trying to keep his brain inside his skull. Words poked at his mind; each word feeling like a seamstress's needle held over a flame and then inserted into the center of his temple: *A policeman is on his way. A detective. You will kill him. You will shoot him dead. You will kill your daughter. Two women will come. You will wait for the two women. You will kill them both. You will do this. This is your duty, flyboy.*

The door to the bathroom flung open with enough force to cause the knob to crack the tiled wall, a gust of wind entered the room, which caused the remaining pieces of mirror blow about in mini-tornados. Making a dramatic entrance, a tarantula roughly the size of a regulation football with legs crept into the bloody hotel bathroom as Doug lay helpless, unable to move within the demon Atwood's grasp. The oversized spider crawled between Doug's trembling legs, walked up his stomach, and came to rest on his chest. The hairy legs of the thing tickled the man's body as they twitched and trembled. Doug's head felt as though it was secured permanently to the floor, pressing itself into the pieces of mirror, causing him to have to struggle to look downward at the weight on his chest.

The massive tarantula inhaled deeply as Doug stared into its disgusting insect mouth, the thing seeming to hold its breath. After several seconds of holding its breath, the giant bug started to vibrate, causing Doug to vibrate also. The two shook as one for about ten seconds, when the room exploded with a deafening pop and flash of light. The tarantula crumbled into several thousand smaller spiders. The brown recluse spiders crawled over the entirety of Doug's frozen body, readying their fangs with venom, waiting on the simple command from their Master.

Doug struggled to muster enough energy to speak, he formed a brief, two word message he planned on screaming: *Jessica, run!!* He heard the words in his mind, he felt them travel through his throat, getting closer to spewing from his mouth. He groaned through his teeth, through the spiders crawling on his lips. He opened his mouth and spoke the words, screamed them, but what came from him was not what he said. What exited his body was an almost inaudible screech, similar to the sound a seagull makes as it soars above the beach, searching for food. The piles of spiders on his chest hissed a series of words into Doug's face, spitting foam from their mouths as they spoke in unison: *this is inevitable this will happen don't fight it don't fight your obligation fucker...*

Chapter 109

CRAIG ATWOOD SAT ON THE porch of his old colonial home in downtown Savannah. He rocked back and forth in his chair, both arms extended outward, the hands curled into a trembling fists. In his right fist, he held the mind of Detective Mike Christianson, gently squeezing; ready to crush it in his hand at any moment. In his left fist, he held the mind of Doug Mason, applying pressure, ready to throw it to the floor and crush under his heel. These two men were his. Atwood owned them and they would pay, one way or another. Part of Atwood's pleasure came from tormenting these poor souls. He would soon release these two men to engage each other and the others; the small one and the two women. The outcome was irrelevant; they would all die, regardless of the victor. The authorities would come and more death would ensue.

The defiant Mexican boy would pay, too. He would pay plenty. Craig would allow the father to arrive, he would allow the boy to think that it was over. The demon would then take hold of his mind. The essence delivered from parents taken by their children would almost be as good as that delivered from the fat head detective. He planned on visiting the boy soon, shortly after the father came to visit; or perhaps he would dispatch a few tiny reminders, just as an indicator that the young boy was still bound to the demon. Craig could feel that the boy's attitude had changed, he was becoming less submissive, he was slowly gaining confidence; his hatred for his father depleting. The demon would allow the boy to continue to think that it was over, that he was free of whatever had control of him. This will enhance the demon's pleasure when he ignites his power over the boy and crushes his soul.

The soldier would deliver what was owed at any moment. This trigger puller was engaging in proactive aggression; the demon was taking full advantage of this fact by providing routine encouragement and guidance in the completion of their collective goals. The drone really only needed a few minor corrections to keep him on task, Craig called these types of proactive aggressors as "fire and forget", he'd provide purpose and motivation and allow them to follow through, which they always did. These slaves always paid off more than reactive aggressors; those who acted impulsively after pulling their trigger. An infected one would always come up with more kills if they had time to plan. Craig intended on paying the soldier a visit soon, once he cut the pilot and detective loose. He wanted to be present for the transfer of essence once the explosion goes off. He would signal the soldier to pull the pin here shortly, just a few more people, a few more patrons needed to fill the lobby of the dirty, brick building.

The demon increased the power of his grip on the two humans, almost feeling their brain's swell within his fists. These were the last few hold outs amongst the infected souls, the last procrastinators. Atwood was becoming slightly impatient; not with the soldier, with the other three. The rest had done their duty in a timely fashion, minimal feet draggers. Once these four minions paid their dues, the demon could relax for several months, maybe even years, having stored enough energy to ensure more longevity. He wouldn't be stagnant for long, however; he couldn't be, it wasn't his nature. Although he needed the nourishment provided from the victims of his humans, he has come to enjoy the kills and murders as they unfolded. Centuries of performing his implants have shown him the true nature of some of this planet's inhabitants, he has seen tens of thousands of humans die and he gained comfort and pleasure from each and every one of them.

Chapter 110

SHERIFF'S DEPUTY MATT WHEELER FLASHED his identification to the Soldier who manned the gate at the Army installation. Matt was the type of person that preferred to conduct business in person, when possible. He wasn't a fan of emails and phone calls unless absolutely necessary. Matt especially hated emails; email messages had the potential to be misinterpreted by the receiver, therefore he only communicated in this method when he couldn't get the person on the phone or go see them in person.

His purpose of this trip was to see his contact at the post's Criminal Investigation Division, Mr. Brett Churchill. Matt met Churchill years ago when he started the process to become an investigator with CID. Churchill had been a mentor to Matt, guiding him in the prerequisites to become an investigator, showing him the ropes. Matt placed his efforts in becoming an investigator on hold in order to continue with his education and the time has slipped away from him. The two remained friends over the years and Churchill had continuously reminded Matt of his initial goal of joining the CID team, trying to hold him accountable for what he originally said he wanted to do when he separated from service.

Matt pulled his Bryan County cruiser into the parking lot of the two story CID headquarters building. He was pleased to see Churchill's truck in the parking lot as he headed through the double doors and up the stairs. Matt had been to Brett's office several times, most people here recognized Matt and greeted him accordingly. Churchill was pecking away at his keyboard when Matt presented himself in the doorway of his office.

"What up, Church?" Matt said, as he walked in and sat in the chair across from the investigator.

Brett's face lit up, although it didn't leave the screen of his laptop, "Hey man! Long time no see! You looking for a job?" Brett said.

"Not yet, I'll get there someday man," Matt said, laughing. "I'm here on business, well, sort of. I'm looking for someone that I think is a Soldier, might be anyway. I have a friend who's on the job in Savannah who has a theory about all the insane assaults over the last three days..."

"I know, it's been crazy. Is he at Savannah Metro? Was he there when the detective shot the place up?" Brett asked.

"Not sure if he was there, but that's where he works. Anyway, he made the connection that everyone that committed one of these assaults were on the same flight from Atlanta to Savannah this past Sunday. He sent me a list of Bryan County folks that were on that flight, I forgot the number, but all of them have done something bad since Sunday. All but two, and I think one of them is stationed here." Matt said.

"What's the name?" Brett said, as he minimized what he was working on and pulled up the website that gave him the access to all personnel on the installation. Brett's credentials and security clearance allowed him to have this information at this fingertips, not everyone had this capability.

"Holloway, Seth," Matt answered, knowing what Brett was doing. Matt had asked for Brett's help in this fashion multiple times in the past, and he surely would be here again someday for this same favor.

"Here he is..." Brett announced. He went on to read the information pertaining to the Army Sergeant's unit, his rank, arrival date, potential date of reassignment, and other basic information. This simply confirmed Matt's suspicions. Generally speaking, people in this area that have a phone number with an area code from another state are usually active duty service members or someone who recently separated from service and decided to stay here.

"I knew it," Matt said, "This guy called me and hung up this morning. Something is up with him, I think. My buddy's theory is making sense. I think we might want to go talk to Sergeant Holloway."

"Agreed. I'll head over there with you. Gimme like five minutes to finish this report and we'll drive over there. I know right where it's at," Brett said.

"I gotta take a leak, I'll be back," Matt said, as he headed down the hall and into the nearby restroom.

Chapter 111

"YOU WANTED TO SEE ME, First Sergeant," SFC Johnson said as he entered the First Sergeant's office. As the senior enlisted man in the company, 1SG Ferbee acted as the Commander's right hand man and advisor, he was responsible for everything that the company did or failed to do. He stood about 5 feet, 2 inches tall, but his physical strength, confidence, and attitude allowed him to tower over his subordinates. Next to him, as he sat at his desk, were two Soldiers that looked slightly familiar to SFC Johnson, although he couldn't quite place from where or in what capacity.

"Any word from Holloway?" the First Sergeant asked, as he stared up at SFC Johnson, who was standing before the desk at the position of parade rest. Johnson knew when to follow proper military customs and courtesies. This was clearly one of those times.

"Not yet, First Sergeant. I have Smith and Ramirez on their way to his house now," Johnson said, as he realized where he knew these two Soldier from. These were the two men that worked the delivery truck from the Ammo Supply Point.

"Who ran the ammo point yesterday?" 1SG Ferbee asked.

"Staff Sergeant Brunick and Sergeant Holloway," SFC Johnson answered, starting to show true concern for what was happening. Sweat was beading on his forehead as he came to the understanding that he was responsible for anything that happened out there at the range yesterday; leaders were always responsible for the actions of their subordinates.

"Get Brunick down here now," the First Sergeant ordered. Johnson said something like roger and stepped outside the office. Grabbing the first person he saw, he sent a runner to head over to 2nd Platoon's area to collect the Staff Sergeant. Once the runner headed out, Johnson pulled out his phone and hit Brunick in his contact list; it was best to cover both angles to find the man. Once Brunick answered the phone, Johnson instructed him to double time to the First Sergeant's office. He reported within fifteen seconds.

"We have a problem, gentlemen," 1SG Ferbee announced to the group, "One of the boxes you turned into the ASP was tampered with. It was missing four blocks of C4. Someone replaced the C4 with dirt, I guess trying to cover it up. Did you fucking inspect each box before you signed the fucking paperwork?" The question directed at Brunick. "Did you do a shakedown? Did you check every fucking Soldier for things they're not supposed to have?" The question directed at Johnson. Both gentlemen gave the same response, "No, First Sergeant."

"Well, we have a fucking problem then. Right now we have missing fucking C4 and a missing Soldier who had access to the missing fucking C4. You two have fucked up royally. Call the two that you sent to fuckhead's house. Tell them to not let him leave if he's there. Get out. All of you. Wait outside my office. Shut the fucking door."

The four men headed into the hallway, Johnson fumbled with his phone, frantically trying to call one of the Soldiers he had dispatched to Holloway's house. The First Sergeant was on the phone with the Battalion Command Sergeant Major. This problem had to be sent up the chain immediately, bad news did not get better with time. This situation required post wide attention.

The color was absent from faces of Johnson and Brunick, as the severity of the situation continued to strike home. They waited outside the First Sergeant's office for the hammer to drop again.

"You didn't notice when he handed you the box?" Brunick asked one of the Soldier's that worked the ASP.

"No. He must've put it on the truck himself. We didn't notice until this morning," the nervous twenty year old said.

"Well, shit. It could've happened after we gave it to you!" Brunick said, becoming frustrated and defensive.

"Easy, we don't know anything yet," SFC Johnson said, "Let's wait 'til they find Holloway. God, I hope he's there. I hope he still has it, if he even took it." The senior NCO rubbed his tense forehead, picturing his career fading away. This type of screw up could easily end someone's career, and their Command Sergeant Major didn't hesitate to make an example out of people.

The training room NCO entered the hallway and spoke to the four men, "Is the First Sergeant in his office, SFC Johnson? There's a policeman and a CID agent out front looking for him."

Chapter 112

SAM AND MARTHA FACED BUMPER to bumper traffic as they crossed the state line, departing South Carolina and entering Georgia. Their trip had been unimpeded up until this stand still. Samantha had tried calling Detective Christianson four times since leaving, to check on the status of his trip to Port Wentworth, each time it rang until the voicemail engaged. She had responded to her daughter's message earlier, which had yet to be answered. Sam's patience for this traffic was depleting rapidly.

"I know you're anxious, Sam," Martha said, "but you need to take it easy. You're going to give yourself a heart attack. We'll get there. The detective is probably driving. You know he won't answer his phone while he's driving."

"I know. I just want to know she's ok. I won't be satisfied until I'm holding her, M." Sam said to her friend as she started to cry. Samantha must've shed a few gallons worth of tears over the last three days. The traffic was creeping forward at a snail's pace, a few inches every few minutes. It was always like this at the state line; the speed limit changed, three lanes became two, and there were several exits and entrance ramps right on top of one another. The ladies still had a long way to go.

Chapter 113

SHERIFF'S DEPUTY MATT WHEELER AND CID agent Brett Churchill stood in 1SG Ferbee's tiny office, along with Johnson and Brunick. Wheeler gave a brief explanation as to the nature of their visit and why they were looking for Holloway.

"He's out-of-ranks, gentlemen," the First Sergeant said, "We have some people looking for him now. There's a much bigger problem going on."

"What do you mean, First Sergeant?" Churchill asked.

"Well, we have reason to believe that he may be in possession of four blocks of C4. He was assisting with running the ammo point at a demolitions range yesterday and there's four blocks unaccounted for. The red flags are starting to line up," 1SG answered, as Command Sergeant Major Wilson barged into the office.

"Did they find him? Was he there?" CSM Wilson asked, surprised to see a uniformed officer here.

"Not yet, Sergeant Major," 1SG Ferbee said, turning to Johnson, "Call them."

SFC Johnson called one of the men he had sent to Holloway's house. He had spoken with them when he was outside the office a few minutes ago, but they hadn't arrived yet. After speaking with Private Ramirez over the phone, SFC Johnson discovered that they two men had just arrived at Holloway's house. The house was locked and there were no vehicles in the driveway.

"He's not there. His truck isn't there either." Johnson said to everyone in the room.

"Can anyone think where he might have gone?" Wheeler asked, knowing that the CSM hadn't heard the conversation earlier, when he explained Christianson's theory. "Was he acting strangely before he took off? Did he seem frustrated or irritated? Anything like that?"

"He told me yesterday at the range that he had to go back to the DMV. I thought it was weird because when I renewed my license they mailed me mine. He said he had to go back to pick his up. Then he didn't show up for the awards ceremony." Brunick said.

"He told me he didn't get his license, said he didn't have two forms of ID. He said he waited all morning, through lunch, and walked away empty handed. He was pretty pissed off. He missed the meeting with the BC. I chewed his ass." SFC Johnson said to the group, thinking about what Wheeler had said about the people from the flight and what they have been doing.

As if the same light bulb sparked over both of their heads, Wheeler and Churchill spoke at the same time, "He's there." Wheeler took over, "Call Hinesville police, get them over to the DMV, now!" he said to whoever was listening as he and Churchill exited the office. The two men ran with a sense of purpose to Churchill's vehicle and sped out of the parking lot toward the installation's back gate.

1SG Ferbee dialed 911 on his cell phone and explained to the operator what they all believed was getting ready to happen. He did his best to convey to her a sense of urgency, although they were really only operating on hunches, without any quantifiable evidence. The four Army men piled into SFC Johnson's mini-van and headed towards the DMV on airport road, all of them hoping that this was all a misunderstanding, praying that their assumptions were wrong.

Chapter 114

THE DEMON RELEASED HIS GRIP on the detective's soul, causing Mike to fall out of his chair, his head bouncing off the hardwood floor of his condo. He laid there for a moment, facing the ceiling, allowing the echo of Atwood's commands to linger within his mind. He was a broken man, helpless and inferior; submissive to the will of the Master. Like a reanimated zombie, Mike rose to his feet and stumbled into his bedroom.

Using a shirt that was on the floor, Mike wiped the bloody drool and vomit from his face and chest. He fumbled through his closet, a blank look across his face as he threw on a random outfit. The hair was matted to the side of his face, crusted there due to the amount of puke that was in it. He donned his shoulder holster and placed his service revolver in its place, along with his spare speed loader. This should be enough ammo, if not he could always do it the old fashioned way. Mike wondered if this is how Grant felt at the end, once he gave in to Atwood; powerless, unable to fight it any longer.

Nothing mattered anymore. Gradually, all thoughts had been removed from the detective's mind, all but one. He was to drive to the hotel in Port Wentworth, the rest would be given to him as he drove. He moved across his condo on auto pilot, almost floating across the room like a marionette, the demon Atwood controlling the strings. He pulled his black dress shoes onto his feet, ignoring the fact that he was not wearing socks, and stammered out the front door, not bothering to close it behind him.

He swept the pile of cigarette butts that were on the seat of his vehicle onto the ground and threw himself inside. The drool began again, as Mike's mouth hung open, sitting there in the morning sun, driver's side door ajar. His dead eyes gazed over the steering wheel and into oblivion as he sat, hands resting lifeless in his lap. Like a bucket of ice water, an invisible open palm slap caught the detective square in the face, knocking him awake. Stars danced in front of his face as he opened his eyes wide and began to regain focus, direction. He knew once again what he had to do. Mike closed the door, started the engine, and headed to I-95 with the intention of heading north towards Port Wentworth.

Chapter 115

THE PILE OF BROWN RECLUSE spiders reformed into the fat tarantula, still laying on Doug's chest. It rolled to its left, using the momentum to completely fall from Doug's body, he then walked at a brisk pace to the area behind the toilet bowl. Doug brought himself to his feet, cutting his knees in the pieces of mirror on the floor, not seeming to mind that he was standing in his own worm infested feces. He didn't seem to mind anything anymore. His days of being defiant were over. He had chosen complete and total submission.

Doug secured his gun from the vanity, pulled the slide back enough to ensure that there was still a round in the chamber, and then let it forward again. He assumed a proper standing firing position, from where he was in the bathroom, Doug would fire over his sleeping child at the policeman who was on his way. He had perfect line of sight through the open bathroom door and over the couch cushion fort where his child currently slept. He would take the policeman and then his daughter. He had been instructed to wait for two women, who he would take once they arrived. He would then be free. He will have earned his freedom and his right to die.

Like an obedient sentry following orders, Doug stood like a statue in the bathroom. He peered across the room, head and eyes fixed on the hotel room's exterior door. The policeman would be here soon, he would kick the door in, like some kind of action hero, only to be greeted with a slug to the chest, courtesy of Doug Mason.

Chapter 116

MARK JENKINS WALKED THROUGH THE halls of Memorial University Medical Center, searching for his son's room. The boy had given him the room number when they spoke last night, but Mark had been a little jet lagged from his flight from Phoenix to Atlanta. He had a long layover in Atlanta, in fact, he would've been here sooner if he had rented a car and just made the drive to Savannah. Having remembered the floor, Mark wandered the halls and eventually found his boy's room.

Amanda Reyes was seated in a chair to the right of Brian's bed, sleeping soundly. She looked as though she had spent the night, which was most likely against hospital policy; however, they often made exceptions to that regulation in cases such as this. The boy was awake, flipping through the seven available channels on the TV mounted to the wall. Mark entered the room, making as little noise as possible as to not wake his son's mother.

"Hey buddy," Mark said, in a voice soft enough to not disturb Amanda. Brian's swollen face had gone down significantly, but this was the first time Mark had seen it, so naturally he was shocked. Swollen or not, Brian's face lit up when he saw his father. The young man felt his worth, realizing the distance that his father had gone to be here now, if only for a few days. His father had put his life on hold; left his practice, left his new family, traveled across the nation to be with his son. The anger and hatred that Brian had for this man yesterday was completely gone. The boy mustered a smile on his fat, wasp stung lips.

"Hey dad. Thanks for coming. How was your flight?" Brian asked, following his father's lead by keeping his voice down.

"It wasn't bad. Nice and short. The layover is what killed me. I hate sitting in an airport waiting to fly. How are you feeling? You look horrible," his father said, pulling the other chair over to the bed.

"Thanks. I feel a lot better. They said I can go home today," Brian said, as his mind went back to when he smashed his entertainment center in his bed room yesterday. He was ashamed and confused by his actions.

"So, what's up? Your mother told me you kinda snapped yesterday? She said you broke some stuff. You're a bit too old for temper tantrums, Brian. What is it? There has to be something else," Mark said.

Although Mark was a surgical doctor, he had taken several courses in developmental psychology and he had an understanding of adolescent behavior. Credentials aside, it didn't take a head shrink to see that there was something under the surface. The boy was in pain, not just physically, and yesterday was the tip of the ice burg. Mark didn't want to see his boy enter into a downward spiral of impulsive, destructive behavior due to angry feelings buried deep in his heart. He needed to learn how to regulate his emotions and talk about his feelings.

Brian was too ashamed to look at his father. He felt like a spoiled little brat, an ungrateful little shit that breaks his toys when he wants attention. He felt like a stupid baby.

"I don't know, dad. I don't know what happened. I just lost it. I started to get jealous. I was jealous about your family. I'm sorry. I feel like an idiot," Brian said, not making eye contact, he stared at the ceiling.

"Don't call yourself an idiot, boy. It happens. You have to learn some self-control. You can't just flip out and break everything when get upset. We can talk about this stuff, you know. I'm always here for you," Mark said, noticing that Amanda was starting to come around.

"Hey Mark," Amanda said, covering her mouth, as she was certain that her breath was offensive. She fumbled through her purse for some gum, "How was your flight?"

"It was alright. Pretty short. You look good. How's everything?" Mark said to his high school sweetheart, who he hasn't seen in nearly seventeen years.

"Oh, I look horrible. Everything's great. Except this. I had no idea he was allergic to wasps. It doesn't make any sense. I didn't even think they would be out in January." She rubbed Brian's hair as she spoke, "It won't happen again, we have the injectors to keep him from reacting like this if he gets stung again."

"That's good," Mark said, "I mean, how would you know you were allergic if you never had a reaction? Some allergies don't manifest until people enter adulthood. It's not unheard of. Don't beat yourself up, Amanda."

Amanda smiled at the father of her son. He was her first love, after all, and it's been said that true love never dies. She would always have room in her heart for her high school sweetheart.

She spoke though her smile, "When are you heading back?"

"Tomorrow night, I have a surgery Saturday afternoon that I have to prepare for," Mark said. "I have another long layover in Atlanta, though. I hate that."

Brian watched the interaction between his parents, he had never seen these two in the same room before, let alone talking to each other. His mother had boyfriends over the years, never anything serious, though. He knew that there was no way that his parents would reunite, but it was still comforting seeing them together. Brian was beginning to feel that everything was going to be alright.

Without warning, every muscle in the young man's body flexed in unison, causing his hands to clutch the sheets of his hospital bed with twisted, crippling fists. White foam formed in the corners of his mouth as he clenched his teeth tight enough to crush a filling. His toes pointed skyward, creating two small tents in the tight blanket of his bed, as he writhed in pain and discomfort. White hot pain penetrated his temples with precision as a familiar voice spoke within his mind. *You will kill them you are stronger than that pussy kill him first then the whore then the whore kill the whore...*

He entered into a seizure so violent he felt as though he would break his own back, veins bulged in his neck and forehead. Losing control of his bodily functions, Brian filled his shorts with the contents of his bladder, followed by a dumping of his bowels, loud enough to be heard from under the blankets of his bed. The rapid vibration of the boy's body caused the bed to rock within its wheels, the small emergency brake almost giving way. The boy's parents cried for help, screaming into the hallway for a doctor or nurse, as their boy struggled and twitched under the control of something that they couldn't see or understand. Mark went into straight doctor mode; taking action until the nurse arrived.

Chapter 117

HOLLOWAY WATCHED THE DMV SLOWLY fill with patrons as he sat in his truck in the back of the parking lot. He was becoming anxious, he wanted to head in and pull the pin right now. The grapeshot charges were directed towards the employees, therefore; Seth believed that the collateral damage would be minimal, which would make the amount of people in line irrelevant. With that thought, Seth departed his truck and headed towards the DMV. To the east and across the street from the building was a bright orange water tower, complete with the word HINESVILLE in black, three foot high letters. Above the water tower, Seth noticed a sporadic group of tiny black specks, much too small to be birds. He squinted as he walked, trying to see what was swarming above this water tower, ninety feet in the air. The distance was too far for him to make a definitive decision as to what was there, but the loud, clicking sound that was starting to hit the air suggested that flock was some type of insect.

He arrived at the entrance and paused for a moment, focusing his complete attention to whatever it was that was assembling across the street. The tiny black dots swarmed in two large concentric circles above the water tower, the swarm got smaller and tighter into the center, and the clicking noise got faster and louder. The objects came together and began to form a human shape, a solid black human shape that had its arms extended upward and outward, much like an Olympic gymnast that had just stuck the landing. From this distance, Seth could not identify any facial characteristics or clothing, but he had an idea who this was.

As he entered into the crowded DMV, Seth had to say "excuse me" to several individuals in order to clear a path into the restroom. Before he entered, he made sure to look over to the counter, confirming that Claudia was still working. There she stood, complete with a stupid, blank look on her face, right where she belonged, behind the counter and aligned with the center most grapeshot charge. He could hear a faint sound of a phone ringing behind the counter, *good luck getting anyone to answer the phone at the DMV*, he thought as he entered the restroom.

He was pleased to see that nobody had tampered with the M81 igniter under the sink and, based on the behavior of everyone out in the main area, there were no suspicions of what was about to happen. Without hesitation, Seth pulled the pin on the igniter, causing the time fuse to begin its one minute burn. Soon the burn would cause the main line of det cord to detonate, which would cause the grapeshots to burst forth with various fragments that would sever the annoying DMV employee's lower half. Seth exited the building and headed towards his truck to watch the fireworks.

Sirens echoed across the open area outside the DMV's main entrance, as Seth began to see multiple police vehicles racing down airport road towards his location. Following the police was what he recognized to be his Platoon Sergeant's mini-van, heading this way at a high rate of speed. The vehicles entered the DMV parking lot though both entry points, two of which secured the far side of the parking lot. Two additional police vehicles tore into the area and came to an abrupt stop directly in front of Seth, as he stood frozen in place about fifteen feet from the DMV entrance.

Police exited their vehicles on the opposite side of the potential threat, weapons drawn, using their cruisers as cover. Seth slowly raised his hands skyward as the men screamed stereotypical police commands at him. He saw SFC Johnson pull his van over on the side of the road, about a hundred feet away. Several uniformed service members poured out of the truck, almost like clowns exiting an over-stuffed clown car, one of which was clearly his tiny First Sergeant. The man on the water tower was still present, staring down on the events transpiring.

The phone continued to ring inside the DMV, employees of this office had learned how to ignore the phone when they were busy with customers, which was all the time. The fat beast Claudia hollered the word "NEXT" as she rested her chubby hands on the edge of the counter, gradually tracing the underbelly, looking for gum she had stuck there yesterday. She had no intention of chewing it again, she just wanted to squish it around with her finger, to waste some time.

Her chubby finger made contact with a foreign object; something that she didn't recognize by touch. This was something new, something that wasn't there yesterday. Confused by what she was touching, Claudia squatted down, and eventually into a kneeling position behind the counter, facing into the small partitioned area designed for leg room. She stared into a reflection of her own fat face in a small piece of broken mirror, a reflection of her face that was bisected with a small strip of black tape. The woman who was unable to show any type of facial expression when dealing with the public now had a look of confusion as she stared at herself within an old silver can.

It was immediately evident that SGT Holloway had used far too much explosive as everyone and everything within the building was instantly liquefied. Mirror fragments and various nut and bolt projectiles were fired into the area behind the counter, as all four charges detonated simultaneously. The counter disintegrated into lethal chunks of wood. Pieces of computers and other standard office items fired in all directions. The solid brick building maximized the concussion of the four pounds of explosive, killing anyone who wasn't riddled with fragments.

The exterior windows at the building's entrance exploded outward, raining glass and miscellaneous objects on the people outside. Everyone took cover behind whatever was available, mostly parked cars. The windshields of cars throughout the first half of the parking lot shattered as the shockwave of the explosion radiated outward. One shaky officer who had his finger on the trigger squeezed off a round when the explosion went off, striking Holloway in the center of his chest, killing him instantly.

Craig Atwood inhaled through his nose as spirits were abruptly torn from their physical bodies, soaking in a portion of the energy as they floated past him on the water tower. The quality of the essence he absorbed had been the best by far; better than the fat head detective and much better than the pretty little teacher. The form of Atwood's body broke back into the locusts that had originally assembled and scattered within the wind, riding it to the next destination, fifty miles north of here.

Manifest

The dust began to settle below, the dull ringing in the air remained in the heads of those who survived outside. Everyone within the old building had died instantly. The members of SGT Holloway's unit ran to the site of the blast, instinct taking over as they tried to implement the life-saving steps imbedded in all service members as part of their combat training. The police officers stopped the Soldiers before they could enter the building, unsure of any potential secondary charges, unaware that any additional charge was irrelevant, as everyone inside was gone.

Chapter 118

Mike Christianson pulled into the Days Inn parking lot in Port Wentworth, GA. He exited his department owned Impala, not realizing that he hadn't put the car in park. The vehicle pushed forward into the concrete wedge that separates parking spaces. Leaving the driver's side door ajar, Mike walked through the parking lot, looking toward the building. He would take the man first, or perhaps the little one. It would depend on how they were positioned in the hotel room. *Which room*, Mike thought. A brisk breeze rolled through the January air, the number 11 whispered in the wind, in a hissing sound that only Mike could hear. Saliva glistened on Mike's lower lip as his mouth hung open.

He removed and checked his service revolver. He kept his weapon lowered to his side while he checked that he still had a full cylinder in reserve in its storage place within his shoulder holster. He then marched towards the door numbered 11, which opened directly into the parking lot. He moved at a brisk pace, taking the most direct route. Mike glided across the distance like a man with a purpose. With his weapon at the high ready position and without breaking stride, once within striking distance he brought his right foot up into the door. In a common law enforcement technique, he kicked the door open, breaking the dead bolt and chain with ease as he crossed the threshold of the door, his pistol leading the way.

A waiting Doug Mason fired a single round, striking the detective in the center of the chest; the force threw him backward into the door's frame, his head jerked back and struck the sharp corner of the entrance's opening. A deafening scream came from under the couch cushion fort, the young lady having been slapped awake with the sound of gun fire. Jessica emerged from under the blankets of her fort and saw her father creeping out of the bathroom. Her dad moved like a person in a trance, this man was not her father. He wore nothing but blood soaked boxer shorts, his body had open sores scattered about its grey, ashy skin. Bones pressed against tight skin, his collarbones nearly poked through the flesh. His ribs were visible through his taunt skin, as were his pelvic bones through his boxer shorts. The man had a demonic look on his face, a look that terrified the young girl. He closed the distance between himself and the detective lying on the floor, with the intention of putting another few rounds through his head.

Young Jessica screamed, "Daddy No!!" as she threw herself on top of the downed detective, putting herself between the barrel of her dad's weapon and the man she didn't know. The little girl, who was smarter than her years, extended her arms outward, shielding the detective from what appeared to be her father's inevitable wrath. "Please, Daddy!! Don't do it. Please put the gun down!!" she cried and begged, looking up into her father's wide, blood shot eyes.

Samantha and Martha entered the parking lot and placed their vehicle next to Detective Christianson's running Impala, shocked that it was still moving against the concrete divider and the driver's door was ajar. The two women exited the vehicle and saw Mike's body lying against the door frame of room 11; his left arm was exposed, resting on the walkway. His revolver was clearly visible within the door's opening.

"Jessica!!" Samantha screamed, her friend Martha grabbing her before she could barge into the room and potentially face whatever had put the detective down. Her friend held her tight, speaking words of reason into her ears, reminding her that she didn't know how safe it was and to wait for her daughter to respond.

"I'm ok mom!!" J bird screamed over her left shoulder as she continued to sit on Mike's body, "stay there! Don't come in!"

The fat tarantula had doubled in size, having to move from the spot in the corner to allow itself more room to grow. It bulged and vibrated, twitching and quivering as its legs began to merge together into human arms and legs. It began to stand erect, hunching and struggling to make it all the way up, placing its hairy insect arm on the counter for support.

Craig Atwood emerged from the bathroom, having successfully occupied and altered the tarantula's body. He stood behind Doug's right shoulder, drawing Jessica's full attention, her little eyes wide with confusion, trying to understand who this man was. *Finish him fucker kill them both the women will come kill them when they do do it now you will do it it's your duty fucker*, the words transferred from Atwood's mind directly into Doug's, each word causing his finger to twitch on the trigger. Atwood's beady eyes pierced the back of Doug's head as he stared him down through the lenses of his dirty glasses.

Little Jessica stared through her tear filled eyes at her father, "Please daddy, don't do it. Put the gun down, please. I love you....I love you, daddy..." she drug the words out as she sobbed uncontrollably, hearing the cries of her mother echoing through the parking lot outside. Doug's eyes slammed shut, squinting as tight as his body would allow. He crouched in pain, as Atwood squeezed his mind with his horrible demonic powers, forcing him back towards submission.

With an overpowering sensation of precious freedom, Doug broke free from the strangle hold that the demon had on his brain, the shackles that once imprisoned him having fallen from his mind. With the unabated focus and confidence of a man regaining a sense of clarity, Doug turned and sighted the pistol on his target and pulled the trigger. The round entered Craig's forehead above the left eye, plastering the area behind him with the contents of his skull. He fell backward onto the floor with a crash, causing more grey brain matter and blood to drain from the 6 inch wide exit wound in the back of his head.

As he fell to his knees, Doug dropped the pistol and wrapped his arms around his terrified daughter, engulfing her with the regained paternal love that was nearly stolen from the demon lying dead on the hotel room floor. Jessica knew immediately that she had her father back. They both cried into each other's body, providing one another with comfort, having avoided tragedy. They held each other forever, displaying a combination of affection for one another and the appeasement of a curse lifted. It felt as though for that moment in time there was nobody else on the planet, as the bond of father and daughter was returned to its proper alignment.

Craig broke the silence as he raised his head from the blood soaked carpet and hissed "You've accomplished nothing!!" in a voice that was not human. The words sounded as if they were traveling through a collection of mud and seaweed. A single centipede covered in blood escaped the small hole that the bullet had left in the demon's forehead and scurried around to the back of its head, leaving a trail of blood behind it. With a thunderous flash and deafening pop, the complete form of Craig's body transformed into an entire pile of centipedes. It held its shape as the insects crawled across each other, fighting for position, as their tiny legs assisted them in slithering about in no discernable pattern. They hung in mid-air for a brief moment before falling to the carpet, splashing in the blood and brain that had accumulated there. Finally, the elongated creatures scattered across the floor and escaped the room through the varying cracks and crevasses that they could find, leaving bloody trails heading in virtually every direction. The bloody centipede trails and the remains of the demon's brain and blood gradually faded away from sight. Doug's affection for his daughter was not interrupted by the dying monster's transformation, his focus remained right where it was, on his little girl. As quickly as he had appeared three days earlier, Craig Atwood was gone.

Chapter 119

DETECTIVE CHRISTIANSON KEPT HIS BROKEN ribs a secret from his superiors. Given the events of the last few days, this was an easy task. When asked why he was struggling to move around the office, he simply reminded everyone about his panic attack and the fact that he had hit the wall in the interrogation room. There were far too many things going on for anyone to care about stinky old Christianson hobbling around the office, therefore; he had no issues keeping his little secret.

As a result of their intimate meeting in the hotel room, he and Doug Mason had a permanent connection with one another, both having been nearly beaten by the demon. Mike had no intention of ever telling anyone that he was shot in the chest by his new friend, he would take it to the grave. There were only three people on this planet that were aware of the bullet from Doug's gun that had been absorbed by the detective's body armor. Samantha and Martha ran into the room after they heard the second shot, the demon having evaporated prior to their arrival. The two women watched her ex-husband's body regain its proper complexion, his weight and physical appearance gradually morphing back into its original state. After they both witnessed this bizarre transformation, the story that Doug told them didn't seem that strange. Sam was just relieved to find her daughter safe and unhurt.

The number of people affected by Craig Atwood over the last three days was immeasurable. Thousands of people lost their lives, each of which donated a small portion of their soul to the demon Craig Atwood. They would never know that they were violated by an evil force not of this world; they wouldn't feel any different in the afterlife, there would be no effect on their standing wherever it was that they went. The monster made sure to only skim from the top, taking just enough to give him what he needed, but not so much that anyone would ever notice. The three days of evil that had tormented the east coast had finally ended.

Chapter 120

TWO YEARS HAD PASSED SINCE Atwood disappeared on a dirty hotel room floor in Port Wentworth, GA. The lives of those affected had slowly returned to normalcy, but they would never be the same. Too many lives were lost. Mike Christianson remained a detective with SCMPD, although he worked much less, having partially retired, a retirement that would change from partial to full within the year. A bond had been formed between him and Doug Mason, much like a union that forms between two people that shared a traumatic event. Similar to that type of relationship, but much, much more. These two men would be best friends for the rest of their lives.

A spark had reignited between Doug and his ex-wife Samantha, once again, a relationship formed in light of tragedy. They had re-kindled the love they had shared so many years ago. The two planned on re-marrying in the near future and little Jessica could not be happier. Actually, she was no longer "little" Jessica. The young girl was quickly sprouting into a beautiful young lady. Mike had been reassigned the affectionate handle of "Uncle Mike" and was a permanent member of the Mason family. Samantha had even convinced the old detective to start doing laundry on a regular basis, although it was usually her that ended up doing it half the time. Sam had also helped Mike quit smoking, which was a mission within itself. He had smoked his last Marlboro nearly eight months ago and he had no intention of ever smoking again. He also started bathing on a regular basis, thanks to the new ladies in his life.

Lawrence Winford had been committed to a maximum security psychiatric hospital in the DC area, which was a request of his son, MAJ Travis Winford. MAJ Winford had been assigned to the Pentagon shortly after the events of January 2014 and he submitted a formal request to remain within a fifty mile radius of the hospital for the duration of his military career. The request is still pending.

Laura Jones was a model prisoner at her Georgia state maximum security woman's prison. She had volunteered to assist with various educational programs within the prison and she arranged multiple programs designed to promote harmony amongst the inmates. The Lifetime network began the beginning stages of a made for TV movie based on the events of January 2014, focusing around Mercer Middle School and the effects of sexual harassment in the work place. Emma Watson was rumored to have been offered the leading role in the idiotically titled "Class Dismissed," due to start filming in spring 2016. Barbara Walters named Laura Jones one of the year's most interesting people in 2014, a fact that disgusted nearly every woman on earth.

PVT Seth Holloway was given a posthumous dishonorable discharge, forfeiture of all pay and allowances, and a reduction to the rank of private. Army officials did not want to hear any talks of supernatural phenomena or any such nonsense. In their eyes, this man was nothing more than a terrorist who murdered thirty two people. Period. He had put a black eye on the Army which would take decades to heal. Staff Sergeant Brunick was reduced in rank for his inability to properly account for the explosive that he was responsible for. SFC Johnson received a General letter of reprimand, which essentially ended his career.

Brain Reyes had a full recovery from his allergic reaction to the wasp stings. He carries his epinephrine injector with him everywhere, not having to use it as of yet. He is currently enrolled in the Savannah College of Art and Design on full academic scholarship. The tiny, two bedroom apartment was still the home for Brian and his mother, Amanda, but Brian knew that he would eventually make enough money to buy his mom the house she deserved. Brian and his father maintained their long distance relationship over the years, visiting one another at least twice a year.

Doug and Sam finalized the plans for their wedding and were remarried in June 2016, the best man was none other than Detective Mike Christianson. They enjoyed a small ceremony at the beach on Tybee Island, a few family and friends were present. Sam's friend Martha was the maid of honor and, of course, Sam's mom was a bride's maid. She was in full remission. Uncle Mike agreed to stay with Jessica when the newly re-weds went on their honeymoon.

Chapter 121

SAMANTHA AND DOUG SET SAIL from Jacksonville, FL a few hours after their intimate ceremony. They had complete faith in Mike when they agreed to leave their daughter in his care while they went on their honeymoon. This little vacation was specifically special for the couple since they hadn't gone on a honeymoon after their first wedding fourteen years ago. This was a well-deserved seven day Caribbean cruise and the couple planned on having the time of their lives. They were fortunate enough to get a state room that had a phenomenal balcony view off the enormous ships starboard side, so said the brochure. They executed the proper embarking procedures and did their best to contain their excitement as they moved quickly through this beautiful floating hotel.

Doug rubbed elbows with a gentleman who was coming down the stairs as he was going up. The man wore khaki shorts and a bright orange Hawaiian shirt. He had a bright yellow old school Sony Walkman on his hip, complete with cheap orange foam covered head phones, next to his hot pink fanny pack. A green tinted visor rested on his head, which kept the sun off his disgustingly smudged glasses. His outfit was complete with a light brown pair of imitation Birkenstocks worn over a pair of dingy white socks with red stripes. The man reached the bottom of the stairs, apparently having already checked into his room. He took up a seat in one of the reclining lounge chairs on the deck, enjoying the view of the pool and the Jacksonville Port Authority building. He removed a wrinkled James Patterson novel from the fanny pack and opened to a dog eared page that was stained with blood. The Captain started to make his announcements as Atwood began to read. The Captain's deep, authoritative voice projected through the speakers at various locations around the ship:

Ladies and Gentleman, let me be the first to welcome you aboard Carnival Possession. This beautiful, luxury cruise ship stretches 893 feet across the Atlantic and today 2,642 passengers will accompany us on this journey. Sit back, relax, and enjoy any of our twelve decks as we set off to Grand Turk, Half Moon City, and Nassau. Our crew, consisting of a team of 1,150 employees, are here to service you, so once again, sit back and relax; let us pamper you, because, after all, it's our duty.

The demon stretched his mouth into a creepy smile, his lips gradually opening to expose his yellow, braces covered teeth; classic Elvis Costello blasted through his head phones loud enough for passersby to hear it. This was going to be a great year.

THE END

Anthony P. Sardina

Made in the USA
Las Vegas, NV
19 January 2023

65913725R00262